ISBN-13:978-0615446578

Acknowledgements

With gratitude and love to

Lonni, Betty, Elaine, Mike and Rachel

CAPTIVES' CHARADE

A Novel by
Susannah Merrill

His words made her bristle. "You can't even take care of yourself, let alone control a man like d'Alava."

"He thinks you're my husband. Wasn't this arranged for my protection?" she rebuked him, her voice on the edge of hysteria.

"'Tis only a deterrent — a charade for which I daresay you are most unqualified."

Her face went white with fury. She snarled, "You are so very confident of my ineptitude."

"Cajoling appreciative males is not your forte. If it were, by now you would have a string of suitors from which to choose a suitable mate ...."

She slapped him hard, the sound of the blow filling the cabin. Both were equally surprised, but Stewart was quicker to recover, seizing the offending limb in a painful grasp.

"As your husband, I would be within my rights to have your hand permanently separated from your arm. You will not strike me again."

Their eyes locked in a passionate struggle of wills. Seconds passed and still the maddening, insufferable contest continued. And when she thought she would faint from the intensity of this wordless battle, Sarah saw that the tinder setting his mink eyes aflame was no longer rage but naked, burning desire.

CHAPTER 1

July 8, 1809

"It's ruined. It's ruined!" cried Lady Juliana Tremont. "And now I shall never be ready in time!" she wailed, making fruitless attempts to free her head from the mass of pink and white silk that made up her gown.

Hearing her younger sister's muffled moans, Lady Sarah Tremont sighed and left her own room to help. "Oh Julie," she chuckled, upon reaching Juliana's doorway, "You are quite the helpless sight, are you not?" Sarah smiled affectionately as she moved closer to the mound of twisting pink flowers. "Just be still now and I will find you."

As Sarah carefully searched for an opening in the gown, Juliana continued her whining. "Oh Sarah, I heard it tear and now I have absolutely nothing to wear to the ball. My birthday is ruined! And it was to be the most special day of my life."

When Sarah placed the neck of the heavily trimmed empire style gown over the mass of honey gold ringlets and pulled it down over her sister's head, she was not at all surprised to see the lovely face of Juliana red with effort and sparkling with huge tears of frustration. For despite all her beauty and the control it afforded her, Juliana was a spoiled and willful young lady and when events did not go according to her carefully contrived schemes, she usually reverted to tears, or rage, or both.

"Oh darling," Sarah replied soothingly. "Your dress is not ruined. See it is only a tiny rend and I will sew it up for you myself." Softly remonstrating her sister, Sarah added, "You should have waited for Tegan to help you. You are much too impatient, you know. Here, stand in front of the mirror and smooth your hair while I get a needle and thread." Sarah deftly closed the tiny pearl buttons at the back of the festive gown.

"And dry your eyes," she called over her shoulder as she left the room. "You would not want Jack to think you've been crying on your birthday."

1

"Jack!" Juliana sniffed as she brushed her fingers across her sooty lashes and pouted at herself in the mirror. "What would he care? He laughs at my tears and treats me like a child!"

Sarah heard her sister's petulant remarks as she crossed to her room. *Oh, Julie,* she thought to herself. *Jack adores you and you destroy him with your tears. He is so hopelessly in love with you. It would serve you right if he found another who would appreciate his devotion.*

As she retrieved her sewing box from the vanity, Sarah thought of Lady Juliana's beau, the handsome Viscount James Harrington, the son of her father's friend, The Marquess of Oxford, and their closest neighbor in the countryside of Oxfordshire. The girls had grown up with "Jack" and while everyone had expected Lord Harrington and Lady Sarah to wed, for they were closer in age and temperament, it was Lady Juliana whom he truly loved.

Sarah bore no hard feelings about this, since she never felt anything more than familial love for the young viscount. But it hurt her to see her fickle sister so abuse this lovesick young man that sometimes she wished that she did love Jack – and that he loved her – just so his poor heart would be immune to Juliana's plotting ways.

Beneath her frothiness, Sarah knew her only sibling was not really as heartless as she often appeared. After all, she was only sixteen today and it would be soon enough that she'd be forced to behave more maturely. But for now, Juliana was gay, impetuous, beautiful and totally without conscience.

Sarah returned to Juliana's room, the sewing box in hand, and smiled as she saw her sister posing coyly in front of the mirror, her lovely face completely devoid of tears.

"Oh Sarah," Juliana turned as she saw her sister's reflection. "It's going to be so exciting, isn't it? My very first grown-up ball and absolutely everyone will be here." She continued rambling as Sarah began stitching the white lace to the pink-flowered silk at the raised waist. "Father said he even invited a Yankee to my party – a man from Massachusetts – and I just know how people will be gossiping about that for weeks! I do so hope he is handsome, for if he is, I intend to show him off to everyone!"

"But what about Jack?" Sarah looked up from where she was kneeling. "Did you not already promise him he would be your escort?"

Without a trace of remorse, Juliana replied, "Oh who cares about Jack? He certainly doesn't deserve my affections, for he toys with me – as if I were a baby. Well, I am not and I will show him tonight!" Juliana stamped her daintily slippered foot, causing Sarah to prick her finger on the needle.

"Ouch," Sarah whispered and pulled her hand away from the fabric so that the blood would not stain the delicate material. "Juliana," she said crossly, blotting her finger on Juliana's petticoat, "you are so cruel to Jack. He does *not* treat you like an infant! He only appears stern because *you* act like a child. You know he loves you and hopes someday to ask Father for your hand. Please, Juliana, be fair to him. He is perfect for you and you know it."

Juliana gave a bored sigh. "I am so weary of everyone playing the champion of 'poor old Jack.' If he is so wonderful, why don't you marry him?"

Sarah stood up impatiently as she broke the thread from the restored gown. "You know the viscount and I are nothing more than friends. If that were not true, you would have both our heads – because you love him madly, even if you will never admit it."

"Well it seems to me," Juliana interrupted smugly as she smoothed her gown, "that it is about time you worried about finding a paragon for yourself, if Jack fails to catch your fancy. Or spinsterhood will not be a choice but a result of your lack of purpose."

Sarah winced; she knew her sister was right. It was becoming harder to believe that the appropriate man would ever find her. Though consciously, she refused to give it much thought, she knew her opportunities were slim, and at 20, her time was running out.

Sarah returned to her room and stood looking wistfully at her reflection in the mirror. The dress she had chosen to wear to her sister's birthday ball was a subdued, though popular, puce color which emphasized her elegant neck and collarbone by

3

bringing a more rosy hue to her pale skin. The expensive silk gown with its empire waist hung in soft folds around her tall, slender figure. The neckline was modest by the day's standards, but Sarah still felt overexposed in the low-cut bodice with cap sleeves that displayed her attractive bosom and slender arms.

Ah, the perfect spinster, thought Sarah, troubled that the image so disturbed her this evening. Her cheeks suddenly flamed and her large blue eyes narrowed beneath thick, dark lashes. She smoothed the gathered skirt over her slim hips, letting her hands rest there. Why did the classic but demure reflection suddenly dismay her so? Had Juliana's cutting remarks finally found their target?

"We are as different as night and day," she sniffed, trying to dismiss the uneasiness she felt. And it was most certainly true.

Juliana, with her wickedly slanting green eyes, her luxurious mane of golden hair, her petite yet voluptuous figure, and effusive tongue, was on a mission to ensure that every single male, young or old, fell victim to her charms. And by the number of anxious suitors, it was not hard to judge that she had succeeded.

Lady Juliana used every weapon in her considerable arsenal of charms to attract and hold a male's attention, while Sarah fought with the same sense of purpose to keep them at bay. She, too, had succeeded, and it was by far the meaner feat, for the older Tremont was as darkly beautiful as her sister was fair. But whereupon Juliana was tiny and used her size to arouse protective instincts in the other gender, Sarah was tall and carried herself with a regal reserve that made all but the most confident males ill at ease.

Sarah chose to disguise her slender yet well-rounded figure with plain gowns that did nothing to accentuate her exceptional coloring. Eyes as deep as a tropical sea, glossy chestnut hair and an English pale but healthy complexion were deemphasized by the tasteful but undistinguished gowns she preferred.

With a disgusted sniff, Sarah escaped her reflection and sought to dismiss the disturbing feelings that threatened her composure. The whole idea of arousing the baser instincts of addle-pated overgrown fops revolted her anyway. Let Juliana say what she wished. Sarah wanted no part of any man who would be swayed only by her comeliness or her skillful manipulations.

Or did she? a small voice asked, as she pulled on elbow-length kid gloves while moving from her bedroom into the upstairs hallway. But there was not time to think about the answer for her mother and father were walking toward her on their way to the grand staircase.

"Are you ready to welcome our guests?" Sarah's tall, dignified sire called out as he and his lovely, petite wife moved closer. They were Alex Tremont and Catherine Woods Tremont, the Duke and Duchess of Weston, and more attractive members of the ton, Britain's high society, could hardly be found. "It appears that your sister is planning to make her grand entrance after everyone has arrived," Weston smiled indulgently, smoothing his white stock and yellow damask waistcoat over which he wore a fine dark blue tailcoat. White silk breeches, stockings and kid boots completed his attire for the celebratory evening. "I have a feeling she intends to break a few new hearts this evening. Far be it from me to spoil her fun on her birthday."

"You look lovely, darling," Sarah's mother greeted her as she affectionately linked arms with her firstborn. As usual, she was a vision, this time in emerald silk, a stunning diamond and emerald necklace enhancing her slim neck and attractive bosom. "Are you looking forward to the party?" Her sweet voice held no trace of the disquiet Sarah knew her mother must be feeling about her daughter's disinterest in the heady social whirl of the ton that most highborn females enjoyed above all else.

Not wishing to upset her, she smiled down at the still beautiful older woman, replying, "I am sure we shall all have a lovely time. Your parties are the most wonderful of all."

"Good evening, Farnam," Weston called as he caught sight of the butler at the foot of the wide staircase.

"Good evening, Your Graces, Lady Sarah," Farnam replied, smiling stiffly, the picture of the perfect butler in his somber, but well-fitted, uniform. "Everything is ready and Silas informs me that our first guests are about to arrive."

"Thank you, Farnam. We will receive them in the ballroom," the Duke said as he escorted his wife and daughter into the softly-lit and ornately decorated ballroom off the tiled foyer.

As Sarah entered through the double doors, a wave of nervousness enveloped her, despite her assurances to her mother. How she disliked these occasions where batting eyelashes, profuse giggling and graceful dancing seemed to be the extent of the expected performance of a young female. With an inward sigh, she steeled herself for the difficult evening to come.

As Farnam had said, everything was ready. The string quartet was tuning up for a waltz, the servants were putting finishing touches on the serving table and the room fairly gleamed – from the newly waxed parquet floor to the three identical crystal chandeliers that hung like sculptured ice overhead.

"I do so love our parties, Alex," the Duchess said breathlessly as they took their places near the door. "They always remind me of what fun we had when you and I were courting."

"Harrumph," replied Weston, in mock consternation. "It reminds you of the fun *you* had, you mean. You played me for a fool while I watched you dance with every rogue in the countryside. My heart still aches when I think of how you spurned me."

"But Alex, you forget that I always saved the last dance for you," the Duchess smiled serenely, her green eyes twinkling.

"Small consolation for the hours of agony I passed waiting for you to make up your mind whether to dance with me at all," Weston replied gruffly, smoothing his handsome dark blue cutaway coat. "My sympathies are aroused for young Lord Harrington when I see Juliana practicing the same wiles on him you so heartlessly used on me."

Aye, so are mine, Sarah sighed dejectedly, thinking that just once it might be a lark to inspire that kind of devotion in a man. But she knew she would do nothing to cause it, for she could have little respect for a man who would fall so easily under her carefully wrought spell.

Despite her reluctance to join in the festivities, Sarah had to admit later that the birthday ball was not unbearable. After helping her parents welcome their guests, she circulated among her friends and acquaintances, doing her best to ignore some of the more assertive young men. While she was indeed perceived as a challenge, not many young men were committed to wasting an entire evening when there were so many more willing and suitable young ladies present. Therefore, Sarah was truly beginning to relax when a compelling presence brought her to a degree of attention and curiosity she had never felt for a member of the opposite sex in her entire life.

Sitting among a group of young matrons, Sarah had just tilted to her lips a second glass of champagne when her eyes were drawn to a man's entrance into the formal ballroom. Never in her life had she been struck with the urgent need to stare, to experience the totally sensual pleasure of admiring the quintessential representative of the species. He was so attractive, so full of an almost animal-like vitality that the room seemed to hush in deference to his presence.

In the crowd of pale-faced peacocks, the man was tanned and dressed entirely in black and white, his superbly elegant clothes fitting him like a second skin. The cut of the rich silk cloth clearly revealed the perfect symmetry of his tall, sinewy build, and set off his patrician features beneath a carelessly arranged crop of springy dark brown hair.

It was not merely his physical size, though that in itself was remarkable. Nor was it the confident gleam in his piercing, brown eyes, nor the arrogant slant to his unruly brows that seemed to mesmerize the throng, and sent a frisson of anticipation stinging along Sarah's nape.

It was the sense of absolute control that marked the man, as if, with no discernible effort on his part, he could have this high-born and influential crowd eating out of his hand. Even at this moment, he was, with practiced skill, returning the curious stares with an assessing gaze that spawned a tittering nervousness about the room.

It was a feeling Sarah was not immune to. When his eyes passed to her, she inhaled sharply, embarrassed by her

7

uncharacteristically impolite and obvious stare. Her cheeks rouged instantly, but before she could bend her head to feign a ladylike cough, she was struck by the brilliantly white, perfect smile he flashed at her, as if he were enjoying her reaction, in particular.

When she had mustered the nerve to look up again, it was to see her handsome father enthusiastically greeting their latest arrival. With a suddenness that caused several raised eyebrows, Sarah leapt to her feet, intent on evading the inevitable introduction. But the sound of her father's voice proved her failure to escape in time.

Feeling more like a lamb to the slaughter than she cared to admit, Sarah straightened her shoulders in the somber gown and walked the short distance to her father's side. Her gaze never resumed contact with the stranger's, but an inner trembling afforded proof that his eyes never left her.

"Mr. Chamberlain," The Duke of Weston bellowed proudly as Sarah approached them. "I'd like you to meet my elder daughter, Lady Sarah Tremont. Daughter, this is Stewart Chamberlain, our guest from the Colonies. Massachusetts to be exact. Mr. Chamberlain is here on business, and I was able to persuade him to join us this evening," her father said as Sarah cautiously extended her gloved hand.

Something in his lazily smiling countenance forewarned Sarah that Stewart Chamberlain's touch was not going to be one she would soon forget. His long, tanned fingers gently but firmly grasped Sarah's gloved hand as he bent to kiss the back of it. She gasped inwardly at the warmth of his lips and shivered, despite her resolve not to.

"My pleasure, Lady Sarah," he intoned in a deep, indolent voice, the sound of which assaulted her senses as much as his grasp. "Your father told me I would be able to meet the two most beautiful young ladies in all of England if I came, and indeed it appears that I have."

With great effort, Sarah summoned an unnaturally bright smile to her face. "Why Mr. Chamberlain, you are much too kind." And then, hoping to undermine his composure, she quipped, "I fear you have been too long at work to believe an indulgent father's opinion of his daughters."

"On the contrary. It is only in business that I have learned whose opinion to trust. And your father's," he replied, casually assessing her bosom, "is unerringly sound."

The nerve! Sarah flushed, feeling a tremendous urge to cover herself from his burning eyes. He had matched wits and then had the audacity to leer at her in front of her father! Weakly, she prayed for escape from the disturbingly virile Stewart Chamberlain and was barely able to hide her relief when Lady Juliana suddenly appeared with young Jack Harrington at her side.

"This, Mr. Chamberlain, is my daughter, Lady Juliana Tremont, whose birthday we are celebrating. And with her is Viscount James Harrington, the son of our neighbor, The Marquess of Oxfordshire.

To Jack, Juliana and Sarah, he said, "This is Mr. Stewart Chamberlain from Boston, Massachusetts." As the Duke made the introductions, Sarah watched Juliana staring at the Yankee with unveiled delight. The fair-haired Jack, having observed this, was finding it more difficult to be congenial.

"Lady Juliana, it is my pleasure to meet you. Birthdays quite agree with you," Chamberlain said as he gave Juliana a dazzling white smile. "And Harrington," he said to Jack, extending his hand, "Indeed you are a fortunate man to be escorting the belle of the ball."

"Oh, Mr. Chamberlain," Juliana tilted her head provocatively, "Lord Harrington may be my escort this evening, but it appears that I have this next dance free. And I think that on my birthday, I should dance every dance, do you not agree?"

"I do, indeed," Chamberlain grinned, offering his arm. "It would be my pleasure."

She smiled, very pleased with herself, and with a wave over her shoulder to the three, Juliana and her partner joined the others already waltzing on the dance floor.

Weston chuckled deeply, "So like her mother, it pains me to remember."

His faced turned a tight mask, Jack turned to Sarah. "Would you care to dance with me, Lady Sarah?" he asked stiffly.

"Of course," she smiled, hoping to find some way to console the poor lad as they walked onto the dance floor.

How they managed to keep off each other's toes was beyond Sarah, since both of them spent the time watching Stewart Chamberlain gracefully sweep Lady Juliana around the gleaming floor, dancing as if they had done this many times before. His dark head bending low to her fair one was a most disarming sight. For totally different reasons, it bothered Sarah and Jack that Chamberlain was such a superb dancer. And oblivious to all stares, Juliana was beaming, having the time of her life.

How can she be so calm with his arm around her? thought Sarah as she plodded through the waltz. *Well at least this is one heart I will enjoy seeing her break*, she said to herself with uncharacteristic vengeance. *Perhaps then he will not be so smug.*

As if reading her thoughts, Jack spoke softly above her head. "For a Yankee, he appears quite at home. I feel sorry for him if he thinks Julie's fascination is real. She is only a little tart playing games," he said with more conviction, obviously, than he felt.

"Now Jack," Sarah replied, feigning a cheerfulness she did not possess. "You know her too well to be jealous. And just think. You have her all to yourself save for these parties. Give her time. After all, she is only sixteen."

Jack sighed as the waltz mercifully ended. "I suppose you are right, Sarah. But there are times when I would prefer to punish her."

"Poor Jack," Sarah commiserated, but she could not help chuckling, too. The thought of Lord Harrington ever doing anything to upset his love was so implausible, it was laughable. Squeezing his hand reassuringly, she excused herself so that he might be better able to recapture Juliana for the next dance.

As she moved toward the terrace doorway, intent on taking some air, she pondered how her young sister had so easily captured Jack's heart. How he suffered because of Juliana! Though when she was not in a position to flirt, Juliana seemed quite in love with her most persistent suitor. Since childhood, he was her staunchest champion, always taking the blame for the misfortunes resulting from her mischievousness. And no matter how often she shunned his devotion, Jack was always there to forgive her fickle ways.

There were times when her affection for the lad almost made Sarah wish that she and Jack had been the ones to fall in love. They were kindred personalities – calm, intelligent, thoughtful – with none of Juliana's selfish unconcern for feelings or consequences. But her *joie de vivre*, so much more compelling than their quieter natures, was one of the reasons they both loved her so much. Juliana was indeed a heartless madcap, but she also provided merriment and calamity to their ordinary lives.

With a clarity that bemused her, for Sarah had not been consciously thinking of the tall, handsome stranger, she believed that Stewart Chamberlain might just be the one suitor whose heart Juliana could not break. Despite her earlier reaction – prompted purely by vengeance – she truly doubted that Mr. Chamberlain had ever been the victim of any woman's charms.

He was no callow youth, if she were any judge of age or experience. The rugged worldliness of his features suggested that thirty had passed him by. By his obvious sophistication, she surmised him to be the type who had sent more than one Juliana crying to their mothers. And not a few fathers declaring that he do the honorable thing and marry their darlings.

Alone on one of the paths through her mother's prized gardens, Sarah laughed aloud at the thought of anyone forcing that Yankee to do anything. Her one encounter with the stranger had already convinced her how absurd the idea was. Chamberlain was his own master, and pity the sorry fool who thought otherwise.

CHAPTER 2

"Care to join me?" The quietly delivered invitation caused Sarah to practically jump out of her skin. It came from a wrought iron bench, beneath a large oak tree. The bench was partially hidden by a hedgerow deep within the garden maze. Before she saw the shadowy form of the man, she spied the dull glow of a pleasantly scented cheroot.

"Y-you startled me," she gasped, her knees turning liquid with the knowledge that the man speaking was none other than the one occupying her thoughts.

"Please, sit down," he beckoned, rising to make room for her on the curved loveseat. Now she could see his face reflected in the torches lighting the path. Again it had a devastating effect as her heart beat madly within her rising breast.

"Thank you, but ...." she hesitated, desperate for an excuse. "I-I am afraid I have grown chilled. I forgot my shawl."

Before she could turn, Stewart had laid his cigar to rest on the bench, had removed his beautifully made tailcoat, and was bringing it around her shoulders. His actions forced her closer to him. To escape she had no alternative but to sit down. "Better?" he murmured pleasantly.

"Thank you," she whispered, an unruly part of her enjoying the fabric, the scent, and the heat of his body still lingering within the folds. The sensations were having a strange effect on her composure.

He resumed his seat next to her, nonchalantly stretching his quite long legs in front of him as he took another puff on the slender cigar. "I had not expected to have such an opportunity to make your acquaintance this evening," he said after a moment. "Your father was quite gracious to invite me on such short notice."

"Are you staying in Town?" Sarah asked politely, referring to London, surprised that her tone sounded normal. The man certainly was impossible to ignore.

"I have been ... until today. Your father and I are going into business together. We are attempting to arrange a trade cartel of American and British businessmen. Do you know something of this?"

She did indeed, but his question surprised her. Most men assumed, and rightfully so, that young ladies knew nothing of what the men in their families did for a living. A woman was a pleasant diversion, the manager of the home, and a necessary partner in the perpetuation of the species. Few women cared, and fewer still were educated enough to discuss business or politics on anything but the most superficial level. Sarah found herself warming to the opportunity of discussing with this man a subject that interested her greatly.

"My father and I have discussed it on numerous occasions," she told him matter-of-factly. "Ever since the Orders in Council were enacted two years ago, we advocated some sort of trade pact between the British and the Colonists, to maintain freedom of trade. Of course," she added, "the Yankee blockade runners were doing an admirable job for a time, despite our restrictions." She smiled provocatively

He tipped an imaginary hat, grinning in shared amusement, "I ask you, what choice did we have? If we wanted to trade with Europe, we had to suffer Britain's 'privilege' of inspecting our cargo beforehand. Your government would have been more honest had they hijacked us on the high seas," he scoffed.

"You have to understand our problem with France," she insisted. "You Americans fail to recognize the principle here, thinking you can trade with anyone, regardless of politics. France is our sworn enemy. You can't have it both ways, Mr. Chamberlain."

"So we have been shown," he chuckled mirthlessly, taking a puff of his slim cigar while he stretched his long body more comfortably on the bench.

The urge to needle him was strong, "Actually I would say your own President Jefferson was a greater problem to you than the French or the British," she offered boldly.

Stewart suddenly leaned forward enthusiastically. "Ah yes," he agreed. "The Embargo Act. I would be much farther along in my business dealings if it were not for that. Imagine, forbidding American ships to sail to any foreign port! The British may not have been able to defeat us, but we've almost done the job ourselves. It is indeed fortunate that President Madison has rescinded the Act, which enabled this visit to England."

Thus set the tone for a lively conversation, politics stumbling over into geography, culture, and before Sarah knew it, the evening had flown. She was so enraptured by the handsome stranger's account of his travels and his native land that it was only the noticeable hush, caused by a break in the musical performance, which made her aware of the passage of time.

"I beg your pardon, Mr. Chamberlain," she pleaded sincerely when she realized the lateness of the hour. "I have sorely monopolized your evening when you should have been inside enjoying yourself."

"Oh, but I have been enjoying myself," he crooned in his wonderfully rich baritone, making no effort to rise. "So much so, I could not begin to tell you."

His appreciative gaze, illuminated by a shaft of moonlight, at once warmed and startled the innocent young woman. It was as if she had only this moment clearly realized the magnetic quality of this dangerously attractive man.

Tearing her eyes away from his, Sarah tensed noticeably, a cautious aura settling around her as real as the shadowy light emanating from the torches near them in the garden. With fingers suddenly numb, she removed his tailcoat from her shoulders, standing as she did. "Thank you," she whispered self-consciously, "for sharing your coat. I-I have to go now ...."

Stewart stood, too, his towering height and broad build overwhelming her. But he made no attempt to reach for the coat she offered with trembling hands.

"Do you ride?" he asked quite unexpectedly. Sarah blinked at the strangely mundane question.

"Ride?" she replied, her surprise obvious.

"Yes, ride?" he grinned in that disarmingly relaxed way. "As in 'ride a horse.' Do you, Lady Sarah?"

"Why yes, of course," she breathed shakily. "Why do you ask?"

"I thought perhaps you would be so kind as to accompany me tomorrow morning. Your father suggested that I might enjoy the countryside."

"You will be spending the night?" she asked incredulously, clutching the silk tailcoat against her bosom. Part of her was thrilled; the other part feared the extended presence of this hypnotic man.

He nodded, smiling. "A week perhaps. Your father has suggested, wisely, I think, given the circumstance, that we conduct our business in relative seclusion." But her question would not deter him from his purpose. "Would you accompany me then?" Noting her wariness, he added, "Being a stranger here, I would appreciate a guide."

How could she refuse him the courtesy? After all, he was her father's honored guest. "Very well," she capitulated, feeling outmaneuvered and quite foolish for agreeing to spend any more time than necessary with this handsome foreigner. How much more could her throbbing pulse endure? "After breakfast then. I will meet you at the stables."

"I shall be counting the hours," he replied smoothly, reaching out toward her, his smoldering brown eyes holding hers fast.

Sarah took a skittish step backward, blushing visibly when she realized he was merely asking for his jacket. Thrusting the rich cloth in his hand, she was again undone by the startling warmth of his fingers making contact with her through her glove.

The unexpected touch evoked an immediate reaction that the stranger could not help but notice. Tearing her fingers away, she mumbled a stunned farewell. But before she could turn, Stewart had grasped her shoulders and pulled her into his chest, his wide mouth meshing with hers in a sudden but gentle kiss.

Her surprise at his unexpected embrace in no way compared to the jolt of excitement caused by his wonderfully sensuous assault. Nervous fingers that had intended to push him away instead contoured with the hard wall of his torso, involuntarily kneading the rich fabric of his white waistcoat.

As his kiss deepened, Sarah felt a mindless urge to cleave to the strong, lean body imprisoning her. In no more than an instant, Stewart Chamberlain had brought her to a level of desire she had never known existed. Her eyes closed, and her entire body trembling with a mysterious anticipation, she was unaware that he had forsaken her lips and was carefully observing her reaction.

Stewart's deep voice shocked her in that she felt the vibrations in his chest before she actually heard his words. "I believe I shall very much enjoy my stay here, Lady Sarah," he crooned, his voice thick with desire. "We appear to have a great deal more in common than I would have expected only moments ago."

With a horrified gasp and a backward lunge, Sarah fell away from the overpowering stranger. "You ... you ... " she stammered, her cheeks flaming with embarrassment. But her fevered brain was no help. With a strangled cry, she spun and flew toward the safety of the mansion, his gentle laughter ringing in her ears.

CHAPTER 3

Mortified by her capitulation, Sarah did not stop running until she had reached the safety of her candlelit bedroom on the second floor. She had taken the servants' stairs to avoid notice, but from the laughter emanating from the ballroom, she knew that the party was far from over. She could tell that many of the remaining guests were well into their cups and the booming voice of her father proved he was regaling the hearty group with stories of his days at Court.

But there was no way she could rejoin the carefree throng. She could not bear to face Stewart Chamberlain again. Whatever had caused her to react so violently to the man, she wondered, pacing the pale rose and blue Aubusson rug beneath her feet. She was no stranger to a man's attention, or even a stolen kiss in the garden. But never had she been so mesmerized by a man's presence. Always she had remained cool and remote toward any would-be suitor, finding their interest in her disgustingly obvious and predictable.

But Stewart Chamberlain had found her weakness – in more ways than one. It was not until they had completed their interesting discussion that she realized what signals she must have been conveying to the rakish foreigner.

And now his kiss revealed that he planned to treat her like ... a woman, Sarah found herself thinking with a sudden clarity. Though Stewart had stolen a forbidden kiss in the garden, she was nonetheless giddy with the thought that he had, at first, seemed more interested in her mind, her wit, than her appearance. And she had responded to that with an enthusiasm that could only have encouraged him.

Quickly removing her dress and donning a pristine nightgown, Sarah bathed her warm face in tepid water from the bowl Tegan had left for her. She then removed the pins from her hair and began brushing the long silken tresses with a vigorousness that made her wince.

But even the slight pain could not take her mind from the man whose company she had so enjoyed. As she considered mentally which riding habit she might wear on the morrow, it was with amazement that despite his indiscretion, she was still eager to see him again. With a perplexed sigh, she threw back the rose coverlet from her wide four-poster bed and snuggled against the lace-trimmed pillows. Thinking how strange it was to be both frightened and excited about their next encounter, she willed herself to let sleep overtake her. But it was visions of the darkly handsome stranger that permeated her last conscious thoughts.

It seemed as though she had just fallen asleep when impatient hands were roughly shaking her. "Sarah, Sarah, wake up. Oh, please wake up! What are you doing in bed?" Through her sleepy fog, Sarah realized Juliana was tugging at her and she moaned as she tried to push her away.

"Julie, stop. Go away," she mumbled, trying in vain to pull the covers over her face.

"Lady Sarah Catherine Tremont," Julie continued, seeming not to care that her sister had been fast asleep. "I have so much to tell you. When did you leave? I have been looking for you everywhere!"

Reluctantly, Sarah slowly propped herself up in bed, knowing that her sister would not go away. When Juliana had something to say, there was no chance it would go unheard. "What-what time is it?" she asked, rubbing her sleep-filled eyes.

"It's 2 o'clock and I came to tell you that my party was a marvelous success," Juliana answered brightly, flinging her pink-clad form unceremoniously on the bed. "I had the most exciting evening of my life and I simply must tell you about it. Why weren't you there? Are you ill?"

"I-I was tired. Too much champagne, I guess," Sarah said, yawning.

"I had too much, too," Juliana giggled, "but it made me feel wonderful and wicked. Oh you'll never believe what happened tonight!" she cried, falling back on Sarah's feet, stretching her petite body languorously.

"Tell me, then," Sarah said sleepily, "what happened that has you in such a state?"

Juliana turned toward her, propping her golden head on her hand, a contented smile turning her entire face radiant. "The Yankee, Mr. Chamberlain? He is the most divine man I have ever met. He is so charming; I was completely swept off my feet. He dances like a prince, and Sarah, he is so romantic. Why, poor Jack was beside himself. But I doubt that I could have turned Mr. Chamberlain's attentions away if I had tried. He is so persistent," she smiled, then giggled. "But I adore a man who knows how to get what he pursues, don't you?"

Sarah's face had gone completely white. "What is the matter, darling? Is something wrong?" Juliana asked sweetly. "I told you I would be with him – if he were handsome – and oh, he has surpassed my wildest dreams! Sarah, don't you think he's magnificent?"

Sarah forced herself to close her mouth, and blinked her eyes to shake her mind of the dread that was forming there. "I-I suppose he is good looking enough. But what of Jack?" she replied, in a desperate attempt to hold at bay the confirmation of her growing suspicions.

Juliana raised her head angrily and slammed her open hand on the coverlet. "Oh, will you please let me forget about Jack one moment?" she shouted. "I am sick to death of everyone thinking he is my beau. He is not! And you can be sure I made Mr. Chamberlain aware of that fact," she huffed, and just as quickly, her face took on its former dreamy look as she sighed, "Stewart. What a marvelously strong name. Stewart Chamberlain. It fits him to a tee, does it not?"

Sarah felt her skin go hot as her teeth clenched in helpless dismay. Of course Stewart and Juliana would be attracted to each other. Why had she so blithely assumed that hers was the only company he sought under this roof?

But then, a fit of jealousy took hold. The nerve of him to woo both his host's daughters in the same evening! He was despicable.

19

As delicately as she could, Sarah attempted to stop Juliana's effusive praise of Mr. Chamberlain's attributes. She certainly did not want to hear any more about him. "Julie, I am very pleased that you had such a wonderful time, but I feel I must remind you that he is only visiting Father for business reasons. It would appear doubtful that you would ever see him again once he leaves."

"Oh pooh, Sarah. The man spends his time traveling all over the world," Juliana shifted her small body excitedly. "He is free as a bird, and if I want him to stay – which I most certainly do – I am quite sure a way can be found.

"Do you realize," she crooned, suddenly changing the subject once again. "Mr. Chamberlain is at this moment in the guest room over our very heads," she sighed and looked longingly at the elaborately wall-papered ceiling. "Father invited him to stay the week and I have no doubt he will be spending all his free time with us. Is that not the most marvelous news? We are going riding tomorrow and Stewart has promised to tell me all about his home and his adventures. Did you know he used to be a sailor?"

"It does not surprise me," Sarah replied through clenched teeth, thinking of the Yankee's duplicity, and not Juliana's ramblings. How dare he ask her to go riding – and then invite Juliana as well? At the moment, she did not know with whom she was most angry: Mr. Chamberlain or herself for being so naïve.

With an unusual desire to mollify her sister, Sarah snapped, "Tell me, Julie, are you not being forward in calling him 'Stewart'? After all, you only met him this evening."

"Oh, but he asked me to. He says that in America, they have become much less formal about such things than we, and besides, we did take a walk in the gardens, so it would be ridiculous to pretend we are strangers," she said smugly, a sly smile quivering on her rosy lips.

"You what?!" Sarah gasped, her cheeks burning. "You let Mr. Chamberlain walk you alone in the gardens? Juliana, have you no sense of propriety? Father would be outraged," she blurted, though she knew her sire could be no more offended than she herself.

"Sarah, for heaven's sake. You are such a prude! The man asked me to show him around. And at the time, I thought I may never see him again, so you can understand I simply had to know what it would be like to kiss him," Juliana said simply, as if her logic were ridiculously clear.

"Juliana, you should be ashamed of yourself. Sometimes you are so bold, I cannot believe you are my own flesh and blood," Sarah railed, horrified by the knot of jealousy tightening in her stomach.

In a bored voice, Juliana replied, "And sometimes you are so cold, I find myself thinking the same." With that, she jumped off the bed and twirled around on the pink and blue rug. "I am as far from ashamed as I can possibly be. Stewart is an accomplished lover and his kisses are divine," she sighed dramatically, reaching for the bedpost and clutching it between her breasts. "If you were not so straight-laced, you might have found that out for yourself."

With that, she planted a loud smack on the carved oak. "And now that I have told you my wonderful news, I am going to bed and pray that morn comes soon. I cannot wait to feast my eyes on Stewart Chamberlain again. Sarah," she smirked, as she placed her small hand on the doorknob. "I want you to know that I envy you."

"After what you just said, how in the world could you envy me?" Sarah said hotly, wrenching herself down under the covers.

"Because," Juliana teased, a thoroughly devilish look on her face, "you have the privilege of knowing that Stewart Chamberlain lies atop you tonight."

With that, she giggled and rushed out the door, just missing the pillow that was thrown at her retreating form.

CHAPTER 4

Sarah awoke the next morning to the sound of cheerful humming coming from somewhere beyond her bed. She knew without looking that it was Tegan, her personal attendant. "What time is it?" she asked huskily, turning her face away from the sun-bright windows.

"Well good morning, mum," Tegan responded brightly. "I feared you would sleep the day away while everyone waits for you to go riding," she said as she stopped to pick up the undergarments Sarah had left on the floor the night before.

"I am not going riding," Sarah declared, pulling the covers up under her neck. Ignoring her, Tegan pulled Sarah's green linen riding habit from the wardrobe.

"Why Master Chamberlain insisted on waiting for you. And Viscount Harrington agreed, though Lady Juliana is as impatient as ever. You are going to ruin a lovely outing if you fail to hurry," Tegan chuckled. "Shall I help you dress?"

Sarah glared speculatively at her maid, who returned a bright, carefree smile. Nothing passed Tegan's notice, though she rarely revealed her opinions unless asked. Usually grateful for the companionship of the petite red-haired young woman, Sarah had a terrific urge to insist that she leave.

The last thing she wanted to do, after Juliana's revelation of the night before, was to spend a morning with any of those three downstairs! Stewart Chamberlain could go to the Devil for all she cared. And Juliana should be ashamed of herself for playing the Yankee against her tender-hearted beau.

It was her sympathy for Jack that finally made her acquiesce. With a look that warned Tegan not to gloat, she hastily removed her nightgown and began pulling on her clothes. When Tegan had finished buttoning the fine white muslin blouse of Sarah's riding costume, she commanded her charge to sit at the dressing table while she fixed her hair.

Sarah plopped on the needle-pointed cushion, willing herself to remain calm, though thoughts of the two-timing foreigner overtook her. How would she face him? Since he was a guest in their home, she would have to be polite, but that did not mean she had to be pleasant. And if Juliana were up to her old tricks, it would be quite easy for them to ignore each other.

That problem somewhat solved, she turned her thoughts to Jack. He must be in agony right now, watching Juliana using her wiles on Stewart. "Please hurry, Tegan," Sarah begged impatiently, "I cannot keep Jack waiting another second."

"There you go, mum. As pretty as a picture you are," Tegan said as she stepped back to let Sarah pass by. "Have a good time. It's a lovely day for riding."

"We shall see," she countered as she stepped from the room, rushing to the stairs. As she caught sight of the foyer, she could hear voices in the front parlor opposite the ballroom where the party had been. Steeling herself for the difficult situation that lay in store, she slowly descended the stairs and made her way toward the entrance hall.

"Sarah!" she heard Jack call as she came into view. There was no mistaking the note of relief in his voice.

As she entered the parlor, Juliana, a vision in a cream-colored riding habit and blue stock, turned and exclaimed cheerfully, "What a sleepy head you are this morning!" She rose from the settee facing the fireplace and moved toward the tall form of Stewart Chamberlain, who was leaning casually against the mantel. "Mr. Chamberlain has agreed that we should all go riding together this morning and Father has even offered to let him use Nubian. What do you think of that?" Juliana said, beaming, her words more a statement than a question.

"I trust, Mr. Chamberlain, that you were forewarned that Nubian is a bit o' blood. Most have found him a difficult mount to handle and not worth the effort. Perhaps you should reconsider."

As Sarah voiced the challenge, she became aware of the fact that Stewart Chamberlain projected an even more dashing image in riding clothes than he had in his formal attire the night before. His white shirt and carefully knotted cravat accentuated

23

his sun-browned skin and flawless white teeth. A well-tailored dark brown tailcoat matched the color of his knee-length riding boots. His lean thighs were covered in fawn breeches and Sarah could not help but notice how tightly they stretched across his sleek, muscular frame. It was obvious that he paid attention to his grooming, but Sarah thought it would be unfair to accuse him of being a dandy. Unfortunately there seemed to be nothing to criticize in the way of his physical appearance and that fact irritated Sarah even as an uncontrollable part of her admired the view.

"Thank you for your concern, Lady Sarah," Stewart responded good-naturedly, though his grin told her that he was not fooled into thinking her remark was prompted by concern. "But my own horse back home is of a similar nature. I would find it a pleasure and a challenge to ride Nubian."

"Very well," Sarah replied much too abruptly and turned to Jack, who was standing beside her near the door. "Shall we go?" Seeing his fair features straining to remain even, she asked, "I am so sorry to have kept you waiting. Have you been here long?"

"Long enough," he ground out under his breath, but aloud he added, "It is all right, Sarah. I had Silas saddle your horse for you already, so we will still be able to get in a good ride before noon."

Hearing Juliana's happy chatter and the deep resonance of Stewart's voice behind her, Sarah was deeply relieved that Jack had not mentioned a picnic today, which is what the three of them usually enjoyed on these outings. Sarah knew she could not bear to be in Stewart's company too long, for his very presence was taunting her with thoughts of how eager she had been to see him again – before Juliana's revelation the night before.

If he were a gentleman, she thought angrily to herself, *he would never think of courting two sisters at the same time!* But it was obvious that Stewart Chamberlain had his own rules of conduct and Sarah was immensely relieved that Juliana was doing her best to keep him occupied – even if Jack was the one having to suffer for it.

As the four stepped down the marble stairs of the entrance to the mansion, they noticed immediately that Silas, the stable master and trainer, was having his troubles trying to control Nubian. The coal black stallion whinnied and skittered, bumping into the other horses and causing them to fret.

Stewart quickly broke from the group and crossed the cobbled drive to where the horse was tethered. Taking Nubian's reins from Silas, he firmly led the stallion away from the others, patting the horse's neck while he spoke soothingly. Even as Jack helped her mount her own chestnut mare, Serena, Sarah could not keep her eyes from Stewart and the stallion. She almost wished the fiery black beast would rear, but after a few minutes, Stewart, with his firm but gentle actions, was settling the horse, causing the mount to pause and gaze at him with wary respect.

"Why Stewart," Juliana addressed him boldly, "I do believe Nubian has finally met his match. Look at the way you have quieted him." She grinned as Jack passed up the reins to her dappled mare, Fancy.

"I think your words are a bit premature," Sarah cut in. "Mr. Chamberlain has not yet mounted. That is the real test."

"Quite right, Lady Sarah," Stewart agreed, without looking up. Freeing one hand, he dug into his coat pocket and came up with a piece of carrot which he held before Nubian's dark muzzle.

The horse readily took the treat and as he chewed, Stewart placed his boot in the stirrup and swung his long leg over the saddle. Nubian reared slightly but Stewart's hands and knees were firmly in control. After only a moment of angry snorting and a few impatient stamps of his huge hooves, Nubian conceded to the large rider atop his back.

"Well done, sir," Jack called to Chamberlain, finding this man difficult to scorn, especially since he had witnessed Nubian besting nearly all his would-be riders.

Sarah turned her head away to hide the disappointment in her deep blue eyes as Juliana gushed over Mr. Chamberlain's success. Lord Harrington, trying to ignore her, nudged his tan gelding forward in the direction of the green meadow beyond the mansion and the others followed.

Once in the open meadow, the group rode four abreast, with Jack and Stewart on the ends, slightly ahead. Sarah could not help noticing how well Stewart rode, keeping the troublesome stallion under perfect control. *He seems to have his way with every creature*, she thought, her full lips pursing in a tight line. It was also apparent that while he was attentive to Juliana's chatter, he was not overwhelmed, as most men were, by her flirtations. In fact, he seemed to accept it as his due. This Sarah found strangely comforting, though she could not guess why.

In time the party came to a ridge from where they could view miles of rolling countryside basking in the light of an unusually cloudless sky. Juliana abruptly turned to the others and said brightly, "I insist we ride on to the Gables today. It is such a gorgeous morn and I am in the mood for a tear."

The Gables was a Roman stone formation Jack and the girls had discovered on one of their frequent jaunts. It was still a fair distance and Sarah was not at all interested in stretching out this ordeal. Besides, the Gables was a secret place, one she had no desire to share with this imposing stranger. An excuse came to her quickly, "Juliana, I cannot possibly go. I am sorry but I have not eaten yet today and I am feeling a headache," Sarah said, rubbing her temple with a gloved hand.

"I will not hear of it," Juliana retorted, her sweet voice a perfect balance of irritation and persuasion. "You eat like a bird anyway and this fresh air will clear your head. Besides," she added coyly, smiling at Jack, "I did promise Jack we would ride today and we must not disappoint him."

"You are quite right," Stewart suddenly agreed and all eyes swiftly turned to him. "But I do have some important letters to post today, so I will be happy to escort Lady Sarah. My Lord, you would not object if we left you and Lady Juliana to ride to the Gables alone, would you?" he asked, his brown eyes guileless.

Jack, not one to hesitate when he had the advantage, returned eagerly, "Of course not, sir. See Julie? We *will* have our ride today." He grinned and before she could open her mouth to form a protest, he added, "Come then, I shall race you to the copse." With that, he turned his horse to face the other side of the ridge.

Sarah, as horrified as Juliana was perturbed, could think of nothing to say to get herself out of the situation she had just created. Before she had a chance, Stewart was pulling up the great black horse beside her as he bid a puzzled Juliana farewell. But Julie was not one to brood for more than an instant and seeing that there might be an advantage for her in all this, smiled brilliantly at Jack and urged her horse ahead suddenly, getting a head start down the bank, her blond curls flying in the wind.

Sarah watched Jack let out a whoop as he took off. Mortified, she turned her horse around, avoiding Stewart's look. As their mounts fell into step, Stewart let out a low chuckle.

Sarah bristled at the sound and snapped her head around to face him. "You are insufferable," she spat, her cheeks hot.

"Why Lady Sarah," he answered, not at all put off by her tone. "I thought you would be pleased that your indisposition did not spoil everyone's ride. Besides," he leaned toward her, his brown eyes crinkling, "I consider it a privilege to escort you."

"Do not insult my intelligence, Mr. Chamberlain," she spat. "I know about you and my sister, and I will not be used by you to make her jealous."

He grinned easily as he settled back in the saddle. "I had no such thought in mind, but it could just as easily have worked the other way," he suggested. "As a matter of fact, I think perhaps it has."

She gasped, her reaction fueled by the obvious truth of his words, though she had never consciously considered it before. "Surely you are not so naïve as to think that my interest in your views last night constitutes anything more significant. And I am insulted that you would presume to manipulate a very strong bond between your generous host's daughters."

"I beg your pardon, Lady Sarah," Stewart replied intimately, "but I have no designs on your sister, though she is an extremely lovely young lady – and appears to know much more about men than her older sister."

"I presume you base your statement on the experience you had with her in the gardens last night?" Sarah bit back and then immediately regretted her pettish words.

"It is unknown to me what your sister may have told you," Stewart answered, his voice still teasing. "And I am not one to discuss my private affairs for the titillation of others. I will say, however, that I had a most enjoyable time last evening, especially the all-too-fleeting moments you and I shared."

Despite her fury, Stewart's words aroused her curiosity and she could not stop herself from carrying the conversation further. "You contradict yourself, Mr. Chamberlain. If you find my sister more schooled than I, how was it that I should have been the one to make your evening more enjoyable?"

Amused at her attempt to hide her interest behind a scowl, Stewart laughed aloud. "Lady Sarah Tremont," he chuckled, "I find your lack of guile refreshing. It appears you truly are as innocent as you seem." Sarah blushed uncontrollably and tried to stammer a defense, but Stewart continued. "And for that, I feel you deserve an answer to your question. You see," he began, his rich brown eyes suddenly serious, "the Julianas of this world – and there are many – put their efforts into the game of enticement. Their wit and charm are a pleasure to behold, but it is only shared intensely with men who are willing to pretend they do not wish it. Should a man be so taken that he must stop pretending and confess his true feelings, the game is over and the woman lost." He paused for a moment while he patted Nubian's withers. "And even if this kind of woman finds a man she truly loves, she cannot deny her flirtatious ways and may cause more hurt than happiness to the man who wins her."

"So," Sarah responded smugly, "you are saying that were it not for the fact that my sister has the power to spurn you, you would wish to have her for your own?"

"On the contrary," Stewart said matter-of-factly. "I was speaking of men in general. Not myself. I prefer women who are not afraid to show passion when the setting is right – as when they are in my bed. It matters not what they are like otherwise." He laughed as he saw bright spots of color reappear on her cheeks, her azure eyes wide with shock. "I see I have offended you, Lady Sarah, but I fear you will have to get used to my veracity. I know of no other way to speak."

"I have nothing to get used to, Mr. Chamberlain," Sarah retorted, urging Serena into a trot, "for you will be soon gone and I will never have to listen to your impertinent remarks again."

Not the least of her anger was caught up in the fact that he was presuming a mutual attraction that she had refused to admit existed. Last night, when they had discussed politics, she had been lulled into thinking that his interest transcended a physical attraction. His seeming lack of attention to her femininity had allowed her own feelings to swell as they had never done before. But now he was complicating everything – and Sarah wanted only to escape.

But Stewart was making that quite difficult, she realized, as he easily maintained his position next to her. "Then your Father hasn't told you? I shall be here often, which is why I have letters to post, so my associates in London will know where I can be reached." Seeing her obvious distress, he added teasingly, "And I thought you would be pleased, for now we will have the opportunity to get to know each other better."

"I would prefer that we do not. Now that you have revealed your true colors, I find I care little about anything you have to say!" With a toss of her head in the direction of the mansion, she harshly stung Serena's flanks with the crop. The mare, unused to such brutal treatment from her mistress, reared suddenly, causing Sarah to lose her footing. As the mare took off in a run, Sarah screamed, feeling herself about to fall.

With a sickening thud, she hit the ground, landing on her left side, and then limply coming to rest on her back, her scream ending in a pained moan. Immediately Stewart jumped to the ground beside her, leaving Nubian to chase after the mare.

"Lie still," he ordered, as she struggled to sit up, pushing his hands away. Frightened by his voice and the force of her fall, she lay back down, tears streaming from her eyes.

"Please go away," she sobbed. "Do not touch me."

Ignoring her pleas, Stewart bent close to her and gently probed her left arm with his fingers. "Do not move until I see if anything is broken," he commanded, his brown eyes following the movements of his hands, his wide mouth set in a tight line.

"Ouch," she whimpered, as he explored the area beneath her heaving breast. Painfully, her hands flew to his as he began to unbutton her riding jacket. "What are you doing?" she pleaded, her voice shaking. He pushed her hands away firmly and continued.

"I cannot tell anything through your coat," he said, and having opened it, slid his left hand underneath the jacket. Forced to suffer while his long fingers carefully moved over each rib, the back of his hand grazing her breast, Sarah screamed inwardly as the tears fell from her cheeks toward her ringing ears.

She thought he would never finish, but his hands finally quieted as he said in a low voice, more to himself than to her, "I think you are only bruised.

"May I please get up?" she whispered tightly, her eyes pinched shut.

"You took quite a spill, Sarah, but I think you are all right, save for some bad bruising," he said kindly, pulling her by the shoulders to a sitting position before removing a kerchief from his coat pocket. "Just sit here for a moment and give yourself a chance to catch your breath."

Despite her pain and humiliation, Sarah could not help noticing that Stewart's large body was suddenly surrounding hers. His long leg was bent close behind her as he knelt to support himself while he wiped her tears. His strong hand cradled her head and neck and his voice seemed to vibrate in her brain as he spoke softly into her ear, his face close to hers.

"It looks like we are going to have to walk back to the house, since our mounts have fled. It is rather far. Do you think you will be able to manage?" he asked gently.

"I-I think so," she sniffed, taking the kerchief from him and wiping her delicately-tipped nose. "I haven't much choice."

"I could carry you," he offered, lowering his lean form opposite her in such a way that their hips touched intimately. An involuntary shiver raced through her and she moved away slightly.

Her red-rimmed eyes looked up from above the snowy white cloth and into his deep brown ones. In a voice muffled by the cloth, she replied, "Have you not put me through enough of your pawing for one day?"

Undaunted, Stewart rested one arm on his bent leg and placed his hand on the grass next to her side. Looking deeply into her eyes, his voice barely above a whisper, he asked, "Sarah, what are you so afraid of? You are a grown woman and I am a man. What is so terrible about the attraction we have for each other?" As he spoke, his right hand came up to softly brush a wisp of hair from her forehead.

Sarah jerked her head away and looked at the grassy green meadow without seeing. "You presume too much when you say we are attracted to one another," she said, her words sounding cold to her own ears. "For I do not like you at all.""Were you not so innocent, you would realize that humans are never more irrational than when their feelings are compelled to surface. Whether you think you like me or not is of no consequence, though in truth I think you do. At least you seemed so last night." He ignored her scathing look. "The fact remains, however, that we are attracted to each other. You feel it. And so do I."

Before she could form a protest, his warm lips had found hers in a kiss as sweet as it was unnerving. Even as she meant to push him away, something deep within her was finding an answer to a question she realized she had been asking herself since he entered the ballroom so splendidly the night before. He was more wonderful to kiss than he was to look upon – and that seemed hard to believe.

Even harder to believe was the fact that she was letting him enjoy the tenderness of her own lips when but a moment ago she had been screaming at him to leave her alone. Disgusted by her weakness, she ignored the pain it caused to move so abruptly, and flung herself away. Her chest heaving from her efforts, she swore, "Damn you for thinking you can kiss me whenever you please. Especially when you made me fall off my horse!"

Shaking his head good-naturedly, Stewart replied, "I fear your temper was the cause of your fall, but if you wish me to take the blame, then please allow me to express my apologies," he said and swiftly bent his head to claim her blossoming lips again. Too afflicted to struggle and too weak from his last assault, Sarah found herself going limp in Stewart's caressing grasp. Her angry moans only seemed to encourage him further and she had a feeling of panic when a strange tingling sensation began to course through her.

To her amazement, for she had never been so boldly kissed in her life, Stewart's eager tongue parted her slackening lips, sliding with teasing abandon along her teeth until she gasped. Pressing his advantage, he met her small, pointed tongue with his own, engaging her in sensuous play until she was swept up securely in the passions he had aroused. Amazed by her own craving for the intimate sensations caused when his body pressed her down onto the sweet-smelling meadow, she found herself ignoring the weakening voice that warned her against this taste of heaven.

Her jacket still unbuttoned, Sarah realized that Stewart's warm hands were touching her through the sheer muslin of her blouse. And even though he seemed to move without thinking, he was very carefully avoiding her bruised ribs. Instead, he intimately cupped her breast, managing to imprison her arms lest she try to resist him.

A cobweb of conflicting emotions sailed through Sarah's fevered mind as Stewart's thumb slowly brushed back and forth across her nipple. Her loins experienced a sweet ache and her ragged breath quickened as his tongue commanded hers to respond. Unobtrusively, Stewart turned her to her side, his right hand trailing down to the small of her back until he firmly pushed her hips toward him so that she could feel that she, too, was having an effect on him.

Shocked by the contact she had never felt before, Sarah moaned again but it only caused him to move slowly back and forth against her. With great effort, she twisted her mouth away from his lips, but before she could speak, Stewart was whispering in her ear, his voice surprising her with its breathlessness. "Sarah ... relax. This is all right," he murmured. "So right."

Listening to his soothing voice as her head was caught in the hollow of his throat, and feeling the body her nearness had aroused, Sarah recognized a fleeting urge to give in to her inflamed senses. But it was Stewart who began to pull away.

With bittersweet longing, his pliant hands slowly moved from her body to her shoulders. Drawing her back and turning her bewildered face to look up into his, he sighed and smiled ruefully. "Sarah ...." he breathed, his thumb stroking her high cheekbone, flushed from his kiss. "I think I would give anything for this moment to continue. But as taken as I am with your beauty, I cannot in good conscience make love to a woman who has just fallen from a horse. Nor can I do it in an open meadow with the imminent threat of intrusion upon us." Reluctantly, his hand drifted from her face as he gave her shoulder a light squeeze, a trace of resignation in his earthy brown eyes. Rising, he picked up the handkerchief she had dropped earlier and returned it to his pocket.

After the shock of his sudden leave-taking, Sarah was quick to regain her composure. Seeking to minimize her own unprecedented surrender, she brushed away his aid and struggled to rise on her own. "Do not touch me! How dare you presume that I would ever *let* you make love to me – here or anywhere! You are no gentleman, Mr. Chamberlain," she sniffed as she briskly buttoned her riding coat. "I am quite sure my father would be interested to know about your penchant for mauling innocent females, and I intend to tell him!"

Chuckling at her tirade, Stewart countered her threat with a stinging insult that pierced her more deeply than she would ever admit. "I doubt that you will tell him anything," he mused. "For he might react with unbridled enthusiasm over the possibility that his spinster daughter may have finally attracted a suitor. He must wonder by now if she is really as cold as she appears." With a smirk that she itched to wipe away with the back of her hand, he added, "I will be glad to vouch that there is still some cause for hope."

Though he offered his arm as she began to stalk past him, Sarah refused to take it, gritting her teeth to stave off the shooting pain in her bruised and battered torso. Tears of anger and hurt welled in her deep blue eyes, as his insult rang in her ears.

What stung her so was not that Stewart had hit the mark about her father's feelings. Though never spoken, she knew he was concerned about her disinterest in attracting a mate. What hurt her more was that the first man to give words to the speculation about her frigidity was the one who had penetrated it.

Having been the first to bring her to the brink of passion, it was a terrible blow to learn that Stewart Chamberlain was, unlike his lovemaking suggested, in actuality a cruel, insensitive man. Had she not stormed ahead of him, however, she might have questioned her own assessment had she seen the curiously distraught look that flashed across his handsome face.

CHAPTER 5

As a limping Sarah and Stewart came into view of the cobbled drive in front of the imposing stone estate, Silas came running to meet them, his wrinkled face revealing pure anguish.

"Saints in heaven! Are you all right?" he cried, laboring to force his wizened body forward. "When the horses came into the yard, I nearly collapsed in fear for your safety." He stopped in front of them, a horrified look on his leathery face. "Lady Sarah, you're hurt!" he cried, as he saw her clutching her left side.

"I-I am perfectly fine," Sarah returned, her face straining to hide her pain. "It was just a little fall – and Serena is not to blame," added quickly, knowing that Silas took full responsibility for the actions of the horses in his care.

"I was about to alert the Duke," Silas replied in agitation. "Oh mum, are you sure you can walk? You may have broken something."

Stewart, towering over them, cut in as his arm slipped around Sarah's waist. "Nothing is broken, Silas. She suffered only bruises, but I think she should not try to walk further." And with that, he gently placed his other arm behind Sarah's knees and pulled her up against his broad chest.

Sarah, stunned by his sudden move but unwilling to show her discomfiture in front of Silas, placed her arm gingerly around Stewart's neck even as she protested weakly. "I really believe I shall be all right."

"Bring her inside," Silas urged, turning to lead the way. "Farnam will send for the doctor."

Feeling Sarah stiffen as she began to protest, Stewart called to the retreating figure. "Silas, I am quite sure she is going to be fine. But perhaps you could ask one of the maids to draw a very hot bath. That, I think," he said, dropping his eyes to look into her blue ones, "will relieve her aches."

As Silas ran off to do as he was bid, Sarah frowned and looked away from his mocking brown gaze. "I can walk you know," she snapped, all too aware of his strong but gentle arms enfolding her.

"It is no trouble," he replied gallantly, a deep chuckle rumbling in his huge chest. "As a matter of fact, I find holding you in my arms much to my liking."

"Well satisfy yourself then," Sarah snapped bitterly, as they approached the stone steps leading to the great front entrance, "for it will be the last time you will find me in your grasp!"

Before he could reply, the door swung open and they were confronted by the worried faces of the Duke and Duchess. "Sarah!" her mother gasped. "My poor darling. We were just told. I could not believe you fell from Serena. You are such an excellent rider. Are you all right?"

As Stewart brought her indoors, she smiled rather impatiently, irritated at the result of her encounter with this domineering stranger. "I am fine," she said wearily. "All I need is a bath and a rest. Father," she added, seeing her father's distraught expression as he hovered in the foyer. "It is nothing, really. Mr. Chamberlain is only carrying me out of courtesy. Actually I can walk quite well."

Before she could insist that Stewart put her down, he spoke above her head to her mother. "Your Grace, she is not badly hurt but walking is painful to her. Could you please lead us to her room and I will see that she gets there without any more strain."

So this ridiculous charade would continue, Sarah thought furiously. And with the blessing of her parents, Sarah saw as her father nodded and her mother hurried up the stairs.

As the Duchess moved quickly up the steps, clucking soothingly under her breath, she did not notice the hot flush on her daughter's pretty face or the calmly assured expression Stewart wore. No one seemed to mind the fact that this over-confident Yankee was violating all the rules of propriety by entering her bedroom, and it irritated Sarah immeasurably that he could so easily manipulate everyone to his advantage.

As the trio entered the rose and blue bedroom, Sarah noticed that her hand-painted porcelain tub was already in place and two young serving girls were pouring steaming water into the flowered vessel. Immediately their eyes widened as they saw the tall, dark stranger holding their mistress easily in his arms. Their nervous giggles seemed to spur Sarah's mother into action.

"Come, come," she called, "let us be quick. Mr. Chamberlain," she said, turning to him. "Put Lady Sarah on the bed – gently," she added, unnecessarily for he was quite careful with his precious bundle. Before she could continue, however, Stewart spoke quietly to Sarah as he straightened over her huddled form.

"Lady Sarah," he murmured, and only she could distinguish the mockery in his formality. "I am quite sorry our ride ended in such an unfortunate way. I hope after your bath and a rest that you will be able to join us for dinner."

"We shall have to see," Sarah responded coldly, all too aware of how his presence had overtaken the entire room. And then for her mother's benefit only, she added, "Thank you for helping me home."

"Think nothing of it." He smiled knowingly. "I am glad I was able to be of service." Then, with a broad wink, he was gone.

"Oooh," Sarah moaned angrily and her mother immediately rushed to her side.

"Oh darling, where does it hurt? Are you sure you do not need the doctor?" Quickly the Duchess began helping her daughter out of the torn and stained riding habit.

Sarah winced and sighed wearily. "I do not need the physician for a few bruises, Mother. I wish everyone would not get so hysterical. It is nothing, really. I have fallen from a horse before."

"Not since you were learning to ride," her mother countered as she untied the stock at Sarah's throat. "You are an impeccable horsewoman, Sarah. I just do not understand how it could have happened. Was Serena frightened?"

Sarah was most unwilling to rehash the events of her encounter with Stewart. Masking her pain, she rose slowly from the bed before her mother had a chance to help her finish undressing. "I-I do not remember. Mother, really," she implored, moving toward the tub. "I am all right now. Just leave me to my bath. I promise I will rest afterward."

"Very well, dear," her mother replied uncertainly, and then suddenly remembering, added, "Where is your sister – and Jack? What happened to them?"

"Oh, they rode to the Gables. I did not wish to go and Mr. Chamberlain said he had letters to post so he offered to return with me. I suppose they will be along soon enough."

"All right, darling," the Duchess said, opening the bedroom door. "Please ring for Tegan if you need anything. I will return later to see how you are feeling. Come on, girls," she called to the serving maids, "let us leave Lady Sarah to her bath."

After everyone had left, Sarah painfully removed the rest of her clothes and went to her mirror to survey the damage. She was startled by the ugly bluish purple flesh below her left breast. Turning slowly, she moaned aloud at the sight of her discolored left hip. Her leg and arm were also blemished by angry bruises, guaranteeing a slow recovery.

"And it is all his fault," she whispered petulantly as she moved to enter the steaming tub, delicately scented with lavender to cover up the vinegar used to treat bruises. But as she sat soaking in the delicious feel of the hot water easing her pains, it was surprisingly pleasant thoughts that crowded her mind. She instead found herself reliving the feel of his gentle hands on her body and the indescribable sensations his closeness had aroused.

But it is wrong for him to force his attentions on me while he seduces my sister as well, she argued to herself. But somehow that fact could not dissuade her from the realization that Stewart Chamberlain was the first man to have appealed to her – and the first man to have evoked a woman's response.

With a horrified start, she realized how sensuously she had been enjoying the warm water's quiet lapping against her swollen breasts as she thought of Stewart's lazy, knowing eyes just before his passionate kisses had overtaken her. "He haunts me!" she cried, smacking her hands against the water, causing droplets to splash about.

Wiping her face with her shaking hands, she knew she had to figure out a way to handle Stewart Chamberlain – or avoid him. And since handling him had been most unsuccessful, she quickly decided that avoiding him was the answer.

Finishing her bath and moving slowly from the tub, she reached for a bath sheet and carefully patted herself dry – more afraid of touching her strangely sensitive body than her painful bruises. Determined to do anything to keep from being near him again, she took heart in her own strength of will and smiled hopefully as she donned a light chemise and a warm, rose-colored dressing gown.

Pulling the pins from her glossy brown hair, she let if fall to her waist and gingerly climbed onto the huge bed. She carefully laid down on her right side and pulled a warm woolen throw up over her shoulders. *I am safe here in my own home, and he is not smarter than I – only more experienced and used to having his way. He will not find it so easy to kiss me again,* she told herself drowsily. Her own words gave her confidence and she found herself drifting easily into sleep.

CHAPTER 6

When Sarah awoke, she found herself immediately alert and aching with hunger. Her bedroom was pitch dark, however, and she realized that she had slept through the entire evening. She vaguely recalled being awakened by Juliana, who had heard of her mishap and seemed to think the entire episode was an amusing diversion to their otherwise uneventful lives.

Carefully she rose from the soft bed, gingerly stretching her wounded body under the dressing gown. *I simply must have food,* she thought to herself, feeling reasonably well and not a bit sleepy. But the ornate brass clock on her bureau showed that it was late and she knew that most of the servants had retired for the evening. She decided to find something for herself and put on a pair of kid mules as she ran a brush through her tangled locks.

Quietly leaving her room, only slightly favoring her injured side, she made her way down the darkened hall to the back stairs that led to the kitchen. Opening the door at the bottom of the stairs, she was surprised to find the huge and usually inviting kitchen so chilled. The fires were banked; it appeared her hopes for a meal were in vain. It was then that she spied a bowl of apples on one of the wide counters and hungrily snatched one.

Resigned to the cold appetizer, she was about to leave when the door to the servants' quarters opened and a small form entered the room.

"Lady Sarah!" a surprised voice whispered. "What are you doing here?" Sarah whirled in surprise and sighed with relief as her eyes rested on the flowing red hair and petite form of Tegan.

"Oh Tegan," she gasped. "You startled me!"

Tegan, dressed in a plain brown house coat, returned quickly, "I startled you? I thought I was seeing a ghost. What are you doing in here at this hour?"

"I was hungry," Sarah replied simply, taking another bite out of her apple, "and so far, this is all I have found to eat."

"You poor thing," Tegan chuckled sympathetically. "You haven't eaten all day, have you? 'Tis a good thing I came looking for tallows. I'll fix you something straight away," she said, bustling into action. "The family had a lovely roast for dinner and there's plenty left over. Would you care for bread as well?"

As she set about making a plate of food, Sarah sat on a stool next to the great preparation surface in the middle of the room. "I don't know how I could have slept so long on an empty stomach," she said offhandedly, glad of Tegan's company.

"Well, I'm not surprised in the least," Tegan replied briskly, "after hearing about your horrible accident. Why, according to Mr. Chamberlain, it was a miracle you didn't break your neck!"

Immediately Sarah was on guard. Just the sound of his name made her heart beat faster. "Now, Tegan," she said, carefully keeping her voice light, "how do you know what Mr. Chamberlain said?"

"Come now, mum," Tegan answered matter-of-factly, "I hardly have to tell you that these walls have ears."

"Well then," Sarah replied, munching daintily on her apple, "you may as well fill me in on all I've missed today."

As she uncovered the leftover roast and began slicing, Tegan went on. "Your mother was quite distressed and begged your father to call the doctor. But Mr. Chamberlain – he's such a commanding figure, isn't he?" Her brown eyes twinkled. "He told them he was quite sure you'd not suffered serious injury and that rest was the best thing for you. He assured your mother that if he should be mistaken, he'd ride for the doctor himself."

"And what of Lady Juliana and Lord Harrington?" Sarah asked, unaccountably gratified by Stewart's show of gallantry.

"They returned much later, looking quite pleased with themselves, if you know what I mean," Tegan said, winking. "But they were shocked to hear of your mishap. Lady Juliana wanted to see you right away, but Mr. Chamberlain said sleep would do you more good than her sympathies. The viscount, of course, was deeply distressed, but Mr. Chamberlain assured him that you were soon to be good as new."

"Did Jack stay for dinner?" Sarah inquired.

"No," Tegan answered as she sliced bread and buttered it none too sparingly. "Her Ladyship whisked him out the door before the Duchess had a chance to ask him. Then," she said confidentially, "and I only heard this, mind you, she chattered all through dinner about her marvelous day – hoping to make Mr. Chamberlain jealous, I'll wager. But it'll never work, you know …."

"Why do you say that?" Sarah asked, hoping her curiosity was not too obvious.

Tegan laughed brightly as she finished arranging the tempting plate of food. "Oh Lady Sarah, you can't tell me you haven't noticed! Mr. Chamberlain has his preference and it is *not* your sister. Aye, and what a lucky one you are to catch his eye."

"I beg your pardon," Sarah retorted, rising stiffly on the stool.

Tegan went on as if she hadn't noticed Sarah's warning tone. "He's an attractive blade and well-versed in the ways of pleasuring women, if I'm any judge at all. Rich as well, I've heard. 'Tis enough to forgive him for being a Yankee, I'd say, if that's what's holding you back."

"Tegan!" Sarah retorted, abruptly pushing herself off the stool. "Hush! Anything you have to say in Mr. Chamberlain's favor is of no concern to me, for I find nothing in him of interest – except 'twere I to learn that his visit was cut short. I find him boorish and most unattractive – when I am forced to take note of him at all!"

"Very well, mum," Tegan replied, completely undaunted. "Would you like me to take this to your room?" she asked, holding up the tempting plate on a small silver tray.

"No," Sarah sighed, her outburst over, though her cheeks were pink. "I think I will eat in the library. I've a feeling I am going to need a book to finish out this night. I slept so long, I am wide awake." When Tegan began to move toward the door, Sarah shook her head and took the tray from the maid. "Go to bed. I can carry this. Thank you."

"Very well," Tegan replied brightly. "Off with you, then. I'll tidy up. See you in the morning. Pleasant dreams," she called teasingly as Sarah shot her servant a scathing look.

"She is such a romantic," Sarah thought of her sweet maid as she slowly and carefully walked down the darkly lit hall to the library, "that she looks for evidence of love in bloom in every occurrence that takes place in this house." Shaking her shining dark head as if to dismiss the train of her thoughts, she quietly entered the library and was glad to see that a fire still burned welcomingly in the hearth before the settee.

After she put her tray down on the table next to the settee, she took a straw from the hearth and used the fire to light it. Turning around to illuminate an oil lamp next to the settee, her free hand flew to her mouth as she muffled a terrified scream. She was not alone!

"A thousand pardons if I have frightened you," the easy voice of Stewart Chamberlain spoke as he rose from the dark leather tufted chair tucked into the shadows of the library.

"My god!" Sarah gasped, trembling uncontrollably. "I-I had no idea anyone was here!" Unbidden tears of shock and relief rose in her eyes. "For an instant I thought you were an intruder." Struggling to calm down after the fright he'd caused, Sarah added, hoping to lighten the moment, "Now it seems I've you to blame for my first gray hairs."

Stewart chuckled as he advanced toward her. Sarah unconsciously took a step backward, the straw still lit in her shaking fingers. "Here," he said. "Allow me." Taking the torch, he turned and lit the lamp for her and a soft light began to chase the shadows away. "Please," he offered, as though he were the host, "sit down. I've no wish to prevent you from enjoying your repast. You must be famished."

"Yes, quite," she replied truthfully yet breathlessly as she moved past him to sink slowly into the far corner of the settee. Suddenly aware that she was clothed only in her chemise and robe, she pulled the material around her legs and asked uninvitingly, "I suppose you plan to keep me company now?"

"Why thank you. I'd be delighted," he replied, settling his lean form in the chair beside her. She immediately noticed how the firelight illuminated his twinkling eyes and long, dark lashes. He was dressed in a dark coat, closely tailored, and his ruffled shirt was unbuttoned as was the top of his matching vest, exposing a peak of his sun-browned, muscular chest.

"I am truly sorry if I shocked you," he said, crossing his long legs encased in tight trousers. "I was looking through your father's books for one to take to bed. The gentle – though enjoyable – pace of my visit here is one I am unaccustomed to and I find it difficult to sleep."

Finding his tone of voice genuinely hospitable and lacking any unseemly innuendo, Sarah relaxed slightly and began picking daintily at her food. "I too find that reading is an excellent potion for sleeplessness. I am grateful that my father encouraged me to read as much as I wished."

"Your father is a wise man," Stewart nodded, "for I've yet to find a soul that reading has harmed. I think you would find America to your liking, since the practice of encouraging young ladies to read is becoming commonplace. I, for one, applaud the trend."

Turning slightly to study her more closely, he asked, "Tell me, Sarah, are you feeling better?"

Casting her azure eyes down to the plate on her lap, she answered lightly, "Yes, much, though I doubt I'll be able to ride for a few days."

"You took quite a fall you know. I hope you will not hold it against me for too long, for I would not wish us to part adversaries," he said gently.

Sarah shifted nervously on the couch, avoiding his deep gaze. "I do not see why it matters so much what my feelings are toward you. I am sure you have plenty of female acquaintances who find your attentions pleasing. One more or less should make no difference, I would think."

Stewart laughed softly, "Ah, but rarely do I meet a woman of your captivating beauty who is intelligent as well. I think we could enjoy each other's company were you to give yourself a chance."

"From what I have observed," Sarah replied haughtily, "you are too little interested in my companionship. You seem more eager to wrench unwilling kisses from me and in case it is not clear to you, I find such behavior arrogant and abusive."

"How long do you hope to deny yourself the pleasures of your own needs, Lady Sarah?" Stewart asked, his words touching her like an intimate caress. "You may not have approved of my boldness, but you must admit you found enjoyment in my arms, for your own response was warm."

"I cannot believe my own ears!" Sarah squeaked. "Have you no sense of decency? We can neither be talking about – nor doing – what you so boldly and knavishly suggest. And where is your pride? Why do you even bother me, when I have told you quite clearly that I do not care for you in the least?"

Stewart seemed unperturbed by her remarks as he responded easily, stretching his long legs before him. "Let me tell you something, Sarah. I learned early in life that a man who is a good judge of character can greatly economize his time and efforts, thereby saving his energies for that which is most important to him. I find you most intriguing, for your dark beauty suits my tastes. You are also quick-witted and lacking in coyness, which I admire in any woman. But all your assets would not have maintained my interest save for one ingredient I deem essential." He paused and Sarah knew she would die of curiosity before she would ask him to continue.

"That quality," he said finally, "is passion -- a true fire that causes a woman to respond in the way nature intended." His mesmerizing voice suddenly turned matter-of-fact. "Perhaps now you can see why I was forward. I wanted to know if you possessed that passion, Sarah, and now that I know you do, I can be more leisurely in my efforts to have you, for I know you will be worth the effort."

Sarah was plainly appalled. Here was this man, a foreigner, a guest in the Duke of Weston's home, telling her in the same tone of voice he would use to read aloud from a newspaper, that he was planning to bed her. Far from an expression of desire, it was a statement of fact, as if he were some sort of fortune teller who could accurately predict their future.

Why, he even looked like some sort of demon sitting there against the shadows cast by the flickering firelight, his dark hair rimmed in a golden glow, his brown eyes dancing with fiery flecks. The handsome cut of his nose and chin was chiseled by the blaze, causing his casual grin to appear menacing.

Frightened by his ominous yet strangely attractive countenance and his overpowering self-confidence, Sarah was at a complete loss for words. Never had she encountered a member of the opposite sex so blatant in his desire for her. And she was of such limited experience that there was nothing she could summon to help her now. Her earlier decision to avoid him had already proved unsuccessful, for here she was, trapped in his lair again.

And then it suddenly dawned on her: Stewart Chamberlain appeared to be an honest man. He frankly desired her, and just as honestly, though cruelly, he had offered his assessment of her father's concern for her spinsterhood.

She was absolutely convinced that her father would only join in partnership with a man of high integrity and trustworthiness. And he was indeed among her father's favorites, if appearances could be judged. Being honest herself, she decided to respond without pretense.

While observing the interesting play of her lovely, serious face as she considered his words, Stewart smiled inwardly and once again pondered his good fortune in having met the Duke of Weston. A man born to wealth and privilege, Weston had begun a trading business by purchasing a few ships captained by men who were willing to take unusual risks to assure England of goods which were most desirable and least readily obtainable. Through his own personal efforts, Weston had added new fortunes to the previous wealth he had inherited. And while his fellow aristocrats may not have approved of his risky and unnecessary adventures, Weston was much too powerful – and popular – to snub.

Now the maverick gentleman, who saw his thriving business as an exciting game, was all too aware of the difficulties involved in trading with the young United States. And yet the market for American goods was never better. Weston, ever a loyal British lord and subject, could not agree with his business associates who felt threatened by America's growing share of trade. "There's room for all of us to prosper," he had told Chamberlain at their first meeting in London, "and I intend to."

Great Britain had enacted the Orders in Council in 1807 which forbade neutral ships to trade with Europe – especially France – without stopping in England first. Intending to strike a blow against American traders, England had not counted on the skill or daring of Yankee blockade runners. The United States still prospered, but grew in their outrage over the British practice of impressments: taking British deserters off American vessels to return them to the stricter and lower-paying jobs of English seamen. Many of these sailors, however, were true American citizens, and were actually being kidnapped to build up the dwindling British navy. President Jefferson retaliated with The Embargo Act, which forbade American ships to sail for any foreign port, a horrendous self-inflicted blow to U.S. trade.

Thousands of sailors were immediately put out of work. Ships rotted in the harbors while merchants stood by helpless, their businesses ruined. Stores of American wheat, cotton and tobacco piled up on the docks, their prices plummeting to rock bottom.

Chamberlain, who had made his own fortune as a shipbuilder and trader, had been lucky enough to escape immediate devastation. But he could not sit idly by while good seamen lost their jobs, fine ships deteriorated in the harbors and much-needed goods sat wasting away without a market. At the first opportunity, he sailed for England, determined to find people who agreed that these economic boycotts were wasteful and ill-conceived and was bent on finding a scheme that would bring some order to all this chaos.

Weston, impressed with the younger man's common sense – as well as his courage to gamble with the world power bureaucracies – immediately agreed to a partnership whereby they would trade under a neutral foreign flag. Together, they had the financial resources, the political influence, and the business know-how to succeed – and both were eager to begin.

But not too eager to leave, Stewart thought, running a long, lean finger across the cleft of his chin as he surveyed the woman beside him in the firelight. In her softly clinging dressing gown, her dark, glossy hair streaming over her firm breasts, she looked like a delicate rosebud, ready to blossom at the slightest provocation. He could almost imagine how tantalizing she would be, writhing beneath him in ecstasy as they jointly partook of the joys their bodies could give each other. But as his dark eyes rose again to her face, it was not the smoky blue gaze he had imagined, but a wide, troubled one.

"Mr. Chamberlain," she pleaded, her sensuous lips quivering slightly. "Please. There is something I must say to you. And it will be much too difficult if you continue to stare at me – in that way." Sarah squirmed on the sofa, pulling her gown more protectively around her slim form.

"Yes?" Stewart replied, blinking to dispel his pleasant reverie. "What is it, Lady Sarah?"

Drawing a deep breath, Sarah prayed fervently that her words would resolve the tension she felt whenever he was near. Hoping her honesty would appeal to his sense of fairness, she began, "Mr. Chamberlain, a man of your vast experience must surely realize that I have led a rather sheltered, quiet existence. I am troubled by your boldness and have so far been unsuccessful in making my objections clear. Since I do not wish to offend my father by being rude to his guest, I would like to propose a compromise – of sorts – so that I can continue living in my own home without fear of losing my virtue."

She stopped then, hoping to gauge his reaction to her words, but Stewart's face was a handsome mask. Seeing her pause, he raised a dark eyebrow as a signal for her to continue.

So he wasn't going to make it easy, Sarah thought, feeling her temper rise. Willing herself to remain calm, she went on, painful though the effort was. "At this time, I have no special suitor. This fact, I know, causes my parents and my sister concern, though I have not given it much care. If you wish to court me – as a gentleman courts a lady – I-I will try my best to give you a fair trial. I only ask that you do not abuse your liberty to act as a beau and that you make it clear to Juliana your intentions toward me. I would not wish to hurt her in any way."

Casually, Stewart resettled himself in the chair, his hand tugging at his mouth to restrain a grin. "Go on," he finally uttered.

Sarah was startled. "Go on? I just told you what I would agree to."

"Sarah, you spoke earlier of a compromise. That means both of us must make concessions. You have not yet told me how you plan to concede. I have already told you what I wish from you, but so far you've made no mention of our physical needs." His dark brown gaze on her was innocent and quizzical, yet his words stroked her as surely as a caress. "What of that?"

"B-but I told you," Sarah replied urgently, feeling the blood rise to her cheeks. "As my suitor – if we find the situation a compatible one—I would not be opposed to some ..." she groped for the word, "affection. And if by some miracle, our relationship were to blossom, we would marry and you would have all you desire."

"Ah hah," Stewart responded and a deep rumbling chuckle escaped from his lips. "I see. So you expect to be wed to me before you discard your innocence?" Ignoring her nod, he continued, "Well, 'Your Grace'," he mocked, "you must surely think yourself some prize to try and extract a proposal of marriage from me just to bed you. I am truly sorry to disappoint you, but the idea of matrimony does not appeal to me. Especially," he emphasized with a wave of his arm toward her, "to someone whose abilities to satisfy a mate for life are completely untested.

"No Sarah, it appears that you have not compromised in the least. I would think you'd be willing to strike a better bargain, when you have so much to gain." Stewart ended calmly, a twinkle lighting up his dark eyes. He knew that he had lit the fuse.

Seething, Sarah sat straight up on the settee, her azure eyes blazing steel. "Sir, the audacity of your tongue far exceeds your crude behavior! I have nothing to gain by your pawing – and a great deal to lose!"

"But you said it yourself," Stewart replied, leaning forward, his forearms resting on his muscular thighs. "You have no suitors at the moment – and at your age that is considered dire. At least my attentions will give your family cause to hope that you can yet attract a husband before one will have to be found for you."

But in truth, Stewart knew, she was far from desperate. Rarely had he met a young woman so beautiful or captivating. Her thick, chestnut hair hung in tumbling waves about her lovely, pure face. Eyes of the deepest blue were encircled by long black lashes and even though, at this moment, her face was contorted by her rage, a fine bone structure beneath the rosy hue of her flawless skin ensured that each expression was as appealing as the last. He remembered the delicious feel of her slim yet soft and pliant body next to his and he knew that if any other man had been able to get as close as he, she would certainly be claimed by now.

Even as he taunted her, Stewart knew he'd be willing to bide his time to have her, for she was surely a prize. But at the same time, it would never do to openly approve of her virginal games, for he certainly did not. He was -- and always had been -- a man of expedience. When he wanted something, he assessed its value and paid the fair price. Lady Sarah Tremont was certainly worth his patience, but she, nor any woman for that matter, was due his name. Bachelorhood suited his temperament and lifestyle, and there was nothing here that he could foresee capable of changing his mind.

His reverie was abruptly interrupted when Sarah suddenly leapt from the sofa, ignoring the pain it caused her to do so. Feet apart, her hands on her slender hips, she spit fury. "In my entire life, I have never been so insulted! Not only have you laid claim to my body – as if I were a trollop – you shamelessly offend me not once but twice today by suggesting that I have neither the propensities nor the means with which to attract a husband!"

Shaking the flowing tresses from her face, she continued, "You are such an inept swain, lacking in the art of seduction, that you must force your intentions upon me like a rutting stallion. And when I counter your attack, you choose to ridicule me to save your own pride.

"Your behavior is despicable, Mr. Chamberlain, and I heartily regret tendering a truce between us. And," she bit off, shaking a finger at his face, unmarred by her tirade, "I will make absolutely sure that our paths never cross again!"

CHAPTER 7

Sarah had never been so furious in her life. Stewart Chamberlain, with his superficial charm thinly veiling a total disrespect for gently-bred women, had affronted her beyond her own comprehension. He was a brute without morals, an unscrupulous cad parading himself as a gentleman of taste, discretion and elegance. She hated and feared his composure and his complete domination of every encounter. He was like a beautiful black panther she had once seen in London – cool, aloof, disdainful – until he scented the trepidation of his prey. Then, without warning, a spring, and in one fell swoop, total annihilation.

Her breast heaving beneath the rose gown, she jerked her blazing blue eyes from Stewart's face, and, forgetting the pain in her left side, stomped off toward the library doors. So overwrought by her own anger and humiliation, she did not realize he was right behind her until she felt his long fingers clamp ever so gently but firmly on her upper arm. Before she could scream for aid, his other hand covered her mouth and pushed her head back against the hollow beneath his chin.

Stewart's uncompromising hold and the knowledge that she was completely helpless to defend herself so shocked Sarah that she could not summon the will to even attempt escape. The panther, indeed, had sprung, and her fate was frighteningly obvious. Simultaneously cursing her own stupidity for being caught off guard and praying for mercy, she did not realize she was shaking and sobbing in his grasp.

"You will not cry out?" Stewart demanded in the quietest of tones. Weakly, she shook her head, a move barely possible because of her imprisonment. His voice, ever so ominous, stirred the hair covering her ear, sending chills up her spine. "You are safe," he breathed, his tone defying her to conjure any doubts as to that fact.

Slowly, his hand left her mouth, slipping to her shoulder as he gently turned her around to face him. Keeping one hand on her arm, he used the other to retrieve a muslin handkerchief from his coat pocket. As he daubed at her tears, still streaming silently down her face, she cast her eyes straight ahead, seeing only his chest. Using his free hand to tilt her chin upward, he sought to repair the damage to her distraught face. Sarah kept her eyes closed tightly, clamping her mouth shut to hold back her sobs, as her mind reeled with anger, fear and foreboding. As if he were merely continuing a quiet conversation, Stewart began speaking in a gentle voice.

"My mother used to warn me that my terseness would someday be my undoing," he said, brushing at her thick lashes clumped into spikes by her tears. "I often wished to show her that such forthrightness had brought me much success in business. But it now dawns on me that she was referring to matters of a much more personal nature – and I fear she was right after all," he said, and Sarah detected a wistfulness in his tone. Her eyes still shut, she listened to the rustle of his coat as he returned the cloth to his pocket and then placed both hands on her upper arms. He was so close that she could feel his warm breath on her upturned face.

"It has not been my desire to woo a lady, for my use of women has been simple and basic," he continued, feeling her arms stiffen at his frankness. "But it occurs to me now that I might have underestimated the value of a woman as a companion – perhaps even a friend."

Sarah, unable to hide her curiosity over his surprisingly conciliatory words, opened her puffy eyes slightly to look upon his face. His flared eyebrows were knit in a thoughtful, serious pose and his brown gaze penetrated hers with an intensity she had not seen before.

"Sarah, I cannot apologize for my words or my actions, for they stem from the truth of this matter between us ... which is a mutual attraction." Sarah quickly dropped her head, stemming the contradiction on her lips. He seemed to know what she would have said. "I know you cannot admit it to me, for you were reared to speak naught of such things. But I would not wish to be spurned before we have had the opportunity to know and understand each other ... and I see that my words have nearly done the deed. For that," he whispered, pulling her closer, "I am truly sorry.

"So," he said rather gruffly, and Sarah sensed this speech was an effort for him, "I will give you my word that no harm will come to you at my hands and I beseech you to reinstate your offer to allow me to court you – 'as a gentleman courts a lady' – I think you said. Whatever springs from our liaison will be because you desire it. Can you agree to this now?"

Her head still bowed and her mind tumbling with a gamut of disjointed thoughts, she answered with the only comment she could honestly make. "I do not trust you."

"I can understand your feelings," he replied. "And all I can tell you is that I am a man of my word. Your father knows this. Look at me, Sarah," he implored and she raised her head slightly to seek his face beneath her thick, black lashes. "You have my solemn promise that your feelings will be considered in this relationship. And if I play you false," he added, his sensual lips curling up in a slight grin, "you only have to tell your father. Indeed I have much to lose that is of no small importance to my future. I trust the terms are fair?"

"Oh," she sighed and her breath came out in a shudder. "I-I cannot say ... I feel 'twould be simpler to drop the whole matter, for it has been going badly for me since the moment we met," she answered, wincing as she rubbed her left hip.

Stewart laughed aloud, visibly relaxing as he looped his left arm through her right one and began moving her toward the library doors. "Lady Sarah, your wit is a delight to my ears. Come; let me escort you to the servants' stairs. You needn't make any decisions tonight, for I have decided to show you what a charming, trustworthy companion I can be. If, by week's end, you find me thoroughly revolting, then you can tell me so and I'll never impose myself on you again."

As he guided her to the door to the back stairs, he continued gallantly, his handsome dark eyes brimming with humor. "Good night, Lady Sarah. Pleasant dreams and I look forward to our next meeting. Until then," he gestured, bending to make a magnificent leg, especially for a Yankee. And with that he turned on his heel and strolled casually back down the hall toward the library, leaving Sarah to gawk at him, a look of total surprise on her innocent, tear-stained face.

CHAPTER 8

True to his words, Sarah could find no fault with Stewart's behavior over the following days, even though at first she tried. During their times together, at dinner and afterwards in the parlor, he was poised, polite, complimentary and the conversations they shared were fascinating to Sarah, who had never ventured farther from her home than Brighton Beach. Stewart was full of stories about the many places he'd visited during his days as a sailor. Minimizing the dangers involved in his exploits, he spoke easily of the many people he had met and the exotic places he had been.

Though she tried not to show it, Sarah was impressed. Stewart had lived a life she had known only through her books. In vain, she sought to quell her curiosity, but because Stewart maintained a certain modesty about his adventures, she found herself asking many more questions that she meant to. The last thing she wanted to do was give Stewart the idea that she was interested in him, but alas, she could not hide it.

Late on the fifth afternoon of his visit, shortly following the departure of Weston's business associates with whom he and Chamberlain had been meeting, Sarah heard a quick rapping on her door.

"Yes?" she responded, marking the place in the book she had been trying to read. The door opened and Tegan stepped into the room, a cheery smile on her rosy face.

"Lady Sarah, Mr. Chamberlain has asked me to see if you would care to join him on a walk to the stables. He feels the need for some exercise, he said, and would enjoy your company."

Sarah was delighted to hear the invitation, but she refused to give Tegan the satisfaction of knowing her feelings. Ignoring the maid's beaming expression, she replied offhandedly, "Tell Mr. Chamberlain I will be down shortly. I should visit

Serena, since I have not seen her since the fall. I wouldn't want her to think I bear a grudge ...."

"No mum," Tegan chuckled, not at all fooled by her mistress's nonchalance. "You wouldn't want that. I'll tell Mr. Chamberlain." As she turned to leave the room, she added, "It's a lovely day. I think all you'll need is a shawl."

As soon as Tegan was gone, Sarah jumped out of her chair, rushed to the mirror and furiously began brushing her dark hair until it shone. As she carelessly pinned it up off her neck, she chided herself for suddenly feeling so radiant. "It's simply that he is someone new to talk to," she muttered to her reflection in the mirror, but she knew that didn't fully explain the glimmer of excitement in her deep blue eyes, or the sudden rosiness of her cheeks. Dismissing the inexplicable thoughts beginning to surface, she abruptly turned from the mirror, grabbed a shawl and bonnet from her bureau and hastily ran from the room.

Controlling her pace just before she reached the stairs, Sarah took a deep breath and slowly descended. Seeing Stewart's casually-attired form, his back to her as he stared out the foyer window, Sarah could not resist the urge to smile. He looked so tall and handsome standing there with his hands behind his back, his curling hair sweeping the collar of his white shirt.

As if he knew she was there, Stewart suddenly whirled about and Sarah had no chance to hide her happy expression. "Good afternoon," he said warmly, grinning pleasantly, his eyes reflecting his approval of her appearance. She was glad that she had chosen this pale green dress. Though simple, she knew it flattered her figure and set off her eyes dramatically. "I am glad you decided to walk with me," he said, coming toward her. "That must mean you are recovered from your spill."

"That's right," she replied, suddenly shy. "I feel nearly as good as before. Perhaps I'll be able to ride tomorrow."

Stewart politely took her elbow and led her to the front door. "I wish I could join you, but I will be returning to London tomorrow. I've an engagement I'm unable to break. But," he added, as they stepped out onto the portico, "perhaps we could ride during my next visit?"

Sarah found it difficult to hide the sudden quickening of her heartbeat. "So you'll be coming back?"

"Why yes," Stewart answered. "I think I told you before. Your father and I have found it much more suitable to arrange our business in relative seclusion. We are not eager to deal publicly at this time, since it might arouse undue suspicion. Therefore, I will be visiting again."

As they walked toward the stables, Sarah asked casually, though she did not feel at all casual with him so near, "You must miss your home and family being away as long as you are."

"Well," Stewart replied as they neared the paddock fence, "I am used to being away for longer periods than this, but since I've acquired some property near Boston, I must admit I do find myself occasionally longing for a visit there. I have a farm and have hired a couple to care for it. It's a peaceful place, a far cry from city life, and I find I enjoy the times I can help with the planting, the harvest and caring for the animals."

As Stewart rested his elbow on the fence, Sarah pulled herself up to get a better look at the yearling Silas was working with in the yard. "I don't understand," she said quietly, studying the spirited filly, "if you enjoy your farm so much, why do you bother pursuing these business interests? You have no need of money. Father told me you've amassed quite a fortune ... for a Yankee," she added, a twinkle softening her eyes.

Stewart laughed easily and leaned a bit closer to her. "Well. I've always enjoyed a challenge and I've been rather fortunate in my pursuits. I still have my life, my health and I am able to live comfortably, when I so desire. But – and your father can vouch for this – life can seem somewhat unfulfilling when there is no challenge, so I keep my hand in business interests I think can turn a profit – and which are beneficial to my country," he concluded, looking away as if embarrassed to express his patriotism.

"I am not so sure I can believe your gallantry," Sarah replied, her eyes narrowing slightly. "You strike me as someone who enjoys nothing more than besting others. That it profits another besides yourself seems inconsequential."

Stewart sighed and seemed to concentrate on watching Silas and the filly. "As usual, Lady Sarah, your judgment of me is harsh. In truth, I share with my countrymen a great love of opportunity and equality for all. And since I have not the burden of family responsibilities, I can spend my time working to bring greater wealth to America."

Sarah stiffened, "So you consider a family a burden?"

"For some," Stewart answered matter-of-factly. "It's not a subject I consider often, since it does not apply to me."

Once again, he had sidestepped the issue of marriage, Sarah noticed with contempt. *He is a rogue to the soles of his boots*, she thought, irritated with herself for even caring. Her feelings for him were an inexplicable mixture of interest and disdain. Every time she tried to dismiss him from her thoughts, something drew her closer. She looked forward to seeing him and yet when they were together, she found herself wary and skittish. His overpowering attractiveness frightened her even as she was drawn closer to it. She could not conceive of a happy relationship with him, and yet she could not deny that she hoped to see him again.

In many ways she was pleased with the way things were between them – happy, congenial, and often companionable with only occasional episodes of tension – as now. It was this basic difference between them – he seeking a lover he could talk to, and she longing for a friendship that might blossom into marriage – that made it impossible for Sarah to be completely relaxed in his presence.

And though she tried not to dwell on it, it bothered her to find her thoughts frequently returning to those moments prior to their compromise when he had held her in his arms, demanding a response from her lips and body she hadn't known existed. In those fleeting moments, he had been able to strip her of her senses, leaving only passion in their wake. He had made her a stranger to herself and she was afraid to understand it – only wishing to deny that it had ever happened. As if she could.

"I seem to have lost your attention," a teasing voice broke into her thoughts. Sarah blushed and turned her face to look up at the man grinning down at her

"I beg your pardon, sir," she stuttered and pushed herself off the fence, landing lightly on her feet. "Shall we go to the stables," she implored, attempting to cover her lapse.

He chuckled, as if he knew quite well the turn of her thoughts, but wisely chose to hold his tongue.

As they entered the darkened stable, they were met by a boisterous whinny from the corner stall. "Excuse me," Stewart said, taking Sarah's arm from his own, "but my friend over here wishes a word with me." Reaching down into the pocket of his breeches as he walked, Stewart pulled out a sugar cube and presented it to Nubian, who was anxiously rustling about his stall.

"No wonder he is so glad to see you," Sarah giggled, moving closer. "It appears you've been bribing him for his cooperation."

"With excellent results, as you can see," he answered, patting the horse's velvety black nose as he devoured the treat. "I've ridden him every day with more success each time. We've become quite fond of each other."

"I am so happy to hear that," Sarah replied genuinely pleased. "Much as he abused his riders, I always took pity on him for being little used as a mount. He is much too strong and proud to be kept only for breeding."

"My sentiments are not quite as noble," came his reply. "I say he must work for his pleasures ... as I have been forced to do," Stewart intoned, giving her a meaningful look.

Her hackles immediately raised, Sarah gasped angrily and whirled away from him. "There you go! Crudely referring to our compromise in the same breath as you mention rutting beasts! I should have known you would mock me at the first opportunity."

Crossing the cobbled stable floor, she reached out for Serena, who was startled by her mistress's angry tones. In doing so, she missed the warning etched on Stewart's handsome visage as the muscle in his cheek twitched, his mouth set in a tight line.

"I was beginning to believe you were sincere in your efforts to treat me as a lady," Sarah continued recklessly, "but now I see the truth: that you consider the whole idea a charade, a comical sketch to appease me so that you can swoop down on me unsuspectingly, like a hawk to some lone field mouse. Well, Mister Chamberlain, I am not fooled, and you can rot for all I care."

Her tirade ended, Sarah leaned against Serena's stall, her fingers shaking as her hand reached up to brush a dark curling wisp of hair from her hot face. She was completely unprepared for Stewart's reply.

"Listen well, Lady Sarah," he spoke, his voice menacingly quiet and controlled. "You have sorely tested my patience in this matter, and I am near the end of my rope. I wish to make it perfectly clear to you that though I have been made to exercise restraint, I will not be gelded by you or any other." His relaxed posture belied the disdain of his words, and Sarah's skin prickled with the fear of it and she refused to face him directly.

"I had believed that there was some room in our compromise for lighthearted banter, but I realize now that even though you are twenty years and, I might add, long past the age of knowledge," he said, his tone tinged with sarcasm, "you are only playing grown-up. You are still very much the child, are you not? Perhaps you should have a talk with your sister concerning the harmless use of innuendo. It seems that you have too much to learn at my expense." With a disgusted snort, he returned to Nubian, who was stamping impatiently for more sugar.

At the mention of her sister's name, Sarah's thoughts immediately turned to anger. She did not wish to be reminded of Juliana's talents as a coquette, especially by Stewart Chamberlain. But at the same time, she knew she had overreacted to his innocent quip. It was his uncompromising virility that continually put her on edge. Haughtiness was the only shield she had to defend herself from his intangible but very real assault.

Mollified by the truth of his words, Sarah let out a trembling sigh, realizing she had held her breath all the while he had spoken. Gingerly, she turned and slowly walked toward him, unable to fathom his thoughts since his back was presented to her.

"Mr. Chamberlain," she began tentatively, and then with more resolve, "Stewart. I-I am very sorry. I fear I reacted more strongly than was called for." Because he refused to acknowledge her nearness, Sarah moved forward and lightly touched his arm, struck by the muscular hardness beneath her glove. "You've been very ... fair."

"Perhaps 'foolish' is a better word," Stewart said dryly, giving her a quick, sidelong glance.

"No," Sarah replied hastily, her fingers tightening involuntarily, "No, I fear there is truth in what you say. You have treated me honorably and I've repaid your courtesies by acting like a child. Will you excuse me?"

Stewart was quite sure Sarah had no idea that her lovely upturned face and those wide innocent blue eyes were so positively convincing. But his ire would not be so easily appeased; he hesitated to reply.

"Please?" she persisted, just as he was about to turn his head away. And then, completely by impulse, she moved closer and, tugging on his arm, reached up and planted a slow, prim kiss on his grimly set lips.

Though her cheeks reddened in shock at her own boldness in using physical means to wield a pardon from this man, she smiled innocently as she lowered herself onto her heels and repeated, "Please?"

With a teasing twinkle suddenly aglimmer in his mink-colored eyes, he shifted his weight to a more casual stance and replied lightly, "At the risk of inciting you again, I think that one more kiss, with perhaps a bit more feeling, might just restore my pleasant mood."

Again surprising herself, Sarah gave a wry smile. Then, placing her arms around his neck, she drew his head down to hers and kissed him again, tentatively moving her ripe lips against his. When he did not respond, she pulled him closer, parting her lips slightly to match his more completely.

It was then that Stewart, warming to her attempts, slowly let his arms slip around her, and with one hand on the small of her back, used his other to gently cup the back of her head.

Though his pace was languid and unhurried, Sarah was overcome by the richness of the feelings he had ignited. It was so easy to bask in the tenderness of his touch, to be filled with the heady scent of his cologne and leather, to feel the hardness of his chest pressing against her tingling breasts. As his fingers wove their way into the loose curls at the nape of her neck, his tongue sought the warmth of her mouth and she found herself overcome by the delicious assault.

Her senses reeling with the ever-building current that passed between them, Sarah longed for the feeling to go on ... and on. His probing tongue set her afire and she knew that she could not pull away from him even if she had wanted to.

Stewart, reveling in the newly-discovered willingness of the delicate pink lips beneath his, was struck by her innocent enthusiasm, quite sure that she had no idea of the effect she was having on him. He felt the familiar stirring in his loins, and wished fervently that their embrace were taking place anywhere but in this very public stable. He would have loved nothing better than to woo her in some secluded forest, where he could lay her down on the sweet-smelling moss and ....

A whinny from Nubian broke Stewart's reverie and he raised his head from Sarah just in time to see Silas leading the filly through the stable doors. Sarah let out an embarrassed gasp, too shocked to move, but Stewart appeared unnerved as he calmly took her wrists in his hands and slowly lowered them from his neck.

If Silas had indeed discovered the ardent couple, he gave no indication as he struggled to control the spirited yearling. "Good afternoon," Stewart called to the man, the assuredness of his voice belying her effect on him. "You seem to have your hands full with that one," he said, holding tight to both of Sarah's wrists as she winced at the double entendre.

"That I do, sir," Silas grunted, pulling the horse toward the stall, "but she's coming around. Afternoon Lady Sarah," he added, pushing the filly into her stall. "Don't tell me you've come for a ride?"

"No-no, not today," she answered much too breathlessly. With a nervous tug, she pulled her hands away from Stewart's grasp. "Just to visit."

Refusing to look into the thoughtful brown eyes that gazed down on her, she hastened to pull her shawl around her quivering shoulders and said, "I think I should be getting back. I have things to attend to before we dine."

"Yes, I do as well," Stewart intoned, his voice stirring her with its gentleness as he placed his hand at the small of her back to guide her toward the stable doors. "Good day, Silas."

"Good day, sir" Silas replied, without looking up. As she walked past the trainer, Sarah's eyes narrowed slightly, wondering how much he had noted, but knowing there was really no need to fear. Silas – and all her father's servants for that matter – were nothing if not discreet.

As they entered the sunlight, Sarah demurely stepped away from Stewart's touch, afraid that she would not be able to concentrate if he continued to walk so closely beside her. "I understand that a special meal has been prepared for this evening since this is your last day with us for a time."

"About this evening," Stewart replied, "do you think you and I could find a few moments to ourselves? Perhaps after dinner? In the garden?"

After what had just transpired, Sarah was frightened by the intimacy of his tone. Her voice caught in her throat as Stewart continued. "You needn't fear my intentions, Sarah, though I'm sure you know that already. It's just that I'm leaving at first light and I won't have another chance to speak with you privately."

"I-I don't know," Sarah rushed on, "I am not sure it is possible, and besides, it would be seen as improper."

"Lady Sarah," Stewart chided teasingly, "you are trying much too hard to thwart our friendship. It is both possible and proper to carry on a private conversation. Why, I believe we are having one at this very moment. So, out with it. What is your real excuse? Are you in the middle of a good book perhaps? Or will a few minutes spent with me disrupt your beauty sleep?"

Sarah's blue eyes blazed as she snapped her head up to look at him, "Do not mock me. I am not a recluse as you are most fully aware."

"Ah," Stewart raised his brows, "then maybe there is a beau who occupies your evenings? I have never seen you dally with the others after dinner. Of course!" he beamed, seemingly proud of his powers of reasoning. "That would explain your absences and aloofness. Tell me now. What young stud has stolen your heart? Is it the viscount?"

Sarah was infuriated by his callous taunts and immediately quickened her pace. "You vex me sorely, Stewart Chamberlain! You are all too aware of the fact that Lord Harrington is practically betrothed to my sister, and that I have no particular beau – at the moment," she spat out. "As for making myself scarce, it is a habit I've only recently acquired," she said, throwing him a meaningful glance.

"Very well, then," Stewart smiled with satisfaction, "you have nothing to keep you from meeting me this evening. 'Tis good, for I have something rather important to tell you."

"If it is indeed auspicious," Sarah said huffily, "then perhaps you'd better tell me now. I really do not know if I shall be able to meet you."

Stewart ignored her reluctance. "I'm sure you'll manage." Before Sarah could utter another word, they had arrived at the mansion. Stewart opened the door with a gallant gesture and Sarah whisked her way past him, the butler's presence closing the opportunity for her to make one last protest.

Smiling politely, she greeted Farnam and threw a farewell to Stewart over her shoulder as she swiftly ascended the grand staircase. Farnam and Stewart both watched her go, smiling fondly, but for entirely different reasons.

CHAPTER 9

Dinner was a festive occasion. The Duke of Weston was in a remarkably fine mood, perpetuated by the fact that his young business partner was soon to set in motion the plans they had so meticulously developed for their new and exciting venture. The Duchess, a lovely and gracious hostess, had arranged a bounteous feast of roast veal, pheasant and all the trimmings, carefully prepared and served by the competent staff. The banquet table in the main dining room was set with the family's best china, crystal and silver on a magnificently embroidered tablecloth made by Sarah's late grandmother, the Dowager Duchess of Weston.

Lady Juliana was, as usual, in her glory whenever a hint of celebration was in the air, and Sarah, who sat beside her, could not help noticing what a vibrantly beautiful woman her young sister was. Juliana's thick golden hair was swept up and away from her face, emphasizing her slender neck and high cheekbones. Her lavender silk satin gown was cut off the shoulder and heightened the attractiveness of her snapping green eyes and creamy alabaster skin. Sarah was fascinated by Juliana's wiles; the way she would raise a finely shaped eyebrow, flutter her gorgeously thick lashes or absent-mindedly run a fingertip across the edge of her revealing bodice when their handsome guest's eyes would meet hers across the table.

Stewart, too, looked especially elegant tonight, Sarah mused. He wore a tailcoat of midnight blue over a silk waistcoat, linen shirt and black stock. His black doeskin breeches hugged his lean form and Sarah could not ignore the handsomeness of his tanned face, nor the way his warm brown eyes bespoke his pleasure when he first looked at her this evening.

Though her dress was not cut nearly as low as her sister's, Sarah was pleased she had chosen the pale blue duchesse silk gown with sparkling beaded trim. The cap sleeves revealed her slender white arms above kid gloves and the beautiful perfection of her bodice.

The Duchess smiled to herself when she first beheld her daughter in the dress, for it was one that Sarah had vowed never to wear. She had ordered it made in serviceable fine white muslin and was completely miffed when it was delivered in its present state. The Duchess urged her to keep it, never letting on that she had changed the specifications herself.

Sarah's luxuriant chestnut hair was held in place by bejeweled combs on either side of the crown and her ears were adorned by tiny marquis-cut diamonds her father had given her as a birthday gift.

Despite the fact that she had not decided whether to meet Stewart in the gardens later, she found it easy to forget her qualms amidst the gay banter around the table.

"But Mr. Chamberlain," Juliana's lilting voice cut into the conversation Stewart was holding with the Duke. "You and my father talk all the time about business in your little country. I want to know what in the world you do for amusement? I've heard that there is a dearth of culture in the Colonies," she quipped, diffusing the sting of her insult with a lovely smile.

Stewart, ignoring her taunting tone, smiled engagingly at the younger Tremont. "On the contrary, I think you'd find America holds the same degree of sophistication you're accustomed to here ... though without, of course, the history. We have the theatre, fine musicians, painters, fashion, exotic restaurants and shops," he answered, and with a mirthful tone, added, "though fighting off the savages curtails the amount of time we have to spend on life's more refined pleasures."

Juliana's jade eyes widened in excitement. "So 'tis true! How positively horrifying. Wild Indians a constant threat. How have you managed to survive?"

Weston bellowed with laughter. "My darling daughter. I am afraid Mr. Chamberlain's ribbing too closely conforms to your romantic notions about America."

"So you're teasing me, Mr. Chamberlain?" Juliana pouted prettily, not taking her beguiling eyes from the man across from her. "And here I thought you were giving credence to the wicked stories we've been hearing."

"There are Indians in my country, but they pose no threat in Boston," Stewart consoled her. "Their savagery is much exaggerated, you know. The race has been sorely provoked by settlers disrupting their homes and hunting grounds. After all, we are not, as some insist, the original inhabitants of the country."

"Have you seen a real Indian?" Sarah could not contain her curiosity.

"On occasion," Stewart answered plainly. "We do conduct business with some tribes. They are unusually fine and fit people to gaze upon and their clothing is wildly impressive. They have a great respect for each other and the forces of nature. I think there is a lot we can learn from them, and I hope someday there will be a more felicitous peace between our peoples," he added, his voice deepening.

"Well I would simply swoon if I ever crossed paths with a painted heathen," Juliana insisted.

"I doubt that," the Duchess interjected dryly, "though the chances of meeting one in Town are rather slim."

"Who knows?" the Duke voiced mysteriously. "Perhaps we *shall* have a chance to view this new country and its people."

"Your Grace?" his beautiful wife addressed him formally, with alarm. "You are not thinking of a voyage, are you? Surely you know that is not possible." Her gleaming green eyes warned him that despite the presence of a guest at their table, she would argue the point, and use all her resources to do it.

It was a well-kept secret that the Duke of Weston was subject to bouts of ill health brought on by a weak heart. The Duchess had made it her role in life to protect her beloved husband from his frailty by rigid adherence to a quiet lifestyle. A voyage to America would be a dangerous test of the Duke's stamina, and he was much too precious to her to risk it, no matter how much the idea appealed to his adventurous spirit.

The Duke shrugged sheepishly, saying, "Calm yourself, dearest. 'Twas merely the germ of an idea our good friend Mr. Chamberlain planted in my gambler's heart. He has invited us to visit his country, and the thought intrigued me."

"Well, I for one am relieved to know that you are not seriously considering it," the Duchess returned, pointedly. "Perhaps Mr. Chamberlain would be so kind as to enlighten us on another subject," Sarah's mother ordered politely as a servant refilled her wine glass. Her stern gaze toward the far end of the table informed her husband that she would brook no discussion, and Stewart did not miss the warning.

"But Mother ...." Julie began impatiently.

"That is enough, Lady Juliana," her father cut in, his eyes telling his wife he had received her message clearly. "Forgive me, Your Grace. The subject is closed."

Sarah, who had been studying the exchange rather breathlessly, was suddenly deflated. She had often dreamed of sailing to unknown shores, but always believed the idea was out of the question. But there, for a moment, her father's interest had opened the floodgates of her wildest imaginings. And now, in the blink of an eye, the dream was again completely unattainable. Realizing her mouth was gaping; she blushed and hurriedly took a sip of wine.

Stewart had not missed the play of expressions on Sarah's lovely face and knew that she had been excited by the idea of seeing his beloved country. He smiled inwardly at her fascination and hoped she would appreciate the news he had for her later, in the garden. Perhaps her gratitude might compel her to please him with another kiss.

Later in the evening, following aperitifs and conversation in the parlor, Sarah rose from the chair she had been occupying by the fireplace to announce her intention to retire. Stewart, who had been drawn by Juliana into a friendly game of faro, quickly excused himself and rose just as Sarah began to walk past him.

"Lady Sarah, I should bid you farewell now since I shall be gone at first light." He casually reached for her hand and gently placed his lips against the back of it. As he raised his dark head, he added, "It has truly been a pleasure visiting you and your family. The Duke warned me that I might find this arrangement much too enjoyable to be called merely business. And after getting to know you and your sister," he smiled lazily,

"I quite agree. I have enjoyed your generous hospitality and I look forward with anticipation to our next meeting."

The gentle pressure of his hand on hers confirmed that he was not referring to future visits, but the one he had proposed for this evening. Unable to impart a scathing glance in the presence of her family, Sarah instead smiled sweetly as she pulled her slim fingers out of his grasp. "You are too kind, Mr. Chamberlain, but I am pleased that your business went well here. Do have a safe journey." She then turned to kiss her parents goodnight and bid farewell to her sister, whose expression resembled that of a very satisfied cat.

"Good night, Farnam," she called to the butler as he passed her in the tiled foyer.

"Pleasant dreams, mum," he responded as she made her way up the stairs, already lost in thought.

As she walked soundlessly down the upstairs hall to her room, Sarah pondered the decision before her. Did Stewart really have something important to tell her? Or was he merely testing his influence over her? Could she trust him? Or herself? Should she be as careless as to risk her reputation on such a rendezvous?

She entered her candle-lit room and walked to her dressing table, sitting down to study her reflection in the mirror. The face that stared back at her belonged to someone Sarah had never really seen. The cool, clear gaze above the mature gown bespoke a sophistication that Sarah had never felt before. The person in the fashionable blue gown was a woman; no longer a timid, easily maneuvered young girl.

This heady feeling of confidence allowed Sarah, for the first time, to ponder her feelings for Stewart Chamberlain with insight and honesty. She had to admit that he was the most exciting person to have ever entered her life. But more than his appearance, his poised and confident manner, his intelligence and his interesting past, it was his effect on her that forced her to see how useless it was to try to maintain disinterest. For the first time in her life, she had a *man* – and one who intrigued her very much.

Stewart was right: The attraction *was* mutual. And though their purposes might be at odds, Sarah decided that this was no reason to keep resisting. They had already achieved one compromise. Perhaps, she mused, this is how happy endings begin.

Resolute, she rose from the vanity, took a deep breath and walked to the bedroom door, picking up a pale blue shawl from her bureau as she passed by. Looking both ways for any sign of a presence in the hall, she stepped quietly out into the corridor, closed the door and tiptoed quickly to the back stairs.

From the empty kitchen, she moved down a short, darkly-lit corridor to the ballroom, where French doors led onto the low balcony that surrounded a large area of the mansion. Furtively walking toward this side terrace, lit by torches on this summer night, her eyes peered down into the darkness of the gardens, hoping for a glimpse of Stewart before he should see her. But the moon was clouded over and Sarah could make out no tall shape that would mark the man's presence. With a growing sense of anticipation, she tiptoed down the garden steps, making her way toward the old oak tree where their first spontaneous meeting had taken place.

Suddenly at the same time the moon chose to peak out from behind the cloud, she heard a delicate, high-pitched voice. With a soundless gasp, Sarah hurriedly stepped back into the shadows. More cautiously, she again moved forward, using the tall boxwoods to avoid observation. The lilting voice continued, though she could not make out the words.

As Sarah inched closer to the voice, she was abruptly struck by the low, gentle murmur of a second, much deeper utterance. All at once it was clear to her that Juliana was the first person she had heard, but who was the man? Jack? Had she stumbled onto a lovers' rendezvous? *Father would be furious*, she thought to herself, but smiled as she crept closer for a peek.

The smile froze on her face as she silently parted the branches of the tall bush not more than a pace from the oak tree. For there, in the midst of a passionate embrace, were Juliana and Stewart Chamberlain.

CHAPTER 10

The pain and shock of her discovery hit Sarah like a physical blow. Uttering a single, short gasp, she released the branches, turned and flew back toward the mansion, mindless of the rustling sound that trailed in her wake as her gown skimmed by the bushes. Over her shoulder, she heard Juliana's petulant voice cry out, "Who goes there?" but Sarah did not hesitate.

Not until she had escaped to her room, torn off her garments, thrown on her nightgown and plunged beneath the covers of her bed did Sarah let the hot, angry tears flow. Muffling her woeful sobs in the pillow, she cursed Stewart's deception and her own vulnerability.

As her wrenching sobs subsided, Sarah tried to picture the sight of Juliana in Stewart's arms as a reprieve from making the worst mistake of her life – but the shocking scene was still too hurtful and her tears sprung anew.

It was not long after her tears had mercifully come to an end that Sarah heard a rustling in the hall followed by a discreet knock on her bedroom door. Sarah burrowed herself deeper in the covers, attempting heavy, even breaths, for there was no one in the world she cared to face. The door opened and she heard Juliana's voice whispering, "Sarah? Are you awake?"

Sarah sensed Juliana's presence closer to the bed. She knew her younger sister was peering into the darkness to see if she really was in bed and asleep. Satisfied, Juliana turned and left the room, closing the door quietly behind her.

Sarah let out a long, shuddering sigh, wondering what Juliana might have wanted. To boast about her encounter with Stewart? To see if she had been their intruder? With a small measure of vengeance, she was pleased to know that Stewart would never know whether she had decided to meet him. She pounded her fist in to the damp pillow, and curled herself up into a tight ball in preparation for sleep ... sleep that on this eventful evening was a long time in coming.

Sarah awoke early the next morning after a fitful slumber. Her dry, puffy eyes burned; she felt exhausted and morose. Straining to pull the bell cord at the side of her bed, she cursed under her breath at the prospect of facing this day with Stewart Chamberlain's damnable behavior still a sharp wound to her pride.

Several minutes passed while Sarah sat motionless amongst her covers, staring into space. When the door opened, she turned to see Tegan ushering in two serving girls laden with buckets of steaming water. "Good morning, mum," Tegan said sweetly as she passed by the bed on her way to bring out the porcelain tub from its closet.

"How did you know I wanted a bath?" Sarah asked numbly, after watching the sudden flurry of activity.

"Had a feeling," Tegan replied casually as she pulled fresh linens from the closet. "Thank you, girls. That's fine now," she said, dismissing the maids. As the two young girls departed, Tegan moved toward the bed and began folding back the covers. "All right then, mum. Here's a nice, hot tub for you. Can I get you something to eat as well?"

Sarah, who had been eyeing the red-headed maid critically ever since she had entered the room, ignored Tegan's entreaties. Showing no sign that she was prepared to leave the bed, she crossed her arms stubbornly and spoke.

"What do you know?"

"Mum?" Tegan's face was an innocent mask.

"You heard me. I asked, 'What do you know?'"

"I heard the question, Lady Sarah. I just can't think what you might be talking about."

"Teeg," Sarah signed impatiently, using the younger girl's nickname. "I can read you like a book. You're pampering me this morning – and for what reason, I surely do not know."

"I spoke with Mr. Chamberlain this morning," Tegan blurted, and seeing Sarah's face contort painfully, hurried on. "He asked me to give you this." And with her words, she pulled a sealed envelope from her apron pocket and held it before her mistress.

Unconsciously, Sarah pulled back, eying the packet warily. "What's this?"

"It's a letter," Tegan said firmly, as if talking to a bumpkin. "Mr. Chamberlain said you must read it. He said I must make sure that you do."

"Oh he did, did he?" Sarah answered hotly, pushing herself up to a kneeling position on the far side of the bed, her thick hair caught away from her face by her night bonnet, her dark hair tumbling over her shoulders. "What else did he tell you?"

"Lady Sarah, Tegan implored. "He seemed disturbed. Said there was some misunderstanding betwixt the two of you and that you would be upset. But this letter explains everything."

With an exasperated jerk, Sarah flung herself off the bed and stripped the clothing from her body. Tossing the garments angrily on the coverlet, she marched to the tub and plunked herself down into the steaming water, ignoring the shock of the heat. "I see the rogue has cast a spell on you, too, Tegan. How dare he wheedle you into playing his messenger? Well I won't read it!" And with that, she began vigorously scrubbing herself with a chip of lavender-scented soap.

"Very well, then," Tegan announced matter-of-factly, breaking the letter's seal. "I shall have to read it to you."

"You will not!" Sarah gasped, slamming the sliver into the water. "That is a personal message to me and you have no right to open it!"

"Mr. Chamberlain told me to do whatever I had to do to make sure you got his message," Tegan replied calmly, a steely glint in her hazel eyes, "so if you won't read it yourself, what choice do I have? 'Tis a terrible position you've put me in." And with that, she withdrew the folded note, preparing to read aloud.

"Tegan, I am shocked at your behavior," Sarah cried. "Where is your loyalty?"

Tegan moved back to the tub, holding the letter before her, her expression sober. "'Tis with you, mum, as it always has been and always will be. 'Tis why I am begging you to read this letter for yourself. Mr. Chamberlain fears you've been upset and needlessly so. And if reading this will ease your mind, as he says it will, then it's my bounden duty to make certain you do."

For a moment, their eyes locked in silent combat above the parchment Tegan held in her outstretched hand. It was Sarah who buckled, torn by the love and concern in her maid's elfish face. "Oh Teeg," she sighed dejectedly, "I know you mean well. It's simply that you don't under--. Never mind," she shook her head vigorously, wiping a slim hand over her brow. "I shall read it ...."

"You will?" Tegan gave a merry jig and attempted to hand the letter over.

" ... *after* I've finished bathing. Now please, just put it on my dressing table and let me soak in peace. I promise you I will look at it presently."

"Very good, mum," Tegan answered happily, tucking the letter back in its envelope and leaning it against the vanity mirror. "Now what can I get you? Some tea perhaps?"

Sarah sighed heavily and sunk lower into the steaming tub. "No thank you, Tegan. I'll send for you later if I wish something. For now, just don't let anyone disturb me. Tell them I'm still sleeping ... anything ... I don't care. I need to be alone."

Tegan smiled confidently as she walked toward the door. "Don't worry, mum. You can count on me."

After Tegan departed, Sarah found herself shaking with unspent emotion. The letter meant that Stewart knew she had been the eavesdropper in the garden. Her cheeks burned with humiliation over the fact that her vulnerability was so apparent to him that he had to make some gesture of redress. Why couldn't he just leave her alone? Besides, what could he possibly tell her — without lying – that would ease her mind? "Nothing," she sighed. "Nothing at all."

Sarah was surprised to feel her reddened eyes brimming with unshed tears. *Oh bother*, she cried, *why should it hurt so? Why did I think for a moment that his interest was sincere? And how did I ever believe he wasn't attracted to Juliana, when every man in the duchy would die for her on the spot.* Sarah knew nobody could love a sister more than she did Juliana, but for a moment, the bitter taste of jealousy filled her mouth, and she nearly choked on the horrid emotion.

Viciously splashing water on her fevered face, Sarah rebuked herself for her momentary lapse. "It's Stewart's fault, not Juliana's! She, too, is an innocent victim of his lecherous games. I've learned my lesson. I will never make a cake of myself again!"

Unfortunately, Sarah realized immediately, it was much easier to declare such a resolution than it was to summon the fortitude to carry it out. The pain and humiliation were still too real, compounded by a sense of longing she could neither understand nor control.

Wearily, she rose from the tub and began drying herself with the sheet Tegan had left nearby. The beige packet taunted her as she performed this task and she found herself propelled closer for a better look. The envelope was unaddressed. Carefully, she allowed her slim fingers to pick it up. As she gingerly turned it over in her hand, she saw on the broken wax seal the impression of a simple, bold "C."

In spite of her reluctance, Sarah's immense curiosity overcame her and with a sigh, she put down the letter so that she could don a wrapper to cover herself and ward off the chill. Tying the cord around her slim waist, she sat down at her dressing table, and, with shaking hands, removed the note from its envelope. Momentarily squeezing her eyes shut, she unfolded the paper, mentally preparing to read. When she finally looked, she was immediately struck by the neat yet dramatic scrawl before her. So much like him, she thought: bold and elegant.

With a growing mixture of anticipation and dread, she read:

> I have not deceived you, Sarah, despite what you may think. But I do not expect you to believe me without an explanation, which I will deliver only in person. Until I see you again, I implore you to postpone judgment and hold dear the thought: circumstances are not always as they appear.

> I look forward to our next meeting with great anticipation.

Regards,

S.

> *P.S. Your father will enlighten you as to the news I had hoped to give you myself. In spite of the cost, I am pleased that you chose to meet me.*

Sarah threw down the letter with an oath. "He tells me nothing! And expects me to harbor warm thoughts until I see him again! Only a true rake would believe such a fairy tale!" But even as she gave words to her bitterness, Sarah's thoughts were racing to discover the truth behind his claim of virtue. *Circumstances are not always as they appear.* But how else was she to interpret the impassioned scene she witnessed in the garden? Stewart and Juliana's embrace was anything but casual. And even Juliana would admit it wasn't the first time they had been so entwined, for she had told Sarah about kissing Stewart in the garden on her birthday.

And the nerve of him throwing back in her face her stupid decision to meet him! "What a little fool he must think I am," she fumed. But how did he know it was she? He must have been sure or he would not have risked writing such an incriminating letter. "Probably some omniscient power given to demons," she remarked, and abruptly rose.

And with that, her answer was dropped at her feet – a small bit of frayed blue silk trim had fallen unnoticed from the letter into her lap. From her gown, no doubt when she had fled the garden.

"Ooh!" Sarah squealed in absolute frustration over his continuing luck and her seemingly endless misfortune.

CHAPTER 11

It was midday before Sarah departed the sheltering haven of her room and then only because she was summoned by her father.

As she entered the library, dressed in a demure flowered gown trimmed in white at the neck and sleeves, her foreboding was masked beneath a pleasant smile and the bright azure gaze she bestowed upon the Duke, who rose from his massive leather chair by the fire.

"Come, come, my darling," he beckoned cheerily, holding out long arms to great her. "You've played the family ghost long enough so I am forced to make an appointment to see you." Father and daughter shared an affectionate buss, and as he released her to return to the chair, he added, "What has become of my constant shadow? The young lady I trip over every time I turn around?"

"Oh Father," Sarah returned warmly, "you have been so busy of late; none of us has enjoyed your company as much as we would like. Is that what was on your mind?" Sarah gathered her skirts and lowered herself onto the settee, her expression teasingly innocent.

"Only in part," he chuckled. "In truth, I am fairly bursting with good news for you and I cannot wait another second."

"Gracious me!" Sarah reacted, raising a hand to the tall white ruffles at her neck in a gesture of mock surprise, "Tell me now. What is it that excites you so?"

The Duke leaned forward eagerly. "You, my bluestocking, are going to America!"

"Did I hear you correctly?" she gasped.

"I am sending you on a visit to the United States of America." Her father, Sarah could see, was practically beside himself with joy.

"But how did this come about? I've never been further than Town in my entire life. What is the reason for such a journey?"

"I wish you to handle the purchase of some property for me there. You know I trust your judgment in land matters, and I am quite sure you will recognize a fair deal."

"But really, Father," Sarah argued. "There are many others much more qualified than I to handle such a task. What about your representatives?"

"They have their place. But if I wish to send my daughter to the Colonies, what is to keep me from doing so? Besides, your powers of observation are keen. I would have no better correspondent than yourself to tell me about this land that I shall never see with my own eyes."

"Oh, Papa," Sarah whispered her childhood name for her sire, her eyes tearful and brimming with love, "I-I don't know what to say. It *is* dreams come true, surely. But to leave you ... and Mama ... and my home? I've never been ...."

Weston quickly interrupted. "I've no doubt you will suffer some homesickness, child. But it is time you begin living a life of your own, and not cloistered here in the Oxfordshire countryside. You need to meet new people. Society may not approve of a daughter of the ton traveling so freely, but" he added with a mirthless chuckle, "I never gave a care for the ton. And you, my darling, are no gabster. I can think of no one I would trust more, or be more honored to send on this voyage."

But Sarah saw something more in his rationale, something she felt compelled to name. She gave him a steady look, thinking back on the day when Stewart Chamberlain had given words to her father's concerns. "I appreciate your modern ideas, but I think you are worried that unless I leave this house, no husband will be found for me. Are you concerned, Father?"

The Duke's eyes did not blink. "Are you *not* concerned?"

Sarah's eyes widened alarmingly and she choked on a sudden intake of air. "Father!"

"Well?"

"No!" Sarah's expression was defiant, but her father's eyes did not waver. It was she who finally broke the stare, as she slumped her shoulders and sighed. "You have always been honest to a fault, haven't you? I beg you not to trouble yourself overmuch, for I shall marry ... eventually."

"That is true," Weston replied sternly, ignoring her defensive tone, "but you've taken no interest in the local crop and you have not helped yourself in London by spending more time in libraries than the salons. So pray tell, where are we expected to find this husband for you?"

Sarah flung her gaze away, rose and walked toward the fireplace. As she whirled around to address her father, irritation was apparent in her furrowed brows and stony eyes. "What does it matter? It is not as though you are in need of sons-in-law or grandchildren, as Uncle Wesley is your heir," she said, referring to her father's much younger brother, who, by the conventions of peerage, would take the place in succession of the son the Duke and Duchess never had.

"If I am destined to marry, I will. But I am not unfulfilled here. I enjoy my life – my family, my books, Serena, helping you, living here. I enjoy my freedom most of all. And yes," she added, thrusting her hands on her hips, "I will enjoy this voyage to America – but only as your emissary – not as some Friday-faced spinster, desperate to marry. Can this be certain between us, Father?" Sarah implored. "For I refuse to go if you expect otherwise."

Weston, who had been watching his beautiful daughter critically, rose slowly and joined her in front of the fire. "From the outset," he began slowly, "our terms have been in agreement. Have no doubt of that. And I remind you that it was you who brought up the subject of marriage. But since you have, I will say one thing and that will be the end of it for all time. Will you listen?"

She nodded, knowing she had no choice.

"You think I want you to marry because that is a gentlewoman's primary function in life. And that we, your parents, would be spared some humiliation if you were to wed. Well, you are wrong," he admonished, "absolutely wrong."

Taking her smaller hands into his great ones, he continued, "I want you to enjoy a full, purposeful life. I simply know that marriage and family should not be underrated in their ability to provide such things. When you choose wisely and make a firm commitment with your spouse to hold to your vows, the world is laid at your feet. Anything can grow from that most sacred bond – an infinite measure of love, courage, compassion, success – and freedom as well.

"Where we differ is that I do not put as much trust in chance as you are wont to. We must go after that which we want; make ourselves available to the workings of fate. So," he concluded, stroking her cheek and tilting her chin to look directly into her misty eyes, "is it permissible for your doting old papa to provide opportunities for you to see what is beyond your own doorstep?"

"Oh, Father," Sarah cried, throwing her arms around his neck and hugging him fiercely. Mumbling into his collar, she sniffed, "I am not sure whether I agree with your beliefs, but your motives are indeed loving and honorable. And I am touched."

As they held each other close, Sarah thought of what a wonderful man her father was. They had been close from the time she could remember. Despite the high value placed on sons and heirs, his every word and action told her that he would not have wished her to be anything but what she was. And because he believed an idle mind was the worst sin of all, he had encouraged her natural curiosity, making sure she learned how to read, write and reason as well as a man.

As she grew, he urged her to take an interest in his business affairs. She learned much about the running of the estate, not to mention the duchy, and eventually was able to offer intelligent opinions. Ultimately she gained a place among his most trusted advisors, a position the two of them held discreetly, since the idea would have horrified most of the men Weston dealt with.

This arrangement suited Sarah perfectly and had made her life interesting and full in so many ways. If only the pressure of a suitable marriage weren't so great, she might be able to enjoy her bounty even more.

But at least she and her father had come to some kind of understanding about that subject, Sarah admitted to herself. And now she could concentrate on the most wonderful opportunity of her life – a journey to America. Immediately, she wanted to learn all the details of her incredible voyage. With one last, brief hug, she stepped away from her father, impatiently wiped the tears that had moistened her cheeks, and said, "You've told me almost nothing about my trip. When shall I leave? How long will I stay?"

"Hold!" Weston interrupted, grinning at the sudden onslaught. "One question at a time. Here now, sit down and I'll tell you the plans."

Eagerly, Sarah returned to the sofa and unceremoniously plunked herself down, her eyes riveted to her father so as not to miss any of his words.

"You will voyage in a month's time. And while I do not expect it will take you long to transact the business, I would hope that you will remain in the Colonies until spring. This will give you ample opportunity to explore and learn. Besides, I would not have you sailing during the winter months for it is not only a freezing proposition, but a more dangerous one as well. I trust you agree?"

"Of course, Father." Sarah's eyes shone with anticipation. "But you have not yet said where I will be going, or who will accompany me. Pray tell."

"Your destination is Boston and I've arranged for a most trustworthy escort – one who is not only familiar with the country, but one on whom you can rely for counsel and aid while you are about your mission. I speak of none other than Mr. Stewart Chamberlain."

Had a shot been fired in the library at that precise moment, Sarah's reaction could not have been more sudden or violent. But even as her mouth dropped open in horror and her face paled, she used inhuman strength to force herself to control her speech.

Knotting her trembling fingers, she replied, "B-but Father! Certainly you are not serious? An unmarried man? I'd be safer traveling alone, surely." Her nervous chatter sounded shrill to her ears. But the idea was so absolutely appalling! Her own father placing her in the care of the one man in the world she feared and now hated. If only she could explain how vile his conduct had been and how knavishly he was wooing both of the Duke's daughters. Being accompanied by him would be tantamount to a virgin sacrifice! "Father," she cried, her tone a combination of outrage and pleading, "it is out of the question. I have reason to believe that Mr. Chamberlain is not a suitable companion."

To her utter amazement, Weston calmly stroked his chin, and with more than a hint of humor in his voice, replied, "You seem quite disturbed, my dear, just as Mr. Chamberlain himself predicted. Would you mind enlightening me as to the cause of your most obvious dislike of the man? I myself have found him to be of unimpeachable character, and a most charming fellow besides. In addition, he is a seasoned traveler. You would be safe in his care."

"Safe?!" Sarah flew from the settee, and kneading her slim hands together, marched to the fireplace. With a gesture of helplessness, her blue eyes wide as saucers, she turned to face her father, beseeching, "Safe? Father, I think no woman is safe where he is concerned. With all due respect for your ability to judge character, I would have you know that Mr. Chamberlain is a blackguard. A rogue!"

"I would ask proof of such a charge," the Duke's tone was suddenly ominous.

Sarah involuntarily crossed her arms over her bosom, hugging herself protectively. "Father, it is unspeakable for me to discuss such a delicate subject. I-I cannot say."

Weston's eyes rose mercurially, but his voice was unchanged. "You *will* say."

Biting her lip, she knew she had no choice. "He-he tried to force his attentions on me." The charges were leveled and she pinched her eyes shut, waiting for the thunderous reaction of outrage and indignation. But instead, her father cleared his voice and spoke quietly, "And was he successful?"

Sarah's tenuous grasp on composure snapped as her eyes flew open. "No!" she demanded. "But that's not the point!

Father, don't you see? He cannot be trusted!" In her anger and humiliation, she began pacing in front of the fire. "He is the least suitable escort you could name!"

Weston slowly sat back in his chair and stretched his stockinged legs before him. Placing his elbows on the comfortably upholstered arms, he touched his fingertips together, seemingly intent on watching his hands flex against each other. "Sarah," he began placidly, "Mr. Chamberlain has confessed to his attraction for you, and did indeed admit to an indiscreet advance." His words caused Sarah to stop in her paces. She looked on her father with a horrified expression. Weston, however, seemed not to notice. "But he also mentioned that the two of you have reached an understanding about this and that it has not – and would not – happen again. Was he correct?"

Shaking to the very soles of her slippered feet, Sarah forced out her reply. "Yes, but you must realize," she implored, "he has you to answer to as long as he is under your roof. There is no telling what might become of me on the high seas – or in America. Father, you are throwing me to the wolves!"

"I have his word that no harm will come to you. And I value his word as I do my own. Surely you would not think of discarding an opportunity to see the United States over a problem already resolved."

"Well I simply do not like him or trust him, Father, and would find his company taxing. How could I feel secure?" she offered desperately.

"Oh, come now, child," the Duke of Weston argued impatiently. "It's not as if the two of you will be inseparable, He will simply be available should you need him. Also, he is making the arrangements for you to stay with his sister and her family in Boston, so you won't be dwelling under the same roof if that is a concern for you."

Sarah realized that if she had any intention of seeing America, she would have to accept her father's terms. But the idea of having to bear Stewart Chamberlain's company – especially after the horrible discovery she had made last night – was almost more than she could handle. But how could she explain any of this to her father without suggesting she felt something for the Yankee? Of course she could refuse to go, but there would never be another opportunity like this.

The dual-edged blade of this dilemma was a physical pain to Sarah, and feebly she attempted to salve her frustration by demanding, "I should hope you will allow a servant to accompany me?"

Weston rose, laughing out loud with relief as he grasped his daughter's rigid shoulders. "Do I hear the last request of a man about to walk the gallows?" he teased. Ignoring her pout, he continued, "Of course, my dear. I supposed you would like to take Tegan? A lovely and reliable girl. I will arrange it posthaste. Come now," he urged, stretching a long arm around her shoulders as he began leading her to the door. "Everything will be grand. You'll see ...."

"Very well, Father," she sighed. And then seeing the flash of disappointment on his face, added, "Excuse me, Papa. You are right. 'Twas a shock you gave me, 'tis all. I suppose I can be civil to Mr. Chamberlain as long as he is accepting the burden of seeing to my welfare." *If only she could believe her own words!* "By the way," she asked, as she placed her hand on the library doorknob, "Does Juliana know of these plans?

"I think your mother has probably told her by now."

"Do you think she will be disappointed that she's not going?" Sarah could just imagine Juliana's ire, especially since Stewart was essential to the journey.

"It is impossible to predict what Juliana's reaction to anything will be," he smiled affectionately, "but if I had to guess, I would say no. Somehow I cannot picture her putting up with the inconvenience of a long voyage. As you might have noticed by her comments at dinner last night, she does not have a very high opinion of the Colonies. No, I suspect her only concern will be that you won't be around to share a confidence ... something I know we shall all miss."

His gaze on her was so bittersweet that Sarah could not resist the urge to hug him once again. "Oh, Papa, I love you so." she whispered. "I miss you already."

CHAPTER 12

Sitting in her room later, Sarah was at a loss to absorb all the twists and turns her emotions had suffered in less than a day. First had come her decision to accept her attraction to Stewart Chamberlain. Then she had found her own sister in his embrace. And to add to her humiliation, her personal maid had delivered Stewart's letter which told her nothing but the fact that he knew Sarah had witnessed their rendezvous.

Then her father presented her with the most exciting proposition of a lifetime – a voyage to America – only to have it tied up inexorably with Stewart Chamberlain. She colored at the thought of Stewart admitting to her father that he had been intimate with her, but that because of their compromise he would still be a suitable escort. She could not imagine that there existed another man in the world who could so successfully turn all events into such good fortune for himself.

She realized now that the voyage must have been the important news Stewart had wanted to tell her himself. At least that was one small triumph for her – he had not witnessed her elation upon first hearing of the news.

Deep in thought, she failed to acknowledge the impatient rapping on her door, but when the portal burst open, Sarah look up, startled.

"You're here!" Juliana stood dwarfed by the doorjamb, looking as lovely as ever in a pale green muslin dress, her blonde hair caught up in curls off her neck and held with green ribbons.

"Yes," Sarah replied, smiling meekly, "I didn't hear you knock. I guess I was daydreaming ... again."

Juliana flounced into the room, pushing the door shut behind her. "I can imagine. It appears you have much more to daydream about than usual."

"Did Mother tell you?" Sarah asked, taking care to convey a neutral tone. It was impossible to judge Juliana's mood.

"She did," Juliana replied coolly, examining her exquisite reflection in Sarah's vanity mirror. "Are you excited?"

"Yes," Sarah said cautiously, "yes I am. Quite. I have always daydreamed about traveling, but never spoke of it. The idea always seemed impossible. And now ..." she shrugged doubtfully, uncomfortable with her sister's blasé attitude.

Juliana gave a bored sigh and lightly hopped upon the bed, close to the window seat where Sarah was sitting. "Well it sounds like a perfectly *awful* way to spend the next six months, if you ask me, especially since the Little Season is soon to begin. I'm certainly grateful for my bacon brain, or Father might have considered sending me." She made an exaggerated shiver, plucking at her gown as if it were suddenly infested. Ignoring Sarah's pained expression, she continued in her haughty manner. "I hear Father has made arrangements with Stewart Chamberlain to be your protector."

"That is my understanding," Sarah replied so faintly that Juliana looked up from her skirt with a jerk.

"Don't tell me this does not please you?" she said mockingly.

Sarah fidgeted uncomfortably. "No it does not. But it is a condition I must live with if I hope to make the voyage."

"Oh, spare me," Juliana cried dramatically, pushing herself off the downy coverlet and floating to the center of the room. "You think I don't know about the two of you?"

"The two of us? Whatever are you talking about?" Sarah asked incredulously.

"Don't misunderstand me, sister," Juliana demanded petulantly, her jade eyes boring into her sister's troubled blue ones. "It is not that I *mind* that Stewart prefers your charms. Heaven knows it's about time you had a beau. But you might have told me yourself. After all, we are sisters, and I have always shared my dalliances with *you*."

Shocked and stunned by her words, Sarah blurted, "Juliana, I-I don't know what to say. You've confused me terribly. I thought Stewart and you ...?"

"Well I won't say I didn't wish it," Juliana sighed. "Even perhaps pursued it," she added over her shoulder as she strutted upon the thick Aubusson. "But I certainly would have saved myself a great deal of trouble – not to mention embarrassment – had you seen fit to tell me that Stewart was courting you all along. If I were the type to feel humiliation ..." she wagged her finger at Sarah, "... and you know that I am not, I might be quite inconsolable over what you've done to me."

"What have I done?" Sarah cried, thoroughly confused.

"You know I had my eye on that Yankee, but you apparently beguiled him right out from under my nose. And all along I thought he was falling in love with me! I don't enjoy playing the gudgeon, Sarah, and now that's exactly what Stewart thinks of me, thanks to you!" Juliana was obviously distraught, for her eyes were stormy and her cheeks flying colors.

She rose and pleaded, "Juliana, please. I don't understand what you are talking about. I swear, I haven't purposely done anything to hurt you."

Juliana stopped her pacing and considered her tall, slim sibling for a moment. Finally, she sighed and slumped into an overstuffed chaise. "Very well. Apparently we have some sorting out to do – though it pains me sorely that I should have to practically swoon before I'm able to find out what's going on." With that, she folded her arms across the swell of her bodice and thrust out her lower lip in a childish pout. "Tell me everything."

Sarah proceeded to tell her, as briefly as she could, about the attentions Stewart had paid her from the time of his arrival. Without detail, she mentioned his forwardness and of the agreement they had reached.

"I first believed, as you did, that he was interested in you. So when he agreed to court me with less ... pressure," Sarah struggled, "I demanded that he make his intentions clear to you. I see that he did not – for his selfish aim was to set his cap for both of us. And I hate him all the more for his deception."

A mirthless smile had begun to play on Juliana's full lips as she pondered her sister's words. Seeing that Sarah would speak no more, Juliana regally raised herself up in the chair and spoke plainly. "Much as it would console my pride to let you believe he is the cad you think, it is not true.

"His interest in you was apparent, but since you did not see fit to tell me of your relationship, I assumed the affection was not returned. Therefore, I pursued Mr. Chamberlain in the hopes that he would turn his attentions to a more, shall I say, willing lady?"

Juliana tipped her chin stubbornly. "Needless to say, I misassessed his cut. Stewart is less reckless than I thought. He does not dally with a woman not of his choosing, no matter how comely and inclined she may be. I learned that lesson quite boldly last night in the garden. So, there you have it, dear one. I have confessed my wanton behavior, with neither regrets nor apologies. What have you to say?"

Sarah gave her sister a sidelong glance. "I should be glad I am your sister and not your rival, then. I truly do not know what to say of this development." Juliana's confessions confirmed that Stewart Chamberlain was a man of his word, and his apparent scrupulous behavior in the face of her sibling's onslaught made him all the more a paragon — for no man had ever refused Juliana before.

"Juliana," she murmured in a troubled voice, "I am beset by this man. I wish I had never met him! Everything was so pleasant and simple before he entered our lives ...."

"And oppressively boring," Juliana snapped back. "I'll be bound, Sarah. I would think Stewart's attention would have you swooning. Instead you are acting like a tabby. If you want to end up like one, you are certainly going about it the right way!"

"Stop it!" Sarah hissed. "I am sick to death of people taking me for more hair than wit, assuming that I shall become a spinster simply because I do not care for Stewart Chamberlain! If the facts be known, he is a most ineligible candidate for the institution. Even if I found him suitable – which I do not – there would be no future in it."

Juliana was completely undaunted by her sister's rant. With a sly smile, she leaned forward conspiratorially and questioned, "So you've discussed marriage? Already? How very interesting ...."

"It's obvious you're up to your eyes in fables and not listening to a word I say," Sarah returned flatly, and with that she turned and walked back to the window seat. Seating herself, she flung her long, slim legs in their white silk stockings and kid slippers upon the cushions and glared at her sister. Seeing Juliana's smug smile, she grumbled, "Think what you will, little sister, but do not expect me to bide your delusions. I'll thank you to keep them to yourself."

"Very well," Juliana chuckled as she rose to make her exit, "but if you believe that nothing will come of your spending six months in the company of Stewart Chamberlain, then you, my green girl, are the one with delusions."

CHAPTER 13

September 6, 1809

The docks were busy but strangely hushed amidst the pervasive gray fog of first light. The post chaise bearing the Duke of Weston, Lady Sarah and Tegan jarred the quietude. Compared to its striking jangling and clopping of the hackneys, the irregular thumps of cargo being moved and the laconic calls of distant sailors and dock workers seemed muffled by the formless clouds.

Though their carriage was moving to within a few yards of the boarding plank of the *Endeavour*, Sarah could barely make out the skeletal outline of the huge ship as she peered beyond the window's heavy drape.

The dank and chilly grayness matched her mood this day. Faced with the prospect of leaving home for the first time, and sailing to a strange country on the other side of the Atlantic, filled her with apprehension. Her stomach churned with the urge to plead to her father to have the coach turned toward home and all the safety and security it represented. But as she peeked at him from beneath her bonnet and long, thick lashes, and saw the pride and excitement etched on his handsome visage, she knew she could never muster the strength to name her fears, for she could not bear to disappoint him. Weston was giving her the opportunity to do the one thing he wanted most for himself – to travel to a vast, young nation and witness the civilization the American colonists had created for themselves – and she was determined he was not to be disappointed by her lack of enthusiasm.

As the chaise came to a halt, Weston pulled on his gray sueded gloves and spoke eagerly to the young women sitting across from him. "Here we are, then. Now just sit for a moment while I check on your accommodations and the whereabouts of Mr. Chamberlain. I shall take Lyon with me," referring to his manservant, "and Silas will remain with the coach."

As he closed the carriage door behind him, Sarah let out a long sigh and huddled beneath her pelisse of royal blue. "I don't know which is worse," she murmured caustically to her maid, "Saying goodbye to my father or having to see Mr. Chamberlain again. Do you think he is here already?"

"I haven't a clue, mum," Tegan returned brightly, "but I don't mind saying I'm glad he's making the trip. Gives a body peace of mind knowing such a fine man is protecting us from who knows what."

Though she was prepared to argue the point, Sarah merely threw her maid a disapproving look and nestled herself more closely into the corner of the carriage. Try as she might, she was unable to keep her mind off the handsome Yankee with whom she would soon be reunited.

Despite the fact that he had visited the Duke's estate a second time, Sarah had not seen him since the night she had found Juliana in his arms. For once, she thought smugly, fate had been on her side. She and her mother had been in Town making the final preparations for her voluminous wardrobe when he'd come to visit her father.

But now the day of reckoning was here, and there was nothing she could do to stop the hammering of her heart as she remembered all that passed between them. Closing her eyes, she prayed fervently that she would be able to maintain her composure, letting Stewart believe that his presence had no effect on her – good or bad.

"Would you look at that?" Tegan's voice suddenly broke into Sarah's reverie. Seeing Teeg staring out the window, Sarah hopped over to the seat facing her and, pulling back the curtain, peered into the smoky haze outside. What she spied was a magnificent coach drawn by a matched pair of dappled gray ponies. The richly-appointed carriage, with its smartly-suited driver, looked all the more spectacular amidst the crude dockside setting, and Sarah immediately decided the occupants must be very important indeed to warrant such grand transportation.

"It must belong to some nobleman, perhaps a member of the court," Sarah whispered excitedly. "Look at the crest on the door!"

As they watched, the coach drew to a stop. Breathlessly, both occupants waited for the door to open. "Whoever it is, he must be sailing with us," Tegan reasoned.

Before Sarah could reply, a finely-dressed coachman appeared from the rear of the carriage and proceeded to pull down the steps underneath the door. As he opened the portal, a tall man in a black cloak, shiny leather boots and a black hat backed out of the carriage. Sarah strained closer, hoping to catch a glimpse of his face, but could see nothing. Immediately, he was followed by an incredibly beautiful woman who was dressed in a most striking pink wool pelisse and gown trimmed in rich, dark brown mink. On her fashionably coifed blue-black hair was an equally shockingly pink bonnet trimmed in mink and feathers. "She's exquisite!" Sarah murmured reverently. "She must be a lady of the court."

As the lovely woman spoke to the man before her, Sarah was impressed by the depth of feeling that showed on her heart-shaped face. Obviously, she was very much in love with the man whose eyes she held with her own. Though she could not hear their conversation, Sarah could tell the words they exchanged were intimate and loving, and their feelings much too warm for such a public setting. The woman continually patted and stroked the man's chest and arms as he held her captive between his body and the side of the coach. When she bowed her head to brush a tear away from her cheek, it dawned on Sarah that only one of them was going on the voyage. Before she could figure out which one, the man pulled the trembling woman in to the circle of his arms and kissed her passionately, right on the lips.

"Teeg, don't look!" Sarah hissed, the blood rushing to her cheeks at the intimate scene before her. Letting the curtain fall, she pushed herself abruptly back in the leather seat and snapped her eyes directly forward, noticing as she did that Tegan had not budged. "Teeg!"

Continuing to stare out the window, Tegan retorted, "If they don't mind kissing that way in public, then I don't mind watching."

"Well, just because they're indiscreet does not mean ...."

"By the saints!" Tegan suddenly gasped, covering her mouth with her hands as she dropped the curtain and sat back abruptly.

Sarah gave her maid a haughty look. "They caught you peeking, didn't they? I told you ...."

"No," Tegan whispered fiercely, her hand dropping to her bosom. Clearly surprised, she seemed unable to speak.

"Well? What is it, Teeg?"

"The man! It-it's Mr. Chamberlain!"

Sarah gasped, her heart thumping. "Are you sure? How ...."

"He's coming this way!"

In a flash, Sarah jumped back into the seat next to Tegan. With shaking fingers, she smoothed her pelisse and skirt, suddenly feeling flushed. "Does he know we're here?" she whispered struggling to swallow the lump in her throat.

Before the maid could answer, Sarah heard the muffled voices outside the coach. With a sinking feeling, she realized that Stewart had recognized Silas and was talking to him. In a moment, there was a knock on the door and Stewart's deep voice called in. "Lady Sarah? It's Stewart Chamberlain. I'm here to escort you to the ship."

Drawing a deep breath, Sarah cleared her throat and answered by pulling down the door handle, allowing the portal to swing outward. Even though the carriage was high above ground, it seemed to Sarah that those handsome dark eyes were level with hers. Disregarding his engaging grin, and fighting the thrill his presence immediately kindled, she said politely, "Good morning, Mr. Chamberlain, My father has gone to look for you aboard ship.'

"So Silas has told me," he replied, his smiling teasing. "I apologize for my tardiness, but I was unavoidably detained."

"No matter," Sarah returned quickly, inwardly seething over what she was sure constituted the nature of his delay. The man reeked of lady's perfume! Plucking her reticule off the empty seat where she had left it, she added, "Would you care to join us? I am sure Father will return presently. The air is rather chilled."

"Thank you," he grinned in that reckless, confident way that always spoke volumes more than his words."I appreciate your hospitality. But might I suggest that you allow me to take you and your maid aboard? I am sure we will have no trouble finding your father."

Sarah turned to look at Tegan, hoping for some support for the excuse she was about to proffer, but the maid's tiny face displayed eagerness. Indeed, she had begun to retie the ribbons on her brown cloth bonnet.

"I-I am not sure that would be a wise idea," Sarah answered defensively. "Father expects to find us here."

Stewart swallowed the urge to smile at her stubbornness by brushing back the curtain and glancing at the ship. He was just in time to see the Duke of Weston waving from the gangplank through the mist. He raised a gloved hand to reply and returned back to Sarah, who had leaned forward to find the object of his greeting. Startled by their sudden close proximity, Sarah pushed herself backward and scowled at him. "I believe the Duke bids us to join him," Stewart said calmly."Is there something you might like me to carry for you?"

"No thank you," Sarah's reply was prim. "Our baggage was put aboard yesterday and Lyon, father's manservant, will take care of the rest. Tegan, you have our case?"

"Aye, mum," Tegan mumbled, slightly surprised by her lady's perversity toward Mr. Chamberlain.

Reluctantly taking Stewart's outstretched palm, Sarah allowed him to help her down from the coach, though she refused to look at him. With a wink, Stewart took the small, leather case from Tegan and handed her down, closing the carriage door behind her. Then they proceeded to follow Sarah, who was already walking quickly toward her father. As she made her way to his side on the roped plank, he cried out a jovial greeting to Stewart.

"Good day, sir! I was just inquiring as to your whereabouts when I saw you at the coach. I trust you are ready to assume the task of seeing to the welfare of my daughter and her maid?" he said briskly, hugging Sarah's rigid shoulders.

"'Tis much less a task than a pleasure, I assure you, sir," Stewart intoned graciously, smiling down at Sarah despite her aloofness.

"Have you seen our quarters, Father?" Sarah's words came out even more coldly than she had intended. Covering her annoyance with a becoming smile, she added, "I am anxious to see where we will be staying."

"I have done that and more, my dear" Looking over her head to Stewart, Weston said, "'Tis a fine vessel you take on your voyage, Mr. Chamberlain. The *Endeavour* is all you have claimed and more. Never have I seen such comfort afforded a cargo vessel. I will rest easier knowing my daughter sails in such grand style."

"Your compliments should go to her captain, sir," Stewart replied. "He would be very pleased to know you are satisfied."

"That I have done already," the older man insisted. "He tells me that you are fully responsible. I suppose a man who travels as frequently as you deserves the comforts of home onboard his own ship."

"This ship is yours?" Sarah's words cut icily into the pleasant conversation. Before Stewart had a chance to respond, her father took on the question.

"It is but one of his many vessels, my child. I thought you knew," he chuckled nonchalantly. "Well, now you do. Come along. I fear the swaying of this bridge is too much for me. I sure hope you do not succumb to seasickness," he commented, prodding his daughter before him. "'Tis a wretched way to travel and I do want you to enjoy your passage."

CHAPTER 14

But succumbing to *mal de mer* was exactly the fate Sarah suffered her first two days at sea. Even though the sailing was calm and the weather clear and sunny, the gentle rolling of the huge vessel was more than her untried stomach could handle and she remained abed, a worried Tegan clucking over her.

After bidding a brave but tearful farewell to her father and meeting the ship's captain, Jeremiah Slade, Sarah, with Tegan, had been escorted by Stewart to an elegant cabin next to the captain's quarters. Sarah noted that it was even finer than the London hotel where they had spent the night before. The compact yet sumptuous quarters contained fitted furniture made of finely oiled black walnut. The dark solid wood lent an overwhelming masculine air to the cabin, relieved only by the flowered coverlet on the wide bunk and the blue and beige Oriental carpets that were spread before the bed, vanity and wardrobe. A vase of fresh flowers bedecked the recessed bureau.

With a pleased exclamation, Tegan immediately set herself to the task of unpacking Sarah's trunks that had been delivered earlier. Mindful of Stewart's presence in the doorway, Sarah turned stiffly and said, "The accommodations are outstanding, Mr. Chamberlain. I am sure my maid and I will be most comfortable. Such quality must be unusual on a cargo ship, I dare say."

With a smile, Stewart propped himself against the door frame and replied, "You are right, of course. But since this is my most frequent address, I wanted to have quarters that would give me a respite from the harshness and monotony of sea life."

"These are *your* quarters?" Sarah's voice rose in astonishment, the thought occurring to her that sleeping in his bed would be tempting fate.

"Why, yes," Stewart replied casually and gestured toward the coverlet on the bed, "though a few things have been altered to make you feel more at home." Ignoring her discomfiture, he added, "Do you like the flowers?"

"Oh yes, thank you." Nervously removing her kid gloves, she looked around, desperately trying to avoid his warm gaze. "I suppose I should get settled."

"Of course," Stewart smiled. "I will leave you now, but will return later to give you a tour of the ship. Besides," he added, quirking a brow in a knowing gesture, "I believe we have some catching up to do. If you need anything, Captain Slade's cabin boy, Ezra, is at your disposal. And my quarters are right next door. I will be bunking with the captain." Touching his fingers to the corner of his brow, he saluted and was gone.

That was the last she had seen of Stewart Chamberlain, though Tegan informed her that he was making regular inquiries about her condition. Sarah was so ill she had refused all efforts of help. No food had passed her lips since the light lunch she and Tegan had shared at noon on their first day. Despite the drinks and broths Ezra had delivered, Sarah remained firm in her singular wish for a swift death, a relief nourishment would not hasten.

On the morning of the third day, after a particularly harrowing night, Sarah awoke to find herself face-to-face with Stewart, who had suddenly materialized at her bedside. "Tegan tells me you are not eating," he warned.

"Tegan talks too much," she croaked, closing her eyes and licking her parched lips. *What was he doing here?*

"No one has died of seasickness, and I will not let you be the first. Not on my ship."

"Go away."

"Not until you take this." He held before her a teacup filed with a vile-smelling liquid.

"No," she whispered as fiercely as she could in her weakened state, turning her head toward the dark paneling which made up one side of the built-in bed.

"Unlike Tegan, I do not fear forcing you. You will take this."

"Go away."

But Stewart was undeterred by her feeble protests. In an instant, he had lifted her aching head from the pillow and was pushing the teacup between her lips. Without the strength to fight him, Sarah knew she would either have to swallow or drown. She chose the former, choking and spluttering as the thick brew burned her raw throat.

When the cup was empty at last, Stewart set it aside, and, with infinite care, began daubing Sarah's cracked lips and green-tinged face with a cool cloth, all the while holding her still with his strong arm. "Do you always resort to brute force?" she finally muttered, her eyes still closed tightly against the sight of his presence.

"Only when you refuse to do things that are good for you," Stewart replied meaningfully. "I guarantee this elixir will have you feeling fit by this noon. And then I expect you to sample Cook's broth. You have upset him terribly, you know. He is not used to having his meals returned untouched."

"My apologies to Cook," she murmured through gritted teeth. "Now may I please be left in peace?"

"Very well," Stewart acquiesced, pushing a stray curl back into her night cap, "but I shall return later and I expect to see you up and about."

"I promise nothing."

"Of that I am well aware," Stewart chuckled, rising from the bed. "But it seems you have extracted a very substantial promise from me," he said, referring to their compromise. "And so I think it should not trouble you too much to allow me the time to clear up the misunderstanding that occurred when last we were together." Ignoring her weak struggles to dismiss the path of his conversation, Stewart bowed and said, "Later, Lady Sarah. For now, just rest and let the potion do its work."

When Sarah awoke later, she was amazed that she felt human again. Whatever Stewart had given her had worked and grudgingly, she admitted that she had been grateful for his ministrations. Throwing off the covers, she tentatively rested her slender feet on the rug. Using the bed for support, she carefully rose to a standing position to find that her stomach no longer rebelled. She did feel faint, however, and fortunately, Tegan, who had been searching through the wardrobe, poked her head out just in time to grab Sarah before she fell forward.

"Gracious, mum!" You are too weak for such sport. Here, let me help you into this chair." With Tegan's support, Sarah walked the few steps to one of the sturdy wooden chairs that sat beside a small round dining table in the center of the cabin

"All right now?"

"Yes, thank you, Teeg. Compared to yesterday, I feel wonderful," Sarah smiled feebly. Rubbing a hand across her face, she added, "But I must look a fright. Could you hand me my glass?"

Tegan passed her mistress an ornately-handled looking glass, cautioning, "A brush and a hot meal will do wonders for you. I'll have Ezra bring in a pitcher of warm water for you, too."

"Egads!" Sarah gasped at the reflection of her snarling hair and sunken eyes. Her complexion, pale and wan, appalled her, especially since Stewart had been allowed to see her this way. "I have never looked so near to a cow's thumb. Help me, Teeg. Quickly!"

It was not long before their efforts considerably improved Sarah's appearance. The water that Ezra had delivered was put to good use as Sarah sponged herself all over while Tegan worked to relieve her dark hair of its tangles. After braiding the thick tresses, she arranged the ropes atop Sarah's head in a smooth coil. Feverishly pinching her cheeks to bring back some color, Sarah bid her maid to bring out a pink gown with the red Spencer that would reflect its rosiness onto her pale skin. The effect was flattering but Sarah still fretted over the dark circles under her eyes and the hollowness of her delicate features. Always a trifle thin, she felt today like a piece of straw.

"Don't you worry, mum" Tegan reassured her, as she moved around the cabin, straightening it. "Cook's soup will have you looking good as new. Ezra's bringing it now."

But it was not Ezra who appeared at the cabin door with a luncheon tray, but Stewart. "Well, well," he beamed, stepping into the room and swallowing it up with his presence. He set the tray before Sarah. "'Tis a miracle I see before me. Never has my seasick remedy worked such wonders so quickly. You look lovely."

Despite her reluctance to treat him kindly, Sarah could not help smiling in embarrassed pleasure at his compliment. "Thank you," she murmured, her eyes downcast, "for your medicine. I may survive this journey after all."

"Of course you will," he assured her, tucking his long legs under the table across from her. "Now eat. I promised your father I would take good care of you and I cannot think of anything that will help you more than this soup." Taking the lid off the small pot before her, Sarah's mouth began to water as she smelled the tantalizing aroma rising form the steaming broth. Her empty stomach growled in anticipation and she was soon spooning down great mouthfuls of the lightly seasoned chicken soup.

"This is excellent," she finally managed to speak between sips, after realizing how closely Tegan and Stewart were watching her. "You have a very fine chef on board. Please thank him for me."

"An empty bowl will be thanks enough for Cook," Stewart told her and taking that as a cue, Sarah kept eating until she had drained the pot.

As if by some prearranged plan, Tegan removed the tray when Sarah had finished and announced that she would return it to the galley herself. Before Sarah could protest, she found herself alone in the cabin with Stewart, a cup of tea the only object between her and the devastatingly attractive man at the other side of the table.

Settling himself more comfortably in the wooden chair, Stewart casually ran a long finger across the cleft in his strong chin and began, "You've had a great deal of time to conjure up the worst thoughts of me since we parted, but I hope I can clear up this misunderstanding between us."

The moment had come and Sarah was still not ready to face it. Juliana had explained the embrace with Stewart. She did not want to recall the pain she had felt. But more than that, she did not want Stewart to know how deeply hurt she had been. He had seen her vulnerability before. She would not let him see it again.

Nervously Sarah fingered her teacup. "In truth," she lied, "I have not been thinking much of you at all." Shamed by his steady gaze, she finally admitted, "Actually you have no reason to explain yourself to me. Juliana confessed."

"Really now?" Stewart was surprised.

"We *are* sisters," Sarah reminded him, "and it would take more than a man to come between us. The only thing I do not understand is why you bother with me when so many others are far more willing."

"I only question why you remain so hostile if you do indeed understand the scene you witnessed in the garden that night," he replied logically.

"Perhaps you misinterpret my indifference to the entire situation."

"I do not think so," he replied. "After all, you *did* decide to meet me that night."

"I was curious about your 'news,' 'tis all," Sarah pouted, nervous beneath his gaze.

"I see," Stewart clipped, muffling his amusement at her obvious uneasiness. "Well, it is important to me that you believe that I was not courting Juliana behind your back. Sparing the details, I would only say that she is a strong-willed, impulsive young lady who is quite skilled at getting what she wants. I had no idea that she was going to follow me into the garden that night."

"I *said* she explained everything," Sarah cut in, her voice rising impatiently. She did not want the shock of that night rekindled.

"Then tell me, Sarah, how might I restore your kinder feelings toward me? We shall be together for quite a long while and the time will pass much more pleasurably if we can be friends. Don't you agree?"

Averting her gaze, she ignored his questions. "My maid and I are both grateful that a seasoned traveler is our escort on this journey. We trust your capabilities as protector and guide. I am also in quite deep to you for curing my seasickness. I did not realize healing was among your many talents."

Stewart graciously accepted her sidestep, even though he had hoped for a more personal conversation. "There were times in my life where I had to practice medicine in order to survive. Any good sailor has a remedy. I am glad mine worked so quickly for you. 'Tis a good sign."

"Aye, I am grateful too," Sarah agreed, a trace of a smile on her pink lips. "Since I have never been on a ship of this magnitude before, I was hoping to see more of it than this cabin."

"I promised you a tour three days ago. Do you feel well enough to accompany me now?"

Pushing her chair back, Sarah rose and tested her stance. Holding her hand up to fend off Stewart, who had risen to help her, she nodded, "Yes, I think I feel fine. Let's see now." She began walking away from him toward the recessed bureau. "Yes, I am a bit shaky but I think a stroll will do me good."

"Excellent!" Stewart cheered her spirit. "Get your wrap, then. The sun is high but the sea air is a bit cool today. As we head further south, the weather will be balmier."

"South? But I thought we were traveling to Boston?"

"Eventually," Stewart answered as she turned to close her red Spencer and take a shawl from the wardrobe. "But we are traveling via the Caribbean route so as to avoid as much intervention by the English monitors as possible ... and to pick up some protection by American ships patrolling the southern corridor."

"But what about pirates in those waters?" Sarah had heard about uncivilized bands of thieves and murderers who plundered cargo ships such as the one they were on. They based their operations out of ports in the Caribbean since they were exiled from their own countries for dastardly crimes both on land and sea.

"Due to present animosities between England and America, we fear British seamen more than pirates," Stewart told her as he took the wrap from her and placed it around her shoulders. "Besides, the pirates are not without scruples. As long as we play by their rules, we can usually pass without incident."

"Do you mean to tell me you actually deal with the pirate bands?" She found the idea of making pacts with thieves appalling.

Stewart's demeanor abruptly turned aloof. "Shall we simply say that we have less to fear from pirates than your Navy?"

Sarah felt a sudden chill. *Did Stewart's fleet consort with criminals?* Perhaps he was not the honorable man her father had insisted he was. All the more reason, she decided, to maintain her distance – both emotionally and physically. Nervously stepping away from his hands, which had found a resting place on her shoulders, she fumblingly pulled the shawl over her bosom and grabbed a bonnet from a peg on the wall. "Shall we go? It will be a pleasure to breathe fresh air for a change."

Hiding a smirk, Stewart opened the cabin door and they departed for the decks.

Sarah found it easier than she expected to tolerate Stewart's tour of his stately three-masted schooner built in Essex, Massachusetts. He was animated and cheerful as he explained the complicated workings of the sails and she was drawn to the modest pride he displayed as he caressed a solid railing here or a taut rigging there. Despite its cargo, it was agile and quick, averaging speeds of well over 20 knots.

As she took in the exhilarating salt air and sunshine, she found herself contemplating Stewart's change of attitude even more deeply. He had always been at ease in any situation, but here, aboard his ship, he seemed even more relaxed and comfortable. Perhaps it was his appearance that prompted this observation. He was handsomer than she remembered, dressing casually in light-colored breeches, black boots, a nautical waistcoat left unbuttoned against the stiff breeze, exposing a linen shirt left open at the neck. His curling dark hair ruffled shaggily, accentuating his strong features already bronzed by the wind and sun. When he smiled, which was frequently, his even white teeth dazzled her and she found herself remembering the pleasure the last time she had been in his arms – in the stable where she had kissed him. Suddenly she recalled the woman at the dock and with a mental shake, she cursed herself for her lapse. She would never survive this voyage if she let her mind wander!

It was then that she found herself on the steps leading up to the bridge where Captain Slade was waiting to greet them. "Lady Sarah! I am glad to see you have joined the living!" he called above the loud rustling of the canvas sails. "I was beginning to wonder whether I would ever have the pleasure of seeing you on deck. How are you feeling?"

"Much better every moment, thank you, Captain," she responded, of necessity speaking close to his ear. "I apologize for my indisposition and any trouble I've been to you and your crew," she added as Stewart drew nearer.

"Pshaw. You've been no trouble at all, except as a distraction to Mr. Chamberlain. He has been fretting over you, you know. Fortunately, we are used to sailing without his help." Slade laughed at his playful ribbing, and Sarah stole a quick glance at Stewart, who had cast his head downward to hide an embarrassed scowl.

Surprised by this uncharacteristic reaction, Sarah was at a loss for words, but Captain Slade appeared not to notice. He immediately began talking to her about the luck they were having with the weather and their course and she used the opportunity to study the man more closely.

He was taller than Stewart, by perhaps an inch or two, and was much thinner and more wiry. Years at sea had given his long, narrow face a permanent ruddy hue that made his crinkly bright blue eyes seem like two turquoise gems. His sandy hair was crushed beneath a captain's cap and were it not for his youth – he was surely no older than Stewart – he would look like the proverbial 'old salt' of her storybooks.

"I trust you've found the accommodations not too uncomfortable," he was saying.

"On the contrary, Captain," she complimented him. "My maid and I are grateful for the comforts and for the fact that you have allowed us to sail with you. I understand that many sailors feel it is bad luck to have a woman aboard."

"In my experience, women have brought nothing but good luck," Slade smiling engagingly. "Until we began our family, my wife sailed with me frequently."

"You're married, Captain?" Sarah asked, surprised.

"But I thought you knew!" Slade replied, looking over her head at Stewart, who merely shrugged. "I am married six years to the most beautiful girl in Boston. Perhaps my brother-in-law neglected to mention it."

"Mr. Chamberlain is your brother-in-law?" Sarah eyed Stewart with an accusing look before returning to the captain.

"That and uncle to our three children as well. Shame on you, Stewart. Didn't you tell her she'd be staying with us in Boston?"

Before Stewart could speak, Sarah answered, "My father told me we'd be the guest of Mr. Chamberlain's sister, but I had no idea that you were her husband." Smiling warmly to assuage the awkwardness, she added, "I am very pleased that I shall have a chance to learn about your family before we arrive. I hope we won't be a burden."

"Now don't you worry about that, Lady Sarah. Peggy and the children will be thrilled. Unlike my tight-lipped partner here, Peggy loves nothing more than company. She will talk your ears off if you permit."

"My sister is a gabster," Stewart finally interjected. And added dryly, "As is her mate."

Slate laughed heartily. "Guilty, as charged. It comes from spending so many lonely nights at sea. What else is there to do but spin a yarn or two?"

"Come, Lady Sarah," Stewart said after clearing his throat. Sarah was surprised to hear him address her formally. "Perhaps you'd like to rest until dinner?"

"Yes, I would," she answered truthfully, suddenly noticing how tired she was.

"I hope you will join me and Stewart for dinner, then," Captain Slade offered enthusiastically, "We will celebrate your resurrection."

"Thank you, Captain," Sarah smiled, genuinely pleased with the invitation, even if Stewart was included. "I shall be looking forward to it."

As Stewart helped Sarah off the bridge, Slade could not squelch the smile that came to his lips as he watched them go. What a striking pair they make! Peggy would be pleased to see her brother in the company of such a beautiful yet unpretentious young woman – someone marriageable for a change. From the way Stewart looked so uncomfortable, the captain was willing to bet that his brother-in-law was more than casually interested in the lady – and yet, with Stewart, one could never really know for sure.

Slade was all too familiar with the carefree nature of his brother-in-law's relationships with women. The two of them had broken many hearts in many places before Jeremiah met and married Peggy. His craggy face softened as he allowed himself a moment to reflect on those rollicking nights they spent in ports around the world.

They had been quite a team in those days. Women would notice Stewart immediately for his dark, aristocratic features made him stand out in any crowd. Even in his sailor's garb, he was always immaculately groomed. As he would coolly survey his surroundings from the vantage point of his height, women would immediately show their interest through coy looks and whispered conversations. Jeremiah, the more gregarious of the two, would be the one to capitalize on the attention Stewart's presence created and in no time at all they would engage in conversation with the mostly likely prospects – always convenients and light skirts – women who were both beautiful and experienced. There was no time for innocents, the hesitant, or marriage-seekers.

In those days, the two were much too busy to consider permanent entanglements. They had met in a Virginia military school and upon graduation, opted to serve their country as blockade runners, unofficially commissioned by the infant U.S. Navy to wreak havoc on the high seas in order that American goods could be transported to foreign markets without interference. At the same time, they were developing their own shipping and trading business, making the necessary European connections that would insure the success of their Endeavours.

It was a complicated, often treacherous combination of allegiances – to country and to their own private interests – but Chamberlain and Slade were equal to the task. Jeremiah had established himself as one of the most able and cunning ship's captains in Atlantic waters and Stewart, a worthy seaman in his own right, possessed an unequaled ability to manipulate the most experienced business and political strategists. In addition, both were charming, dashing characters, able to make themselves at home in any situation.

As their reputations as sailors, businessmen and rogues grew, so did their status. In nearly every capital, Stewart and Jeremiah became sought-after guests to men of power and women of influence. When in port, they began to mingle with society and royalty in private clubs and homes; Jeremiah the engaging and quick-witted conversationalist; Stewart, the charming, yet remote and mysterious young blood.

But that free-spirited and more-often-than-not dangerous life was long over for Jeremiah and it happened the day he met Margaret Chamberlain. He had fallen in love with her the moment he'd first seen her in New York City, where she was attending school. She was a beauty, with her curling black hair and fair skin, but what had most attracted Jeremiah was the spark of mischief and defiance in her warm, brown eyes. Unlike most young girls, she was incapable of feigning shyness or reserve. Instead, she unabashedly stared at anyone who caught her eye and struck up immediate conversations with strangers, regardless of whether she was properly introduced or not. Her questions were direct and she made uncommonly astute observations about the people who caught her attention.

When Jeremiah first approached her party during intermission at a theatre, on the pretense of saying hello to an old schoolmate standing near Margaret, she immediately extended her hand to him, saying, "Sir, it is about time we met." Ignoring her friends' uneasiness, and finding her boldness refreshing, he took her gloved hand in both of his and squeezed it affectionately, a gesture that did not seem to offend her.

"I most heartily agree," he answered, grinning warmly. "I am Jeremiah Slade and ...."

"I know. You are a frequent topic of conversation in our home. I would have recognized you anywhere."

"I am sure the same will be said of you, if only I might know who you are," Jeremiah replied, pleasure showing clearly on his attractively weather-beaten features.

"I am Margaret Chamberlain, Stewart's sister. Are you surprised?"

"Delightedly so! Your brother barely mentioned your existence, let alone described your beauty. I now see clearly why he did not wish to arouse my curiosity."

Peggy smiled happily and made no move to take her hand away from his. "He's told me that you are a scalawag. But I am sure that is not the sole facet of your character."

"I appreciate your generosity. I hope you will allow me the opportunity to prove you correct."

"With pleasure, sir. If you are free, you may call on me tomorrow at the St. Regent, say 11 o'clock? We have a great deal to discuss, don't you agree?"

"Most heartily," Jeremiah responded, giving her hand a final pat as the lights dimmed to announce the end of the intermission. "Until the morrow then."

And from that moment on, there was no other woman in the world for Jeremiah Slade. He was so intrigued by her beauty, her wit and her strong will that he would have done anything to make her his. She, too, was swept up by the dashing, yet sentimental and kind captain, who had been her brother's most trusted friend for many years.

After a six-month courtship, made up mostly of long and loving letters, Jeremiah asked, indeed begged Peggy to wed him, promising to give up his responsibilities as captain, if only she would consent. Much to his amazement, she refused, declaring she would find no happiness with a "landlubber." But, she countered, if he promised to allow her to accompany him, she would accept his proposal.

Despite his concern for her safety and well-being, Jeremiah loved her too much to lose her, and finally acquiesced.

But the road to matrimony was further impeded by one irate and overprotective brother. Jeremiah sighed to himself as he remembered the one time he had ever seen Stewart completely lose his temper.

"I'll see you planted twenty leagues under before I allow you to wed my sister!" Stewart had bellowed. "You conniving lecher! You may have fooled Peggy but I know you better than anyone alive and I won't have you stealing her virtue – if you haven't already, you bastard – and breaking her heart because of your penchant for warm brandy and hot women." His tirade had continued with a detailed description of all his vices, capped by the exhortation that no decent captain would ever marry and leave a sea widow. When Jeremiah explained what Peggy wished to do, Stewart had become more belligerent, accusing his partner of further charming her out of her senses.

The epithets continued until the calm, controlled Slade was forced to play his ace. "I am sorry, Stewart, that after all these years you have found not one virtue within me that is good enough for your sister, but the matter, quite frankly, is out of your hands. Your father has already given his consent."

His waning control shattered, Stewart reacted out of blind, senseless rage. Before Jeremiah could even recognize the threat, Chamberlain had smashed him square in the face with an incredibly forceful blow from his right fist. While picking himself up off the floor, Stewart had fled. Fortunately for Jeremiah, a broken nose was the only damage and it mended well in time.

Jeremiah had been willing to forgive and forget the whole episode, understanding that Stewart was moved by an extraordinary love and concern for his sister, as well as a firsthand knowledge of Slade's dubious past. But Peggy was livid. It was a year before she would read any of Stewart's letters and even longer before she acknowledged that the affection between them was greater than the rift they had suffered.

In those first two years of Peggy and Jeremiah's marriage, Stewart removed himself from the business and on an impulse, signed up as first mate on an independent Spanish trading schooner, managing to see the world and learning a great deal about emotional and physical survival for a young man completely on his own.

When he finally returned to Boston, his entire family, including Peggy, Jeremiah and their infant son, young Jeremiah, found it easier than they expected to convince the wayfaring Chamberlain to take up his life exactly where he had left it.

He found Jeremiah eager to continue their business relationship. And even though there was to be no more bachelor camaraderie as in the olden days, both men found their partnership as enjoyable as before ... and even more profitable.

CHAPTER 15

Sarah took special pains with her appearance that evening on the rather weak excuse that dining with the captain demanded elegant attire. But deep down, she hoped to see the light of approval flicker in Stewart's warm, brown eyes. She had the disturbing notion to compete with the beautiful woman he had so passionately kissed at the dock, and yet, she was still quite certain that she must, for her own safety, spurn Stewart's attentions. This conflict made her uncharacteristically cross and poor Tegan was forced to bear the brunt of her moodiness.

"'Tis a blessing to see you looking so lovely again, mum," the maid encouraged as she skillfully coiled Sarah's glossy locks into a fashionable chignon. "I'm sure Mr. Chamberlain will have trouble keeping his eyes from you in that gown."

"Then I shall change forthwith," Sarah snapped, plucking the low-cut bodice of the sapphire-hued gown of silk satin. "The last thing I need is Stewart Chamberlain ogling me in front of Captain Slade."

Tegan sighed patiently. "You haven't much time, mum. Besides, I doubt there is a dress in your wardrobe that would not become you. You and the Duchess took ever so much care to make sure those Colonists ...."

"Don't remind me," Sarah huffed, moving her head away from Tegan's last-minute pats. "My mother insisted on putting me in such immodest costumes. Sometimes I wonder about her sense of propriety."

"You are a young woman," Tegan said fondly. "'Tis only natural that you should dress like one."

"Spare me, Teeg. I understand completely my mother's designs. She wants to arrange me as window dressing for sale to the highest bidder." Sarah frowned. "She thinks I would be happy as a wife, a life I cannot see for myself. Who wants a partner who would rather read than prepare teas? Or prefer to go riding rather than ... than ...." Tegan smiled broadly and Sarah knew she did not have an ally. "Than ... never mind. But thanks to her, I own not one costume that any could call 'maidenly' anymore."

A knock at the cabin door silenced her complaining and immediately a nervous lump rose in her throat. "Get the door," she whispered, cold fingers pulling up the material that barely shielded the swell of her firm young breasts.

Tegan did as she was told. "Good evening, sir," she smiled warmly at the tall figure dressed in a dark blue coat and white shirt with a conservatively tied stock. How her mistress did not melt at the very sight of him, Teeg would never understand.

"Hello, Tegan. Is your mistress ready?"

Before Tegan could reply, Sarah snatched a cloak as she crossed the room and announced, "Yes, Mr. Chamberlain. Shall we go?"

If Stewart were surprised by her curtness, he did not show it. Taking her cloak as she passed him outside the door, he skillfully draped it over her shoulders before she moved out of his reach. Sarah walked the few steps to the captain's quarters and looked back at Stewart, who was eying her quizzically. "Well?" she intoned, wondering why he had not followed her.

"Jeremiah was detained slightly. He asked that I entertain you while he finishes dressing," Stewart said pleasantly as he came toward her. "Shall we take a stroll on deck? It's not too cool."

Sarah nodded, shielding her embarrassed flush by turning toward the stairs. Silently she cursed herself for her haste. If she'd stayed in the cabin, Tegan would have saved her from being alone with this disturbing man.

But as they stepped onto the main deck, Sarah was immediately distracted by the luscious beauty of the evening. A full moon bathed their surroundings in silvery white light. The gentle roll of the ship and the rhythmical voices of the schooner singing through the calm waters created a relaxed, almost intoxicating, atmosphere, and Sarah gasped at the wonder of it all. "I have never seen a setting so exquisite," she cried, forgetting her nervousness and her restraint as she moved swiftly to the railing. "Look how the ocean reflects the light. 'Tis as bright as a winter's day!" she whispered, completely in awe of the fantastical vision seen only by those at sea. The air was pleasantly cool and smelled clean and fresh; a soft breeze stirred the tendrils around Sarah's face as she arched her slender neck to catch the lovely sensations.

As she drank in the setting in silent reverence, Stewart allowed his gaze to rest on her dramatic profile. She appeared a part of the scenery in her ice blue gown, the moon glowing white on her pale, delicate skin. It was so bright he could actually see the vibrant blue of her eyes, fringed by those impossibly thick eyelashes. She was indeed a diamond of the first water, exquisitely beautiful and rare. Such a vision was she that his breath was nearly taken away by a sudden and tremendous urge to touch her. Never had a woman affected him so spontaneously and he wrestled silently with his masculine urgings.

Turning to hide his struggle, he leaned against the railing, his coat sleeve lightly teasing her arm. Reawakened to his presence, Sarah inclined her head slightly to glance at his moonlit profile. She had not looked directly at him until now and was again struck by his classical handsomeness. The strong features were softened somewhat by the curling dark hair that gently blew round his face and the strangely vulnerable expression he wore. Was something troubling him perhaps? She had thought him happy to be on this voyage, sailing for home after such a long absence. But obviously he was not at the minute the carefree soul she had always believed him to be.

Somehow this realization strengthened her, allowing her to relax in his presence in the beautiful moonlight. "I never knew the high seas could be this peaceful, this inviting," she offered tentatively.

With a blink, the boyish look was gone. The old confident Stewart reappeared, his voice deep, assured. "The seas hold many nights like this, which is why some find it difficult to live their lives without it."

"Are you such a man?"

"I was," he replied, his eyes sparkling in the full light, "when I was younger. But no longer. I prefer the adventures to be encountered in business. The sea can extract too dear a price."

"Meaning?"

"My duties kept me onboard for long periods and rather than moving from port to port, we simply stayed to sea for as long as we were able. Our primary purpose was to throw a rub in the way of any who would thwart America's interests. When one's life is stripped of all elements save survival, it is not the kind of existence I would call 'rewarding'." He turned his body toward her, still leaning on the railing. "But this," his voice softened as he stretched his arm out to sea, "when you are sailing for home in so fine a ship in the company of friends and fair weather? Well, you see for yourself. It would be easy to become half-sprung with pleasure."

"Aye," Sarah agreed, feeling again the companionship they had ever so briefly shared over a month ago. She knew a strong desire to tell him how excited she was to be on this voyage, how much she was looking forward to the realization of her dreams; that his presence was much less a curse than a comfort to her. But it could not be. Her confession would make her vulnerable and that was something she could not afford, especially in this overwhelmingly romantic setting. "Do you think Captain Slade is ready for us now?"

"I think we've given him enough time," Stewart answered. "I hope you've regained your appetite," he continued, offering his arm to her. "Cook's prepared a feast for us, I understand. And as an old seafarer to a new one, I recommend that you eat hearty for the food becomes less appetizing with each passing day. There are only so many fresh provisions we can store."

Sarah rested her hand lightly on his coat sleeve as he guided her toward the hatchway. "How long will it take us to get to Boston now that we are not on a direct path?"

"If the weather continues and the winds are in our favor, we will be there before the month is out; probably sooner with Jeremiah so eager to be with his family. He pushes the ship and crew to the limit when he's homeward bound." As he handed her down the wooden steps, he added, his lips disturbingly close to her ear, "So don't be offended should he leave us suddenly during dinner. We're at full sail and he likes to make regular inspections."

CHAPTER 16

As Sarah listened to the banter between Stewart and Jeremiah, while Ezra cleared away the remains of the delicious meal, she realized she should not have worried that this intimate supper might cause her discomfort or stress. The gentlemen on either side of her were quite experienced when it came to putting a lady at her ease and she found herself thoroughly enjoying their company. Jeremiah was eager to answer any questions she had about their travels, their family and the strange, new country she was soon to visit. Stewart, too, seemed pleased with her presence; more relaxed and candid than she had ever seen him. He joked, laughed, and, she was relieved to note, did not chafe her with any smoldering glances or accidental touches that she would have found impossible to ignore.

With Ezra gone, the three shared a second decanter of Madeira and talked until Jeremiah needed to check their course with the watch on the bridge. After he left, Stewart turned his full attention to Sarah, noticing at once how the wine had added a blushing hue to her fair skin. "Perhaps you'd care for a little fresh air?" he offered kindly. "It's gotten rather warm in here."

"Oh yes, please," Sarah sighed, pressing a napkin against her damp forehead. Rising with a nearly imperceptible lurch, she accepted Stewart's strong hand on her elbow as he guided her to the cabin door. Trying to ignore her sudden lightheadedness, she walked very carefully to the wooden stairs, chattering all the way. "I had not realized it was so stuffy inside. Dinner was lovely, ever so much more sumptuous than I expected. Tell me, Mr. Chamberlain," she continued as they moved toward the railing, shining white in the moonlight, "do you and Captain Slade always use bone china at your meals? I had envisioned dining at sea to be somewhat less ...."

"Tin cups and trenchers?"

"Why yes," Sarah agreed, wide-eyed in the darkness.

"Usually our meals are taken a bit more rustically, but this was a special occasion. It's rare that we have such a lovely guest on board and we did want you to feel at home. I hope we've succeeded ...."

"Indeed you have," Sarah gushed, eager to show her pleasure. "I am finding my adventure much more comfortable than I anticipated. I thank you for that." She emphasized her delight with a genuine, if slightly lopsided, smile, and Stewart knew then for a certainty that she was quite drunk.

"I cannot promise you such luxury for the entire voyage, I'm afraid, especially should the weather turn. In that event, all hands are needed and our meals are not quite so leisurely."

"Oh, I understand completely. I do not expect or wish to be catered to. It is enough that you have given up your quarters to me and my maid. We are so comfortable, I'm sure it was quite a sacrifice."

Stewart gazed at her, a mirthful expression on his handsome face. "Only in that I could not share the comforts with you." To his surprise, Sarah giggled, and looked up at him, her eyes shining mischievously, no offense taken.

"I am sure Tegan would be pleased with that arrangement. She is forever remarking on what a reassuring presence you are." Delighted with her coyness, Sarah held onto the railing and threw her head back, giggling again. Stewart had never seen her so devil-may-care and the vision was enticing, but he cautioned himself to tread lightly, for he had seen before how quickly he could arouse her suspicious wrath.

"And do you agree with her assessment?"

Sarah gazed up at him, scrutinizing his tanned face in the moonlight, attempting to formulate an evasive answer. Flirting with him might be fun after all. But her mind could not, for some reason, focus on anything more than those dark eyes that expressed a desire her own body suddenly felt helpless to repel.

How lovely it would be to sample the tenderness of his lips again, to feel the strength of his well-muscled arms, to be pressed so close as to nearly suffocate in his passionate grasp. All her carefully reasoned arguments flew as she felt her own heartbeat pounding in her ears knowing that she could not struggle anymore. Turning slowly to face him, her arms seemed to move of their own accord to his shoulders and she closed her eyes to accept his lips on hers.

If he were surprised by her boldness, his response did not convey it. With slow sureness, Stewart's warm lips captured hers as his arms enfolded her. With a moan of pleasure, she opened her mouth slightly to allow his tongue easy access. Pressing herself closer so that her breasts were crushed against his unrelenting chest, Sarah caught her fingers in the curling hair at the nape of his neck, as it to thwart any attempts he might make to move away,

Stewart's mouth slid from hers to her cheek, to her ear, the perfumed softness of her neck and then back hungrily to her waiting lips. Moved by the dizzying urgings of her body, her delicate tongue possessed his with a passion that surprised them both, Stewart's skilled fingers caressed her hair and finding the combs Tegan had so carefully put in place, removed them so that Sarah's luscious dark tresses tumbled over her shoulders, filling the air with its subtle fragrance.

With her hair unbound, Sarah's response seemed to take on new fervor. She moved instinctively now, planting hot kisses on Stewart's face, ears and neck as he lost himself in the sweetness of her shining locks. Pressing her closer, his mouth left a searing trail down her pale skin to the heaving flesh just above her ice blue gown. She reveled in the sudden tremors of desire that shook her when his lean fingers molded themselves to her firm breasts, massaging the peaks beneath the heavy fabric as his lips and tongue lovingly caressed the straining mounds of flesh. For a moment, she cursed the gown that had earlier seemed so immodest, but now was holding her breasts captive from his searching mouth.

Sensing her frustration, and feeling not a small amount himself, Stewart tenderly slid his hand up to her chin, and tipping her flushed face up, gazed wistfully into her puzzled, tormented blue eyes. With a sigh, he lightly kissed her passion-reddened lips and the tip of her slender nose. Pulling her head against his chest, he gently stroked her neck beneath the tousled brown hair, and spoke. "Oh Sarah, what a bewitching temptation you are. You almost made me forget our setting is public. And I am too selfish to allow any other man to view your charms."

Only beginning to realize the abandonment of her actions, Sarah stiffened at his words. "I'm quite sure I don't know what you're talking about."

She felt, rather than heard, the rumbling of a chuckle deep within his broad chest, "Surely by now you can tell when a man wants to make love to you. I think you want it as much as I"

"Sir, you are mistaken. I have no such thoughts," Sarah responded breathlessly, pushing herself away from his silken touch. But he was not yet ready to let her out of his grasp, and held her slim fingers captive in his stronger ones. "Please, it's late. I really must go."

As if he hadn't heard a word she uttered, Stewart brought his arm around her waist and held her close to his side, ignoring her resistance.

"Beautiful, innocent Sarah," he murmured. "You must be very careful not to offer what you are not willing to give ... especially to me." The threat was unmistakable.

Struggling against the effects of the wine and his kisses, Sarah realized the foolishness of her incautious actions, but her pride would not let her admit her deep longing for his caress. Defensively, she muttered, "Are you so weak that you cannot control your own lusts?"

"Are you?" he whispered seductively, his warm breath tingling her earlobe as his hand molded itself against her ribs.

"I was foolish to allow myself to be alone with you. I assure you it will not happen again!" She struggled to remove herself from his viselike hold but to no avail. "Unhand me before I scream."

"Are you sure you wish to cause such a disturbance? You forget this is my ship. No one will interfere when they see you are with me. Besides, you should know you are quite safe. Didn't I give your father my word that no harm would come to you?"

"Your promise was only too clever," she sniffed haughtily, though a slur marred the confident tone, "for you do not consider your ravishment of me a danger. But I tell you this:

My father would not hesitate to ruin you if I am returned to him in a-a trifled state." Sensing that her threat was ineffectual in the face of this well-connected and highly resourceful man, she cast her eyes downward, struggling in vain against his powerful arm.

"Then I suggest you take pains to bridle your desires, my sweet, for I cannot continue to protect you from yourself." With a disgusted snort, he added, much to Sarah's surprise and consternation, "'Tis ironic that you should be the one to warn me against trifling, since it is your game, not mine. I would do better to confine myself to women who are honest about what they want."

"Like the woman at the dock?" The bitter words left her mouth before she had a chance to think. Stewart did not seem surprised, but neither, to her chagrin, did he comment.

Releasing her for a moment, he took her hand and placed the combs, stolen from her hair, into her palm. "Off you go, little one. It's late and you need your sleep."

Incensed by his paternal dismissal, Sarah snatched her hand away and with a burning look, flung her tangled mane over her shoulder and stalked off with what she hoped was great dignity. But his short, deep-throated chuckle told her the show of bravado was lost on him.

Had she been able to see the disquieted look in his dark eyes, she might have found some whit of satisfaction to take to her bed. But as she did not, there was nothing to comfort her; only silent tears of anger, humiliation and a sense of frustration she could neither name nor understand.

CHAPTER 17

Just as Stewart promised, the weather as they edged southward grew increasingly warmer. Despite Tegan's warnings, Sarah spent a great deal of time reading on deck, allowing the hot sun an occasional peak at her face.

"Your mother would dismiss me forthwith if she could see those sunspots. You look like a dairy maid," she scolded Sarah one afternoon as they were having tea in their cabin.

"But it feels so good," Sarah argued, "Besides, they'll fade before we're home again."

"Perhaps, but those colonists will have a hard time believing you're the daughter of a Duke with your cheeks ruddy and all," Tegan insisted.

"Captain Slade tells me his wife goes without hat and gloves all summer when they stay at their country home. And he thinks she's beautiful."

"What does Mr. Chamberlain think? 'Tis his opinion you should be worrying about." Tegan eyed her pointedly.

"I care not one fig for his opinion," Sarah replied sharply, "but if you must know, he says he thinks a woman should do whatever she wants. So there."

"I thought you and Mr. Chamberlain would have hit it off better than what I've taken in so far," Tegan remarked, without so much as a warning.

Sarah returned a suspicious look, her blue eyes glinting dangerously in the sunlight that streamed through the porthole in their quarters. Tegan had definitely struck a nerve. "God help me, I don't know where you get your notions. Mr. Chamberlain does not appeal to me in the least. I have told you that before. You saw him in London with --- that woman. I'm sure he has others all over the globe. What use would I have for a man like that?"

"A man with experience makes a better husband. Gets his sporting out of the way before he's wed, not after. Besides, you'd get the benefit of all that skill in pleasing woman, if you know what I mean," she answered, her eyebrows arching suggestively.

"I swear you are impossible," Sarah shot back, her cheeks burning with embarrassment. "You talk as if *that* is all that matters. What about trust, mutual interests, honor, respectability? Mr. Chamberlain is a scoundrel, I am convinced. Would you have me marry a pirate?"

Tegan laughed brightly. "There goes your imagination again. Do you really believe your own papa would send you off with a scalawag? Seems to me you are looking a tad too hard to find the muck. His only faults are that he's a bloody Yankee – which you can't blame *him* for – and he treats you like a grown woman."

"If you only knew ...." Sarah began, and then, her eyes smoldering with disturbing memories, changed the course of her words. "How in the world did you manage to get on the subject of marriage to Mr. Chamberlain? 'Tis a dead issue, Teeg. He has declared he does not wish to marry, and besides, I find him intolerable! Please, can't we discuss something pleasant? Like ...."

Just then, the women were startled by shouts from above and the sound of heavy boots running in every direction. "What in the devil?" gasped Tegan, stiffening in her chair. Never in all their days at sea had they heard such unexplained chaos.

A prickle of fear stung Sarah's nape as she strained to hear what the voices were shouting, but it was impossible to make out words above the clamor. Her heart thumping nervously beneath her blue-flowered day gown, she moved hesitantly toward the porthole, but could see nothing save the incredibly blue water shimmering in the light of the hot afternoon sun. Edging toward the door, she practically jumped out of her chemise when a loud pounding commenced. "What is it?" she cried?

"It's Ezra, Lady Sarah. I have a message from the Cap'n."

In her relief, she lurched toward the door and fell back again, the latch in her hand. "Come in, Ezra! Tell us, please, are we in danger?"

The young boy, his face flushed with a combination of fear and excitement, panted, "A ship's been sighted ... no colors ... could be pirates. Cap'n says you're to stay here ... keep out of sight and quiet. I'll lock the door from without when I leave ... don't Make your presence known, understand?" The women nodded in dumbfounded silence. "Not a peek. Cap'n and Mr. Chamberlain have keys. They will let themselves in if there's any need. Got that?" Again, the women nodded. "I'm off then ... don't worry," he added, though not quite convincingly.

"Ezra," Sarah pleaded as the boy backed out of the room. She could see the sailors rushing past behind him, their faces grim. "What's going to happen?"

The boy's young face was straining with emotion. "I do not know, Lady Sarah. I've only been to sea for nigh six months now. It's never happened before ...."

Seeing the fear in his eyes, and remembering how kind and polite the cabin boy had been, Sarah was moved to grasp his arm in a brief squeeze. In a voice much more confident that she was, she said, "We will be fine, Ezra. Captain Slade and Mr. Chamberlain know what to do."

Finding comfort in her words, the boy smiled with a bit more assurance and closed the door firmly, staying only to bolt the lock.

But the bravado used on Ezra disappeared the second his footsteps were gone. In their shock and fright, Sarah and Tegan clutched each other for a moment, unable to think what else to do. "My God, Teeg," Sarah whispered, trembling, "this is a merchant ship. We're at their mercy!"

"Maybe," Tegan prayed, "maybe it's not pirates. We've got to believe that it's not."

"But they are not flying flags! Stewart told me that all friendly vessels show their colors. It's the code of the sea."

Suddenly the women heard footfalls coming from the stairs, and then, the sound of the captain's door opening and slamming. Together they inched toward the wall that separated the two quarters, hoping to eavesdrop. Sarah immediately recognized Captain Slade's voice, but the wall, covered with built-in furnishings, was too thick to hear specific words. At one point, however, she distinctly heard Stewart's baritone scowl her name, and fervently hoped that he would come through the door and rescue them from their terror. But in a few minutes, the men left the cabin and rushed back on deck, not even pausing to shout a word of reassurance through the door.

The young women waited for hours, it seemed, in interminable silence, huddled together on the floor of the wardrobe. Hidden by the heavy doors and yards of fabric from Sarah's gowns, the panic-stricken women perspired from both the heat and their raging fear stemming from a fate unknown.

Pirates! Sarah's inner voice screamed, as the sweat trickled down her back and between her breasts in the overwhelming blackness. Robbers, murderers, rapists, all! There was no hope for salvation. Desperate, evil men had no respect for human life. They would take what they wanted from this defenseless ship, killing anyone who would stop them. Killing for sport if there were no resistance. Oh yes, she'd read about their wretchedness.

As a mewling cry escaped her lips, Tegan hissed, "Don't think!" and clutched Sarah's damp fingers in the darkness. "Pray! God and Mr. Chamberlain will take care of us. He promised!"

Suddenly the distant sound of quickening footfalls rang like thunder in their ears and, in their horror, the women grabbed each other tighter, oblivious to the insufferable heat and airlessness of their prison. The metal scraping of the lock being opened at their cabin door increased their trembling as they imagined the worst – that pirates had take over the ship and were in search of their captives.

"Lady Sarah! Tegan! Where are you?" The voice. *Whose?* Before they could react, the wardrobe doors flew open, exposing the cowering women to fresh air and light. Fearing the worst, the women hid their faces, pushing themselves farther back into the recesses of the closet.

"Gooses, it's me, Captain Slade. Come out now before you perish of suffocation." Grasping both of them firmly by the arms, he pulled their quivering bodies from behind the mass of muslins and silks. In their relief, they clutched him tearfully, hiding their faces in his rough shirt. "There, there you two," he chuckled kindly. "It's going to be all right. Come. Sit down. I must talk with you." Pushing the terror-stricken women into their chairs, he noted their pale, sweating faces and the hot spots of color on their cheeks. "I wish I'd had a chance to talk to you before. You needn't have hidden yourselves away. You might have died in there!" His wide mouth turned up into a grin, but Sarah could see that his crystal blue eyes did not share the humor.

"We are in grave danger, aren't we? Please Captain, tell us what is happening!" Her hands trembled as she brushed clinging tendrils of hair from her drawn face, feeling weak from the ordeal.

"It's a pirate ship all right, but don't you worry. We will all be safe, as long as you do as I say. Tegan, quickly. Grab your things, bundle them up and give them to Ezra when he returns. Hurry, I'll explain everything to your mistress." With a second of hesitation, Tegan leapt from the chair and set about the task.

"Lady Sarah," he said quietly, taking her hands and looking sternly into her eyes. "We know who the pirates are and as long as we give them what they want, they will leave us in peace. But they are going to make us go with them to their island because their hold is full and they can't take on any more cargo. I know because it's happened before. I am eternally sorry for this change of plans, and for your fears. We didn't expect to meet up with them this time of year, leastways not without an escort. But our blockaders must have met with some misfortune. They never appeared."

"Thank God. At least we are safe," Sarah gasped, her body slumping in relief and fatigue.

"Well," he cautioned, "you will be as long as you and Tegan do as I ask." The tone of his voice aroused a new fear in her, more ominous than before.

"What, Captain? We'll do anything you say, of course."

"I do not want to alarm you unnecessarily but the fact that you and your maid are aboard makes our situation dicier." He paused, and the visions Sarah had imagined earlier came back to haunt her even more vividly. "These men have been known to take female hostages, though it has never happened to me when

Peggy sailed with us. Even in their lawlessness, they have some respect for the institution of marriage."

"What are you saying?

"I am saying that I want Tegan to disguise herself as a boy. She is rather slight and plain. Ezra's clothes will fit her but, though I hate to suggest it, you will have to cut off her hair."

"Oh no, you can't ...." Sarah cried, but Tegan, overhearing the conversation, interceded.

"Captain, we'll do it. It's got to be. But what about my lady?"

He looked at Sarah speculatively, though his eyes spoke of a decision already made. "There's no way we can disguise you, Lady Sarah, even though you are slender. Besides, we would never be able to get rid of your belongings in time. There is only one solution."

As he spoke, he removed a packet from his shirt pocket. Sarah's skin prickled with apprehension. "This document," he said evenly, unfolding it with maddening care, "will serve as your protection. It's a Special License for your marriage to Stewart dated the day of our departure. It was prepared by the Archbishop of Canterbury while we were in London. Stewart and I felt the need for this 'insurance policy' should your safety be in question.

"I don't mind telling you how I regret the inconvenience of this charade on you, but it is the only way we can guarantee your protection. Now if you will just sign ...." he said hastily, rising to locate an inkwell and quill.

Stunned, Sarah stared blankly at the parchment, seeing nothing but the fierce black signature of Stewart Chamberlain and a blank space where a second name was required. "Th-this isn't ... legal, is it?" she spoke in a hushed, breathless tone when Jeremiah returned.

"It is absolutely legal. But please, Sarah, do not fret now. As soon as we are rid of these rascals, the document will be destroyed and as far as all are concerned, the union never took place."

"But why do we need proof? Can't we just tell the ...."

"Simon d'Alava is the name of our hijacker." He added wryly, "He is a sly fox. He will accept our ruse with better grace if Stewart can show him the license. We are actually helping him save face by providing it. Among his men might be those who wish to challenge whether you and my brother-in-law are legally betrothed."

Seeing that she did not understand, Jeremiah added, "I don't want to alarm you, Lady Sarah, but these pirates can be quite dangerous. D'Alava will see that his men respect the fact that you belong to Stewart; they'll leave you alone as they did Peggy. But without Stewart's protection; without his right to be near you at all times ... well, I don't even want to give words to what could happen."

Without a moment's hesitation, Sarah signed.

CHAPTER 18

Married! Without a proposal, a ceremony, or even a look at the groom, Sarah had entered paper nuptials. Everything had happened so fast, she was only now beginning to realize just how far this incredible charade might have to go.

After Jeremiah left, with the signed document tucked safely in his pocket, Sarah had taken the scissors to Tegan's beautiful copper hair. Through tears of sorrow and fear, she clipped the burnished locks into a shaggy style while Tegan sat in stoic silence. They placed the cuttings, along with Tegan's dresses and accessories, into a weighted bundle which Ezra took to heave overboard after he delivered a set of his own clothing to their quarters. "They're not much, but everything's clean," he said, shaking his head sadly at the twist of fate befalling the poor lady's maid. "I want you to know," he added fiercely, "that Cap'n Slade's men, all of us, will make things as easy for you as possible. 'Tis a shame and we are all sorry for you, but we'll make it up to you by keeping you safe."

Tegan thanked him warmly, as did Sarah, and, after he left, she proceeded to change into the rough shirt, jacket, breeches and boots the boy had provided. Though Tegan was rather small-breasted, Sarah insisted on binding her chest with linen strips, just to make sure she looked completely boyish. After pulling a moth-eaten knitted cap over her eyebrows, Tegan finished the disguise by dipping her fingertips in soot from the warming stove, getting black under her short nails. "'Ow is that for a ratty urchin stowaway?" she asked with a trace of humor as she turned to her mistress for inspection.

"You still look like my dear Teeg," Sarah uttered, clutching her in a farewell hug. "I wish so much this hadn't happened. I'll be exhausted with worry over you."

"Now don't you think on it another minute. I took care of myself most of my life. And I can handle this, too. In a day you'll forget I was ever a girl!" With a glint of mischief in her hazel eyes, Tegan left to take up her station, in the kitchen with Cook. Jeremiah had assured them before he left that she would be practically unnoticed there, at least while they sailed for the pirates' island.

Now Sarah was alone, pacing nervously, waiting for what she did not know. She tried desperately to keep her mind off Stewart Chamberlain, but as usual, found that exercise futile. He'd been distant ever since that first night they had dined with the Captain; polite but aloof. She found it quite easy to avoid being alone with him, since he seemed to ignore her unless she was accompanied by Tegan or Captain Slade. *Which was just as well.* Since that night he had kissed her and then humiliated her, she vowed he'd never touch her again.

But the pirate overtaking had changed all that. She was married to Stewart now, so, as Jeremiah had said, he would have the right to be near her at all times. The idea disturbed her nearly as much as their hijacking.

How would he play his role in this travesty? Would he be considerate of her plight? Or taunt and mortify her? Would she be ignored? Or overwhelmed? Wringing her hands in frustration, she scorned her need for his protection and the burden it placed on her to put up with whatever treatment she received. Why couldn't she disguise herself as a boy, as Teeg had done?

But she knew that Jeremiah was wise not to suggest it. Even if she could somehow camouflage her womanly curves, her face was much too soft and pretty to hide her sex for more than an instant. Her mannerisms, too, would quickly give her away. When she, her sister and Jack used to make-believe, the others always insisted she take on the feminine role, for her actions were ever delicate and graceful, not fit for the part of a king or soldier.

"Damn!" she whispered fiercely, falling onto the flowered coverlet that overlaid the wide bunk. Hot tears of fear and helplessness stained the fabric as she beat her fists into the pillow. But her outpouring was short-lived as she heard heavy footsteps outside her door and the key fitting into the lock. Sitting up quickly, she brushed her hem across her nose, pulled it down and pushed a straggling curl back from her wet cheek, her body taut with anxiety.

It was Stewart. Locking the door behind him, he strode to the writing desk, only glancing at her on his way by. His demeanor was purposeful and he neither smiled nor spoke as he searched for something in a hidden drawer she had never noticed before.

Openly observing him, Sarah could not help admiring how fiercely masculine he looked in his rugged clothes. His pale blue shirt was opened nearly to the waist, exposing his tanned rippling chest. His natural-colored canvas breeches clung damply to his flat belly and sleek, muscular thighs, filling the room with a salty tang. Was this truly the same man whose sophisticated elegance brought a hush to the ton at her sister's birthday ball? It all seemed so long ago. Her concentration was so intense that she failed to notice the he had stopped searching and was looking at her instead.

"Your appraisal is rather bold for such a timid bride. Have I met with your approval? Or do you wish a closer inspection?" Ignoring her look of utter shock, he continued calmly, "Be patient, my love. We will have time for intimacy later. Right now I have to deliver this manifest to Señor d'Alava, who is most eager to assess his plunder."

Struggling to regain her composure, Sarah spat, "We are not truly married!"

His cool response served only to infuriate her. "Oh, but we are, or did my brother-in-law not make the terms clear to you? You would be wise to accept that fact, and my husbandly attentions, or your safety will be most ... uncertain." Biting back a response when she saw the cold warning in his eyes, she dropped her view to her tightly clenched fists. "Come now," he prodded her, walking toward the door, "freshen up a bit. Our captor is eager to meet you."

After he left, locking the door behind him, Sarah knew a cold, creeping fear in the pit of her stomach. So he was going to carry his performance to the hilt, and force her to comply by reminding her of her desperate need for his protection? *Some protection!* Walking mechanically to the commode, she splashed tepid water on her feverish face. Removing the pins from her thick hair, she brushed the wayward locks absently until they shone, lost in contemplation of her fate.

As she began recoiling her hair in order to pin it up again, it suddenly occurred to her how impossible it would be for her to dress without Tegan's assistance. Nearly every one of her gowns was closed by dozen of tiny fastenings up the back. Angry tears of frustration threatened to appear as she once again was reminded of the helplessness her gender had imposed on her. Out of sheer bitterness, she put her hands to the back of her neck and tugged until the light fabric gave way. Buttons began popping off on the carpet as she stretched and strained to free herself. Gasping in foul temper, her bodice finally fell away from her shoulders at the same moment Stewart chose to re-enter the compartment.

"What in the devil...?" he muttered, staring at her contorted face in amazement.

Horrified by her immodest display, and infuriated by his sudden appearance, Sarah clutched the gaping material to her corset and chemise, screaming, "Get out! Get...!" But before the next words could be uttered, Stewart had eliminated the space between them, clamping one huge hand over her mouth and the other around her bare shoulders.

In a furious whisper that very nearly singed her ear, he demanded, "Blast it, woman! You'll have the whole criminal mob breaking down the door if you continue your shrieking! And how do you propose to explain that your devoted husband is the cause?" His fingers bit into her arm, forcing her to pay close attention to his words. "I suggest you very quickly get used to the idea that I am your spouse. It is doubtful that you would *be* a loving wife, let along know how to play-act as one, but I swear on your father's title it is your only chance. And if you don't have a care for your own life, please consider that we are *all* in danger – a peril far more deadly should anyone discover our charade. One does not make a fool of a pirate. Do you understand?" Brown eyes bored menacingly into frightened blue ones. Satisfied when she nodded, he released her, noticing then the buttons under his boots. "What the devil...?"

In a voice cowed by his harangue, she faltered, "I-I was going to change my gown ...."

He turned her away from him and sighed when he saw the dress rent halfway down her back. His fingers nimbly loosened the remaining buttons. "And well you should. This one is ruined."

Only too aware of her nakedness and the feel of his knuckles grazing her back, Sarah held her arms firmly across her bosom. "I don't have Tegan to help me anymore."

"So your plan is to destroy your wardrobe instead of asking me for assistance? I admire your independence but what did you have in mind when all your dresses are ruined? In the future," he continued sternly. "I will help you when you need it. There," he muttered when he had finished. "Change your clothes. And hurry. Simon d'Alava does not like to be kept waiting."

Sarah glanced at him over her shoulder and saw that he had already turned to the writing desk on the opposite wall, It was clear that he was not planning to leave the room and after the tirade he had just leveled, she was too afraid to suggest it. With a shudder, she dashed to the wardrobe and hid herself as best she could behind one of the tall doors. Keeping one eye on Stewart's broad back, she scurried into a gown, the white bodice cut to show off her neck and shoulders, the empire skirt sprinkled with embroidered cornflowers.

"Are you ready yet?" he called out, not looking back at her.

Demurely she stepped from behind the door and, eyes downcast, walked silently across the rug to stand behind him. "The buttons?" she pleaded humbly and noticed his scowl as they both turned around.

Stewart completed the task efficiently and without comment. But before Sarah could breathe a sigh of relief, he put his broad hands on top of her shoulders and touched her ear with his lips. "Please remember this, Sarah," he warned. "Even though I expect you to follow my lead, you are my wife, not some overly obeisant serving girl. You'll only arouse suspicions if you fail to show your mettle."

His words pricked her sharply. He seemed to relish jerking her around in her emotional distress, completely inconsiderate of her plight. Squaring her shoulders, shrugging off his hands in the process, she vowed at that moment to show him, despite this trial heaped upon her, that she would do more than survive. She would triumph.

CHAPTER 19

Walking into the blazing brightness, Sarah, having forgotten her parasol, shielded her eyes momentarily as Stewart led her to the bridge where Simon d'Alava was waiting to meet her. Except for the ominous presence of the pirate ship off starboard, nothing impressed her as being different. Sailors still walked freely about, though there was little to do since the ship was anchored, all sails furled. The seagulls still soared and squawked overhead; the breeze was still warm and rustled the hair that had escaped Sarah's careful pinning.

Everything was so calm, in fact, that much of her nervousness left her. Was piracy on the high seas always so civilized, she wondered to herself as Stewart handed her up to Jeremiah, who was waiting to introduce her. "Sarah," he began, intentionally leaving out her title, "This is Señor Simon d'Alava. Señor, may I present my sister-in-law, Madame Chamberlain."

"Señor," she intoned serenely, giving the stranger an even, benign look. The man who took her proffered hand and kissed it was quite different than Sarah had imagined. Of medium height, the Señor was stout, had a rigid bearing and carried his weight well. His face was cruelly handsome, Sarah decided, in an exotically foreign way. Blue-black hair streaked with premature gray, engaging black eyes fringed in the longest lashes she'd ever seen on a man, white teeth marred only by the presence of a gleaming gold-capped incisor, and a thin, aristocratic nose above a carefully waxed moustache were his most prominent features. Though she somehow had the feeling he was approximately the same age as Stewart, constant sun had darkened and weathered his skin, giving him the appearance of an older man.

His clothes were comical; a collection of different ill-fitting uniforms taken, no doubt, from other unfortunate mariners. Scores of medals were scattered across his chest and, she noticed, he was heavily armed with two pistols and a sword and scabbard hanging from a silver inlaid leather belt that stretched across his girth. All in all, his presence was disturbing in a most inexplicable way.

"My dear Señora Chamberlain," he exuded in a thick, though charming Spanish accent, "I am enchanted to meet you and most humbly sorry for this minor inconvenience. Had I known my old *compañero* Stewart had taken *su novia* board, I may have decided not to trouble all of you with this unpleasant business. But on the other hand," he chuckled at his own cleverness, "I have my job to do and, as you can see, so very many mouths to feed." As he waved his hand toward the other ship, she saw for the first time that the deck was crowded with an assortment of wild and dangerous-looking men. D'Alava's gesture set off a profusion of cheers, jeers and obscene remarks from these ruffians, most of which were about her. Instinctively, her face paling, she stepped backward and was relieved to feel the comfort of Stewart's strong arm as he placed his hand on her waist, pulling her close in a husbandly gesture.

"You must excuse *mi tripulación*," d'Alava referred to his crew, seeing Sarah's retreat. "They have not seen *una mujer* in weeks, and never such a beautiful one. They will not be so very happy when I inform them that you are married to our friend, Stewart, for many of them know what a possessive rascal he is."

The familiarity surprised Sarah and she raised her eyes to look up at him curiously. Stewart, his face set in a dark scowl, did not return her gaze. "But this time," d'Alava was continuing, "I cannot blame you. The lady is not only your bride; she is by far the loveliest creature my eyes have ever beheld." Sarah cringed inwardly as he first raked her with a bold leer, and then held her eyes prisoner with her own. "Captain Slade," he remarked casually, grinning at Sarah, "I think I shall remain aboard your ship for the duration of our voyage. I am weary of my tiresome, brutish crew and the lonely life I have led these past months. I would much prefer to spend these days with old friends ... and new ones, I fervently anticipate." His beringed hand reached out to grasp her fingers again and she used inhuman strength to keep from pulling back in disgust.

"As you wish, Señor," Jeremiah said evenly. If he were surprised at this turn of events, Sarah could not detect it in his voice. "You'll take my quarters of course."

"I do not mind sharing them with you. We should all be as comfortable as possible, don't you agree? Turgot!" A hulking scar-faced man suddenly materialized at d'Alava's side. "See to our business here. I shall return shortly with additional crew members, and we will set sail immediately. Captain. Stewart. My dear Señora Chamberlain," he bowed slightly and was gone.

When Stewart held open the door to the quarters, Sarah nearly fell into the nearest chair, quaking with the emotions she had been holding at bay. Stewart quickly came up with a bottle of brandy and poured her a liberal dose. "Drink this," he ordered. "It will help." She gulped the amber liquid and nearly choked to death on the burning sensation that scalded her throat. He patted her back until her coughing ceased and then brought her a glass of precious water. Sitting down beside her, he gave her a vacant glance before tossing off a shot himself.

Feeling the warmth of the brandy beginning to take effect, Sarah ventured, "D'Alava ... is he ... are you..?"

"Are we friends? Is that your question?" Sarah nodded.

"Hardly," Stewart sneered. "He is a snake. Fortunately, I know his traits quite well At one time, we served on the same ship, a Spanish trader. But that was before he chose to officially depart from the law." Twirling the glass between his tanned fingers, Stewart seemed to talk more to himself than to her. "He's not making things any easier for us by deciding to sail on this ship. He's an extremely cunning, if somewhat impulsive man. I do not relish having to put up with his moods. Nor do I like you being subjected to his attentions. It's obvious he wishes nothing better than to settle an old score."

"An old score?" Sarah leaned forward.

He looked at her narrowly, then back at the glass. "A woman. Someone who shared her favors with both of us, if you know what I mean. When we learned that fact, he challenged me to a duel. It was stupid of me to accept, for the girl meant nothing. But at the time, it seemed important to save face. I intended only to wound him, but the gun misfired. I nearly killed him."

"So that is why you're enemies?" Sarah was amazed by this revelation.

"We're enemies because after I shot him, I sent word I never wanted the girl and if recovered, he could have her." A humorless laugh escaped his lips. "I was somewhat more reckless then than now. She made things worse by refusing to go to him even though I made it clear I wanted nothing more to do with her."

His coldness disquieted her and she rose to escape, looking out the porthole as an excuse.

"You *did* ask," he said gruffly, sensing her disapproval. "Besides, it might help you handle this situation more sensitively if you know some of the history involved."

Sarah turned around to see his dark gaze upon her. She shuddered involuntarily out of ... what? Fear? Or was it her body's unbidden response to his overpowering magnetism? It seemed no matter whatever else transpired around her, his very presence forced the quickening of her heart, the breathlessness, and the incapacity to speak or act normally. In the brief second before he spoke again, she redoubled her pledge to somehow shake his domination, even under these new and adverse circumstances.

"You may find him charming, even fascinating," Stewart was saying, "but remember this: He is a malevolent cutthroat. I have seen him torture and kill and for much less than a ship's bellyful of goods or a beautiful woman. We are fortunate that he seems more interested in whatever fellowship we can offer ... for the time being. But make no mistake. It is always possible that he will change his mind about his intentions to confiscate only our cargo and leave us alone. We must try to cater to his whims, without letting him think we are doing so." He gave her an intense look, but it seemed he was considering their situation rather than her.

Suddenly, with an oath, he slammed the glass down on the table and stood up, his eyes glazed and furious. For an instant, Sarah thought he had gone mad, so keen was his wrath. "That viper! How I detest the power he wields over us. I should have killed him when I had the chance!"

Pacing before her, his hands clawed his unruly hair as he struggled with his impotence. Abruptly he stopped, his index finger poised only inches from her nose. "He wants you. You must know that. God, if only you weren't so naïve! You can't even take care of yourself, let alone control a man like d'Alava."

His words made her bristle. "He thinks you're my husband. Wasn't this arranged for my protection?" she rebuked him, her voice on the edge of hysteria.

"'Tis only a deterrent – which has been considerably weakened by the fact that he will be in our midst. A man can get mightily hungry looking overlong at the food ..." His eyes dared her to blush. "He will find your innocence enticing. He'll press you for some sign of approval which, of course, you cannot give. And because of your obvious revulsion and virginal indignation, he'll be provoked into action, if only to save face. What we are about is a charade for which I daresay you are most unqualified."

Her face went white with fury and her blue eyes narrowed into shards of steel. Through tight lips, she snarled, "You are so very confident of my ineptitude."

"Cajoling appreciative males is not your forte. If it were, by now you would have a string of suitors from which to choose a suitable mate ...."

She slapped him hard, the sound of the blow filling the cabin. Both were equally surprised, but Stewart was quicker to recover, seizing the offending limb in a painful grasp.

"As your husband, I would be within my rights to have your hand permanently separated from your arm. You will not strike me again."

Their eyes locked in a passionate struggle of wills. Seconds passed and still the maddening, insufferable contest continued. If the entire crew of the pirate ship were to burst through the door at that moment, Sarah's pride would have still forbid her from turning away, so intense was her cause. And when she thought she would faint from the intensity of this wordless battle, Sarah saw that the tinder setting his brown eyes aflame was no longer rage but naked, burning desire.

Slowly, without blinking, his head bent to capture her lips. But in a last, desperate striving to win, she turned her face away, only to find it returned by his free hand which had closed around her jaw. Every fiber in her body screamed for release as his burning kiss stung her mouth. Only by forcing herself to recall his taunts was she able to remain rigid and unresponsive. Still he persisted, teasing her with his tongue, compelling her body to mold itself to his. Her heart pounding, her breath rapid and shallow, Sarah knew Stewart sensed she was weakening, and for once the realization fortified her.

His inflamed senses were finally penetrated by her implacability. Stewart dropped his hands, enabling Sarah to peel herself away from him, her blue eyes smoldering above fever-stained cheeks. "Perhaps I underestimate your skill in handling yourself," he said quietly, the anger completely gone from his voice. Sarah dropped her eyes to consider what she had actually seen in his strangely poignant expression. But when she looked up again, he had turned away and was leaving the room.

CHAPTER 20

Señor d'Alava did not return to the captured vessel for over an hour, giving Stewart the time he needed to move his belongings into Sarah's quarters. After curtly demanding that she make some room for his clothes in the wardrobe and bureau, he did not speak again as he worked quickly, leaving no doubt that they shared the cabin. From her position at the table in the center of the room, Sarah watched him furtively, a sense of trepidation gnawing at her stomach. Seeing his belongings mingled familiarly with hers made her situation all the more real.

On his last trip between the adjacent quarters, he put away the last of his possessions and without a warning, began removing his shirt. Sarah's eyes widened as she caught her first glimpse of his completely naked flesh. Even as her cheeks burned, she found something awesomely appealing in the sight of his broad shoulders, the well-defined muscles on his bronzed back and the fact that his tapered waist appeared so hard and lean, without an ounce of bulk. Surely he was the strongest man she had ever seen, capable of defending her if the need ever arose. She was mesmerized by the play of his muscles as he washed himself at the commode, the clean smell of the soap he used wafting toward her.

When he completed his toilette and turned around, Sarah ducked her head away quickly, angry with herself for being so curious that she'd risked being caught staring ... again. Stewart used one hand to briskly towel his damp, curling hair dry, and with the other he unexpectedly pulled out the chair next to her and sat down. Sarah turned to look at him slowly, hoping the blush was gone from her cheeks, but the nearness of his naked torso caused her to tremble. She saw that his brown eyes registered the involuntary movement, but he did not comment. He sighed, and then, almost to himself, said, "If only my mother could see me now – a married man."

Awed by his solemnity, Sarah murmured, "Your mother ... is she...?"

"She died last year of a fever. My father is a widower." She studied Stewart intently as he stared at the table, looking strangely tired, pensive. For some inexplicable reason she wished he would tell her more. But she dared not ask, disturbed by the intimacy such talk could lead to.

It was then that Stewart pushed his chair back and stood up, clearing his throat and muttering a gruff dismissal under his breath. Quickly he began pulling clothes from various places, his intention to change in front of her becoming quite clear. Abruptly Sarah rose from the table and scurried toward the door, mumbling her plan to take some fresh air on deck.

"Don't open that door." The voice from the far side of the room was cold, threatening. Biting her lip and squeezing her eyes shut in a mixture of futility and outrage, Sarah rested her cheek against the doorframe, her fingers locked tightly around the latch. As she listened to the unmistakable sounds of boots and clothing dropping to the rug, her embarrassment nearly caused her to choke out loud. Surely he must recognize the indecency of what he was doing! When he finally spoke, Sarah shivered with the fear that he might come closer, or worse, force her to turn around. But he did neither.

"You are not to walk *anywhere* on this ship without me or Jeremiah at your side. Not only is d'Alava a threat to your safety, he's bringing aboard a pack of those felons who, only a short time ago, expressed their sordid interest in your charms. Would you rather take your chances alone with them ... or with me?" His last words held an unmistakable note of conquest that infuriated her.

Through clenched teeth, she snarled, "You offer a choice when there is none. What difference does it make who rapes me? The defilement would be the same."

"Are you being rhetorical, or merely naïve?" he asked incredulously while he dressed, undisturbed that it was her back that he spoke to. "Rape is what you'd suffer at the hands of one of those barbarians out there who wishes only to satisfy his animal urgings. On the other hand ...."

"There is no other hand!" she spat, pressing her cheek against the door. "Rape is taking a woman against her will. *Any* man who touches me is a *rapist!*" Hoping her warning was clear, she waited breathlessly for his reply, nearly fainting when his hand suddenly clamped on her forearm before flinging her backward against the door.

The space between was charged with a degree of tension Sarah found oppressive, fueled all the more by Stewart's calm, almost lazy posture as his hand rested casually on the latch. It was all she could do to keep from scratching the sardonic grin off his bronzed face. "*Any* man, Sarah?" he finally said, his brown eyes piercing her. "Surely you are not so ignorant as to believe that rape could exist between a husband and wife?" Her eyes widened in shock as she clutched her hands to her breasts in a protective gesture.

"You wouldn't dare!"

He shrugged nonchalantly. "I would be within my rights ...."

"This marriage is a charade," she hissed, her cheeks burning with emotion. "Surely you understand that any in-intimacy would only complicate the situation." Finding courage in her logic, she added, "As you've managed to remain a bachelor for this long, it appears you've prejudged the consequence of your dalliances correctly. Would you lose your freedom for a foolish mistake?"

To her irritation, he chuckled, "Perhaps you give me more credit than I deserve. Until today, it was mostly luck that spared me from captivity – matrimonial or otherwise. Now I find myself imprisoned by a hated foe and married to a beautiful but prim and unrelenting shrew." His face hardened. "One whose undisguised loathing for me bodes ill for our chances of being released unscathed."

With a sigh, he rubbed the back of his neck in a gesture of capitulation. "I won't rape you Sarah. I've no wish to further complicate our situation, or my own life." His eyes lifted, boring into her blue gaze. "But I warn you: Unless you act like a real bride – warm, loving, and reasonably content – our chances of fooling d'Alava are nil. He is dubious enough to find me married at all; let's not arouse his suspicions further by suggesting that our union is anything less that blissfully passionate. Men like me don't marry for any of the usual reasons ...."

Before she could offer a suitable retort, he was gone.

Sarah's reluctance to cooperate was quickly daunted when the seriousness of the situation became clear to her at dinner that evening. Although their captor was pleasant, indeed gracious and charming, she immediately sensed an unpredictability bordering on madness which emanated from him. It was obvious that Simon d'Alava was capable of anything and would certainly retaliate if he believed they were toying with him.

Forgetting her pride, her bitterness and her innocence, Sarah plumbed the depths of her experience and observations to become exactly the kind of woman Stewart told her she was not: a happy bride, a loving wife and a skillful manipulator of men.

Fortunately she was not lacking in examples. Her own mother was a most devoted wife, and a gracious hostess besides. Her coy sister, Juliana, was a perfect model of a woman who could evade without alienating. And her father, a shrewd and perceptive businessman, had been her mentor for years. He had shown her how he observed others astutely to gain the knowledge of their strengths and weaknesses, and to use that knowledge for personal advantage. Now her life depended on how well she could incorporate those skills into her own behavior, a realization that gave her the motivation she needed to overcome her natural inclination to withdraw.

As the men shared a bottle of cognac following an unusually delicious meal of freshly-caught fish, Sarah allowed the sherry she was sipping to relax her a bit. The evening had gone well so far. D'Alava clearly wanted his captives to relax, and so directed their conversation toward matters having little bearing on their present situation. Sarah was frankly amazed at his abundant store of information, until she considered that his profession might keep him better informed of current events than an ordinary criminal. He certainly played well the role of raconteur. She smiled to herself as she pictured the pirate holding hostages at gunpoint while he quizzed them on the latest European political developments.

Thinking her smile was for him, d'Alava beamed. "So you approved of the idea of extending your *luna de miel* by spending some time on my little island?"

Keeping her wits about her, Sarah replied demurely, giving Stewart a radiant look. "We plan to live our honeymoon forever, if possible, Señor, but you must know that I am eager to meet Stewart's family and see my new home."

"But my dear, you have your whole life for such things! Surely you will allow me the opportunity to make amends for so rudely interrupting your journey? I can offer you the comforts of home as well as absolute privacy in the finest tropical setting you'll experience anywhere in the world. Tell me, how many brides could boast of such a romantic beginning?"

"Señor," she responded silkily, with just the appropriate amount of persuasion in her voice, "already you have made this interlude most unforgettable. But you would not mind it if I preferred our freedom to your hospitable gesture?" She gazed at him sweetly.

D'Alava laughed heartily, filling the room with his deep voice. "Stewart, you will have trouble denying this woman anything, most assuredly!" Eying Sarah appreciatively, and noticing once again her pleased acceptance of her husband's affectionate touch, he continued, "How I detest pressing the issue, but as it is difficult to get good help these days, I must beg your collective indulgences – at least for a fortnight or two. You see, my island paradise suffers from, how do you say, benign neglect. And if the work were left entirely to my rather small *tripulación* and the local *residentes*, it would take more time than we could afford to devote to it. Captain," he said, turning to Jeremiah, "I assure you that your men will not be worked overhard and that their rations will be considerably more bountiful that even you provide."

Slade knew, of course, that he had no choice, but he did risk one request. "May I ask that they not be jailed, Señor? My crew is loyal and will obey the orders I give them. I will take full responsibility for their cooperation."

"Your beautiful sister-in-law has put me in a most benevolent mood, Slade," d'Alava replied, nodding to the sweet-faced lady at his side. "I will say *si* for the time being. But if any one of your crew should step out of line, they will all be punished." The gentleness of his tone made his words all the more ominous, and Sarah forced back the urge to shudder.

"Agreed," Jeremiah responded firmly.

"Señor," Sarah interrupted softly, giving his coat sleeve the slightest touch, "would you mind terribly if I asked Stewart to take me for a short stroll on deck before I retire? I am afraid the smoke has given me a slight headache."

"But of course, Señora Chamberlain. You should have said something earlier," he scolded, stubbing out his expensive cheroot. "Come, let us all go. A night such as this should not be wasted," he said, taking her hand to help her rise from the chair.

This was definitely not her plan, but Sarah hid her disappointment behind a grateful smile and moved past d'Alava to the door held open by Jeremiah. They filed out, and upon reaching the main deck, d'Alava grasped Sarah's arm and linked it with his own, intending to be her partner on the walk. Sarah glanced back to see Stewart's eyes narrow in the moonlight as he fell in step with Jeremiah. She turned back just as d'Alava's man, Turgot, appeared out of nowhere to speak with him. She gasped in surprise; the large, ugly man was frightening in any case, but more so when suddenly materializing in the dark.

"Turgot," d'Alava said sharply, as Stewart came up to Sarah's open side, "your timing is abominable, as usual. What is it?"

As the problem involved the ship, Jeremiah left with their captors, allowing Stewart and Sarah a few moments alone. After d'Alava's touch, she was grateful for Stewart's possessive arm around her waist as they strolled toward the bow of the ship. They spoke ever so softly, sensing rather than seeing the presence of the pirate crew. "Did you expect d'Alava to keep us on his island," Sarah whispered, looking up into Stewart's eyes and feeling the softness of his velvet lapel against her cheek.

"I'm not surprised, but I had hoped we could have avoided it. Every extra minute we spend in his hold creates opportunities for something to go awry." Feeling her stiffen, he pulled her closer, running his hand up and down her sleeve. "I'm sorry. I don't mean to frighten you." His tone was so sincere, she had no wish to back away as he drew her to his chest, resting his chin on her scented hair. After all, they were newlyweds. The crew would expect no less. Gazing out onto the moon-spangled water, he spoke gently, "We will all reach our destination sooner or later, no small thanks to you."

She raised her head quickly, expecting to see a sarcastic sneer, but his eyes conveyed his sincerity. Lifting her hands to rest lightly on his waist, her voice trembled with skepticism. "What do you mean?"

As his hands had been hovering about her all evening, it did not surprise her now when he took her upturned face between them, brushing away a stray curl that had been caught by the breeze. "Your performance has been impeccable. You are ever a delightful surprise, Sarah. D'Alava is enchanted ... and so am I."

Later she was to reflect that it was the first honest kiss they had ever shared. Its sweetness sprang from mutual respect. Stewart was proud of her, and she was pleased to know he was not above admitting it. The gentle pressure of his lips was not intended to light a fire, but it did, and he knew it. But he chose not to press his advantage, and for that she was grateful. He seemed content to nuzzle her face, holding her close, letting her find comfort and strength in his nearness, which she did but could not understand why.

Anticipating d'Alava's return, Stewart suggested, after a bit, that they might be wise to head back to their cabin, thus sparing her having to deal with the Señor again that night. They gained the haven safely and Stewart informed her that he would make the necessary excuses for her as he lit the lamp next to the berth.

The bed. There was only one and though it was hefty by ships' standards, it could not be considered large enough for two, comfortably. Sharing it with Tegan had been barely adequate.

Sarah blushed to think what a tangle would result if Stewart's long body joined hers on the linens. He would simply have to sleep on the floor, she decided, but for some reason, could not summon the will to speak aloud, quite certain an argument would ensue.

As Stewart moved easily about the barely lit room, Sarah slumped on the bed and began removing her shoes. What should she say? Every idea that popped into her head would surely destroy the rather pleasant truce that now existed between them. So busy were her thoughts that she didn't notice Stewart had stopped looking into drawers and had gone back to the door until he spoke. "I'm going to lock the door from the outside while I'm off to join Jeremiah and d'Alava. I may be gone for a while. Do you need anything?"

"No," she answered meekly, deciding to postpone the inevitable. "Thank you. Goodnight." But as the door shut, she remembered one very important detail, and rushed to the door, tripping over her shoes on the way. "Ouch. Stewart?" she called, slapping the door with her palm. He reappeared, looking surprised and much taller now that Sarah was in her stocking feet.

"What's happened? What's wrong?"

"Nothing ...." she looked up momentarily, then, embarrassed, cast her eyes down at her wriggling toes. "My gown ... the buttons?"

"Of course," he replied, stepping back into the room and closing the door. "Turn around." Despite the darkness, his speed at unbuttoning was twice as fast as buttoning, a skill in which experience played a major part, Sarah allowed, with some degree of wry humor. "There you go. Goodnight," Stewart offered pleasantly, adding a playful pat on her bottom. Sarah whirled around, a cross look on her face, but Stewart was already closing the door.

Knowing he would give her adequate time, Sarah carefully prepared for bed, donning her most voluminous nightgown, leaving on her chemise and silk stockings. She washed her face, brushed her hair until it shown, and tucked it under a gauzy nightcap.

Susannah Merrill

She threw back the flowered coverlet and climbed into the semi-soft bed, lying down stiffly on the outside edge. There! That would discourage him from thinking she planned to share. But what if he tried to crawl over her? She wriggled over to the inside, huddling herself against the wall. Now *that* was an open invitation, she decided. Cursing under her breath, she rolled to the center, beating the pillows as she attempted to make herself comfortable. Lying rigidly on her back, she raised her head, peering left, then right, in order to judge her position. What she discovered was that Stewart would have just enough room to sleep on either side of her, if he were so inclined.

"Blast!" With an exasperated grunt, she sailed one of the pillows to the carpet, and followed it with the coverlet, which landed in a heap on the floor. Flopping kitty-corner on the berth, she punched her pillow and wrenched her nightgown free from its hopeless tangle around her body, muttering, "If he's too thick to figure *that* out, he's no threat to me!"

CHAPTER 21

Sarah awoke to the feeling of bright light pressing against her eyelids. Rubbing away the sleep, she forced her mind into wakefulness, wondering why Tegan did not call out her usual greeting. She started to rake her hands through her hair and felt instead the nightcap. Pulling it off, she considered it sleepily, not sure why it had been on her head.

At the sound of a deep cough originating from the center of the room, Sarah froze, reality coming back to her in one great leap. *Stewart!* Turning her head abruptly, she took in his long form seated casually at the table. His back was to her but she could see that he was studying a map laid out before him. He was dressed in his usual daily attire: fawn breeches, a linen shirt and knee length boots. Remembering that she had thrown a pillow and blanket on the rug the night before, she looked to see evidence that he had slept in the designated spot. Her stomach lurched when she noticed the pillow next to her head and the coverlet draped neatly over her body. Surely he hadn't...? She could recall nothing.

Stewart looked over his shoulder just in time to catch the perplexed furrow of Sarah's delicately arched brows, and he smiled with sure knowledge of her thoughts. "Good morning, my sweet. Would you care to join me for a cup of hot chocolate? Compliments of our generous pirate."

Sarah raised herself up tentatively making sure the blankets stayed snug around her neck. A sleepy yawn escaped her, momentarily erasing the worried set of her face, but it reappeared immediately as she nervously pushed her dark hair back from her face. "Can I fetch your dressing gown?" Stewart asked pleasantly, pushing his chair back and rising to stand next to the bunk, his left elbow supporting him as he lounged against the gleaming casement.

His looming presence and self-confident manner were nerve-wracking, and Sarah found herself responding breathlessly.

"In the wardrobe ... on the door." With a nod, he walked across the room to her closet. Sarah took the opportunity to peak under the covers to see if she was still intact. Yes, the nightgown was securely buttoned and she could feel the soft chemise next to her skin. Her toes wriggled in their white stockings. Relaxing a small whit, she lowered the covers to find Stewart calmly watching her.

"Looking for something?"

His smugness infuriated her and she snatched the robe from his fingers, punching her fists through the sleeves as she struggled to don it. With a chuckle, Stewart resumed his seat and turned to pour a cup of chocolate from the china pot on the table. Sarah scurried to climb out of bed, straightening her clothes and securely tying the wide sash around her tiny waist. Eying him suspiciously, she took a chair opposite him as he set the cup and saucer before her.

"Did you sleep well?" was his cheerful remark.

"Did you?" she snapped.

"Not a wink," he replied calmly, his eyes trained on the paper he was folding.

Sarah softened a bit, feeling more comfortable. "I suppose it might have been difficult, getting used to the floor."

"But I did not bed down on the floor." A mirthful expression crossed his face as he saw her blue eyes widen in horror. "Really, Sarah. We are supposed to behave like newlyweds. How could I explain my having to sleep on the floor when my beguiling bride is so enticing, even in repose?"

"What a rakehell you are to take advantage of our situation!" Sarah's cheeks blazed as she grabbed the edge of the table in a futile effort to control her fury. "No one would ever know what our sleeping arrangements are, and if they did, you could have made an excuse. Damn you, Stewart Chamberlain!" she hissed, her wrath full blown. "You are so clever when you want to be, but you opt for a dim-witted tack when you know it will compromise me! And stop laughing, you loathsome lecher!"

"Are you always such a spitfire in the morning?" Stewart's tone was cajoling, enragingly serene. "I will be mindful to keep my distance until you've have a chance to wake up completely. Now if you will just rest from your exercise of jumping to conclusions ...."

"You actually expect no protest from me?" she charged. "Lest you forget, I am a *lady* ... in both title and character. Not some dockside convenient or enterprising courtesan. Yet already I have been subjected to a humiliating lack of privacy that would brand me a Paphian were anyone to find out. You are ruining me, Mr. Chamberlain, and I won't stand for it!"

"Are you finished?" His answer came in the form of two slender hands raised in claw-like fashion accompanied by the hissing sound of a cat. With maddening tranquility, he proceeded. "I did not sleep because I spent the entire night in a rather challenging game of cards with d'Alava and our captain. Your complaint of a headache was all I needed to gain a seat in the match. Otherwise they would have thought it strange that I would prefer gambling to your hypnotic charms. You see? I am not completely unsympathetic to your plight," he added with a cherubic smile.

"You let me believe ...." Sarah began, her voice rising in choler with each world.

"Tut, tut," Stewart rebuked her good-naturedly, getting up from his chair. "You leapt to conclusions my dear ... one of your more tiresome habits." Sarah chose not to respond, feeling for the moment that her relief was enough satisfaction, but having a great urge to poke out her tongue at him. With a haughty look at his retreating form, she turned her attention to the cup of chocolate before her, but was forced to take note of him again as he leveled a parting comment at the door, his brown eyes dancing. "I might add, for future reference, that when I do sleep with you, you won't be wondering in the morning if it truly occurred."

As usual, he was right. This fact was proven to Sarah the very next night, after the ships sailed their way into the tangled maze of islands that created a safe haven for d'Alava's pirate kingdom. After disembarking from the long boats, the crew was sent under Jeremiah's watchful eye to dilapidated quarters off the southern shore. Sarah's heart lurched when she saw the meager form of her maid trudging wearily beside Ezra, who stoically pretended not to watch out for her.

"Stewart," she whispered pleadingly, as the two watched the proceedings from the deck. "We can't let Tegan stay in that hovel with the others. Is there anything you can do?"

"We're going to try to get her duties in the kitchen," he replied softly, observing the sailors' march. "Then perhaps she'll be allowed to sleep in the main house where we will be staying. But we can't press for too many favors, Sarah," he added, his arm coming around her shoulders in a comforting gesture. "It would arouse suspicions, which would be more harmful to Tegan than her present situation. Come now, sweet," he murmured, pressing his cheek against her soft hair. "Hide your distress. D'Alava is approaching."

"Are you two lovebirds ready to disembark?" The Spaniard's voice boomed cheerily behind them as he made his way to Sarah's side. "I believe you two might be looking forward to a night on dry land, where the only rolling is of your own making." He laughed at his own joke, even more so when he saw the embarrassed blush spread across Sarah's cheeks.

"Your dwelling is well hid, Señor," Stewart interjected, and Sarah was so grateful for his intercession that she moved back easily against his chest as he turned toward the pirate. "I see no trace of a settlement from here."

"'Tis the advantage of a tropical jungle, Mr. Chamberlain, as well you know. Believe it or not, my home is but a short walk from the beach. The village stretches to the west." He pointed over the lush greenery. "Come, I see the longboat is returning. I'd like to show you around my humble abode before nightfall. The natives will unload the cargo in the morning."

Humble was right. Not in size, for the main house was three stories high and had two double-storied wings attached to either side. But unlike any home Sarah had ever entered, d'Alava's mansion was almost completely without ornamentation. The walls were plainly white-washed and there was not a trace of fine moldings or paneling throughout. Roughly–constructed bamboo shades took the place of draperies in some rooms, but most rooms were without any window adornments, or even glass. D'Alava's "palace" was kingly only in its spaciousness and the haphazardly-scattered array of rugs, furnishings, and silver and gold artifacts his piracy had netted him over the years. Sarah noted, too, with a shudder, that the house was in need of a thorough cleaning.

"Have you servants, Señor?" she asked, hoping her tone was casual.

"Of course, my dear. But I've no need of them unless I am in residence. Turgot has gone to round them up from the village. Let me show you to your rooms, and I'll have one of the maids draw you a bath when she arrives."

With a paternal smile, he took her arm and led her up the wide staircase to a door on the southern side of the large foyer. Stewart followed, carrying a small case containing some of their personal items. "This," he announced, opening the double portal, "is your sitting room. See how lovely the breeze? It's shaded here so we've dispensed with window coverings."

"And with furniture as well," Stewart drawled upon entering the room. It was true. Aside from a huge Persian rug, the entire room was bare.

Waving away Stewart's comment, d'Alava sputtered impatiently. "That will be taken care of in good time. There are plenty of settees and chairs around here. We don't have guests very often, so this room was never decorated. What do you care?" he added, his voice changing suddenly to a teasing quality. "You won't be spending much time in here." With that, he sprung open the doors to the bedchamber, and gestured for his guests to follow.

Sarah wandered reluctantly into the room, stopping dead in her tracks when she spied the thing which d'Alava was so eager for them to see. She would have stayed riveted there were it not for Stewart pushing her ahead of him. "Eh? You are speechless, no?" the pirate chuckled, clapping his hands in pleasure. "'Twas a gift from the French. And as you know, their skill in bed making is exceeded only by their expertise beneath the covers. Well, what do you think?"

It was a massive twisted-walnut bed, the elaborately carved and gold-leafed posters reaching nearly to the high ceiling and supporting a frighteningly heavy wooden canopy. Six people could recline comfortably within its confines, so wide was the mattress. And six people probably had, Sarah thought, swallowing hard as her eyes rested on the dingy linens. "It is most unusual," she finally murmured through gritted teeth.

"Ah, but look closer!" d'Alava encouraged gleefully. Throwing a helpless look at Stewart, who seemed to be taking quite an interest in the bed, Sarah tiptoed nearer and saw that the handwork was not some abstract design, but detailed representations of amorous nudes. Not wishing to show offense, or shock, she grimaced weakly and made to test the bedding with her gloved fingertips.

"It seems quite comfort--." A movement directly above snagged her attention. Peering upwards, she gasped at the sight of her own surprised face reflected in the Venetian mirror tiles lining the canopy's interior. Mortified by the indecency of the carnal couch, and feeling all the more agitated by the two men staring at her, Sarah felt a terrific urge to scream out her indignation. Fortunately, Stewart surmised her distress and placed himself between his wife and the Spaniard.

"I think my wife is somewhat overwhelmed by your surprise, Simon," he said laconically. "Her upbringing has been sheltered, as you might imagine, but I am sure she will come to appreciate your gesture of hospitality. Won't you, darling?" He clasped his large hand over her trembling one and pulled her next to him.

"Of course, Señor." Her voice startled her with its assuredness, for she felt anything but calm. "Tell me, do you have fresh linens for us?"

D'Alava smiled knowingly. "So! You are eager to sample the delights of this love nest, *no*? But of course. There is a bathing chamber through here, see?" He pointed to a door opposite the bed. "I believe it is well stocked with all you shall need, including netting to ward off mosquitoes, if memory serves me correctly. But you needn't trouble yourselves. The maid will take care of everything."

As soon as d'Alava departed, Sarah released the shudder of revulsion that had been building up, and backed away from the bed until she found herself leaning against the window sill that spanned the length of the far wall. Aiming a gloved forefinger at the monstrosity, she declared, "I will die before I sleep in that hideous thing! It's not fit for a brothel!"

Stewart was unperturbed as his hand carelessly traced the carvings on one of the posters. "I did not realize you were familiar with the décor of a brothel. Actually, this would fit in rather nicely, I believe." His eyes examined her leisurely, for she presented a startlingly pretty picture in her violet day gown, firm breasts heaving in her discomfiture. The afternoon light softened the rosy hue of her skin, and her chestnut hair shone where it was touched by dappled sunlight.

"I fail to see the humor," Sarah snapped, crossing her arms in defense of his gaze. Obviously she was not aware that in so doing she was presenting him with an even more provocative view. "This place is unlivable, though it seems not to bother you one iota."

"Since we have little else to do, perhaps we can remedy that somewhat. Unless, of course, you find housecleaning an offensive chore."

"Filth offends me, sir, as does your smugness," she muttered, removing her hat and gloves and pushing up her sleeves.

The two attacked the bedroom and bathing chamber, using strips torn from the bed sheets to knock down cobwebs and dust the few pieces of furniture in the rooms. Stewart managed to pull the mattress to the small balcony on one side of the room, beating the feather-stuffed ticking soundly to free the dust and stale odors. By the time he returned it, Sarah had shaken out the clean but musty linens and the two proceeded to make up the bed. He laughed aloud when she produced a bottle of toilet water from her case and liberally sprinkled the sweet-smelling perfume on the sheets and pillow cases. "Now I am convinced you know something of brothels. 'Tis a very effective means of freshening up between customers."

She was about to level a scathing retort when a knock sounded at the door. Stewart went to open it and found himself confronted by a shy young black girl loaded down with a pail of water, linens and various cleaning items. "Come in," he smiled engagingly, taking the heavy bucket from her. "We've taken the liberty of starting without you."

The girl gave him a puzzled look, but her eyes widened in surprise as she saw the very beautiful lady, her dress wrinkled and damp with perspiration, face flushed, and hair tumbling in sweaty ringlets, coming round the end of the bed.

The look made Sarah conscious of her rumpled appearance, but she was much too preoccupied to do more than rub her sleeve across her brow. "How do you do?" she asked briskly, taking in the girl's simple, flowered dress, skinny ankles and bare feet peeking out from beneath. With a smile, she added, more kindly, "What is your name?"

"Galena," the waif replied nervously, in a strangely-accented voice. "Come to m-make nice."

"I am so glad," Sarah answered. "Here, come with me and we will have this place spotless in no time."

"No!" the girl implored. "I clean. You not work. Señor not like you work."

"Well he'll never know, will he?" Sarah smiled sweetly, taking the girl's arm and pulling her toward the bathing chamber. "You are going to need our help if you're ever to finish before nightfall."

It was some time later that Sarah found herself finally relaxing in a heavenly warm and fragrant bath that Galena had prepared for her. It had been a long time since she had exerted so much physical effort and her muscles ached with satisfying fatigue. Stewart had gone off to do some reconnaissance so she luxuriated in her privacy, knowing that she'd be undisturbed until dinner.

She found Galena to be a competent, willing maid, eager to demonstrate her skills that were rarely in demand in d'Alava's mansion. Galena had managed to find a new dress for Sarah to wear, since her trunks were still aboard ship. It was a trifle too daring – an extremely low-cut empire-styled gown in a pale blue silk that clung most provocatively – but it was clean and fitted her tall, slim figure. The shy girl was an excellent hairdresser, Sarah was pleased to discover, and worshipfully clucked and fussed over her glossy, smooth tresses, so unlike Galena's own crimped, short hair. As she finished up her task of placing a fragrant camellia in the upswept style, Stewart entered the room.

"I see clothes have been found for you, too," Sarah said casually, though her heart raced with a sudden thrill at seeing Stewart immaculately attired in white breeches, hose, shirt, stock and vest and a rich green cutaway coat. His face seemed darker, more handsome, and his pearly teeth dazzled as he smiled his approval of her décolletage.

"Yes, our host is eager to please," he replied ruefully, holding the jacket open for a moment. "It seems he has enough clothing here to outfit the capitals of Europe." Turning for a moment to the reticent young girl, he spoke gently. "Galena, your handiwork is truly appreciated. My beautiful wife has not looked quite so ravishing since we first began our voyage." Both women blushed under Stewart's lazy perusal, but for entirely different reasons.

"Now may we have a moment of privacy? I'd like to speak with Mrs. Chamberlain before dinner." The maid bowed briefly, then beat a hasty retreat, a happy expression on her dark face. Sarah, on the other hand, frowned slightly, finding it uncomfortable to be alone with this tall and disturbingly handsome man. Pretending to fuss with her earrings in front of the looking glass on the dressing table, she spoke offhandedly.

"And where did you manage to find a bath?"

Walking up behind her, he directed his reply to her reflection. "There's a rather delightful lagoon but a minute's walk from this wing. Remind me to show it to you tomorrow." He bent his head close to hers. "Perhaps you might be encouraged to join me in my next partaking?"

Annoyed at his implication, Sarah hastily slid off the hassock, and occupied herself with smoothing the clinging gown. "I prefer something more civilized if you don't mind. Tell me; were you able to get Tegan out of the sailors' quarters?" Her concern for her maid appeared in a sudden widening of her azure eyes.

"Much to my surprise, d'Alava is being amenable to practically our every wish. Jeremiah said he found the idea much to his liking, after he told d'Alava she – he – was responsible for our meals aboard ship. I guess his own chef is average at best. I just hope ...."

"Stewart, you don't think d'Alava would demand to keep her here, do you?"

He raised his hands in a placating gesture. "Now Sarah, don't go borrowing distress. We will deal with any problems as they arise, not before. We have every reason to believe that we will be on our way in a fortnight – with the entire crew intact. Jeremiah and I looked over the work that d'Alava wants done, and it's not extensive. Now just worry yourself with continuing your convincing performance, and we'll take care of the rest." As he spoke, he had gained her side and was putting his arms around her. Sarah cowered for a moment under his captivating onslaught, then began to struggle.

"My role begins out there," she muttered through clenched white teeth, pointing her chin toward the door. "Not in here!"

Brown eyes caressed her face, then dipped to the nearly immodest display of creamy white skin above her bodice, while all the time his arms held firm. "My only wish is to help set the proper mood. Is it too difficult for you to imagine what d'Alava believes we are doing every hour we are alone?" He chuckled at her gasp of embarrassment. "It's important that you look like a sated, thoroughly enraptured bride, fresh from her marriage bed yet stimulated by musings of the next joining." She thrust her face away, her body hot yet stiff with indignation at being spoken to with such intimacy. Undaunted, Stewart pressed his face against the arched and straining neck she presented him and between titillating kisses thereon, he murmured, "Since you're as yet unwilling to feel like a real bride, at least let me light a fire in your eyes ..."

Try as she might, Sarah could not control the racing of her heart nor stop her ragged breathing. Stewart's lips were communicating with a part of her far more willing than her mind. Each touch of his mouth on her neck, her throat, her cheek, her ear, brought waves of pleasure that made her struggles seem sensuous rather than defensive. In a final effort to stop his experienced seduction, she nudged her upturned face toward him, choking, "Don't ... please ...."

It was a fatal maneuver, for his lips captured hers and held them prisoner while his tongue Endeavoured to probe the sweet depths exposed to him. She was lost; overwhelmed by the need he had so skillfully brought to the surface. With a defeated moan, she brought her arms, which were suddenly freed, around his neck, and leaned her body closer to his hard form. He held her so for a moment, letting his hands run at will up her bare back and down to her softly rounded hips. Then he took a step forward and she ached with the blissful feel of his thigh pushing against the flimsy skirt covering her legs.

When it became apparent that he was as much aroused as she, Sarah was surprised that her own reaction was one of satisfaction rather than revulsion. So she, too, had the power to stir. The thought so overpowered her that she failed to realize he'd guided her to the bed until the back of her legs hit the cool wood and she dropped softly to the mattress, Stewart's arm gently cradling her, as his other broke their fall.

Immediately she stiffened as a gasp of panic escaped from her partially covered mouth, But Stewart persisted, carefully working to erase her fears with sweet, gentle kisses on her lips and face, his free hand taking her fingers that were pushing against his chest and returning them to his neck. His eyes, black glimmers in the dim candlelight, allayed her struggling somewhat, as they were warm and loving, with no trace of their usual arrogance.

Finally she relaxed again, twining her fingers into his wavy hair and letting her delicate tongue and teeth join her lips in pursuit of passion. It was then that Stewart allowed his leg to drive casually across her hips and in this sublime captivity, she felt his hand come up between them to the exposed flesh of her bosom. Her eyes flew open as his burning fingers explored the edge of her low bodice to find the ribbon fastening her chemise.

She pulled him closer to her hoping to thwart his attempts, but her strength was feeble and she felt the undergarment give way.

With a voice gentle and persuasive, he began whispering endearments, and between kisses and feather-soft nibbles, he encouraged her acceptance of his caress. Her whole body shuddered when his strong but gentle hand pushed the bodice away from her shoulders, slid beneath the corset and brought forth a full, rounded breast, the rosy nipple peaking with excitement. He kissed her lovingly while he massaged her, his palm bringing excruciating pleasure until this moment unknown to her. When she thought she could stand it no longer, he took the tender tip between thumb and forefinger, rubbing it until she felt she would drown with longing.

As Stewart boldly exposed her other breast, his lips left her slackened mouth, burning a trail down the hollow of her neck to come to rest on a swelling bud, which his moist tongue teased mercilessly. A sob escaped Sarah's spoiled lips as her senses went numb with shock, his actions so unimaginably persuasive. But at the same time, with her heart thumping so strongly that her ears rang, she awakened to the indescribable ache of passion in her loins – a phenomenon so new, so exciting, that she was rendered completely helpless by the effects. Unbidden, her trembling hands pressed Stewart's head closer against her bosom as she basked in the heat of his lean and hard body, his hips moving ardently against her thinly-clad shape.

Sarah didn't hear the knock on the door, but when Stewart suddenly raised his head, leaving her moistened skin vulnerable to the air, her mind reeled in shocked confusion. Stiffening when he calmly called out an inquiry, she held her breath as she heard Galena announce dinner through the closed door and then leave nearly as silently as she had come.

With a displeased growl, Stewart returned his gaze to the woman beneath him, expecting to look into dazed, navy blue eyes. But instead, Sarah's fair face was contorted by surprise and horror as she saw, for the first time, the reflection of twining bodies and her own bare flesh on the looking glass overhead. With a cry, she began frantically pulling up her somewhat limp dress, casting her eyes up and down, embarrassed as though the glass were a shop window rather than a mirror.

Stewart chuckled indulgently and captured her flailing hands in his steel grasp, forcing her to glare at him when he still managed to fondle the heaving mounds she was bent on hiding. His slim, warm hand caressed her, and even though Sarah still burned from their lovemaking, his sardonic expression humiliated her and an angry, remorseful tear slid from her eye.

"What's this? Tears?" he asked, an indulgent note in his deep voice. "I too am sorry we've been so rudely interrupted, but later ...."

"Stop it!" she sobbed through lips that felt too swollen to speak. With a lunge, she attempted to rise but the result was completely unsuccessful, so great was the weight above her.

"Sarah?" Immediately his voice was again warm and concerned as he moved to cradle her against him, his magical fingers brushing the tear away, just as another formed in the other eye. "What is it, love? What's wrong?"

"*This* is wrong!" she gasped. "This tawdry setting. And you! Haven't you an ounce of decency in your black heart? I am not some cheap light-skirt, and I see no humor in your conquest." Ignoring the warming glint in his observant eyes, she added with a vengeance, "And don't make it even more sordid by pretending you care about my feelings. It is quite obvious you do not. Now if you'll allow me the dignity of covering myself ...."

His tone was instantly tough, sarcastic. "What? And risk changing your low opinion of me? Perhaps I should take your clothes away and force you to parade for my pleasure ...." His eyes burned her flesh with their smoldering perusal even as his words caused a tremor to engulf her. But when he saw the hurt and fear in her expression, knowing she believed absolutely that he was capable of heaping such humiliation on her, Stewart abruptly rolled away and swung himself up from the bed, angry, no longer with her, but with himself for his dark humor.

Sarah scrambled off the mattress and away from the stark reflection of herself in the mirror. Her limbs felt weighted and numb as she shakily repaired her dishabille. Feeling sharp brown eyes boring into her back did little to ease her troubled spirits. She knew Stewart was very angry with her and this made her earlier pleasure seem all the more vulgar and tragic.

But what did he expect of her? To have her fall happily into his arms, heedless of the consequences? His triumphant, disquieting mood had convinced her that his domination of her physical body was the only appeal she held for him. Where would she be left once she had made the ultimate sacrifice? The answer was more troubling than she cared to ponder.

But briefly, spurred on by the hot glow left by his skilled touch on her innocent flesh, she realized what a tender trap he had set. The awakening of this primitive need prompted an almost desperate longing for more caresses incautiously accepted. How long could she remain strong when she was forced to share intimate quarters and these all-too-dangerous private moments?

The threat was not even abated when they were in the company of others, Sarah realized dejectedly. For a man who held such a dim view of marriage, Stewart was an enthusiastic and convincing husband – affectionate, considerate, proud and protective of his bride – the perfect mate. His words, breaking into her thoughts, startled her.

"Are you ready to go?" It was impossible to tell what he was feeling, for his voice was even, unemotional.

"Y-yes," she stumbled, not daring to look back at him lest her eyes give away her pain and confusion. She slowly began her walk to the door, willing herself not to flinch when his large hand embraced her bare elbow as he gained her side.

In silent agreement, both assumed their roles with seeming effortlessness as soon as they joined their host, despite the new level of tension between them. Survival was a great compromiser, Sarah mused cynically as she lovingly returned Stewart's warm gazes and spoke with the confidence of a woman used to her husband's cherished adoration. But why? Why did his supple fingers grasping the curved wine glass have the capacity to remind her of their other, more formidable talents? If she couldn't steel herself against such forbidden memories, how would she ever survive his persistence?

Though d'Alava and Jeremiah did not perceive it, and could have no way of knowing, the narrowly wed couple was keenly and desperately aware that their relationship had altered considerably in this short space of time since arriving at the pirate island. But neither could name the change sufficiently nor foretell its ultimate consequence.

CHAPTER 22

The bright dawn broke through bare bedroom windows, its brilliance only partially dissipated by the thick jungle foliage outside. Sarah stretched languorously, feeling hot and uncomfortable in her heavy, long-sleeved gown unsuited for this tropical climate. But quite necessary under the circumstances, she told herself, pushing a damp ringlet away from her flushed face. Her head turned tentatively on the pillow and her eyes rested first on the long bolster she had insisted on placing down the center of the wide mattress. The overhead mirror caught her attention and she could not help but look up, immediately taking notice of the long, partially draped body on the other side of the barricade.

An involuntary shiver possessed her as her eyes took in the bronzed chest, and more shockingly, a length of leg, muscular and firm, which had somehow lost its sheet. Quickly raising her view, she was surprised to find herself gazing into sleepy brown eyes that noted her observation with casual indifference. Snapping her eyes shut, Sarah rolled onto her stomach, pressing her hot face into the pillow.

Why had he commanded that they sleep in the same bed, she mused angrily. Hadn't she unselfishly offered to take to the floor? The bath? But in his irritatingly reasonable manner, he had bade her to consider that the net-hung bed was the only place she would be truly safe from mosquitoes and other hungry insects. Her retort that such discomforts were preferable to his nearness signaled the end of his patience, and he had threatened to tie her within the grotesque chamber if she uttered another refusal. In mute defiance, she had flung the bolster down the center of the abhorrent bed, her steely blue eyes daring him to cross the boundary. With a chuckle he had shrugged, saving his final salvo for much later, when she had all but drifted off to sleep. "Don't let this bag of cloth and feathers lull you into a false sense of security, my dear. I'm merely too tired to fight you – tonight."

A knock at the door ended her bitter remembrances and she raised her head just as Stewart tossed the bolster above their heads. "Galena may not understand your perverted habits," he grinned lazily. Without warning, he filled the void with his own body, bidding the maid to enter at the same time he slipped a sinewy arm beneath his wife and pulled her close to his bare chest.

"You brute!" she hissed between clenched teeth, enraged at his clever entrapment. There was not a moment to struggle but she made a discreet attempt to lift her cheek from the hollow beneath his chin only to find him using strong fingers to pin against his chest the hand she had used for leverage.

Therefore, when Galena entered with a breakfast tray of coffee and sweet breads, her eyes took in a most romantic scene. The bride, cuddled so close to her strong, handsome husband, looked flushed and embarrassed behind the gossamer curtains. Galena smiled at their inability to keep their hands off each other, though it was not surprising. Never had she seen such an attractive, devoted couple. With a pleasant smile and a happy greeting, she set the tray next to the bed and proceeded to push aside the netting.

"You hungry, yes?" she asked sweetly. "But not for food, I think. I leave now. Not come back."

"Thank you, Galena. We appreciate your ah-understanding," Stewart drawled with a wink, which turned into an imperceptible grimace of pain when delicate fingers beneath his own secretly plucked out a hair from his sleek torso.

"Galena," Sarah spoke up suddenly, inwardly smiling at her small revenge, "I would like a bath ... and as soon as possible, if it would not be too much trouble." Her shining blue eyes artlessly wide, she added, "I am not yet used to this heat. A bath would be most refreshing."

As if noticing her attire for the first time, Galena stared at Sarah and a lilting giggle escaped her. Pointing to the enveloping gown, she said, "Dress not needed for sleep here. Too hot. Everybody sleep raw. You too now, yes?"

"I will n---," Sarah began heatedly, but a painful pinch on her firm derriere warned her, " ... consider it," she ended meekly, training to keep from clawing the perpetrator.

"*Bueno!*" Galena beamed. "You sleep better. Better for Señor too," she tossed out with a wink before hustling out of the room.

The latch of the door had not even clicked before Sarah tried to wrench free of Stewart's all-too-familiar grasp. But she hadn't counted on his wish to prolong the contact, and instead of breaking his hold, she suddenly found herself smothered by his warm, hard body pressed over hers.

"Not so fast, my beauty," he commanded silkily. "You've kept me at bay all night. Surely you can't refuse your husband a simple good-morning kiss?" Through fiercely brilliant eyes, she observed his tousled hair, the dark shadow of whiskers on his unshaven jaw, the humorous pliancy of his wide mouth, and the appreciative twinkle in his expressive brown eyes. His powerful shoulders were overwhelming in their nakedness, so close that she could press her lips there if things – everything – were different.

"Why do you torture yourself so?" she muttered sarcastically. "You know our marriage is a farce and will be dissolved as soon as we leave this place. Why do you persist in your quest for husbandly rights when you're no real husband at all?"

"Let's just say that I have never done anything halfway," he murmured, pressing an unwanted kiss on her temple and nuzzling her dark hair. "By force of habit, I am compelled to play my role to the hilt. Besides, can I, a mere man, be blamed for wanting you?" His warm breath tickled her ear and sent reluctant shivers thumping through her body.

"Yes --- you can," she returned breathlessly, unable to stop his firm lips from grazing the side of her trembling mouth. "For your job is to protect me. And so far –" she moaned, trying to turn her face away from his tender onslaught,"—you are the only man I have reason to fear ...."

"Are you saying ...." he whispered, touching his lips to her face with unrelenting purpose, " ... that you enjoy my caresses?"

"You will never hear me say that." The retort was cleverly worded, for there was a mindless, entirely involuntary part of her that responded to his touch with such exuberant wanting that it left her reasonable, logical side in a dazed, breathless shambles. His every look, gentle touch or fierce possession alerted her shameless body to his firm yet sensual mouth, and especially the searing brown eyes that beneath their thick lashes, turned dark with obvious lust, branding her with a promise she could not let him keep.

Of course, he knew what she meant by her scathing denial. The mad pounding of her heart beneath her breast and her unbidden gasps told him she was far from unmoved by his slow, experienced assault. And for an all-too-uncomfortable moment, Stewart debated the merits of offering this irresistible young woman a permanent claim on his name just for the opportunity to salve the hot male stirrings her nearness caused. She possessed a goodly number of the qualities he found attractive in a woman – beauty, intelligence, spirit and passion – and certainly being the daughter of a member of the peerage, and his business partner, did not lessen her allure. Few marriages were contracted without the economic advantages in mind. But despite these powerful inducements, a flash of reason prevailed, even as his demanding lips stormed the target of her soft, now yielding mouth. Marriage was suitable for some, but the idea of a permanent liaison did not exactly appeal to his restless nature. He supposed that love might make somewhat of a difference, but in two score and ten that emotion had eluded him. For the best, he quickly added. Even this captivating young girl, so bewitching despite her valiant efforts to deny him, had elicited only a fondness from him. That he wanted her desperately had, he knew, very little to do with love.

Besides, he was not entirely without entanglements. Hadn't he only recently expressed his devotion to the beautiful Lady Amberling? Funny, but he'd barely thought of the raven-haired vixen since leaving her, in tears, at the London dock. Not that Felicia expected him to remain faithful to her, for she herself was a somewhat adventurous and insatiable confection, a member of the serious Queen's gay and frivolous court. The intimate words that fell from his lips in the heat of passion were, of course, not binding, but the two were considered a pair, enough so that Felicia would not react lightly to the news of a sudden marriage. Knowing the reaches of her pride, Stewart could imagine the lengths she'd go to discredit his name in their circle of influential friends. No, Felicia deserved more than that. She had been good to him over the years; he was not about to infuriate her if it could be avoided.

His ardor somewhat cooled by these thoughts, Stewart avoided the surprised blue eyes, and with a sigh, shifted his weight off Sarah, covering his eyes with his forearm as he rolled onto his back beside her. Confused and naggingly disappointed by his abrupt release, she lay still for a moment, feeling her heartbeat slowly return to a more normal pace. What had she done ... or said? And why did she care? She stared at his reflection overhead, willing him to say something, anything, to give her a clue as to his inner thoughts. But his dismissal held fast, and with a jerk, she arose to prepare for her bath.

"I trust this ordeal has not been too hard on you." Jeremiah's voice was casually inquisitive above the briskly lapping waves of the incoming tide as he and Sarah strolled along the beach before dinner. It was the eighth day of their captivity and things had settled into a pedantic routine, at least for Sarah, who had little to do while the crew worked long, hard hours in the sun.

"No, Captain," she smiled reassuringly. "I might consider this a holiday were it not for the knowledge that we are here against our will. I just wish I could be more helpful in attaining a quick release ...."

"Now don't you worry about that. You have been invaluable to us," he said, helping her step over a scrap of driftwood lodged in the sand. At her questioning gaze, he explained, "D'Alava is more acquiescent that we ever believed possible, and I am convinced that it is because he wishes to make a good impression on you. I have every reason to hope we'll be on our way in a week or so."

"Your wife must be very concerned." Sarah voiced the subject tentatively, not wanting to upset him. But Jeremiah's response was matter-of-fact.

"I have always been careful not to provide definite dates when I write of homecomings. Peggy knows it's impossible to foretell weather conditions. Besides, she is not immune to the dangers of a life at sea. She has been through a pirate overtaking herself, though it did not involve this much of a delay. She's a strong woman, my wife," he added, his eyes glowing with pride and pleasant memories. "I am assured that she does not waste time pining and fretting, or I'd have given this up long ago."

They walked on in quiet companionship for several minutes before Jeremiah spoke again. "Tegan seems to be handling herself well. The kitchen staff has borne no complaints about the little urchin we foisted on them. As a matter of fact, I think they're pleased with the help she's – he's – been."

"Oh, yes, you are quite right. Did I tell you I was able to speak with her today?" At his look of surprise, Sarah hastened on. "Don't worry, Captain. It was quite by chance that I ran into her, and I am sure no one saw us." She proceeded to explain that they had chanced to meet in one of the parlors near the dining room of the great mansion. Sarah had gone there to examine some rare paintings d'Alava had confiscated from an unlucky Dutch freighter. Tegan had spied her as she rummaged through the treasures, still in their packing crates. "She looks well, considering the strain. And she told me she's pretending she is mute so she doesn't have to lower her voice. Clever, isn't she?"

"Very," Jeremiah agreed. "Your maid is quite brave and resourceful ... and a fine cook, as well. But please be careful, Sarah. It would be hard to explain your having a conversation with a mute servant. If anyone should ever see you together, it could put you both in jeopardy."

Sarah sighed, looking longingly out to sea. "I understand. But I feel so sorry for her, so alone and working so hard. While I've been treated like a princess ...."

"Now, I cannot blame you for concerning yourself with your servant. 'Tis a situation I chafe under as well seeing my men give their all for that demon d'Alava and his ill-gotten realm, while we bask in the comforts he's deemed to pleasure – or should I say – imprison us with," Slade sniffed defiantly. "But it does no good, Lady Sarah, to dwell on life's inequalities. We will just have to take what comes for now and make reparations when we are able."

With a pensive sigh, Sarah agreed. "I suppose ...."

To ward off her impending melancholy, Jeremiah attempted to change the subject. "You'll forgive my impertinence if I compliment you on what a convincing Mrs. Chamberlain you've become. I would give anything for Peggy to see her bachelor brother take so wholeheartedly to his role as a devoted husband. It would do much to restore her flagging hopes about him." Sarah cringed at the mention of the Captain's brother-in-law, but was determined not to show her discomfiture, nor the blush that threatened to rise.

"It is amazing our capabilities when the consequences of failure are so dire," she replied somewhat stiffly.

But Jeremiah was not satisfied, unwilling to let her evasiveness stand. "Even so, you two seem quite compatible."

Sarah laughed without humor. "Is that what you think? Perhaps we should become play actors if our charade has convinced you otherwise. Mr. Chamberlain and I have very little in common, and have never gotten along very well." Nervous fingers knotted and unknotted the ends of the light shawl draped around her slim figure.

"Now I am surprised," Jeremiah returned and Sarah readily picked up his ill-concealed interest. "My brother-in-law speaks little of his acquaintances to me, but I found you to be the exception. He seemed quite impressed with the Duke's enchanting daughter, and now, having met you, I can see why." The tall man chanced a sly glance down at Sarah and was rewarded with an obvious blush.

"He-he must have been referring to my sister, Lady Juliana," Sarah replied. "She is the family beauty, and was quite taken with him, I know."

"She may have been taken with him, but you were the one he spoke of," Jeremiah insisted. "His delight over the Duke's decision to send you to America was obvious."

Sarah's response was curt, though the Captain's words had their impact. "Mr. Chamberlain is proud of his homeland. I daresay he would be eager to show it off to any Brit. Besides," she added, a feeling of perversity overtaking her whenever Stewart was discussed, "is it not an expression of good faith on the part of my father that he would entrust my protection to his new partner? 'Tis the heady compliment he basks in, nothing more."

But though Stewart's nature was not completely fathomable to anyone, Jeremiah knew him best of all. Stewart bore the self-assurance of a man used to being respected, but never beguiled by the power it gave him. Jeremiah was quite sure Sarah was wrong in her assessment, and was equally convinced she knew it as well.

A knowing smile threatened to break across his lips, but the Captain suppressed it by voicing the suggestion that they return to the mansion.

Her obvious relief at the change of subject was all it took to convince Jeremiah that, like Stewart, Lady Sarah Tremont was afflicted with an attraction that made their unusual circumstances all the more interesting. Wouldn't Peggy be pleased if he could be the instigator of a real marriage for the footloose Chamberlain?

The idea brought an amused and satisfied chuckle to his lips, which was quickly doused by the queer look Sarah tossed up at him. "I was thinking," he blurted to cover his real thoughts, "were your father to learn our exact circumstances, Stewart would be basking in the substance more resembling boiling oil than glory. It is a small comfort to know that he assumes our safety."

"Aye," Sarah replied pensively, disturbed that she had not, until this moment, considered her family and their anticipation to learn of her safe arrival in the United States. Stewart Chamberlain seemed to have overtaken all her thoughts, conscious or otherwise.

CHAPTER 23

Their captivity had stretched into two weeks, then three. Three endless weeks of a masquerade that had, in many ways, become reality. The rancor that Sarah had felt at being, not only d'Alava's captive, but Stewart's as well, was all but gone. It was almost as if they had settled into the not-unpleasant routine of a long-married couple.

The night he had touched her so intimately had marked the end of his physical pursuit, though it had taken Sarah several days to relax her guard, and several more to divest herself of the niggling disappointment over his cooled ardor. Every explanation was painful: Had he tired of her? Had he found her physically lacking? Was she no longer a challenge or a prize worth winning? He still seemed to enjoy her company, even away from d'Alava's keen observance. But his compliments sounded perfunctory and his gazes were no longer leisurely or smoldering. Stewart had overnight become positively brotherly in his actions, and it was only then that Sarah could honestly admit to herself that she had enjoyed his caresses, or she would never have given into them.

The acknowledgement was frightening at first, for passion was not an enviable trait in a gently-bred young woman. But admitting she possessed this shameful flaw, Sarah found, did make it somewhat easier to overcome. And now that Stewart had dismissed her, her pride kept her longings at bay.

Of course Sarah had no way of knowing that Stewart's desire for her had, if anything, heightened in the time since he last held her. He was possessed of much experience when it came to hiding his feelings and now he drew heavily on this talent. She could never know that his uncharacteristic pang of conscience barred him from breaking down her defenses, making her prove that she was every bit the sensuous woman he thought she could be. And it was not his loyalty to Felicia, as he had once told himself, that held him in check. It was Sarah, and something she had reminded him of on that night she had been close to being taken.

Stewart Chamberlain, the man who was so sure of everything, was for once not so sure how he would feel after Sarah had become his lover. He had become fond enough of her to know that he did not wish to hurt her. What if she were right? What if he grew tired of her after the game was won? Experience dictated that a strong possibility. Hadn't it always been that way? And though Lady Sarah Tremont was as intelligent as she was beautiful, her innocence made her too vulnerable. She would never marry without her virginity, of that he was nearly sure. And he did not want to be responsible for forcing her into spinsterhood. Let that crime be on her *own* head!

And so, he thought ruefully, stretched out comfortably on the bed while Galena expertly dressed Sarah's shimmering tresses, the monk and the virgin shared a name, a room, a bed, and a companionable, if not honest, relationship, while all the time his body was tormented by the irony of it all.

"If Galena finishes soon, darling, would you care for a stroll by the lagoon?" His gentle voice wafted toward Sarah and she smiled at his handsome reflection in the dressing table looking glass.

"Oh, I would. I've not been outside all day. Hurry Galena, or we won't have time." Sarah loved the serenity of the hidden lagoon where Stewart bathed. But on his orders, she never dared go there by herself. Some of the pirates, including d'Alava himself, frequented the lush haven, making it unsafe for a lone female.

"I done. See? So pretty, yes?" Galena adored dressing Sarah's hair and worked diligently to please her mistress. The results were always perfect. Tonight Galena had created a sleek coiffure, with Sarah's dark hair secured firmly at the base of her neck in a stylish chignon. It suited the black low-cut gown perfectly, making Sarah look and feel much older and more worldly than her 20 years.

A hot flicker of approval momentarily lit Stewart's brown eyes when she turned for his inspections, but he masked it quickly, rising from the bed and pulling on his well-fitted black cutaway coat. "You rival any Spanish princess this evening, my dear," he offered with more politeness than warmth. "Galena, a splendid job, as usual." The dark-skinned maid lowered her eyes in embarrassed pleasure as she quickly put away Sarah's combs and brushes.

They reached the lagoon by way of a narrow path that began directly beneath their balcony. The early evening sun cast long shadows across the wide, azure pool, an oasis in the dense tropical flora surrounding it. Picking their way across some flat rocks on the leeward side, they came to an area where fallen palms had created a natural bench on which Sarah settled herself. She breathed deeply of the heavily perfumed air, and was about to comment on the beauty on the spot when something unusual caught her eye.

"Stewart? What is that over there?" She pointed to an area on the windward side still dappled by the fading sun. "It looks like someone forgot to retrieve his clothes." With an impish smile, she raised her eyes upward to where he stood in front of her, adding, "Perhaps we've frightened off a bashful pirate."

Stewart winked. "I assure you, my dear, there is no such thing. But let me take a look." He passed in front of her, but instead of remaining, she rose to follow.

"I'll come with you," she murmured, concentrating on holding up her full skirts and following his long-legged stride. So intent was she on picking her way between the mossy bank and the tangled foliage that when Stewart stopped suddenly only a few feet from the mysterious mound, she bumped full force into his broad back. Clutching his arms to steady herself, she giggled a pardon, peaking around his shoulder to see the reason for his abrupt halt.

"Go back, Sarah!"

"What is it?"

"I said go back!" Shaking off her hands, Stewart strode over to the spot and Sarah watched as he knelt and parted the leaves around the object. Inching forward, she peered until she realized that he was handling not a bundle of clothes but a lifeless body. Even as the shock nearly paralyzed her lungs and heart, her mouth suddenly dry, Sarah was mesmerized by the sight and continued forward. "Sarah!" Stewart's head snapped up and angry eyes shot sparks into her horrified blue ones. "Not one step further, do you hear?"

"Who is it?" She heard the voice, but it did not seem her own.

With a leap, Stewart was on his feet and rushed to hold her back. Still staring beyond his arm, she struggled fiercely, knowing yet not knowing what he was keeping her from. "Stewart, tell me! Who is it?" Her words spilled out in a horrified gasp brought on by shock and the effort made to cut loose from Stewart's firm grip. Finally, he managed to wrap both arms securely around her, forcing her to look up into his face as she pleaded, "I want to know, Stewart. You must tell me."

Looking into her wide, frightened eyes begging for yet repelling the truth, Stewart knew a moment of utterly devastating remorse. She had been so young and so well shielded from the harshness of life. And then he entered into her safe, secure world and nothing but misery had been her lot since. He had never meant to cause her so much pain. "Sarah," he whispered, holding her so close she almost lost her breath, "It's Tegan. She's dead."

She stared at him as if she were still waiting for him to speak. And then, the tautness left her body and she slumped against him, so suddenly that he nearly lost his balance holding her up. Pressing her head against his shoulder, he gently caressed her slender neck, murmuring, "I'm sorry, Sarah. I'm so sorry."

She rested against him for what seemed like an eternity, her mind a complete blank, her body as rigid as a stone carving. Then in a quiet, tearless voice, she spoke, "I want to see her, Stewart. Take me to her."

"Sarah ... someone's killed her. I don't think ...."

"I want to *see* her." The voice, though faint, was charged with a fierceness that brooked no denial. Reluctantly he took her by the waist and led her to the spot where Tegan lay.

That impish face, always so pleasant and full of life, was pale and marred. Tegan had been strangled by strong, bare hands, and by the look of her disheveled boy's clothing, Stewart guessed other atrocities had been committed as well. He wondered if Sarah were concluding as much. Slowly, mechanically, Sarah sank to her knees beside her trusted maid and friend and began gently brushing the shaggy auburn hair from the tiny face. Stroking the cool cheek, she whispered, "No one had a more loyal servant or friend than I, dear Teeg. You cared for me, expecting nothing in return. How I will miss you ...."

Moments passed until finally Sarah raised her head, looking up at Stewart with dry, serious eyes. "We must bury her before anyone can find her body. Will you help me, please?"

For a second, Stewart hesitated, left speechless by her calm, rational mien. But he recovered quickly, saying, "Sarah, I can take care of this. Let me take you back to the house."

Her brow creased impatiently and she shook her head, not meeting his eyes. "No, there isn't time. I will see this through, so you needn't try to stop me."

They worked quickly. Stewart found a spot in the jungle where the sandy soil was loose, but with only shells and flat stones with which to dig, it was impossible to clear more than a shallow grave. Meanwhile, Sarah lovingly straightened Tegan's tattered clothes, silently decrying the fact that the plain girl must go to her final resting place in breeches rather than a dress. With her handkerchief, she washed the smudges from Tegan's face and arms, a burning lump rising in her throat as she touched the ugly bruises on the maid's neck. But she willed herself not to dwell on anything but the task at hand.

With infinite care, Stewart laid the small form in the pit he had dug and Sarah turned away while he completed his task. When he was finished, she helped him camouflage the grave with sand and fallen palm leaves so that the area might have resembled an animal's lair if one ever came upon it. In wordless agreement, they bowed their heads in silent prayer and then Sarah placed a kiss on the matted leaves.

"We must hurry," she ordered, picking Stewart's coat from a branch where he'd hung it before beginning to dig. "You'll have to change your shirt and breeches before we go to dinner."

They raced back to the haven of their chambers, mercifully unseen, and while Stewart removed and hid his soiled clothes, Sarah took his high top boots out on the balcony and brushed them till they shone again. She returned just as he was tying his stock.

He turned from the looking glass as she came toward him. Her face was a determined mask. "Sarah, you needn't join us for dinner. I'll have Galena bring something up if you're hungry."

"Don't be ridiculous," she said abruptly, refusing to meet his gaze, "I must go or d'Alava may suspect something is wrong. And have you considered that he may know something of this? It behooves us to show him that we've made no discovery."

"I have considered these possibilities, Sarah. That is why I think it's best that you avoid his company. It may be very difficult for you ...." His concern for her threatened her composure; she made an angry gesture of dismissal.

"There's no time to waste arguing. I shall dine with the others. Are you coming?"

CHAPTER 24

Dinner was a truly unique affair from Stewart's point of view. In awe he watched Sarah, as gay, witty and charming as ever. Never did she miss a beat of the conversation while he, amazed by her remarkable performance, lost track of the banter not once, but twice during the course of the evening. D'Alava appeared not to notice, but Jeremiah, attuned to his best friend's ways, sensed that there was much more going on than met the eye.

At one point, d'Alava commented that the meal was less tasty than usual. Stewart stiffened at this reference to Tegan's cooking, forgetting all else but that it was a clue to how long ago she had been murdered. But Sarah immediately cajoled their host, offering that in three weeks, this was the first poor meal, and that every cook has a bad day. She then proceeded to change the subject to her regular reminder to d'Alava of how overlong their captivity was lasting. He took great delight in offering excuses to her, which she, in turn, charmingly refuted.

The evening continued as usual until it was time to repair to the parlor for an after-dinner aperitif. This night Sarah begged fatigue and asked to be excused. D'Alava countered that if her pre-dinner promenades were so exhausting, perhaps she should forego them in order that he might enjoy her company longer.

She smiled bewitchingly, despite the painful reminder. "Even in the Tower of London, Señor, prisoners are allowed their daily exercise. Would you be so cruel as to deny us that small taste of freedom?"

"You wound me to the quick, *mi dulce*," d'Alava lamented. "Have I not been the most benevolent of jailers?" He stroked her hand lovingly while Stewart inwardly seethed.

"But of course, Señor. And that is why I begged to take my leave, without fear of reprisal." She gazed at him demurely, waiting for his permission.

With a hearty laugh, he caved in, giving her hand an intimate squeeze and kissing it soundly. "Fare thee well, enchantress, while I piece together the bits of my rapiered heart." Sarah nodded to Jeremiah, reached up to give her unsmiling husband a quick kiss and left hastily.

She was met by Galena in the adjoining sitting room, but after the maid helped her unlace her evening gown and corset, she dismissed her, looking back only to add a kind word when she noticed the fearful disappointment on the young girl's face.

At last Sarah was alone. Stepping slowly out of the beautiful black gown in the candlelit bedroom, she considered how appropriate the color for the task she had earlier performed. She waited for the tears, but none came.

With a sigh, she removed her undergarments and foregoing a nightgown, slipped into a light wrapper which she belted loosely. Any other night she might have found the garment too thin for modesty, but tonight she did not care.

Sarah sat in front of the dressing table mirror, mechanically removing pins until her dark brown locks fell free. She brushed and brushed, staring at her haunting reflection, waiting for the tears. But none came.

Why? Tegan had been brutally murdered and all she could do was ask herself why she could not cry? She felt empty; there was no pain. She was numb and nothing seemed worthy of her attention. Only that fact: She was too cold, too dead, to cry. The idea should frighten her ... anger her ... something. But there was no feeling at all.

She thought about her performance at dinner. It should have been difficult, even impossible. But it was easy because it did not matter. She had had nothing to lose. She could have continued on; she wasn't really tired as she had told d'Alava. Simply weary of their numbing charade.

Carelessly she dropped the brush and it clattered noisily on the vanity. Rising, Sarah strolled to the balcony, staring aimlessly until she spotted the bright moon peaking between the palm fronds overhead. Resting her head against the doorframe, she hugged herself tightly, trying to capture her body's own warmth. But she felt cool, detached from herself. With her blue eyes locked on the bright ball in the sky, she tried to conjure up thoughts of Tegan and all that the young woman had meant to her these many years. When that failed to evoke a reaction, she tried to picture the abused, lifeless body. But her mind would not rally to the task, as if it had nothing to recall. And still she could not cry.

Sarah decided she was losing her sanity. Where was the girl who wept at the drop of a hat? The girl with empathy and understanding for those she loved? The temperamental shrew that plagued Stewart so? Or the passionate woman that only he had discovered? Who was this cold, heartless, mindless shell?

When Stewart found her, she was still staring dry-eyed at the moon. He threw off his coat, draping it on a chair as he rushed to her side. "I got away as soon as I could. You should not be alone. But d'Alava found satisfaction in detaining me."

"No matter," she replied dully, her eyes still rigidly fixed on the sky.

"I brought you some brandy," he offered kindly. "I thought it might help you." Studying her profile in the moonlight, he was reminded of another night on board ship when the sight of her bathed in moon glow, her blue eyes shimmering beneath dark lashes, had stirred him profoundly. But something was different this night, despite her breathtaking beauty. Her eyes. They were empty, devoid of expression. "Would you care for some brandy, Sarah?"

She sighed, then blinked, sliding her eyes toward him as if he were hardly worth noticing. "I don't care."

Taken aback by her indifference, he reached for her arm, shocked to find it as cold as ice. "Sarah, you are freezing, despite this heat. Come, let me warm you." He pulled her to him, wrapping his long arms around her, hoping to comfort as well as soothe away the chill. But he might have been caressing a marble statue, so still and frigid was her slender body. He looked down on her and saw that the glassy stare had now fixed on his chest. She neither knew nor cared what was happening to her.

Enraged that her pain was so great that she could not even suffer, he snatched her up, forcing a breath from her body, and dropped her unceremoniously on the huge bed. After throwing a blanket over her, he retrieved the small bottle of brandy from his coat pocket and, lifting her head, forced the bottle between her slackened lips. Finally, she was compelled to swallow the burning liquid, feebly coughing as she did.

Satisfied for the moment, Stewart set the bottle aside and quickly removed his clothes, the thought crossing his mind that her anger might rally at his immodesty. But even if she noticed, there was no reaction. With a sigh, he crawled into the bed, pulling the sheet over his nakedness. Sliding his long body next to hers, he propped his head on one hand, using the others to reach beneath the blanket to bring her arm around till she faced him. The smell of the brandy was heavy on her lips and without thinking, he kissed her, taking the taste into his own mouth. But he might have been making love to the bottle itself, so still and cold she lay.

Stewart raised his head in frustration, his attempt to evoke some response, even anger, having failed. She continued to stare at him, not seeing his darkly handsome features nor the pain in his troubled eyes.

"Sarah," he whispered insistently, "where are you?"

As if making the greatest human sacrifice, she finally responded, sighing, "I feel nothing ... I care even less."

He smoothed her hair, running his thumb along her slender jaw line, gently stroking her ear. "'Tis the shock. It has been too much to bear at once."

"Where are the tears? Have I gone mad?" Her thin voice was devoid of emotion. "I am as dead as she."

"No, no!" he whispered fiercely, gripping her shoulders, his imploring brown eyes illuminated by the moonlight. "This won't last. You've been under such a great strain that nothing seems real anymore. But we are alone now. You can let go."

A mirthless laugh escaped her tight lips. "Of what? There is nothing inside. Nothing."

"You're wrong," Stewart argued, yanking away the bedclothes and molding himself to her thinly-clad body, still so cold and taut. "There is a passionate woman inside, who feels, who cares, who is grieving. Let me help you, Sarah. Let me comfort you."

With the greatest care, as if handling a tender babe, Stewart rolled her unresisting form to her stomach. Lifting her thick hair aside, he began gently massaging her rigid neck, shoulders and back. If only she could relax, he believed the trance-like state would end. Then she would be able to deal with her pain. Diligently he worked, his hands skillfully manipulating the tense muscles beneath her thin wrapper, lending her the warmth from his fingers.

Unmoved by his ministrations, Sarah lay in silence, staring at the balcony doorway, seeing nothing. An eternity passed, or so it seemed, and still Stewart worked tirelessly, praying she would give into the brandy and the massage, for he could think of no other balm.

At last, his efforts began to bear fruit. Without warning, Sarah shivered involuntarily as a sudden warmth poured into her. The abrupt feeling of life was disconcerting and without knowing why, she felt an overpowering urge to cleave. In a voice barely audible, she pleaded, "Hold me ... please hold me."

It was the sign Stewart had been waiting for. Immediately he dropped beside her on the bed and took her into his arms, not unaware of her tender flesh where the wrapper had twisted away. Impatiently she pushed against him, wrapping her arms around his neck, whimpering his name in a pathetic, childlike voice. Far from disturbed by her first encounter with Stewart's naked flesh, she reveled in its warmth and strength that seemed to seep from his body into hers. Nothing mattered except that she was feeling again and would do anything to keep the sensations alive.

Her desperate wriggling caused the wrapper to part and Stewart knew excruciating agony as a tender, swelling breast pressed against his hard chest. Her silky thighs molded themselves to his lean legs, giving rise to his manhood despite his attempts to will against it. In torment over his predicament, he tried to alter his position but Sarah relentlessly clung to him.

Were she any other women, his course would be certain. But Lady Sarah Tremont was not any woman. He had known her too dearly, had come to respect her reasons for chastity, even if they sorely conflicted with his own opinions and desires. That she had suddenly made herself a willing partner for his own lusts forced him to question her obvious, if inexperienced, overtures.

Would making love to her increase her anguish, complicate her suffering? Or would rejection? God, if only he could be certain! Everything about her this night confounded him – her calm control in the face of an unspeakable personal tragedy, her superlative concealment of her knowledge and emotions in d'Alava's menacing presence, the cold withdrawal and now her passionate pleading. Had she gone mad, as she feared, or would a wrong decision on her part be the sway?

The misgivings persisted even as Sarah found his lips, kissing him wantonly, digging her nails into his broad shoulders and squirming until her supple body was pinned beneath his. And she truly felt his undisguised hardness pressed between them and knew that no matter what trauma had brought her to this point, nor what outcome would transpire, she wanted, needed, to experience the culmination of desire with this man, and no other.

"Take me ... take me, please. Make me feel again." The whispered supplication ripened into a demand, so emphatic that all Stewart's uncertainties took flight. She wanted him, as he had always wanted her. But he was determined to be patient and to stop his caresses should she suddenly change her mind. In soothing tones, he murmured of her beauty, his desire and of the act they were about to share, all the while removing her robe, teasing her body with gentle, persistent fingers. He kissed her, reveling in the unrepressed response of her delicate lips and tongue.

As his mouth sought the sweetness of her peaking breasts, Sarah pressed his head closer to her bosom, thrusting her hips toward him in urgent need for release from this exquisite torture he had aroused in her loins. Her will was gone and in its place was burning, aching desire to experience whatever lay in store.

Stewart was overwhelmed, struck by the intensity of emotion he had never sustained until this night. She was splendid in looks, taste, touch, scent, sound. Her barest quiver fanned the flames of desire, but to his surprise, selfless caring was by far the stronger impulse. As much as he wanted her, had always wanted her, he could not put his needs before her own. Tenderness, gentleness, patience had been mere words until this moment. And the realization that he possessed such traits only added to his reverent adoration of the woman beneath him.

His warm, pliant fingers teased and fondled every inch of her body until coming to rest on the soft mound between her legs. Drawing his leg up to separate her limbs, he retreated when he discovered resistance there. Raising his head from the deep hollow at the base of her pulsing neck, he sought the reason for her reluctance. Her hair had fallen into a dark, magnificent cloud around her face and framed her eyes, which, when she opened them, were soft, a luminous navy blue. Immediately her hands rose to cup his lean face, pulling him closer till their lips met in a rapturous kiss that both thrilled and confused him.

Again he pressed for access to hidden places and still she resisted, all the while gasping in breathless wonder at the powerful waves of pleasure overtaking her. If only she knew the course of this heady passion! Where was its crowning? How was this "act," of which she knew virtually nothing, supposed to be accomplished? Eyes brimming with tears of frustration, Sarah wordlessly damned her prim and sheltered existence, fortified by her own stubborn desire for ignorance in all things sexual. For now, when she wanted to experience everything, she found herself a prisoner of her own purity.

His tender, husky voice broke into her recriminations. "Is it pain that you fear? 'Twill be small and not what you remember of this night, I promise."

Hiding her eyes from his intense gaze, she spoke, her words muffled, "Not that ... I would relish the pain. But I-I am without ... I don't know what ...." Her embarrassed confession, so arduously attempted, melted Stewart's heart as it cleared his confusion. He had forgotten how unschooled gentlewomen were in the art of love, so long had it been since he had come across a true innocent.

Lifting her arm from across her face, he delicately kissed each eyelid, savoring the taste of her salty tears. As his hand caressed the firm yet supple swell of her buttocks, he whispered reassuringly, "Take ease, my darling. Open yourself to me and your body will show you the way ...."

Tentatively at first, her knees came apart as his lips traced searing patterns on her ear and the slim column of her throat. Very gently his hand again approached the untried territory between her thighs, causing her to flinch, more from surprise than from fear. But he would not be swayed, methodically stroking the moist flesh, continuing to nibble and whisper in her ear of his pleasure and her charms.

Wave upon wave of hot desire washed over her and Sarah felt suspended, apart from her own body, yet pulsing and breathless with longing. His masterful fingers played her like a fine, precious instrument. Unconsciously she spread herself beneath him, pushing and straining as her mouth and tongue sought the strong possession of his.

And then he withdrew, raising himself above her in naked splendor, a dark rippling panther so close yet much too far. In agonized disappointment, she moaned, wrapping her pale arms around his neck in silent pleading for his return. Stewart bent his head to kiss her again and in so doing, slowly lowered his body until his throbbing manhood tested the warm, wet heat of her portal. Dark sea blue eyes rose in confused panic, but earthy brown eyes were strangely reassuring despite their burning intensity.

Never had Stewart known such a desperate craving to find release for his too-long, pent-up urgings. But to move hastily would surely prove a grave gesture, for Sarah was so tense that he would undoubtedly inflict immeasurable pain. His arms trembled under his weight but his manner was calming, subtly moving his hard, warm body against the soft curves beneath him.

Sarah felt herself responding to his deliberate movements, relishing the way his muscular chest taunted her aching nipples in feverish delight. Breathlessly she waited for his thrust which would surely end the incredible pleasure that, thanks to his skillful and considerate lovemaking, had nearly all been hers, or so she believed. But still he took his leisure, kissing her with controlled passion, discovering every inch of her mouth with his relentless tongue until his arm had gone around her and his heavy body was pressing hers into the soft mattress. She thrilled to the touch of his hand as he traced a molten path down the length of her trembling flesh, coming to rest on the downy softness of her inner thigh. With gentle pressure, he pushed her limb further outward and the other followed willingly.

Then, and only then, did Stewart press his lean hips closer. Sarah's legs tightened involuntarily at this encroachment, but surprisingly, there was no pain, only an ardent fullness that nearly took her breath away. Regaining her eagerness, Sarah sighed and pulled Stewart's head closer, nuzzling her nose in the thick waves of dark hair about his ear.

Incapable of prolonging this sweet agony, Stewart rocked gently back and forth, moving imperceptibly deeper with each thrust of his burning shaft. A more experienced woman would have known that entry had only just begun. But Sarah, lulled by Stewart's rhythmic page, thought her initiation complete and satisfying.

But her feeling of drifting contentment ended abruptly when Stewart's gentle probing turned helplessly more demanding. Surprised and frightened by this change, his ragged breathing burning her ear, Sarah instinctively sought to resist him. But Stewart had gone too far to turn back now, pressing himself deeper and deeper into her gentle flesh. The discomfort she felt alarmed her and made her less open to his thrusts, which now seemed capable of ripping her body asunder.

She cried out, whimpering, pleading, begging him to stop his conquest, but either he did not hear or no longer cared for he drove himself relentlessly between her quivering thighs. Sarah squirmed and twisted, pummeling his broad shoulder with her fists but her efforts were totally wasted on this strong animal who imprisoned her so completely.

Betrayed and helpless, Sarah rolled her head from side to side, the tears flooding her flushed face. Meekly she sobbed, only remotely aware that the rending pain had subsided and in its place was a bittersweet ache as Stewart's rhythmic invasion continued. And then, a very strange sensation crept over her, more mysterious because she had expected only to endure. It was as if her body were rekindled; she tingled with a feeling of indescribable anticipation for something that defied explanation. In burning response, her hips rose of their own accord to meet Stewart's plunging stabs. The pain no longer mattered and his labored sounds were suddenly music to her ears.

She gripped him, molding his body more tightly to hers, feeling as if she were about to burst into millions of glimmering stars. She felt faint, weak, yet strangely powerful, driven.

But it was a short-lived tumble of sensations for just as suddenly as her passions had risen, he stopped, and in the next instant, she felt his spasmodic tremors deep within her belly.

Stewart lay so still and heavy atop her that for a moment, Sarah thought he had suffered an attack, or had lost consciousness. A torrent of conflicting emotions engulfed her – concern, relief, curiosity, confusion, and fulfillment. None would take sure hold, yet none could she dismiss. Her eyes, still wet, filled again with unshed tears.

It was then that her lover, for that was surely what he had become, raised his head and with eyes aglow, carefully took in every detail of her lovely face, clearly defined in the white shaft of moonlight. With tender care, he brushed a damp ringlet from her temple, lovingly kissed her tears, stroked her high cheekbones, her slender nose and outlined her swollen lips with feather-soft touches.

Sarah returned his stare, her wide blue eyes and expressive brows revealing her myriad thoughts as if they were spoken aloud. "You are feeling many things," he murmured, "but I sincerely pray that regret is not among them."

"No ...." she replied hesitantly and then with conviction. "No, regret is not one." The realization impressed her, and her spirits lifted a little. "What of you?"

He pondered his answer carefully, then spoke in a low voice. "If I could have given as much pleasure as I have found this night, then I would be the happiest man on earth. Would that I could have spared you the pain ...."

She put her finger to his lips. "Don't. 'Tis a maiden's lot, that much I knew."

"Do you know that you have never looked more beautiful than this moment? Do you know that your body was made for a man's caress and that your innocent passion stirs me more than I can say?" Her eyes lowered in shy delight that this aloof, often arrogant man should be moved to speak such heady words of praise. Stewart kissed her again, gently, lovingly, reluctantly removing himself from the warm shelter of her body, though his arms still enfolded her in newfound familiarity. "Tired?"

Sarah thought a moment, not quite sure of the relationship she now shared with the strong, handsome man who lay beside her. She considered it ironic that their intimate actions did not naturally evoke a comfortable openness between them. But she forced herself to speak honestly, although she could not look at him. "I-I am confused mostly ... I don't know how this," she gestured, "happened when I should be pulling my hair out with grief. I am thinking I must be a terrible person."

"No, never that," Stewart interjected soundly, pulling her close to his broad chest, his hands sending warm shivers through her body. "Some things would be devastating if we considered them too soon. You will grieve when you are ready. And I will be here to comfort you."

His words brought a peacefulness to her that she had not felt in a very long time. Too weary to contemplate why or how, she sighed, closing her eyes and soon was sleeping easily.

But Stewart lay awake for a long time, staring up at the mirrored canopy and the reflection of himself and the tender child-woman curled up so trustingly next to him. It was a scene he had long pursued, and now, having won it, was strangely uncertain about the wisdom of it. She was so vulnerable and it pained him to think that he might have made a mistake, an error that would compound her suffering when he had only meant to ease it. *I should heed my own advice,* he thought irritably, *and not consider it fully too soon.*

Sarah stirred, brushing her eye in sleepy annoyance, then huddled closer to Stewart, her leg moving comfortably between his, as if sleeping in his arms were a pleasant habit. In the darkness, Stewart smiled, then placed an affectionate kiss on her perfumed temple. A pleasurable wave of contentment overrode his reservations and he, too, dozed off into a sound slumber.

CHAPTER 25

The intense screaming raised gooseflesh on Sarah's feverish skin. She ran forward, then whirled around, not sure whether to find or escape the source. Blinding tears caused her to stumble. Jungle foliage impeded her frantic attempts to rise. The screaming continued, louder and more agonized than before. Then a voice, a sweet consoling, feminine voice very close to her ear said, "Don't worry, mum. Mr. Chamberlain knows what to do. Gives a body peace of mind knowing that such a fine man is protecting us."

Sarah's head snapped around. There was Tegan, her impish face beaming with confidence beneath her shaggy auburn locks. "There, there mum. See? Nothing to fret about. Mr. Chamberlain's taking good care of us." The boyish figure in ragged seaman's clothes walked easily through the tangled underbrush, away from the spot where Sarah had fallen.

"Tegan! Teeg!" Sarah sobbed. "Come back. Don't leave me here, please!"

"You're in good hands, mum. And what a lucky one you are to catch his eye!" The maid was gone, swallowed up by the unforgiving tropical forest.

"Oh my God! Tegan, come back. Please don't leave me here," she choked, her heart breaking at the loneliness that engulfed her. "Don't leave me. Please ... don't leave me!"

"Sarah! I'm right here. I won't leave you. You're safe ... I'm here." But it was not Tegan's voice consoling her, nor Tegan's hands grasping her shoulders. It was a man, a warm, compassionate figure hovering over her in the moonlight.

"Stewart!" The relief of recognition swept over Sarah like a cooling ocean wave. Sobbing helplessly, she flung her arms about him, seeking the sheltering haven of his powerful body. Wrenchingly she confessed her misery, crying ceaselessly into his warm flesh. "Stewart ... I saw her ... I saw Tegan ... but she's dead. It was only a dream. She's dead, Stewart. Teeg's dead!"

She wept, her outpouring overwhelmingly tormented. The pain was a physical torture as well as an anguished guilt. That sweet, fearless Tegan should be killed so undeservedly when she was merely doing the bidding of others ... the atrocity was too much to bear.

The memories flowed, each one more discomforting than the last. All these years, Sarah had considered her sister, Lady Juliana, her closest companion, and yet it was Tegan she turned to, confided in, depended on. And now she was gone, leaving Sarah alone ... with no one.

But even as the pain, the guilt and the loneliness coursed through her, bringing a physical ache to her very soul, Sarah was not unaware of the comfort she found in the body she clutched so desperately. The very same man who had been the source of turmoil in her life was now the one lending her strength, for she had none of her own.

With whispered words and gentle touches, Stewart eased her misery. If only a whit, it was more than Sarah expected, and she was grateful for his nearness. Finally, when her wrenching sobs dissipated into feeble, involuntary shudders, she opened her swollen eyes, seeking the words to express her jumbled, exhausted thoughts.

"I-I am sorry if I woke you. The dream ... it was so real. It made me remember ... e-everything ... and I c-couldn't help m-myself." As new tears threatened to fall, Sarah covered her face with her hands, embarrassed by her weakness.

"You needed to cry. And I told you I would be here, so you needn't apologize." Stewart pulled her closer, prying her fingers away from her wet face, kissing each digit tenderly. "Tegan was your friend. The memories will haunt you for a long time."

That fact she agreed with completely, and her body responded with another quaking sigh. "What are we going to do now?"

"I need to speak with Jeremiah, to find out what he knows, if anything at all," Stewart mused. "There was no opportunity this evening. "D'Alava made certain of that." He studied her wide-eyed, confused and heart-broken stare, and added, "Besides, I was more concerned about you."

Her gaze dropped then, for she was suddenly taken with remembrances of his tenderness toward her, a gentleness that she was not quite ready to trust, even now that they had become lovers.

Observing the vulnerability in her mien, Stewart was moved to place a consoling kiss on her brow, only too aware of her compliant form beneath him. He considered easing himself away from this silken temptation, but was hugely relieved when she raised trembling lips to find his, her arms persistent in their wish to hold him fast.

After the many battles provoked by his desires and her reluctance, this newfound intimacy was all the more addictive, a bond nearly won yet still tenuous. It was this uncertainty that compelled Stewart to proceed cautiously, hoping he would do nothing that would cause her, in confusion, to turn away from the comfort he so wanted to offer.

Sarah, on the other hand, her emotions still raw and shaky, had not yet achieved objectivity, responding only to the deep and fervent call within her. The rightness -- or wrongness -- was for now not the issue. Only the need to be possessed, to be completely and utterly distracted from the fear and misery that Tegan's death perpetuated. Even now as his molten kisses and practiced caresses thrilled her, his consuming embrace was a profound solace, a measure of relief she had never expected, but cherished just the same.

And responded to, she realized, as her body arched and writhed in anticipation. As his tongue played havoc with the sensitive tips of her breasts, she knew that she would endure any amount of pain to hold him within her, to find that release she had been so close to discovering before. His learned fingers stroked and petted her, sharing a knowledge of her body that mystified as much as it delighted her. How could he perpetuate this longing with such ease and skill? It was ironic that he seemed intensely familiar with the body that was a complete stranger to its very owner.

But these random thoughts flew quickly when he raised himself up to enter her. She gasped with pleasure that the time had come, and he quickly dismissed the semblance of restraint he had planned. So it was that their coming together was urgent, filled with need and lacking reservation. Their warm bodies meshed and swayed in response to ancient rhythms dictated by the sweeping, consuming desires that overtook them. Sarah, propelled into enthusiasm by the surprising absence of pain, reveled in the blissful surrender to this lean, hard man who was still as much a stranger as her lover.

His every touch was fire; his whispered endearments reverberated in her mind, his powerful thrusts she welcomed with unabashed relish. Again she experienced the tumultuous and wildly exciting phenomenon of her body taking on a life of its own, a sensation so bold and conquering that she was left a gasping voyeur of her own actions. But unlike before, there was no abrupt end to this unearthly rapture, only a blazing, devouring intensification, like a fire gone out of control. And she, the willing, nay, eager victim of this holocaust, clung to its purveyor, his name torn from her lips in a smoldering kiss, riding like a shooting comet to the summit of fulfillment as his throbbing rejoinder found surcease.

Minutes, or was it hours, passed before Sarah found the strength or desire to wrest from the fusion of their damp bodies. The high blush provoked by her fevered capitulation had waned into a translucent glow, making her smoky blue eyes appear even larger and more prominent than before. As Stewart slid himself to her side, she burrowed her face into the hollow beneath his chin, hoping to cloak from his observant brown eyes the utterly complete surrender of her will and resistance to him.

For now she realized that her virginity had not been the prize she had been guarding with haughty disapproval. No, it was this deep and overpowering enslavement that had overtaken her body long before she gave it, this inability to govern herself, to fend off the lusting desire she felt for him.

And now the truth was even more awesome than the fear, for her very soul had betrayed its most potent secret, one that even she had not learned until this night: Her body would always be his no matter how her mind balked or her actions refuted it. He knew what he had done, and just as surely would bring her to this helplessness again. It was no less than blackmail and it was with shame that she admitted willingness to pay the price whenever he exacted it.

Expecting his smugness over her total submission, Sarah was surprised when he whispered in a compassionate tone, gently running his fingers up and down her side as she lay cradled in his arms, "You've known the full measure of a woman's response. 'Tis not always the way, especially for one so ... new." *Another betrayal!* Even her lack of experience had not prevented her from proving her consuming lust for him. When she did not speak, he continued, "Now I am surely the happiest man alive, for you have known the full pleasure your body was meant to enjoy."

Her silence filled the room and he pushed her back into the pillows in order to see her face clearly, though she was reluctant to match his gaze. "Does your passion embarrass you?" It was much too simplistic an explanation, but it seemed a harmless one to admit to and would curtail his probing. She nodded. His lips curled into a benevolent smile before coming to rest on the sensitive skin below her ear. "Well, my darling, it is your right to enjoy lovemaking as much as any other. Your perfect body demands perfect fulfillment, and I will do my best to satisfy you."

And I you, she wanted to say, but could not let him see how weak and servile he had made her. Something warned her that humble devotion would not please him, though she would gladly offer it if it would. Fighting back tears threatening her composure, she kissed his strong jaw and nestled her head on his muscular shoulder, feigning exhaustion. But long after the sound of his breathing had become regular, Sarah lay forlorn and sleepless, watching the black night fade into early morn.

CHAPTER 26

The morning sun was harsh, an unwelcome intruder into the unshaded bedroom where Sarah lay, groggy and uncomfortably warm. The twisted sheet clung to her naked form and her tangled hair lay matted against her fevered cheek. Rubbing her face in sleepy annoyance, she struggled to figure out the reason for her pervasive lassitude.

But of course! The sun was high; she had slept uncommonly late. Sarah sat up quickly, the sheet falling away to be quickly replaced by her heavy tresses. She studied the room in confusion, wondering why she had not been wakened at the usual time by Stewart or Galena's stirrings.

Stewart. The drama played out the night before came back to her in one fell swoop. Her lethargic body was no longer innocent of a man's passions; it was a body schooled and fevered by womanhood — new, enticing, and terribly frightening, Sarah though, bringing her knees up and hugging herself protectively. How could she face him, his cool arrogance, now that she had given everything away?

She did not have long to contemplate this thought, for the door suddenly opened and in he walked, looking relaxed and confident in fawn breeches, dark boots and a cool muslin shirt buttoned halfway up his expansive chest. His manner was so well-composed, nearly indolent, that it was difficult for Sarah to imagine that this was the same man who had alternately cradled and comforted her, then brought her to the peak of undisguised passion only hours before.

The incongruity disturbed her and she warily eyed his advance, pulling the sheet more tightly around her, though he seemed undaunted. "I'm glad you're awake," he smiled lazily, coming to stand beside her. "Galena is positively fidgeting to attend you. I did not know how much longer I could hold her off." Casually he seated himself on the bed facing her as she suppressed an urge to shiver as his stirring gaze took in the view.

Embarrassed by her disheveled state, though his eyes spoke of pleasure at the sight, Sarah hugged her legs more tightly to her. "I told her you weren't feeling well today, and that I would see to your needs."

"Thank you," she murmured docilely, unable to meet his direct stare.

"I thought you could use the extra sleep," he continued. She blushed at his reference, but not nearly so much as when he added, "Besides, I did not want her to tidy up just yet. The bedclothes bear certain ... evidence that would compromise us dearly." His lack of embarrassment was unnerving, even more so because physical proof of her virginity was something Sarah had not considered at all, making her feel insurmountably naïve. Her crimson hue failed to wane when she felt his warm lips on her naked shoulder.

Struggling to maintain her poise, she replied, "I'll see to the bedclothes ... if you'll keep Galena away for a while longer."

"'Tis done," he murmured offhandedly, more intent on nuzzling the tender sweetness of her slim neck. "Galena won't appear without my summons."

His meaning was perfectly clear and Sarah found her body already responding to the proposition. But her mind was deterred by too many reservations, not the least of which was the fact that it was broad daylight and she felt in dire need of a grooming. Pulling away from the long arms that threatened to surround her, she spoke up, somewhat breathlessly. "H-have you had a chance to speak to Captain Slade about Tegan?"

He stopped his advance, giving her a long, indiscernible look, which she forced herself to match. Finally he spoke, running his hand smoothly up and down her arm. "Jeremiah knew nothing of the murder, but he's checking with the crew as discreetly as he can. If d'Alava knows anything, he's doing an excellent job of keeping it to himself ... and that is not a comforting thought, for it can only mean that he plans to use the information."

"In what way?" Sarah bit her lip expectantly.

"As proof that we've deceived him ... a reason to challenge other truths, or to punish." Stewart gave her a hard look as his mind considered other things. "He's been much too compliant for much too long."

"What are we going to do?" she asked nervously, frightened by Stewart's cold appraisal.

"We're going to continue as before ...."

"But if he knows, if he's planning to punish ...?"

Hard fingers captured her arm, forcing her to cut short her words. His stern voice brooked no argument. "We shall continue as before, Sarah. That is all you need to know."

She realized that he was keeping something to himself and it angered her to think she did not merit his confidence, especially now when so much had happened to draw them closer. Apparently he did not share her feelings and it hurt her more than she was willing to admit. Coolly she raised her clear blue eyes to his and snapped, "Very well. Now would you mind unhanding me so I may prepare for a bath?"

Again he looked at her, his brown eyes curious but uncompromising. "I thought we had seen the last of the shrew after last night."

"You treat me like a child," she bit back.

"Only when you behave as one," he returned dryly, his eyes flickering with mischief as he gave a light tug at the sheet she clutched to her bosom. "Perhaps you would show me that the woman has returned." His dark head bent to place a tantalizing kiss on the hollow between her breasts where the sheet had slipped.

Sarah closed her eyes, aching with longing yet desperately needing his assurance that her body was not the only part of her that pleased him. "I can help, you know," she murmured, a sullen note creeping into her quiet voice.

"Mmm," Stewart assented, his warm lips traversing the softly-rounded crest of her nearly exposed breast, 'by not talking ....'"

Wounded by this obvious dismissal, and fighting for control of the quivering sensations he was producing, she choked, "How long will it be before my body holds as little interest for you as my opinions do now? And what then?"

With maddening slowness, Stewart raised his dark head, his piercing eyes inscrutable as they were held in the wide, uncertain stare that challenged them. *Don't you see?* she wanted to cry, *that I have to believe that we are still companions, equals, as we were before last night? I've won your respect and trust, or at least I thought so. But now, because I cannot deny you anymore, because I need your body as surely as I need breath, I have become nothing more than an amusement, a diversion, as dozens of others before me.* But pride kept her silent, even as his disruptive gaze bore into her.

Finally, in a controlled yet sarcastic tone, he spoke. "Ah yes. I see your game. The virgin sacrifice demands reciprocity, does it not? And I was so overwhelmed by your beauty, I forgot the price." His lean fingers grasped her trembling hands in an iron grip. "Marriage, wasn't it?" Her blue eyes raised sharply in surprise, while his eyes flickered in sinister amusement. "I see I've remembered correctly. Marriage will assure that even though I grow tired of your opinions and your body," he mocked, "you need never worry that you have forfeited too much."

His cruelty threatened her composure as she gulped to hold back the angry, hurt tears. "But as you'll recall," he continued mercilessly, "that matter has already been taken care of. You are my wife, Sarah, unconditionally so, now that our union has been consummated, and as such," he added, his voice a disturbing mixture of ire and seduction, "you have no right to deny me anything."

"No!" she cried, yanking herself away from his hands and plunging toward the foot of the huge bed, oblivious to her nakedness. Misunderstanding her simple need for respect, it was clear that he believed she was after legal ties instead. Hot, fitful tears rained down her distraught face as she crouched on her knees to face him, her dark hair falling wildly about her pale, tense, yet breathtaking, body. "Did you think I would hold you to that paper? We spoke no vows to each other, and – and last night," she struggled feebly, "last night changed nothing."

But it had changed everything. Sarah feared he would see that fact in her eyes and hastily wiped her tears with the palm of her hand. "I-I made you do what you did last night. I admit it," she choked. "You are absolved of all responsibility for my weakness."

"And if there's a child?" His calm voice introduced the thought matter-of-factly as he looked at her with polite interest, the anger completely gone from his handsome face. But Sarah was far from controlled, her mind reeling from this sudden thought – a possibility she had never even considered.

"No! There will not be a child!" she bit back.

"And why not?" Stewart voiced with indifferent curiosity, though his eyes softened with humor at her declaration.

Sarah's mind had been racing to answer this question even before he asked it. She tossed her head petulantly as if to hide her lack of certainty, "Because – because I don't *want* a child!" she snapped at him.

He laughed out loud, infuriating her, as he lifted his legs onto the bed and leaned back against the carved headboard, completely relaxed. "Were that a reliable method of preventing conception, Sarah, there would be no bastards."

His last word brought a diversion to mind and she quickly used it. "And how many bastards have you sired, sir?"

If she had hoped to shake his self-assurance, the attempt failed, for he responded evenly and without hesitation. "None."

Inexplicably she was relieved, but even as the conversation was becoming increasingly embarrassing, Sarah fought to parry. "Then I would assume you are incapable of fathering children."

"Let's just say I have been careful not to," he replied undaunted by her insinuation.

Unsure of his meaning, her knowledge grossly lacking in this delicate area, she was compelled to ask, "And were you ... careful ... with me?"

"No." His calm, offhand admission hit her like a blow to the stomach and she expelled the breath she had been holding in anticipation of his reply.

Desolate with dread and confusion, but determined to hold her head high in the face of his coolness, Sarah squared her shoulders and responded stiffly, "We have both been rather foolish, don't you think?" He shrugged at her grim judgment.

"But if there is a child, I will manage. You need not fear ... an entanglement."

Staring down at her hands clenched nervously on her bare thighs, feeling the full weight of her body's lustful misdeeds, she added, "You made your intentions clear from the beginning. It was I who-who," she faltered miserably, "lost my head." Ashamed of her confession and her tears, Sarah hung her head, letting her thick hair protect her from his penetrating appraisal.

In an instant, Stewart closed the distance between them, placing his hand under her trembling chin, forcing her face up until her tearful blue gaze met his. "Damn your pride," he whispered gently, his voice holding none of the vehemence of his words. "Do you actually believe I would desert you if you carried my own child?" Her mournful eyes told him that she did. "And that you were solely responsible for last night?" Wryly he commented, his thumb softly stroking her stiff jaw. "After all this time and the things we have been through, you still believe me to be an ogre, don't you?"

"Your words are sometimes ... cruel," she whispered, helplessly affected by his nearness and his sudden switch to tenderness.

"Your skepticism of me provokes a mean temper," he admitted, lifting her tangled hair to reveal a supple breast, which he touched with burning fingers, his eyes never leaving her face. "But enough of this pointless bickering. Can we not find a peaceful truce ... as lovers?"

A shuddering sigh escaped her sagging lips as she found herself responding to his practiced caress, her eyes closing with the deliciousness of the warmth spreading through her. "This is madness," she gasped. "We are not being wise .... There is so much to consider ...."

His lips found the delicacy of her slender neck. "Some things, my darling, are meant to be. No amount of reasoning could make me stop wanting you now," he whispered, pressing his lips to hers. "And you feel the same ... or would you deny it?" he added teasingly.

"No," she whispered truthfully, the last ounce of restraint crumbling as his lips took full possession of their tender target.

She was actually humming. After all that had gone wrong, all the confusion, the tragedy, the grief, her complete surrender to Stewart's power over her, and the new, intensely precarious situation she now found herself in, Sarah was humming! Even this realization brought a melodic, tinkling laugh to her lips as she luxuriated in a soothingly tepid bath.

"You feel better, yes?" Galena smiled happily, entering the bathing chamber. "I worry you be sick, but good now, yes?"

Sarah smiled guiltily as the maid walked by with fresh linens. "I think the heat finally took its toll," she lied, splashing the fragrant water on her arm, "but this is so refreshing, I feel wonderful. I may just stay here all day."

"Oh no," Galena replied seriously, turning from her task. "The Señor ask for you. He want you come to dinner, or he worry!" It was clear that Galena considered d'Alava's every wish her command.

"Oh, Galena, don't fret," Sarah smiled nonchalantly. "I was merely joking. Besides, if I stay in here much longer, I shall be all shriveled."

"Very good," the servant beamed, her white teeth contrasting starkly with her dark skin. "I wait outside to dry your pretty hair."

"Fine," Sarah answered sweetly, if somewhat absently. "Thank you very much."

Grateful when the door closed and she was once again alone, Sarah sank more comfortably into the pleasant bath, closing her eyes in dreamy contentment as she contemplated the previous events of the day.

She could still feel the tingling excitement of Stewart's knowing touch, blushing at her ardor surprisingly unhindered by the lack of darkness. She had amazed herself with her boldness in helping him remove his clothes and the way she had returned his kisses with feverish longing. Again the magical, mysterious moment of complete and willing capitulation had seized her as she lay breathless beneath his long, perfect body, listening to the eagerness with which he rasped her name.

And then, later, as she was cradled in his protective embrace, he had carefully explained why he had chosen to withhold information from her. It was not, as she feared, because he did not trust her intelligence, or her silence. "The less you know of our plans, the easier it will be for you to deal with d'Alava," Stewart had explained. "Quite surely, he believes you to be the weak link, for his regard of women has never been high while his confidence in his ability to charm them is great. We expect he'll use whatever he knows or may learn against you to get to us. If you know nothing, your safety is much more certain. I simply do not want you placed in a position where you may be compromised, so, my sweet, ignorance will be your best safeguard."

"I should not be this content," she giggled, raising a long, slender leg, letting the water trickle downward, "but I simply cannot concentrate on anything but the change that has come over me ... now that he is my ... lover." The intimate word brought a sigh to her still passion-swollen lops and an attractive blush to her cheeks.

It amazed her that the reality of the situation was practically meaningless to her. Here she was, a crazed pirate's captive, her life in danger. She had loved ones who may never see or hear from her again. Her maid was dead, brutally murdered. Not only that, but she was pretending to be married, enjoined in an illicit affair with a man who never even professed to love her, flirting with the possibility of producing a child and all its disastrous consequences, and yet, she had never felt so alive or happy.

"Well Father," she whispered, poignantly recalling the day he announced his plans to send her to America, "you wanted me to be available to the workings of fate, to see what was beyond my own doorstep. But somehow I cannot believe you had all this in mind."

CHAPTER 27

More than six weeks had gone by since Simon d'Alava had confiscated Stewart and Jeremiah's ship, and despite the ever-present sense that events were coming to a head, nothing seemed to change.

It had been two weeks since Tegan's death and still there was no indication that the pirates had discovered anything amiss, even though the meals had become decidedly mediocre and tasteless. Often Sarah pushed away her barely-touched plate, nauseated by the undercooked meats and overdone vegetables, not to mention d'Alava's grating good nature. It was obvious he was aware of much more than he divulged, enjoying to the fullest his power over his statured guests.

The interminable waiting was taking its toll, heightened by the blind chess game being played out by victim and captor alike. Jeremiah, ever pleasant and receptive, had acquired the steely gaze of a man about to lose his patience, though his voice never betrayed the tension that etched deeper lines into his craggy features. Stewart was more transparent, occasionally letting slip a barbed comment that might have done harm if only d'Alava had chosen to take it as an insult, and not a jest. When such a lapse in Stewart's ironclad control occurred, Sarah would catch his hard gaze, holding it warmly and reassuringly in her own, until she saw the muscles of his jaw relaxing.

She knew there was more than impatience at work here. Stewart and Jeremiah were exhausted. For the past four nights, Sarah had awakened to find herself alone in the huge bed, Stewart having gone on some mission of which he dared not speak. She would doze fitfully until it was near daylight when he would fall heavily into bed beside her, wrapping his tired limbs about her as he fell asleep almost instantly. Several times she had almost blurted one of the many questions wracking her brain, but she sensed that her mute trust meant a great deal more to him than any curiosity or offer of assistance. So she chose to hold her silence.

Her new lack of contrariness surprised her. Gone was the need to assert herself in the face of Stewart's powerful presence. Instead she exuded an air of calm strength and quiet affection, a part of her nature only her family had known intimately.

And if this change bemused her, then Stewart was completely bewildered. More than once she noticed his demeanor prepare for battle, only to relax in stunned disbelief when she cheerfully acquiesced. He never commented on this change, but she could not help but notice that he watched her more carefully, as if struggling to match the complacent woman before him with the mutinous girl he had come to know so well, one whose return he expected at any moment.

In a way, she was comforted by his skepticism, even though there was no longer any need of it. She had become addicted to his lovemaking and his tenderness toward her, but thankfully he did not seem to take this for granted. Her pride had been so totally banished that she knew she would give herself to him under any circumstances, but he continued to woo her in a way that made her feel unique and special. Even though she had now joined the ranks of the many comely wenches who had passed beneath him.

That was the dark side of this affair, she admitted reluctantly. No matter what he said about his own complicity, or responsibility, with the last vestiges of her self-respect, she knew she could never hold him to her. She could not deny finding solace for her conscience in the marriage they acted out under d'Alava's watchful eye, but its duration was temporary, even if its consequences were permanent. Stewart's freedom, his independence, was something she vowed never to be liable for taking away. She renewed this daily pledge in the tearful aftermath of their passion as she lay nestled in Stewart's arms while he caught precious minutes of sleep before setting about his nocturnal business.

In these moments, she would hungrily fill her memory with the handsome, almost boyish innocence of his face in repose, the feel of his chest against her soft cheek, the way strong legs and arms possessively surrounded her, and the uneven thumping of blood through her veins as her body slowly recovered from his complete mastery of it.

At such times, she prayed for the strength of character to demand nothing more of him, and hoped that these sensory remembrances would be enough to see her through the years of impending spinsterhood, for despite her innocence, something told her that it would be a fruitless search if she hoped to find another with whom she could achieve such blinding rapture.

And there was more. This was the love of her life, she had finally admitted, and though their time together was fleeting, at least she had been spared the emptiness of going through life without ever knowing such rapture.

But more often, the future was a reality that Sarah kept naively at bay. Held in the warmth of Stewart's approval and his physical need of her, it was hardly a chore to push the pain and uncertainly aside. She had finally accepted what he had known all along: that she was a woman capable of great passion, and he was the tinder that set her aflame. The fact that he did not love her generally seemed of little consequence, for when caught in the throes of his all-consuming desire, it was easy to believe that her love for him was enough. It was the only secret she had left, and she guarded it with fierce possessiveness.

CHAPTER 28

"Señor wishes to see you." Galena was nervous. Her huge brown eyes and fidgeting fingers made it obvious. Sarah returned a calm but frowning look as she absent-mindedly returned the book she was reading to the table beside her.

"Mmm, I wonder why," she replied casually, hoping that her wish for a clue was not too apparent. She strode to the dressing table, patting her hair in feigned interest.

But Galena, usually happy to talk to her new mistress, was uncharacteristically elusive. "I tell him you resting, maybe?"

Sarah returned a quick, studied look, though her voice gave away none of her sudden apprehension. "Don't be silly, Galena. I'm not resting. Tell Señor d'Alava that I will be there presently."

For an instant, Galena stood riveted to the spot, struggling, it seemed, to speak. But when Sarah turned to give Galena her full attention, the wiry girl abruptly nodded and whirled around to leave.

A wave of fear broke over Sarah's calm demeanor and she had a strong urge to press the puzzling maid for some clue as to why she was so upset about making this summons. But she had never allowed herself to compromise the maid's loyalty in the past, and she would not now, despite a clear foreboding that something was amiss, something that Galena very much wanted to help her avoid.

D'Alava's request in itself was unusual, Sarah reflected, watching the small girl hastily leave the room. He had never intruded on her privacy in the many weeks of their captivity, even though it would have been easily within his ability to single her out for his company, since Stewart and Jeremiah spent long hours with their crew restoring the pirate's dilapidated kingdom.

Rarely had she ever been alone with him, and never for more than a short time. Some evenings, while she and the pirate were engaged in a friendly game of chess or backgammon in the parlor, Stewart and Jeremiah would retire to the adjoining promenade, smoking expensive cheroots and talking casually, though never loud enough to be heard clearly. D'Alava was outrageously flirtatious at these times but never seriously threatening. But now Sarah wondered if that were only a ruse to gain her confidence.

An involuntary shudder passed through her as she smoothed the skirt of her bright blue lawn dress, chosen for its cool sleeves and light fabric. With a steadying breath, she pulled open the bedroom door and walked determinedly through the sparsely furnished sitting room to the wide hallway.

As she entered the parlor, d'Alava turned from the promenade doorway, smiling eagerly at the sight of the young woman whose presence enhanced any space she happened to occupy. The stout pirate was dressed casually in a loose muslin shirt, dark trousers and boots that did much to hide the faults of excess that his leisurely life on the island perpetrated. His crackling black eyes and debonair moustache furthered his image as a swashbuckler, and were it not for the ominous-looking pistol and dagger hooked to his wide leather belt, Sarah might have found it easy to smile at his imposing character. As it was, she matched his gaze with a benign expression. "You wished to see me, Señor?"

"Not a moment has passed since we met that I do not wish to see you, Señora," d'Alava replied dramatically in his heavily-accented voice, reaching for her hand and kissing it warmly. She winced at the contact but steeled herself against revealing her discomfort at his noxious caress. "Would you favor me with a game of chess this afternoon, *querida?*" he inquired smoothly as he reluctantly took leave of her slim fingers.

"I'd be delighted, Señor," Sarah replied coolly, though his simple request did nothing to quell her foreboding. The Señor bore the look of a cat contemplating the consumption of a defenseless canary. With resounding conviction, Sarah knew that chess was not the name of the game he had chosen to play this day.

"*Mirabilis*, perhaps?" he offered her the beverage politely after she had seated herself at the ornate marble chess table, its jewel-encrusted pieces standing up as a formidable-looking, though ineffectual, barrier between them. A clear head was essential, but to refuse would invite his scrutiny.

"Lovely," she smiled pleasantly, examining the board in feigned interest. "Shall I begin, or is it your turn to open the match?"

He chuckled, his back to her, as he poured the golden liquid from a crystal decanter on the buffet. "Eager to conquer me again? Perhaps my playing will surprise you today," he murmured potently.

No doubt, Sarah thought to herself as she felt her stomach muscles tightening with tension. "So you've been toying with me, Señor? And I thought you were not the kind to let others win."

A leering smile creased his swarthy face as he set the flute before her and took his place across the board. "You know me well. But the war's the thing, eh? Battles?" He gave a gesture that showed his unconcern for whether a little skirmish ended in his favor.

Willing her fingers to refrain from the barest hint of trembling, Sarah sent her first pawn on its course, knowing with deep-seated but inexplicable conviction that the end of the war was upon them and that the enemy had already begun to taste the fruits of victory.

A full half hour went by without a word passing between them, a most uncomfortable change of habit. But what was unsaid reverberated with fierce intensity through the expansively cluttered room. Anxious for the Señor to tip his hand, Sarah struggled to quell her desire to open the conversation, remembering her father's advice that the party forced to break a pregnant silence lost his advantage. Never in her life had she needed the upper hand more desperately; stoically she held her tongue.

"Never have I seen you play with such intensity," d'Alava said, his indolent voice at last breaking the oppressive silence.

Sarah raised her sooty lashes, her deep blue eyes betraying nothing of her inner turmoil. "I intend to win."

His next words brought a wave of fear that prickled the smooth skin below her hairline. "I think perhaps that is out of your hands." To emphasize his statement, d'Alava moved, trapping her king with consummate skill. "Check."

Fury and terror mixed a potent brew within her that constricted her chest. It was all Sarah could do to mask her emotional upheaval with an inscrutable smile. How could he have done this to her when she'd been watching so carefully? But it wasn't over yet. *Please God, not yet!*

So intent on the board, Sarah did not notice d'Alava rising and practically cried out when his thick hand rested on her arm. "More *licor*?"

Her cheeks bloomed with color as she struggled to maintain her composure. "No, *gracias*."

He chuckled and walked to the buffet, lazily calling over his shoulder, "Are you ready to concede, *querida*?"

"But Señor," she pouted coyly, "the game is not over."

Exuding a powerful degree of self-confidence, d'Alava leaned his bulk against the buffet, crossing his arms upon his wide chest and perusing her with studied pleasure. "You disappoint me, *Señora* Chamberlain. I have always considered you to be one of the few members of the fairer sex to be blessed with a clear sense of reality." His hand reached up to lazily stroke his chin. "The game is *terminado*."

He knows! There was no doubt of it for the truth that she was not Stewart's bride and the pirate's glee over discovering their captives' charade was glimmering in his gaze of burning coal. And how he intended to proceed on this information was evident in his undisguised expression of lust. So that was the reason for Galena's distress; she knew his summons would lead to malevolence.

"I beg your pardon?" The mock curiosity was proffered with the greatest effort as Sarah's thoughts raced to plan a defense against horrors too hideous to contemplate.

"Would you deny your farce and insult me further, *mi dulce*?" d'Alava asked nonchalantly."My good friends were foolish to take advantage of my honorable nature. They know my plundering does not extend to another man's wife." His voice dropped seductively. "But you are the bride of no man, are you, Lady Sarah Tremont?"

Her breath paralyzed in her throat, Sarah rose stiffly, a haunting sense of doom threatening to destroy her composure. With a quiet control she did not feel, she replied, "I do not know why you feel you have reason to doubt my marital status, but I assure you, Señor d'Alava, Stewart Chamberlain and I are in every way husband and wife."

The pirate snickered. "I do not doubt Chamberlain's been riding you well. I can attest to his hearty appetite for feminine flesh. And women do find him rather irresistible, though I cannot see why." She cringed at his crudity. "But marriage? Pfuh!" He pushed himself away from the table and began moving toward her.

"Stewart would no sooner strap himself with baggage than I, though I cannot blame him for not wanting to share you." His eyes burned her with their wicked perusal, and she stepped back just as his hand rose to touch her cheek. He shook his head as if to mock her attempts to avoid him. "Your stallion is a jealous rake." He scratched his wide chest beneath the shirt. "I have proof of that, but you will see soon enough."

As much as it wracked her to maintain her poise, Sarah knew it was her only chance. Somehow she sensed that d'Alava would show no mercy to a shrinking, pleading hostage. Better to maintain her dignity if only to buy much-needed time.

"Señor," she bit back in righteous indignation, keeping a safe distance from him, "I had not thought a man of your considerable intelligence and charm would find it necessary to resort to intimidation to find appeasement for his lusts. I do not know what reasons you have for believing this nonsense, but Stewart is my husband. Touch me and you are a dead man, Señor." Ice cold blue eyes lent emphasis to her chilling threat, but d'Alava was unperturbed.

"Spirited words for a helpless – and I might add, lying – wench," the pirate chortled. "Do not toy with me, *Señorita*, for I have waited for your charms much too long ... and unnecessarily." His eyes narrowed ominously. "It would not take much to provoke me into punishing you for your deceit." He viewed her hungrily. "'Twould be a pity for such lovely flesh to suffer permanent disfigurement ...."

"Stewart would kill you." It was a weak defense, despite her venomous delivery, but Sarah knew of no other way to gain a reprieve. Furtively she judged the distance between where she stood and the parlor doorway behind her, depressed by what she saw.

D'Alava grinned obscenely. "He has already been given that chance ... and failed. Your lover will not have such an opportunity again."

"You underrate my husband's will if you think harm to me will go unavenged."

"But, *querida*, you forget. Chamberlain is also my prisoner, *no*? Do you think me so careless that I would leave myself unprotected from a jealous rival?" He waited patiently for his words to sink in and laughed, when, with a start, Sarah realized just what he was saying.

Gripping her hands together to quell their shaking, she demanded, "What have you done to him? Where is Stewart?" The room threatened to swim past her as she waited for his answer. That Stewart might be powerless to rescue her was something she had never once considered. It had been the basis for her bravado, and now, for the first time, naked terror engulfed her as she saw the evil depths in d'Alava's malicious black eyes telling her to believe what she could barely give name to.

"Now you are frightened, *no*?" he announced, casually smoothing his moustache across his sneering lip. "*Buena*. Perhaps you will not be so defiant, *querida*, now that you see the inevitability of your fate."

"What has happened to Stewart?" she whispered, mesmerized by the horror overtaking her. "Tell me."

"A pity," he replied in mock sympathy, slowing moving toward her. "It was an accident, I believe. One that often befalls prisoners who try to escape." He nodded his reluctant assent to the heart-rending misery etched on her strained features. Taking her suddenly limp arm, he led her, unchallenged, to a settee, talking most pityingly all the while.

"Did he vow never to leave you? It pains me to tell you that that was exactly his plan." Searching her wide, vacant eyes as he seated her, he added hastily, "But of course he meant to come back for you ... perhaps," insuring the rooting of the seeds of doubt.

"You haven't told me," she murmured dully, her lips barely moving. "Is he ...?" *Don't say it. Please don't say it. I could accept his leaving me, but please don't tell me he is ....*

"Dead," d'Alava finished solemnly. The groan that escaped her lips might as well have been perpetrated by a blow to her stomach. "A nasty duty I have accepted for myself, *no?*" d'Alava continued, seemingly oblivious to her pain. "Galena offered to bear the bad tidings, but," he pontificated, "I am the master of this island, and thought it only fitting ... my sweet, you are as pale as a ghost. Some sherry, perhaps?"

She nodded unconsciously. Anything to stop his incessant patter, anything to mitigate the fierce churning of every fiber in her body. A blackness threatened to overwhelm her and she bent her head, doubling over to ward off a swoon. *Stewart dead?* Her chest ached with unspent tension; her limbs were devoid of feeling, like heavy logs attached to her quivering torso. His handsome face flashed before her, brown eyes crinkling a greeting as they awoke in each other's arms. *Was it only this morning?* His pleasant, almost ironic humor as he prepared for the day, clothing his splendid sun-ripened body in tight breeches and a loose shirt as she watched secretly, shyly admiring the lean rippling flesh, his muscles stretched and honed by his labors.

Huddled pathetically there in d'Alava's parlor, the reality that he had planned an escape without her created a suffering nearly as scorching as his death. And had he succeeded, she would still be here, dreading the insidious plans the malevolent cutthroat had made for her.

Only Stewart would not be dead, a voice deep within her soul cried out. Was this the price for loving? That he could use her to survive, then leave her defenseless, and she would still grieve his death? *Yes,* she admitted with humiliation that threatened to make her physically sick. Sarah clamped her hand over her mouth, clutching her waist with the other as the room began to spin around her. With an inhuman cry, she stumbled off the couch, raced unheeded through the parlor doors out onto the promenade where she hung over the balustrade, violently ill.

After a time, she heard sauntering footsteps from behind and knew that d'Alava had joined her. Too weak and feverish to protest, she suffered silently while he patted her forehead with a dampened handkerchief, then tucked the cloth in her dangling fingers so she could use it to tidy her face.

"So you did care for him," d'Alava stated not unkindly.

"He was my husband," she answered blandly, unable to pick her elbows off the railing.

"Maybe he promised you marriage, *querida*, but that was the extent of it. I do not bluff to learn the truth, only to make others admit it."

"I do not know what you're talking about."

D'Alava sighed laboriously and moved to a half-sitting position on the balustrade. "There was another woman onboard your ship," he offered matter-of-factly, "though the credit for her discovery goes to my faithful servant, Turgot." Sarah tensed apprehensively, but continued to lean over the balcony, staring at the dense foliage beyond, her body pounded into languor by the heaping of one nightmare upon another. "You see, Turgot had a weakness for young boys ...." and when he saw her clutch the handkerchief over her mouth, added, "Not unusual for a man too long at sea, though Turgot carries his fetish wherever he abides. He was most satisfied with the arrangements your captain made to put the waif to work in the kitchen. Saved him the inconvenience of seeking the 'boy' out in the prisoners' quarters." Sarah's heart plummeted with the realization of their role in Tegan's murder, and suddenly her eyes were blinded by tears. D'Alava continued, mindless of her torture.

"He courted your little mute unsuccessfully – though one who can't utter a protest is as good as willing in my book, *no*?" When that failed to arouse her, he accelerated with force. "And what a surprise?" D'Alava laughed gleefully and it was all Sarah could do to keep from being sick again.

"He-he raped her?" she choked, the tears sliding down her ashen face.

"Well you don't think after all her hard work, she was going to acquiesce without a protest?" the pirate rejoined playfully. "But Turgot has a short temper and just enough brains to detest being made a fool. That girl paid dearly for your saintly lover's cunning ... just as you will pay, *sí?*" His black eyes narrowed threateningly.

But Sarah was past the point of caution. "You loathsome, disgusting bastard!" With a swift movement that belied his cumbersome size, d'Alava gripped her wrist, spinning her body to press against his. She struggled but every maneuver seemed to bring her closer to his repulsive form. Finally, she tossed head aside and stood rigidly still, willing back the nausea that threatened to engulf her. "Watch your tongue, *querida*," he warned, so quietly yet with so much menace that a cold shiver raced up her spine. "There is nothing between you and unspeakable torture save myself. You would do well to placate me with the same favor you dispensed to your self-seeking rake. Perhaps this time you will fare better ...."

Bowing her head in submission, her body too frail to resist and her mind grief-stricken and confused, Sarah was nonetheless relieved when d'Alava released his grip, allowing her to cling to the railing of the promenade. Eager to gloat still, the pirate continued his account of the discovery of their charade. "Seeing that Chamberlain had disguised the identity of one female, it was only logical to assume the other was engaged in pretense as well."

"You examined the marriage documents, did you not?" Sarah rejoined without spirit, knowing that it was hopeless to even dare believe that wedlock would save her now, now that she was ... a widow. *God, what a hollow, heartless word.*

"Oh, the Special License serves the letter of the law," d'Alava snickered, "but not the spirit. Chamberlain take a wife? I had my doubts from the beginning, but you seemed such a sweet, sheltered dove, I truly did not wish to see you suffer the crudities of a pirate hijacking.

"Call it a character flaw, if you will," he beamed proudly, "but you aroused certain ... how shall I say ... fatherly ... instincts. Besides, I had no desire to vent aggression on close friends after

215

such a successful tour of duty." His equanimity was revolting. Sarah knew a great longing to lean farther forward and fall the eight feet to the hard earth below. Perhaps God in his mercy would assuage this torture with a fatal broken neck. But she was too much of a coward. Admitting it brought more cold tears to her tangled lashes.

And still the pirate kept up his relentless monologue. "I was perfectly content to play the gracious host, even if it meant giving you and that horny stud free reign to carry on your ill-fated little tryst. I might have offered the same hospitality even knowing the truth about you," he added, in a tone that forced her to cast an eye toward his face.

He surprised her with an angry, smoldering look. "You smug, little whore!" Her breath caught sharply in her throat and she sidled away in renewed fear. "The both of you, laughing at my stupidity as you tumbled in my bed!" His chest was heaving with the effects of his sudden wrath, and Sarah saw the dark, mad glaze of his beady eyes. "Nobody deceives me and lives to tell about it ... at least not until today."

"Wh-what do you mean?" Sarah choked, grasping her shoulders, hugging herself tightly to stop the shaking of her limbs.

"Chamberlain paid for his sins ... lying, making a fool of me, and trying to escape," the Spaniard replied. "Why should both of you suffer the same fate? Why should I punish myself for your conniving, when your torture could be my rapture?" His stubbly hand reached out and pinched her chin, forcing her to stare straight into his burning black eyes. "For as long as you amuse me, you'll do your penance flat on your back."

"No ... no, please ...." she whispered tragically, her blue eyes wide and glassy with sickening horror. Never could she endure his cruel touch, his disgusting, selfish embraces, his vile possession of her tender body. But was there any choice, now that she was so desperately alone and helpless? Feverishly her brain struggled to bring forth a defense, even a stall, anything to keep this barbarian at bay. But it wasn't until he leaned forward to press sneering lips to the crawling flesh of her neck that the thought occurred to her.

"Please don't hurt me, Señor," she pleaded in a small voice. "I beg for your mercy. You see, I-I carry a child."

CHAPTER 29

D'Alava stopped in midpoint, his pitchblende eyes searing right through her. Immediately Sarah regretted her rashness, for there was no basis for the statement's truth, and the pirate would know soon enough that she was lying. But she had committed herself and returned his look with all the assuredness she could muster.

His thick fingers dug into the smooth flesh of her jaw before he carelessly flung her away to allow himself a thorough inspection of her tall, slim form. Concentrating on her well-rounded breasts, tiny waist and slender hips, he spat, "You are lying. And I thought you had more sense than to attempt to deceive me again."

"'Tis the truth," she implored, "though the time has not been long."

"How long?" he bit back impatiently.

"T-two months, perhaps less." Seeing that he was completely unconvinced, she hastily added, "I-I have not been well, so I am still ... rather thin."

"Too thin," he muttered cruelly, grabbing her arm in a biting hold, "for me to believe your feeble story. And it makes no difference anyway. I want you even if you are harboring Chamberlain's *bastardo*!"

"Señor, I beg of you," Sarah choked, the tears streaming down as he maliciously pulled her quaking form against his chest. "Please do not kill my baby. It-it is all I have left."

"Did Chamberlain stop his nightly exercise because of your 'delicate' condition ... if indeed you are so encumbered," d'Alava sneered. "I think not!"

"My God, Señor," Sarah whimpered hysterically as his teeth sank into the sensitive flesh of her shoulder, his arms rendering her helpless against his merciless assault. "Do you care so little for what has happened to me? Can you not give me some time?"

His head shot up and he spoke as if possessed by demons. "Time? You want time? After all the days you have stolen with your treachery? You prevaricating, high-born bitch! You will learn soon that *I* dictate the moment, and it is *now!*"

With a contemptuous yank that nearly removed her arm from its socket, d'Alava dragged his terrorized prey back through the balcony doors into the parlor. Gasping and stumbling blindly in his wake, Sarah was in no way prepared for the scene that followed when they reached the great foyer, whose stairs would lead them to d'Alava's private chambers.

It was a dream, she was sure, as sure as she could be of anything in this hideous nightmare she was living. A presence, so pervasive, so real that she screamed before she actually saw the shadowy form of a man stepping silently from beneath the winding staircase on the other side of the three-storied hall.

Alerted by her cry, d'Alava whirled about, instinctively forcing her back against his chest as his free hand drew the pistol from its sheath. He aimed it at the slowly approaching figure. "Let her go, Simon, and make peace with your Maker."

The voice. So familiar. Cruel, unforgiving. Yet, a balm for the senses. Sarah stared, her emotions rising to joy and falling to despair with each furious beat of her heart. Had she lost consciousness? Was it a nightmare, this dear, sweet vision of the only man in the world who would ever have her love? "Stewart," she whispered tearfully, prayerfully, hoping against hope that the portrait would not fade away at the sound of her voice.

"A cruel act of fortune that you somehow escaped your intended demise," d'Alava uttered coldly, his breath pricking as it stirred the hair above Sarah's ear. "For now you will suffer a slow, painful death as you observe the submission of your harlot to her new lover." As if to emphasize his words, the pirate's restraining hand rose from Sarah's waist to clamp painfully on her breast. Impulsively, she struggled, but it was useless. His grip was too strong, too hurtful. The man, who looked so much like Stewart, did not flinch, though his dark eyes narrowed imperceptibly, dangerously.

"You have one shot, d'Alava." The confident, resonant voice seemed to reverberate throughout the house, sending chills

219

of trepidation through Sarah's abused body. "God help you if you miss."

Fearlessly, the unarmed man moved another step closer, his mystical arrogance having a sure effect on the couple before him.

Suddenly, without warning, d'Alava turned the barrel of the pistol inward so that it stuck painfully into Sarah's ribs. When she gasped, the pirate jerked her back more closely to his chest. "One more step and she and the child are dead!"

That warning, so desperately offered, stopped the apparition cold, an unearthly glint of pure, unadulterated loathing seeping from every fiber of his being.

Never had Sarah seen such a ghoulish, heinous sight as the total aura of revulsion that emanated from this man. It wasn't Stewart, and yet, it was. Her body shook from the effects of the malevolent hatred passing over her to the man who clutched her more tightly to him. D'Alava sensed it too. She could feel his body cringe. *Did this mean ... could it be ... was it really?*

A blackness pulled at her eyelids. Her knees buckled, given unannounced to a will of their own. The floor was suddenly there to meet her cheek as a gunshot echoed about her.

"Sarah! Wake up. There's too little time. Wake up!" Insulted by the quick, painless slap on her cheek, Sarah's eyes flew open to see a thin, brown face creased with worry hovering over her.

"Galena?" She frowned in confusion. She had expected d'Alava to be the perpetrator of such abuse. "Where-where is ...?"

A relieved grin swept away the maid's clouded expression. "Señora, you awake! She be awake!" The last statement was directed toward another presence, and Sarah closed her eyes again, swallowing weakly, praying for the blackness to return. Anything to postpone the inevitable.

"No you don't," a deep voice warned her gently. "There's no time for you to leave us again."

Daring to believe her ears, Sarah gingerly turned her head, which was pillowed in Galena's lap, her eyes fluttering open once more. "Stewart?" Her childlike voice verified her disbelief.

"At your service," he chuckled wryly, his brown eyes warm and reassuring, "and not a moment too soon." His large, warm hand found her smaller, cold one and he gripped it firmly as it to prove that he was real and not a ghost.

"Stewart," she whispered reverently, "I thought you were ...."

"Thought d'Alava did me in, eh?" he mocked her playfully. "You never did have much faith in me."

"No, you don't understand ...." she protested, trying to rise.

"Easy now," he ordered pressing her back into Galena's lap. "Are you ready to get up?"

Sarah nodded, and with their help, was lifted shakily to her feet. Galena scurried off the floor behind her. Only half out of need for support, Sarah twined her arms around Stewart's waist, resting her head on his comforting chest, reveling in the safe feeling of his arm about her shoulders. Her head was clear, knowing no dream, no matter how beautiful, could match the intensity of her happiness at this moment. "Thank God you're alive."

"And d'Alava dead!" Galena rejoiced, clapping her hands in glee.

"He is?" Sarah asked, looking from one face to the other for assurance.

"Your man be the best pirate I *never* saw, the way he use that knife." The maid offered eagerly. "Bastard killed with he own blade, just so!" She made a slicing gesture beneath her chin, adding a sound effect for emphasis. "I see everything. Great show! You miss best part. But that all right. You still see what left." She pointed to a place behind Sarah's shoulder, to which Sarah began to turn until Stewart stopped her.

"I don't think Sarah's quite prepared for the sight of a corpse, Galena," knowing his guess was correct when he felt her shudder. "Besides, we have to go."

"Where are we going?" Sarah looked up curiously, drinking in the sight of his gloriously handsome face.

Stewart shook his head disbelievingly. "You don't think we've gone to all this trouble to stay on the island? Sarah, we're escaping. We're going to America."

It must be a dream. So much had happened in the past few hours that escape had paled in comparison to survival. And now she was to have both! "Can Galena come with us?" the spontaneous question was met by Stewart's speculative glance.

"I think that is up to her, Sarah, though we would be happy to welcome her."

"Galena, will you come?" Sarah pleaded, reaching out to squeeze the dark-skinned young woman's arm. "I-I don't have a maid any longer," she told her sadly, "and you've been so good to us."

"Señora," Galena smiled warmly, returning the affection, "you make me very happy. But I not want to leave my people. I safe here now that bad pirate gone."

"Are they, Stewart?" Sarah asked, her face echoing concern for the waifish girl. "Is she safe remaining here?"

"D'Alava and Turgot are dead and they were behind all this." He spread his arm to indicate the mansion and the feudal system it represented. "Galena told me the other pirates are more or less peaceful, accepted as members of the community. I think she's safe," he reassured her, smiling at the grinning maid. "Perhaps she can now enjoy a life of her own, among her people. We could not give her that in my country."

"I shall never forget you, Galena," Sarah murmured tearfully, turning from Stewart to give the girl a heartfelt hug. "Your kindness and friendship have more than made up for our captivity."

"You be here always for me," Galena replied, pressing her hands to her breast when Sarah had released her. "Go now, quick!" She gave the other woman a hasty push, waving tearfully as Stewart pulled Sarah toward the front door.

Outside, Stewart made a careful assessment of their jungle surroundings, silently cautioning Sarah not to speak as he led her quickly down the path that ended at the beach. She was brimming with a sense of well-being so pervasive that it never occurred to her to be afraid, not with her small hand tucked safely in Stewart's much larger and stronger one, seeing only the reassuring breadth of his muscled shoulders before her. He was alive and whole, and her crushed and battered soul was resurrected and soaring.

He stopped suddenly and Sarah saw that they were at the edge of the jungle which overlooked a wide expanse of light sand separating them from the slowly incoming tide. Farther out, looking much like a skeletal statue cast about on the restlessly lapping blue waters of the natural cove, was a ship. Stewart's ship. "Damn," he hissed impatiently, "the longboat is gone. We'll have to swim." He turned back to her, his look of preoccupied seriousness leaving her somewhat unsure. "Can you swim?"

Not wishing to disappoint him, she answered, "I-I used to, as a child ...."

With an angry toss of his wind-ruffled hair, he ground out, "This is no bloody wading pool, Sarah. Listen and do exactly as I tell you, do you hear?" She nodded, wide-eyed. "We're going to make a dash for the tide. Don't look around. Just run for your life, do you understand?" She nodded. "As soon as we are well in the water, I want you to climb on my back. Hold on to my shoulders and as your life depends on it, don't let go!" He again surveyed the coastline, and then pulling her up beside him, asked, "Are you ready?"

"I'm ready," she offered firmly, hoping her confident timbre did not reveal the doubts that threatened to unnerve her. The ship seemed a speck on the horizon and the tide would fight their efforts all the way. Stewart was undoubtedly a strong swimmer, but could he make his destination with her clinging to his back?

At least she could run swiftly, as Stewart was soon to note when they began their dash to the sea. Her long-legged strides nearly matched his own and when her skirts threatened to prove an encumbrance, she pulled her hand from his. Without breaking rhythm, she yanked her petticoat from beneath her gown until they pulled away with a ripping sound.

Quickly understanding her action, Stewart grabbed the white material falling out from underneath her blue-flowered skirt and she fairly flew out of the constricting folds, stumbling only slightly over the heap. Her slippered feet hit the chilly waters only seconds before his and she made a high-stepping dash for as long as it was possible in the rising, choppy waves. Feeling strong and exhilarated by the cool, salty water, Sarah dived into the approaching wall of water, landing back on her feet in the shoulder-deep brine. She looked for Stewart and found him a few yards to her side, whipping the droplets from his suddenly straight hair. When he'd wiped his eyes, he spotted her, calling, "C'mon you brazen mermaid. Hold on to me and let's hope Jeremiah sees us before the pirates do!"

Bouncing up and down on the soft, sandy bottom, she navigated her way to him, grasping his shoulders without another word. Taking one last deep breath, Stewart plunged them into the swirling blue waters and took off in quick, powerful strokes. Sarah, painfully aware of her role as a hindrance, did her level best to hold on tight. But it seemed the longer Stewart swam, the farther away the ship lay anchored. How long could his determined arms and legs propel them before he reached exhaustion?

And then, almost without warning, Sarah spied a vision that was imminently more threatening than the limits of Stewart's endurance. A long boat was coming toward them at great speed. Six or eight men, she could not tell for sure, manned the oars. Pirates!

She must have cried out, for Stewart momentarily broke his feverish pace, casting his gaze about until he, too, spotted the swiftly approaching vessel. There was no way they could reach the ship before they were captured, but Stewart was bound and determined to try. With inhuman fortitude, he forced his fatigue-shaken limbs to move them onward. But even he was forced to admit defeat when the unmistakable ping of gunshot sprayed about them in the treacherous waters.

"Hold your breath," he sputtered over his shoulder and when she nodded, he plunged headlong into the brackish sea, swimming underwater until Sarah thought her chest would explode. Surfacing again amidst a spray of bullets, he repeated his command as Sarah gulped convulsively for life-giving air. Bent on playing this desperate game of hide-and-seek, the swimmers were unaware that another boat had entered the churning waters, fast on a course that, if successful, would cut off the pirates from their prey.

It was a miracle, nothing short of it, Sarah decided when, after she broke water for what could only be the last time, she witnessed the strange scene of one pirate, then another, and still another, falling overboard. They weren't diving, but screaming and plummeting awkwardly. But how ..?

It was Stewart who realized they had been rescued at last, suddenly pulling her arm so she slid off his back, then holding her by the waist as they treaded water. They had been sighted by Jeremiah and it was the *Endeavour's* longboat crew that had been responsible for the shower of bullets, holding off the pirates from their quarry until they were within range to murder.

"We've been saved," Stewart managed to gasp as he watched the lopsided skirmish. The speeding pirates' boat had suddenly become a ghost ship as its crew was annihilated before any had a chance to turn tail and run.

And then they could make out the poised, commanding figure of Captain Slade standing at the bow, two pistols in his hands, directing the oarsmen toward them. Bedraggled, nearly drowned, the two clung to each other, lacking even enough energy to hail their rescuers. And when the vessel finally made its way alongside them, and Sarah felt Jeremiah's steady hands pulling her up, she managed a small "thank you" before falling into a peaceful unconsciousness she wanted to last forever.

CHAPTER 30

It was evening. The dull golden glow of a lantern swinging silently with the rolling ship made dark, yet strangely warm and comforting shadows about the spacious cabin. From among the snuggling folds of the downy comforter draped over her in the oversized bunk, Sarah eyed the familiar surroundings peacefully, knowing full well where she was and that she was safe.

But she was tired, so tired her muscles ached, and there was a briny taste in her mouth, as well as a gnawing emptiness in her stomach. Still the physical discomforts did little to assuage the numbing restfulness that came with knowing all was well.

Or nearly so. As full consciousness was regained, a painful germ of unhappiness fought for dominance of her thoughts. She was safe, rid of the terrible fears that had engulfed her when d'Alava sought to claim her for his own, but the fact remained that divine intervention had saved her, and not the man she loved with all her heart. Oh, it was true that Stewart killed the horrible pirate and had risked his own life to spare hers, but the miserable truth was still a soul-searing reality: Stewart had planned to leave her behind.

But why? Did he really consider her such a burden that she was not worth rescuing? She had made it clear that he owed her nothing for her rash but glorious capitulation. She'd avoided talk of the future, making no demands. Surely he knew she'd gone into their affair with open eyes, and that the conditions she'd so naively laid down months ago had no bearing on their future.

Was he simply a cruel and selfish man? No, her mind argued as a single tear dropped from her lower lash, No, she had experienced too much patience, too many kindnesses at his hands to believe that to be true. Then what? *Why?*

As if on cue, the object of her aggravated thoughts suddenly appeared in the room, coming out of the shadows to

226

carefully study her troubled yet brave smile. "Are you feeling all right?" His deep baritone filled the space between them, making her feel warmer and happier than her previous thoughts had given right to.

"I'm fine, really," she answered quickly, brushing a hand across her dampened cheek and lifting herself up hastily, then smoothing the blankets round her slender form.

"Then why the tears?" he challenged, his dark eyes expressing concern though his jaw held stiff in an inscrutable, distant way, pricking Sarah with wariness. *Was he angry?*

"I am relieved ... exhausted ... I don't know," she shrugged with an attempt at lightheartedness. "Silly of me."

"You've been through quite an ordeal," he announced soberly. His aloofness was understandable in light of what she knew, but no less hurtful. Her mind strove to find something to relieve the tension.

"Are you all right?" By appearance, he looked dashing, carefully groomed and clothed in a thick black jersey and breeches, his complexion robust despite the lines of fatigue on his finely chiseled features.

"That swim was a bit much," he grinned, suddenly lighting up the room, his teeth gleaming white in sharp contrast to his darkened figure, "but otherwise, I am fit. Glad to be off that damned island."

"I, too," Sarah replied shyly, studying her nervous fingers as they fumbled with the hem of the bed sheet. "However did Jeremiah and the crew retake the ship? I thought the men were under constant surveillance."

"It's a long story," Stewart sighed. "Would you rather eat something? You must be hungry."

"I am not nearly as hungry as I am curious. I think I have waited long enough to learn the facts."

Stewart's eyebrows arched slightly, but his voice remained cool. "I was merely seeing to your needs. There's a broth warming on the stove. May I suggest you eat while I talk?"

Sarah blushed, replying demurely, "That would be fine."

He left her bedside for the shadows on the other side of the room, returning moments later with a steaming, fragrant bowl of soup on a small tray, which he placed on the pillow she had arranged on her lap. He then turned to pull up a chair beside the bunk, settling himself comfortably while she spooned the first delicious mouthful. "Mmm. This is lovely," she murmured in response to his questioning gaze. "So tell me, please, how did you and Jeremiah recapture the *Endeavour*?"

Stewart snorted derisively. "Well, in many ways it was like taking candy from a babe. For pirates, d'Alava's men were a strangely complacent rabble. On the nights when they bothered to form a watch, the crew would be counted on to sleep through it. They cared little about holding prisoners. After all, they expected our freedom eventually, just as we did. Why should we try to escape?

"At any rate, as our captivity stretched on interminably, Jeremiah and I decided to act on the assumption that d'Alava had no intention of letting us go, at least not in the near future. But when Tegan was ... discovered," he uttered the phrase carefully, but Sarah still flinched upon hearing him, "we saw that our time was running out. No telling how soon he would learn the truth."

"He *did* know," Sarah interrupted. "He told me that it was Turgot who-who ...." She was unable to finish. Stewart quickly reached out a comforting hand to rest on her covered leg, a familiar intimacy so natural neither noticed the impropriety of it.

"I know, Sarah," he soothed, leaning forward. "And if it makes you feel any better, Turgot paid dearly for his crimes." Her saucer-like eyes stared into his for the answer. "Ezra, God bless the lad, finished him off, saving Jeremiah's life in the process. But I'm getting ahead of myself. Are you certain you want to hear all this?"

"Please go on," she murmured. "I really do want to know everything."

"Well, you knew we were up to something," he continued conspiratorially, his hand still touching her leg, "with me leaving every night. I can tell you, dearest, that was sheer torture." His voice bathed her intimately, and she struggled to ignore his tone. She studied the bowl of soup on her lap, her heart throbbing at his verbal caress. "We managed to prepare the ship for sailing, stocking up enough supplies to get us to Charleston, we're estimating. Fortunately, we even managed to recover some of our weapons, or you and I would not be here discussing our victory," he added, referring to the frightening ambush at sea.

"But how did the crew escape ... and in broad daylight?"

"As I said, the guard was practically nonexistent," Stewart continued. "We were able to hide away almost half the crew over the four nights without anyone noticing ... or perhaps 'caring' is a better word. D'Alava and Turgot hadn't nearly the loyal band they thought. Most of those pirates wanted nothing more than to live peacefully in the village. D'Alava had enough booty to last them all a lifetime, though it doesn't appear he was fair in dividing the spoils. The only time the men got halfway decent treatment was when they went on raids, which, I suppose, is why they even bothered to go. That and the thrill ...." Stewart sighed, raking his hand through his darkly waving hair.

"So what happened? What went wrong?" Sarah knew she was venturing into painful territory, but she needed to hear the truth from his lips.

"We had planned to leave tonight," Stewart went on, absently plucking at the blanket covering her legs. "Everything was perfect – the winds, the tide, the weather – everything that is, except our cover. We knew d'Alava was suspicious, but we hadn't planned on him making his move today."

As if she were reliving a dream, Sarah whispered, "He said you were d-dead." Her body shivered with remembered anguish.

"Had things gone as he expected, I would be," Stewart told her simply. "I was ambushed on my way to the worksite this morning. Knocked over the head and tossed down a ravine on the other side of the lagoon." At Sarah's look of horror, he added, "Good thing my executioner didn't check his work, or I might very well be dead."

"But you must have been hurt terribly."

Stewart shrugged. "A knot on the head, a few bumps, bruises. Obviously somebody wants me alive," he chuckled, "for it was hard to believe I survived either the blow or the fall. Quite a stretch of time passed before I regained consciousness and managed to climb back up the ravine. In the meantime, Turgot had gone after Jeremiah, but hadn't counted on Ezra coming up behind him or his skill with the sabre. We might have lost our able captain were it not for that brave boy." He added, his voice softening. "I think his courage was borne out of the need to avenge Tegan's death. He took it personally, you know."

"Poor Ezra," Sarah sighed sadly. "He promised he would protect her, but it wasn't his fault." Pausing briefly to gather courage for her next words, she whispered, "I wanted to thank you for rescuing me. I know things did not go quite as you'd planned ...."

"Now there's an understatement," Stewart rejoined swiftly, causing her troubled eyes to grow wide with surprise. She hadn't expected him to admit so readily to his decision to leave her behind. But she had misunderstood, as his next words proved. "When I caught sight of that bastard dragging you off, I realized just how close we'd come to bungling the whole escape." His dark eyes bore into her with a look of both anger and sorrow, an odd combination, impossible to judge. "Did he hurt you, Sarah?"

The pain could not be disguised. "Not physically," she replied through clenched teeth, using every effort to hold back the tears. The fact that he had gone rigid and aloof did not make it easier.

His voice was cold, "And what is that supposed to mean?"

"Meaning," she breathed heavily, "he showed me what a fool I had been to trust others when my life is at stake."

Stewart's tone took on a strangely eerie quality, as if he could not quite believe what his ears were hearing. "You ... a fool? For trusting me? What did d'Alava tell you, Sarah?"

Suddenly, Sarah realized she did not want to hear either his confession or his lies. She fumbled for words to extricate herself from the force of Stewart's gaze. "Please. The past is over. Let's not bother to talk about it anymore."

With the grace and speed of a cat, he had leapt from the chair and was sitting beside her on the bed, his strong hands grasping her wrists as the tray rattled off her lap, sloshing the remains of the soup about as it slid to the bed. She struggled to hide her tearful face, but he persisted, pulling her arms away until she was forced to look at his steely countenance. "It seems you've more than one secret to hide from me, Sarah. Now tell me, what did d'Alava say?"

"He said you'd planned to es-escape without me, th-that you'd no intention of t-taking me with you...!"

She thought she would drown in her own sobs, as the words were wrenched from her, and it took many moments to realize that Stewart was holding her close, comfortingly, as if her accusation meant nothing. It felt so good to have his hard chest beneath her cheek, to be soothed by his practiced hands stroking her tangled hair and wet face, that she was almost willing to let the truth pass.

Almost, but not quite. With a sudden lunge, she pushed herself away, only to find herself mesmerized by his smiling brown eyes, his hands still holding her shoulders firmly.

"Whatever will it take," he chuckled infuriatingly, "to make you trust me, and not the words of any slimy snake that has nothing to lose by discrediting my poor, dead soul? Did it ever occur to you that d'Alava might have said that to make his own cause more appealing?" Her troubled look stood as her answer. "No," he sighed, "I guess not. But can you not believe in the facts: that we rescued you and you are safe?"

"I am not ungrateful," she blurted, hurt by his mundane argument. "It is just that you told me nothing ... and I-I ...."

"I told you why as well," he reminded her, as if talking to a tiresome child. "Heaven help you if d'Alava had suspected you knew about our escape."

"He said you were going to leave me ...." she sobbed, her confession burning her tongue.

His head shot up as he leveled an angry gaze. "Not *one* of us would have gone without you – for *any* reason. My word means a great deal, though apparently not to you. I promised you

– and your father – that I would keep you safe, or had you forgotten?"

She shook her head. "So much has happened I did not expect. I was confused and afraid. I let d'Alava convince me that you could not be trusted. I'm sorry," she added contritely. "Will you forgive me for doubting you?"

"That depends," he answered, a trace of warmth returning to his features, "on whether I can believe you trust me now."

"I-I guess I always have," she stammered, not quite knowing what he expected. "Whenever I was unsure, it always turned out that you were telling the truth ...."

"Sarah," he interrupted her, shaking his head, "I'm not looking for contrite speeches. If you mean what you say, shouldn't you be telling me what I have a right to know?" She looked at him, puzzlement creasing her smooth, delicate features. *Did he suspect she had fallen in love with him? And if so, was she obliged to tell him? But whatever else could he mean?* Her answer came in his next shocking words. "The baby, Sarah. D'Alava threatened to hurt you and the child. *My* child."

His dark eyes were angry, but it was the fierce possessiveness that stunned her, the same unearthly determination that seemed to pierce her very soul when he had confronted d'Alava as the pirate sought to claim her earlier that day. She swallowed, shaking her head to rid herself of that vision. "No," she murmured breathlessly, unable to meet his eyes. "You misunderstood ...."

"*Don't!*" His fiercely intense command struck her like a physical blow and she realized his upraised hand was shaking. "Don't – lie to me." Immediately he was in control again, leaving Sarah to think she had imagined his sudden outburst, and the possessiveness that aroused it. "We knew this might happen. I am prepared for the consequences, as I told you before."

Instantly she was furious. As if accepting parenthood were his own personal sacrifice, and had nothing to do with her! "I sincerely apologize for dashing your hopes of playing the martyr, *Mr.* Chamberlain," she spat sarcastically, "but there is no child. I was lying to buy time, not that it would have done any good. I think d'Alava would have enjoyed jeopardizing the life of your offspring."

"Are you sure?" His voice was incredulous.

"Of course I am sure," she sniffed, crossing her arms over her breasts and leaning back against the pillows. "I told you I did not want a child."

He laughed, though a little preoccupied. "Forgive me. I forgot your method for preventing conception. Anyway, 'tis just as well. After what you've been through today, you might have lost the child, endangering your own health as well."

She didn't mean to speak aloud, but the statement came out before she could stop herself. "You were worried."

For an instant, Stewart looked almost sheepish, but he quickly recovered, leaning forward to give her hair a playful tug before he moved away from the bed. "Of course I was worried, you little vixen. I've grown rather fond of your sharp tongue, not to mention your other, more pleasing attributes." With a swiftness that literally took her breath away, he bent to place a long, lingering kiss on her open mouth, stopping just at the point when she would have curled her arms around his neck.

Embarrassed because she still wanted him so badly, Sarah sought to cover her desire with words, as Stewart was pulling away from her. "Do you think ... does Jeremiah know ... about us?"

Stewart shook his head, leaning over to recover the tray that had fallen from her lap, seeming intent on his task. "No, but it would be better for us if he did. We could share my cabin. As it stands I'll be waking up to that old sea dog, unless . ... " he paused and she offered up a silent prayer that was quickly dashed, "you can be convinced to thumb your pretty nose at convention and let us continue as we were."

She wanted to scream at his shallow, hedonistic attitude, but managed to control herself. "That is impossible, as well you know. The luxury of living for the moment is passed. 'Tis best we forget what's happened and resume our former roles." Even to her own ears, the words sounded clipped and forced.

He gave her one last stirringly sensual look before leaving her alone with her troubled thoughts. "Resume our former roles? I suppose that is sensible. But forget?" His eyes held hers with smoldering intensity as his words caressed her. "Forget, Sarah? Never." And then he was gone.

CHAPTER 31

More than two months behind schedule, Sarah was thrilled by her first glimpse of Charleston, South Carolina. Though she knew America was somewhat civilized, she was unprepared for the modern, bright and bustling view of the southern city as they made their way up Charleston Bay. Even in November, the weather was moderate and greenery abounded beyond the white sandy beaches that greeted them.

Dressed in one of only two decent dresses she had been able to collect from the poorly provisioned ship, a rather nondescript dark brown, high necked gown of serviceable linen, and her green wool pelisse, Sarah stood on deck to observe the excitement of her first docking on American shores.

Everywhere there was movement, but it was the commanding figure of one man who held Sarah's attention most raptly. Stewart, looking tall and lean, stood at the bow, signaling directions to Jeremiah on the bridge, giving Sarah's heart ridiculous little twinges of nostalgia as she remembered how very close they had once been and how very much she longed for that intimacy again.

But even though Stewart's eyes occasionally told her he, too, wanted that intimacy again, his manner toward her was beyond reproach, a turn of events she found ridiculously frustrating. Accustomed to spending so much time alone with him, Sarah found it increasingly difficult to accept the fact that he was deliberately avoiding such situations now. Jeremiah, warm and congenial as ever, seemed to have attached himself to Stewart's coattails. All their meals were taken together, as well as any other time Sarah could hope to talk with Stewart alone. She knew, of course that this was for the best, but that did not make it less frustrating.

The *Endeavour* was no stranger to Charleston Harbor, Sarah soon learned. Berthing was met with cheerful greetings called from sailors working on the ships anchored alongside, as well as from earthy-looking dock workers, all eager to trade the latest news. But business came before pleasure. Jeremiah's crew worked swiftly to put the ship abed before anyone was allowed to disembark.

But at last the moment came. A carriage had been summoned and when it pulled up alongside the gangplank, Sarah felt a hand cupping her elbow, turning to find Stewart smiling beside her. "Well, my fair English rose, are you ready for your first walk on Yankee soil?"

"Oh yes," she beamed happily. "It seems like a dream."

Bending his dark head so that his words were for her ears only, Stewart whispered teasingly, "Should you require pinching to ascertain the fact that you are not dreaming, I will be only too happy to accommodate you." He laughed at her surprised gasp and the attractive blush that suddenly colored her fresh face. "Come then, Lady Sarah, let's be off. The comforts of a warm bath, a decent meal, and a soft bed await you." Stewart walked her down the gangplank, handing her carefully to the driver of the carriage waiting on the street.

Immediately Stewart was converged upon by an assorted group of men milling on the dock. Without turning around, Sarah heard him promise them all a full report after they'd had a chance to settle in. "The Ram's Head at nine, then?" a drawling voice called as Stewart followed her into the carriage.

"Where else?" he replied jovially, poking his head outside for a final farewell, "I've been hankering for Belcher's ale since New Year's last."

"Not as much as Belcher's daughter's been hankering for you!" a crude voice interjected, followed by a chorus of raucous laughter as the driver pulled the horses away.

Surprised by the familiar banter, Sarah sat across from Stewart in the comfortable coach. Seeing that he was not going to explain the remark, she observed, "I didn't realize you had so many acquaintances so far from your home."

"In my business," he responded casually, "the entire Atlantic coast is more or less home. Jeremiah and I come here frequently, which, by the way, is fortunate for you."

"How so?" she asked, her curiosity overtaking her.

Stretching a long leg onto the seat beside her, he exhaled comfortably. "Because I can promise a replacement for your wardrobe posthaste. Am I correct in assuming that you're in need of some things before we arrive in Boston?"

"Oh yes!" she cried, delighted, her reticence gone. "I must admit I was none too pleased at the prospect of meeting my hostess in these well-worn rags, but they happen to be the best I have at present. But how will you manage it?"

"A very dear, old friend," he replied easily, "in the business of dressing beautiful women. I can summon her this evening if you like."

"Can you really? Oh, but ...." her face fell with quick realization.

"Don't tell me you've somehow made other plans," he cajoled her.

"No," she hesitated, feeling quite uncomfortable. "It's just that I-I haven't any funds. D'Alava confiscated the money my father provided for me."

"Now don't you worry about a thing, Sarah," he reassured her, reaching over to pat her hand paternally. "Our cargo was heavily insured and I have connections with the Charleston bank. I was planning to get some cash for you first thing in the morning. We'll settle the rest when we return to Boston. Feel better now?"

"Much," she sighed, relieved with the knowledge that she was not his financial burden. Somehow it would have made her situation ... awkward.

The Back River Inn was palacial and Stewart was obviously no stranger there. Despite their rather mundane appearance in sharp contrast to the glamorously-attired staff in silk and fine cotton, their entrance was met with warm hospitality. "Welcome to Charleston, Mr. Chamberlain," the stately desk clerk offered in his pleasant drawl. "It's been nearly a year, hasn't it?"

"That is has, Mr. Henderson, and I am more pleased to return than you could imagine," Stewart replied as he accepted the quill from the older man. As he registered, Sarah standing quietly next to him, he continued, "Is the Carolina Suite available by any chance? I'd like Lady Sarah Tremont to have it if possible, and rooms close by for Captain Slade and myself."

"Of course, sir," the gray-haired man agreed without hesitation and Sarah had the feeling that there was nothing Stewart could ask for that would not be granted. "I'll summon Mr. Mason to handle your luggage."

Stewart chuckled unselfconsciously as he finished writing. "I'm afraid there's precious little of that on this trip, Mr. Henderson. Our crossing was met by a rather greedy band of pirates. We're here only to reprovision before heading for Boston. Which reminds me," he added, glancing at Sarah. "Could you please summon Madame Petit to Lady Sarah's quarters this evening? She'll be needing some things rather quickly."

"Consider it done," Henderson replied, offering Sarah an understanding smile. Then turning his kindly gray eyes back to Stewart, added, "Your suites will be ready shortly. Perhaps you'd like to wait in the dining room? They're serving tea."

"Thank you," Stewart said. "I'm sure Lady Sarah would like that after our rather uncivilized voyage." Offering Sarah his arm, he called over his shoulder as they began walking toward the dining room. "Should Captain Slade arrive, would you please tell him where we are?"

"Certainly sir," Henderson promised and then his eyebrows suddenly shot up as he remembered something. "Mr. Chamberlain, excuse me!" Stewart and Sarah turned around at the sound of his anxious voice. "I nearly forgot to tell you. This is quite a coincidence. There's someone in the dining room who's been asking for you, though we had no idea you would be here."

"Did he give his name?" Stewart asked, though Sarah thought him surprisingly indifferent.

"No sir. He and the lady, his sister I believe, only arrived yesterday. She seemed quite concerned for your whereabouts. I believe now they're trying to arrange passage to Boston in hopes of finding you there."

"Well, thank you, Mr. Henderson," Stewart replied, his brow furrowing as he considered the desk attendant's words. "We'll see them now."

Unable to contain her curiosity, Sarah wasted no time asking questions. "Do you know who it is, Stewart?"

"I have my suspicions," he drawled, a frown creasing his handsome features, "but it makes no sense."

"Stewart! My darling!" They had arrived at the entrance to the dining room and the few heads present turned in surprise as the beautiful woman, dressed in billowing lavender silk, flamboyantly bolted from her chair and rushed to the couple standing there. "My God! I can't believe you're here and you're safe!" By this time the strikingly gorgeous lady had flung herself at Stewart, and oblivious to all, was crushing him in an intimate embrace, which, Sarah noticed, was met without resistance. Indeed Stewart was smiling, nearly laughing, a fact that disturbed her more than she was willing to admit.

"Felicia, you are ever full of surprises," he crooned as he held the raven-haired beauty by the shoulders, looking her over as one would examine a familiar but cherished ornament. Obviously he was pleased with everything he saw, Sarah surmised as she turned her gaze to the woman, who was touching him as if she were searching for broken bones. And that was what jarred her memory. Of course, the woman at the London docks! The very one he had so passionately kissed before setting sail. *But what was she doing here?*

"We heard your ship was captured," Felicia was exhorting, her sultry voice sounding carefully anguished. "Captain Lattimer saw the *Endeavour* being escorted southward upon his return from the West Indies. When he told us, I made Ross book us passage on the first ship to America, a wretched but speedy little freighter bound for Charleston." She sniffed in tearful remembrance and Sarah had a malicious thought that indeed she was a very good actress for her features were unmarred by tears. "I simply could not wait to hear if you were all right. We were just this morning searching for transport to Boston to see if you'd arrived there, and if not, well, darling, you know I would have searched the *world* to find you."

Stewart's brown eyes twinkled with mirth. "Somehow, Felicia, I find it difficult to feature you bearing the discomforts of the sea life simply to find me, but," he added, cautioned by her pretty pout, "I am grateful for your concern. As you can see, we're unscathed."

At the mention of "we," Felicia turned her attention to Sarah, her beautifully-shaped almond eyes narrowing perceptively at the much younger woman standing to the side. Despite her plain attire, she was still stunningly beautiful. "And who might this be, dearest?" she asked sweetly as her arm encircled his waist possessively.

"Lady Felicia Amberling," Stewart had suddenly affected a formal tone, "may I present Lady Sarah Tremont, daughter of the Duke of Weston. Weston is a business associate. Lady Sarah has come to America with me to represent her father in a legal transaction.

"Lady Sarah," Stewart turned to her, "Felicia is the widow of the Duke of Hartwick. She serves Queen Charlotte at the court of King George. She and I have been friends for many years." The women exchanged a formal, and somewhat cool, greeting. Sarah could not help but notice the catbird gleam in the dowager's jewel-like violet eyes. The spark told her a great deal more about her relationship with Stewart than his introduction.

And the way Stewart had introduced Sarah served as a vivid reminder that their charade was over. How cold and impersonal he had sounded. Even knowing it was in her best interest, Sarah was miffed, the noxious green stone of jealousy sitting heavily in her stomach.

"I am charmed to meet you, my dear," the Duchess purred in a superior tone. "Such a terrible experience for one so young. Is this your maiden voyage abroad?"

Her well-chosen double entendre shocked the younger woman, particularly under these strained circumstances. "Yes it is, Ma'am," Sarah replied tightly.

"Oh, do call me Felicia, won't you? These colonists have a charming disdain for titles, and I wouldn't want to draw undue attention," she confessed with honeyed sweetness. *As if she didn't go out of her way to draw attention*, Sarah thought spitefully. "May I call you Sarah?"

"By all means," the younger woman smiled without warmth.

At that moment, they were joined by a dapper and good-looking young man, almost as tall as Stewart, though of a slighter build. His dark hair was neatly clipped and straight, combed away from his face to give notice to expressive eyes of forest green. Giving Stewart a friendly clap on the back, he announced in an engaging tenor voice, "May I say how delighted I am to see you safe and sound, Stewart, old boy, for Felicia would have dragged me 'round the world in search of you, and I can think of much better things to do ... like being introduced to your lovely companion," he added with a flirtatious wink in Sarah's direction.

"Ross, good to see you again," Stewart smiled, shaking the younger man's hand. "You are looking none the worse for wear."

"Neither are you, Yankee, though my sister had us believing the worst. Pirates, eh?" But before he could continue, Felicia broke in effusively.

"Ross darling, this is Lady Sarah Tremont, daughter of the Duke of Weston. Sarah, this is my precious brother, The Earl of Rossing. Our mother was married to his father, the Marquess of Shaftsbury." She was obviously proud of her brother – and his bloodline. "Now do be a gentleman, Ross. You can see she's no more than a child. Please help her to get some tea before she swoons."

Taking Sarah's proffered hand, Ross graciously kissed her on the glove as she murmured a stiff greeting. "The pleasure is all mine, Lady Sarah," he said, ignoring his sister's call to dispense with titles. "Please come and join our table, won't you? As an Englishwoman, you must be rabid for tea." Taking her arm, leaving Stewart and Felicia to follow, he whispered, "Felicia has absolutely no manner when it comes to our Mr. Chamberlain. You should have been seated at once. You must be quite exhausted."

Far from immune to his friendliness, Sarah's spirits recovered with the balm and she answered brightly, "It must have been quite a shock to you both to see Stew – Mr. Chamberlain here. I can understand her excitement."

Ross bent his head to her ear, murmuring, "Between you and me, I think the shock was seeing him with such a lovely lady.

'Licia is insanely jealous, especially of beauties with youth on their side."

Sarah laughed nervously as a blush rose to her cheeks. "Your sister is far from old and it's clear Mr. Chamberlain adores her." Unfortunately that seemed to be true, Sarah thought as Ross seated her where she could see the handsome couple approach. Stewart's hand rode her small waist as Felicia cuddled against him, a look of pure bliss on her aristocratic features. He, too, was smiling easily, as if Christmas had come early.

As soon as they were all seated, Felicia practically moving her chair onto Stewart's lap, a waiter appeared with a fresh pot of tea, cakes and extra cups for the new arrivals. Felicia poured as if she were born to hostessing, which must serve her well at Court, and the conversation hummed gaily, although Sarah found it difficult to match the lively mood of the three friends.

Felicia cleverly directed the flow of words toward mutual friends and the goings-on at Court, subjects of which Sarah cared precious little. But Ross was kind, finding ways to include her even though his sister refused to change her tactics. Occasionally she looked up from her teacup to find Stewart's gaze on her, but he never spoke directly to her, and that was the most alienating thing of all, as if she were suddenly an unwelcome stranger to him.

How it happened, Sarah could not recall, but all at once the conversation shifted to their abduction and the pirates' way of dealing with them. Felicia was suddenly most interested in Sarah's welfare and began pressing her for details.

"I've heard the most hideous stories about what ugly men do to women they capture. However did you survive?" The woman's eyes fairly danced with curiosity.

"I-I was extremely fortunate," Sarah answered carefully. "I was not harmed."

"But that is incredible," Felicia probed. "I would think they would go mad to have a lovely girl like you."

At Sarah's shocked expression, Stewart interrupted sternly, "Felicia, Sarah was spared but the ordeal was very difficult. Aren't you being rude to press her?"

"Oh my dear," Felicia babbled apologetically. "I did not mean to upset you. It is just that I have never met any woman abducted by pirates, though I daresay it could happen to anyone who sails these beastly waters. I only thought that if you could tell me how you were spared, it might help should I ...."

Again Stewart cut in. "We convinced them that Sarah and I were married. I knew the leader and he respected our situation." Shocked by his admission, Sarah gulped as Felicia gasped, but whether in outrage or merely surprise, Sarah could not tell.

"Why, this is fascinating!" the black-haired beauty finally uttered, her violet eyes flashing. "The two of you posing as man and wife. How terribly clever of you, Stewart," she cried with a slightly malicious gleam before turning her full attention to Sarah. "Did you actually share the same quarters?"

It was impossible for Sarah to stand this malevolent interrogation and to the surprise of all, she abruptly rose, stammering, "I-I really am feeling – rather tired. If you will excuse me ...." She bolted for the exit, oblivious to the sounds of Felicia's feigned concern and Ross's quiet but angry rebuke.

Just as she reached the area of the registration desk, realizing that she might have nowhere to go if her suite were not yet ready, Sarah felt the rock hardness of a sinewy hand on her arm. She whirled about, a furious expression contorting her smooth features, crying, "Don't touch me!" to her tall, grim-faced captor. But Stewart's grip was immovable as he silently pushed her toward a vacant cloakroom off to the side of the hotel lobby.

With resolute firmness, he pinned her shoulders against the wood-paneled wall and held her there until, with an angry moan, she ceased her struggles, glaring at him with naked anger. "You shouldn't have run off like that," he said coldly, his brown eyes piercing.

"What?" she screeched, livid over his insensitivity. "You heard her! She was dying to embarrass me with her scurrilous insinuations," she hissed, her breasts heaving. "I do not have to take *that* from the Queen *herself!*" she spat as her blue eyes turned molten. "And you! Admitting our ploy as if you wanted to make her jealous! How could you compromise me so?"

Stewart's demeanor was as though he had not heard her barbs. "You shouldn't have run," he repeated quietly. "Had you stayed, I would have handled everything. Now Felicia thinks you have something to hide."

"That is all you care about," she sobbed, furious with herself for starting to cry. "Would Lady Amberling be so glad to see you if she had known you were unfaithful to her?"

"That was *not* my concern," he rejoined sharply. "You are the one who worries about appearances. You could have spared yourself Felicia's suspicions if you hadn't acted so rashly ...." For a moment he stared at her. "Whatever happened to that clever woman I was captured with?" His sudden switch to cajolery did more to destroy her composure than his anger, and with a swift yank, she pushed his hands away, covering her bleary eyes with shaking hands.

"Sarah?" he murmured, his deep voice a mixture of surprise and concern. "What in the world is bothering you? Surely Felicia's cattiness was not that devastating, unless ..." he speculated aloud, his fingers brushing a curling tendril from her shoulder, "there's a bit of jealousy involved ...."

"Your arrogance astounds me, sir!" she bit back as her head snapped up to glare into his gently mocking brown eyes. "You would love to believe that, wouldn't you? Well, you are wrong! I don't care who has shared your bed, only that I was unfortunate enough to be one of them!"

Her barbs seemed to have no affect on him. In fact, a teasing smile played on his firm lips. "Perhaps I should remind you that you once assured me you felt no regret over our affair. Indeed, you were a most happy and eager lover, and my memories of those moments are quite good." He paused, holding her gaze. "I think yours are too."

He was making love to her right there in the cloakroom, with his soft words and caressing eyes. They seemed to penetrate her very soul. Sarah knew if she were not vigilant, she could easily lose herself to his overpowering mastery. But if nothing else, she had learned to be careful. "You knave," she spat.

"Bringing that up when your – your mistress is in the very next room!"

He was undaunted, speaking quite calmly. "She is not my mistress."

"You deny you are lovers?"

"Our relationship is none of your business, you know," he warned. "Neither is what happened between us any business of Felicia's as she is quite aware."

"Do you think for one moment I would have tumbled into your bed had I known you were ... involved?" she whined, feeling overwhelmed by his rational mien.

"Only you can answer that, Sarah," he answered quietly. "But I tell you this: Felicia is my concern, not yours. And I have no regrets, I assure you." Before she could level another retort, he said, "Come now. Let me take you back to the others."

"No!" she hissed, pulling away the hand he had tried to capture. "I cannot go back now. Don't you understand?"

His insistence was infuriating, but his logic was sound. "It will be worse if you don't. Felicia isn't the only one who'll be asking you questions about our ordeal. Though," he admitted, "I daresay she is the most indiscreet. Now is as good a time as any to learn to manage these inquiries." With a brotherly squeeze, he encouraged her, "I have seen you handle yourself better under more trying circumstances. I have every confidence in your abilities."

He was right, of course, though she was loathe to admit it to his face. With a fearsome look and an angry sniff in his direction, Sarah pulled a handkerchief from her sleeve, dabbed her eyes, then squared her shoulders and marched ahead of him out of the cloakroom. But she almost lost her nerve when, as they reentered the dining room, her eyes fell on the hostile, jealous stare of the raven-haired beauty across the room.

It was obvious she had counted on Sarah not returning. But Stewart's broad hand was pushing into the small of her back and she was forced to suffer Felicia's insulting gleam until Stewart had seated her again next to Ross.

"I apologize," she said before anyone else had a chance to speak, "for making a scene." Fortunately her voice was unaffected by her wildly beating heart, and this gave her the confidence to continue. Looking directly at Felicia, who was eying her with new interest, she explained, "My maid, a very dear woman, was killed during our ordeal, and it's rather difficult for me to discuss our captivity without remembering her misfortune ...."

"Sarah ..." Ross interrupted sympathetically, but she held up her hand to quiet him, giving the handsome man a soft, pleading look.

"Were it not for Captain Slade, who suggested that Mr. Chamberlain and I pose as newlyweds, I would surely have suffered a similar fate." She glanced at Stewart and was encouraged by his admiring gaze. "Our charade made it possible for Mr. Chamberlain to protect me from harm ... and I am grateful to him for his sensitivity to my plight."

With a charming blush that only she and Stewart knew was born of a lie, she added, "I have led a very sheltered life, and was embarrassed by Mr. Chamberlain's admission of our ploy, although I have no reason to be." She awarded him with a sweet smile, as one would give a kindly uncle. "He was most understanding and spared us both a great deal of awkwardness. And, of course, I cannot understate the fact that he saved my life."

"Why darling, how gallant of you!" Felicia cried, delightedly, patting Stewart's check with a well-buffed hand. "Sarah, I am so sorry if my inquiries disturbed you. And your poor maid. Please forgive my terrible *faux pas*," she churned. "Stewart is quite the devil at times. I naturally assumed ...."

"Would you like more tea, Sarah," Ross quickly intervened, giving his sister a killing look, though Felicia's expression of triumph remained.

"No thank you," Sarah replied, returning Ross's kindness with a grateful smile. "I really am quite tired. Mr. Chamberlain, do you think perhaps our rooms are ready now?"

"I'm sure they are," he answered, rising to escort her, much to Felicia's chagrin.

Ross stood up, too. "It has been a pleasure meeting you, Sarah. Will we see you at dinner? I believe serving begins at eight." Sarah's eyes went to Stewart, noticing the tiny frown that creased his brow.

"I thought Sarah might prefer dinner in her suite. There's a dress maker coming to help her replenish her wardrobe, since we weren't able to take much with us. But if you'd rather ...." he turned questioning eyes to Sarah.

"Perhaps we can dine together tomorrow?" she begged Ross sweetly, pleased that Stewart had offered a perfect excuse to avoid Felicia. Too bad that Lady Amberling suddenly looked so satisfied. "Maybe by then I will have another dress to wear," she grinned sheepishly at her own vanity, but Ross's manner was understanding.

"May I ask who is doing your clothes?" Felicia inquired, perfectly at ease in her chair while everyone else stood around her.

"A Madame Petit, I believe," Sarah replied, glancing at Stewart for verification. His nod was accompanied by a faint tic in his cheek muscle, and Sarah soon learned the reason for his tension.

Felicia dimpled provocatively. "Madame Petit! Why darling, isn't she the one you had design that positively wicked gift you gave me for my birthday?" Ignoring his stern look, she bubbled, "Of course. I do so love it. Sarah, if the woman is half as good with a bolt of muslin as she is with a foot of lace, then you shall be well pleased, I'm sure!"

Without flinching at her immodest revelation, Sarah replied, "I will let her know she comes so highly recommended. Now if you will excuse me?" With a pleasant nod to Ross, she departed, not giving a damn whether Stewart followed her or not.

He did, of course, and she waited until he had secured the keys to their rooms before giving him a disapproving look, her ire slightly cooled. "Your lady friend is quite out to disarm me. If it is impossible to avoid her, might you suggest that she sheathe her claws? Her possessiveness is nearly as tiresome as her lack of breeding."

To her surprise, Stewart gave a hearty laugh. "I daresay Lady Felicia would be outraged to hear your opinion of her. Her breeding is impeccable as she will be glad to tell you," he said, guiding her up the main staircase. "Believe it or not, she is the darling of the Queen's court. The ladies can't wait to hear what she'll say next."

As they made their way to the Carolina Suite, Sarah mused, "Perhaps the Queen finds her amusing, but it is beyond me to picture you with a woman like that. She seems rather ... overwhelming and frivolous."

"Don't let Felicia's poor manners deceive you. She is a very strong woman, and a sharp judge of character, not that I expect you to become fast friends," he grinned, seeing her lip curl distastefully. "Here we are."

CHAPTER 32

The Carolina Suite was an elegant oasis after Felicia's barbs, Sarah mused later as she padded noiselessly on thick pile carpeting in the main salon. Fresh from a soothing bath and a languorous rest, she perused the stately suite as she finished a meal of fresh lamb and vegetables prepared especially for her. Pale ivory walls and rich cotton drapes of cream and black *toile de Jouy* gave the suite a decidedly European flare. The sitting room was made comfortable by furniture crafted of fine native woods. A cream and black striped silk sofa faced the lighted fireplace and thickly cushioned chairs of cream velvet banked either side. An elegant scriptoire nestled in one corner of the beautiful room, while a well-supplied liquor cabinet lined the opposite wall. Fresh flowers spilled from delicate crystal vases and a welcoming bowl of fruit and nuts sat just out of reach on the small dining table.

As her large blue eyes took in the elegant paintings of Southern gardens adorning the walls, Sarah found it hard to believe all that had happened to bring her to this comfortable setting. The serenity and cheerfulness made it difficult for her to fully comprehend what a dangerous existence she had been living. And if anyone had ever suggested that she would have tasted the fruits of a forbidden romance, or worse, would have fallen so hopelessly in love with a man she could never have – well, it was simply beyond her powers of understanding. She was not the type to have brought this sort of folly upon herself.

As she passed by the table, she allowed a self-indulgent sigh of pity to escape her lips. Her father had always preached accountability; blaming fate is a poor excuse for failing to handle oneself properly, making deliberately wrong choices. On the island, everything had seemed so inevitable, so right. But now? Sarah pressed a hand against her trembling mouth as she gulped back an urge to sob. As everyone shifted into their previous roles in proper society, the grievous blunder she had made weighed heavily on her conscience.

But what hurt the most was Stewart's ridiculously calm acceptance of the past, and the ease with which he seemed to have forgotten her. At this very moment, he was wining and dining Lady Felicia, picking up that affair as if nothing had happened since their passionate goodbye at the London dock.

And tonight, Sarah mused bitterly, *she will be the one reveling in his embraces, warming to his touch* .... Aloud she scolded herself, "I must stop wanting him, loving him ...."

A brisk knock on the paneled door brought an immediate blush to her pale cheeks. Nervously she wiped her eye where a tear was beginning to form and cleared her throat before answering, "Yes?"

"Lady Sarah Tremont? It's Eliane Petit. Mr. Chamberlain sent for me."

"Yes, of course," Sarah answered, already slipping the latch on the double doors. "Come in, won't you?" The doors swung open wide to reveal a petite older woman cloaked in a full-length cape of rich navy velvet, a serious-looking young girl laden with two cases behind her. "I've been expecting you."

Madame Petit and the girl marched quickly into the room, leaving Sarah to close the door. "I hope we're not interrupting your repast," the older woman said politely. But obviously she wanted to get down to business, motioning the girl to begin unpacking. As if by way of explaining her helper's activity, she added. "We haven't much time to prepare a wardrobe. Mr. Chamberlain informs me you'll be sailing in a week."

"Oh?" Sarah responded. "I hadn't realized arrangements had already been made." *Damn him for leaving me the last to know.* "M-May I take your wraps?" she offered as the dress maker briskly unbuttoned her cape, reveling a plain but richly tailored gown of the same material.

"No-no, dear," the woman waved her off, as her small, bright eyes narrowed to make a lightening assessment of Sarah's tall, slender shape hidden somewhat by the rather unbecomingly wrapper she wore. A faint, but pleasant smile softened her hawkish features which were framed by graying hair escaping from a severe bun at the nape of her neck. "I shall enjoy outfitting you," she stated matter-of-factly. "I weary of hiding figure flaws, though I do it well. You, my dear, are perfect for my creations – softly rounded, tall and not ashamed of it."

"My neck is --."

"Your neck is splendid. Ruffles at the throat and décolletage equally become you, I am sure. Remove your robe, please," she ordered, bending to extract a measuring tape from one of the cases the helper had opened on the floor. "I will take your measurements now."

Thus commenced a flurry of activity as the three women discussed fashion, shuffled through fabric samples, selected trims and made arrangements for fittings and purchases of suitable accessories. Despite her severe nature, Madame Petit was an appealing woman, one moment charming, the next commanding, but always wise and professional. She knew her business and accomplished it posthaste. The young girl, whose name was Rachell, turned out to be the niece of Madame Petit's late husband, and despite her solemn countenance, she was pleasant and accomplished at assisting her aunt. They were a discerning, efficient pair and Sarah was more than pleased that Stewart had selected them to replenish her wardrobe.

Sarah helped them pack up swatches of material and trims with some regret. Their visit had turned out to be a welcome respite from her otherwise troubled evening. It was only now that she again thought of Stewart and Felicia and how *their* evening was progressing. Giving herself a mental shake, she stepped back from the case she was filling, allowing Rachell to close it up. "Thank you so much for coming at this late hour," she addressed Madame Petit warmly. "I cannot tell you how much I appreciate your help. I was not looking forward to journeying to Boston with but two gowns – and one not even my own."

Madame Petit patted Sarah's hand affectionately. "When Mr. Henderson summoned me on behalf of Mr. Chamberlain, we came as quickly as possible. He's always been a favorite patron." And before Sarah could speculate, Eliane added, "This will be the first time he's been to Charleston without purchasing a gown or wrap for his sister. But under the circumstances, there simply isn't time to design one, let alone make it."

"Mrs. Slade will be disappointed, I'm sure," Sarah murmured regretfully, wishing she had not been the cause of her hostess's deprivation.

"Margaret Slade?" Madame Petit interjected sharply. "My dear, she is the kindest, most unselfish woman you're likely to meet in this country. Her husband and brother indulge her only because they adore her, not because she requires such consideration. Unlike some others ...." Her last words hung without completion only for a moment, leaving Sarah no time for speculation. "Excuse me please, Lady Sarah." Helene recouped briskly as if irritated with her slip into the realm of gossip. "It's been a pleasure to meet you, but Rachell and I must hurry. No doubt my driver is anxious to complete his duties for the evening, and we have much work to begin tomorrow morning."

With a flourish, Eliane Petit donned her cape, gave Sarah's proffered hand a final squeeze and bustled Rachell into the hall. "Fear not, Lady Sarah," she called from the doorway, "we'll have you a wardrobe fit for the crowned heads in no time. Good evening." And with a wave, the women were gone, leaving Sarah somewhat breathless over the older one's display of energy and confidence.

"It's all right, Sarah. It's only me."

Sarah had awakened with a start, the presence of a shadowy form bringing her to full, frightened consciousness in the quiet, fire-lit bedroom.

"What are you doing here?" she hissed, her eyes adjusting to the dark as she looked on Stewart's silhouette crouched before the fireplace.

"Your room is cold," he stated matter-of-factly. "I was putting another long on the fire." Rising, he added, "I didn't mean to awaken you."

"Well you did," she mumbled crossly, though secretly pleased to see him. "You shouldn't be here," she added for propriety's sake.

"Perhaps not." She sensed that he was smiling, though she couldn't see his face at the foot of the large bed for the light was behind him. "But I wanted to make sure you were all right."

"Quite," she replied pettishly, remembering with whom he had spent his evening. "You'd better go." Decorum did not dictate her words nearly so much as a trembling desire to invite him closer. *Would this torture never end?* Being ever so close, yet unable to taste the sweetness of his kiss, the hard longing of his body?

He showed no penchant for leaving, choosing instead to lounge casually against the sturdy bedpost. "Madame Petit. Was she to your liking?"

"Yes, of course. We accomplished a great deal. She has quite an eye for color and design," Sarah rambled, somewhat breathlessly, unnerved by his presence. "Why didn't you tell me we'd be sailing next week?"

"An oversight, for which I apologize," he intoned lazily, refusing to explain further. Pushing himself away from the bedpost with his shoulder, he drifted to a seat near her on the high bed. Instinctively, Sarah curled her legs closer to her body. Any physical contact, she was sure, would be her undoing.

In the short silence, Sarah had a chance to wonder why Stewart was here, and not with Lady Felicia. The question was on the tip of her tongue, but knowing he would realize her jealousy prevented her from being direct. Instead she forced herself to break the pregnant pause with a benign inquiry. "Your evening, did it go well?"

"We had a pleasant meal in the hotel dining room, if that's what you're referring to," Stewart replied.

"Did you go to the Ram's Head after?" she asked, remembering his promise to the sailors at the dock.

His darkened face studied her. "No, Ross and Felicia's unexpected appearance precluded those plans."

Without another word, his hand came up to brush a stray lock of silky hair from her face. Nervously, she turned her gaze away, but his fingers remained to caress the sweet-smelling tresses. "Has it been difficult for you," he murmured gently, his voice barely audible above the crackling fire, "sleeping alone after all those weeks on the island?"

"Please go," she begged, turning to clutch the pillow beside her head as if it were an anchor against the storm that was raging inside. He appeared not to hear her as his lean fingers traced the pulsing artery beneath the plush softness of her skin.

"You are a bonafide addiction, Lady Sarah," he whispered. "More than once I have awakened to find myself searching for your tender body to warm my own." Stewart's searing lips gently tempted the sensitive spot behind her delicate ear as he murmured, "I want you, Sarah. God, how I want you."

He was already pushing the loose chemise away from her shoulders when Sarah cried out with her last vestige of sanity. "You're mad to come here. Leave at once or I shall scream." With a burst of strength, she twisted herself to a sitting position before him, realizing too late that her own undergarments had betrayed her by falling away from her heaving breasts. Her gasp was at once swallowed by Stewart's firm mouth, his tongue wasting no time exploring its target.

Angry and frightened of the power he held over her, Sarah struggled but her slender arms were pinned uselessly by her shift and his strong arms wrapped around her. His fine wool waistcoat brushed intoxicatingly against her peaking breasts. Sarah moaned at the overwhelming temptation of his practiced assault.

His kisses were relentless, gentle yet with a persuasive fervor she could not hope to ward off. His coming here was wrong; their entire intimate relationship was wrong. But knowing, admitting that, was still not helping her now. She loved him and her love made her weak, a slave to his undeniable passion.

His hands had released her from the imprisonment of her chemise and now he seemed bent on holding her close while loosening his own clothing. Finally forced to release her in order to throw off his vest and shirt, she gasped tearfully in a final attempt to stop him. "Felicia is here for you now. Can't you finally leave me alone?"

It was as if she had slapped him. His dark eyes grew narrow and a metallic glint pierced her soul. His jaw worked ominously as he stared down at her. "You think I have come only to ease some primitive desire? Something that any comely wench could satisfy?"

Shaken by his crudeness, she nonetheless could not give words to a lie that would stop his callousness. "You've given me no cause to think otherwise," she choked, knowing she was forcing an issue whose outcome would bring her no satisfaction. Stewart did not love her, had no desire to marry her, and would not pretend simply to continue his seduction.

His defensiveness suddenly turned to resignation. Combing his fingers through his freshly trimmed hair, he sighed, "I believe whatever our feelings are for each other, they are not the same ... or else we would not be discussing them now."

The silence that followed was broken momentarily by the crackling fire and the disconsolate hiss of burning sap. For Sarah, it seemed to mock the sound of her breaking heart. Straightening his clothes, Stewart rose, offering, "I apologize for my indiscretion. I have no right to be here, as you say."

His head bent while he gathered his waistcoat and put it on. She could not see his eyes. "I was going to inform you later, but I may as well tell you now." Sarah pressed her arms around herself, curling up tighter as she sunk behind the covers, knowing she would be wounded even deeper by what he had to say.

"I will not be accompanying you to Boston." His voice was clipped, precise, showing no emotion whatsoever. "I've decided to finish some business here and join you and Jeremiah later." Shocked, never even entertaining the possibility that Stewart would be absent, she simply stared at him, a glaze settling over her vivid blue eyes. He added, "You may now feel utterly safe."

Despite her own pain, Sarah could see that Stewart was not pleased with himself. His parting words seemed to prove her correct. "I somehow felt," he began tentatively, "that what happened between us on that blasted island was mutually agreeable – and that it could be put into perspective – not completely forgotten." He shrugged his hands into his trouser pockets, locking her eyes in a serious gaze. "But as society does not allow women to enjoy life with the same appetite as men, nor enable them to entertain fond memories of a past, I promise this night never to subject you to any recollections of shared intimacies. What transpired, I assure you as a gentleman, did not. Good evening, Lady Sarah."

It was over. He was gone, leaving Sarah to suffer through the longest night of her life.

CHAPTER 33

The journey to Boston was miserable, and only partly due to the frigid weather. Jeremiah, Sarah and the crew sailed in the bleak coldness of November, following a sumptuous farewell dinner with Felicia, Ross and, of course, Stewart. Each attempted a lighthearted mood, but it seemed, at least to Sarah, that only Stewart and Felicia were truly enjoying themselves. Jeremiah, she knew, longed to be in Boston with his darling Peggy and the children. Ross might have had a better time if Sarah had been able to respond to his kindnesses more receptively. But she was homesick, she explained, and found herself feeling worse as she told him some of her family's Christmas traditions.

Sarah prayed that somehow by now her parents had learned that she was safe in America. She had posted letters the day they'd arrived in Charleston. She knew the posts should reach them well before Christmas, and it lightened her heart somewhat to know that the good news was on its way back to England.

During the voyage, Jeremiah sensed that all was not well with Sarah, and though they shared the special closeness of people who have weathered grave danger together, he did not pry and she did not seem to want to discuss any personal matters with him.

At one point, he had tried to tease her, in hopes of bringing a shine of humor to her strangely sad eyes. "So how does it feel to be a free woman again?" he had asked cheerfully.

"Free?" She had responded, confused. Obviously her thoughts had been somewhere else. "Oh, you mean free of d'Alava."

"Actually," Jeremiah replied, "I meant free of the bonds of matrimony. The paper you signed ...."

"Oh, that!" Sarah answered, a flash of raw emotion – was it pain? – momentarily crossing her features. "It has been destroyed, I trust?"

"Stewart took care of it," Jeremiah assented. "You must be happy that the charade is over. I know it was a difficult thing for you to do, and I, for one, am truly apologetic for the inconvenience of it all." He added softly, "I knew from the moment we met that some women's penchant for deception was foreign behavior to you. But you are quite a survivor – and you and Stewart performed masterfully. It was almost ...."

Sarah at once interrupted with an almost hysterical laugh. "Oh, Captain Slade, I am just glad the whole ordeal is in the past. And yes, it does feel better to be free again. Much better ...." And then she had suddenly excused herself from the conversation, looking even more woebegone than she had before.

Jeremiah had been distressed, to say the least. She looked older, he decided, and not well. But this he attributed to their harrowing experience, Tegan's death, and the current frigid conditions for sailing. It made him all the more eager to be reunited with Peggy. She would care for Sarah, and bring the bloom of youthfulness back to the Englishwoman's cheeks. Sarah, after all, was the daughter of a wealthy and high-ranking family. She had led a pampered life and was most likely suffering from the lack of daily luxuries.

When the *Endeavour* berthed in Boston Harbor, it was snowing. The cold white flakes brought a muffled hush to the darkening city and only the warm glow of window lamps pierced the hazy winter atmosphere. "We're just in time for the evening meal," Jeremiah beamed happily as he lifted Sarah into a hired carriage. "I can't wait to thaw out in the bosom of my family." His ruddy face split into a grin that was positively adorable, Sarah thought, responding to his infectious anticipation.

Her down-trodden mood had lifted considerably with the prospect of reaching her destination and meeting this wonderful family Jeremiah was so fond of discussing. She knew that he and Peggy had three children – young Jeremiah, who was six; Ethan who was four; and Rebecca, who would be a year old on Christmas Day. Jeremiah hadn't seen them all for six months and was quite sure that Rebecca would be virtually unrecognizable.

The Slade home was a gracious, white colonial structure on a heavily-populated hill overlooking the harbor. It took only minutes to arrive there, but Jeremiah was so impatient, it seemed as though he was almost ready to jump from the carriage and run the two blocks. Sarah was sure he would have if she hadn't been in his care.

As Jeremiah restlessly paid the driver and began grabbing one of Sarah's cases, she touched his arm, demanding, "Please Captain Slade. The driver and I can manage my things. Go greet your family."

With a grateful smile, he wheeled around, dashed up the snow-covered walkway and took the front steps two at a time — as fast as his lanky legs could carry him. Sarah hung back in the carriage, watching as he opened the door and hooted a huge greeting to those within. The chattering of women and children commenced at once and before the door closed, Jeremiah was surrounded by loving kin.

The glimpse of the warmth inside the home brought tears to Sarah's eyes and she choked with, it seemed, both happiness and misery. Happy for Jeremiah and his family, surely; but miserable because this family reunion was one she could only observe from afar. Her heedless plunge into the depths of love had been taken alone; Stewart would never see her as Jeremiah saw Peggy – his one true love. There would be no other, and now she felt only a shell of her former self. The memories of Stewart's kisses, his touch, his bravery and humor, were more painful, not less, and the realization that he was happy in Charleston with his Felicia made the torture even greater.

"Can I give you a hand, miss?" the driver was asking, and Sarah quickly scrubbed her eyes with her gloved knuckles. *I must stop this nonsense,* she urged herself as the kindly driver helped her down to the snow-covered sidewalk.

As she turned to take the small bag the driver handed her, a lilting feminine voice called from the portico. "Lady Sarah, are you coming?" Sarah turned to gaze up to the doorway to the sight of a young woman, her head and shoulders covered in a light shawl. Not waiting for an answer, she picked her way down the stairs, heedless of the snowy cold.

Concerned that the woman would catch her death, Sarah skittered toward the figure calling, "Oh please, Mrs. Slade, you needn't come out here. It's freezing."

"But I cannot wait to welcome you," Peggy called, moving as fast as she could on the slippery walk. "I can't tell you how happy I am that you're here!"

They were almost within reach of each other when the inevitable occurred. Peggy slipped, and Sarah, attempting to steady her, found herself tumbling as well. With a whoop and a thud, they landed in a heap as the amazed driver looked on.

Sitting up and finding themselves in each other's arms, they both giggled, laughing at the absurdity of the situation. It was the warmest of welcomes, in spite of the cold.

"Lady Sarah," Peggy panted as she pulled her shawl away from her face where it had twisted. "I'm Margaret Slade, and I think it's just wonderful that you've come to visit us." And with that, she hugged her bedazzled guest as they again rocked and laughed in the snow.

"I think under the circumstances," Sarah gasped, "you should – you must – call me Sarah."

"Peggy," Margaret responded in kind, gripping her companion's hands as they attempted to rise together. "Careful – careful now. I don't think I'll be able to get up again if we fall."

"Lucky for you, you've got Mike Temple here to help," a jolly voice broke in. "I've never seen anything like it," the driver teased as he helped them steady themselves. "The two of ye will be in bed till March if we don't get you out of this snow bank."

"Thank you, Mr. Temple," Sarah puffed as she dusted the clinging wet snow off her fur collar and cuffs. "Would you help Mrs. Slade into the house? She hasn't the proper footwear to trek without slipping again."

But by then, Jeremiah had burst on the scene and amid a blustery scolding, swooped the petite Peggy into his arms and carried his giggling bundle back into the house. Temple helped Sarah and they all finally managed to gain the foyer.

"Good gracious," a buxom, uniformed woman introduced as Mrs. Leland, the housekeeper, fumed as the troupe entered. "Get the both of them before the fire. 'Tis no wonder the children have no sense when they see their mum behaving so."

As the two women were settled briskly before the huge stone fireplace in the cozy parlor, three pairs of round, astonished eyes observed the proceedings with interest. "Children," Peggy chided them lovingly, "don't look so alarmed. Haven't you ever seen snowmen before?"

Realizing their mum was all right, the children relaxed a bit and grinned shyly at the newcomer. Little Rebecca crawled up close until she could fall into her mother's wet arms, just as Jeremiah pulled a lap robe over his wife's shoulders. "Sarah," Peggy beamed, her pert features glowing and moist, "I'd like you to meet our children. Jeremiah, Ethan, I'd like to present you to Lady Sarah Tremont who's come all the way from England to visit us."

The boys bowed politely, reluctant to take their eyes off the striking and friendly-looking woman who'd been literally dragged in from the snow. "And this is Rebecca," Peggy added, pulling the babe out from under the blanket where she was hiding. Her dark curls and brown eyes, unlike the fair-haired boys, attested to her resemblance to the Chamberlain side of the family, and Sarah thought she'd never seen a child so beautiful. "Please don't mind her shyness," Peggy insisted. "Once she gets to know you, you'll never keep her from your skirts."

"I shouldn't mind that at all," Sarah responded softly, mesmerized by the toddler's precious countenance. This is what Stewart's children would look like, she found herself thinking, a flash of pain crossing her blue eyes. But she hid it quickly by lifting her hands to remove her hat. "Your children are lovely," she beamed and turning to the boys, added, "Your father's told me so much about you, I feel as though we're friends already."

The boys grinned and looked happily at their towering father, who was beaming with obvious pride, glad to be home at last.

CHAPTER 34

The Slades were a loving family; their gaiety and devotion to each other was extended to their foreign guest, enveloping her in a downy cocoon of warmth and caring. It was exactly the kind of balm Sarah needed to assuage her heart's grief over her lost love.

Well, nearly so. After a month in Boston, the dark circles under her eyes had dissipated, the bloom was returning to her cheeks and she had regained some weight, but occasionally, when she thought no one was noticing, the pain was still apparent in her dark blue eyes.

It flashed whenever a kind word or a gentle touch was passed between Jeremiah and Peggy. Or when the children – those beautiful children – spontaneously dived into Sarah's skirts for a quick hug, their giggles filling the happy home with a deep sense of joy.

And it was most apparent the day Peggy innocently asked Sarah to accompany her to Stewart's home, a block away. "I just want to make sure the seasonal decorations are completed," Peggy said as they awaited entry to the imposing colonial home on a quiet street above the Slades' home. "Since Mama died, Papa and Stewart rather depend on me to supervise their help." With a glittering smile, she added, "Not that anyone needs to oversee Mrs. Hubbard. She's quite the matron here."

And with that, the door was opened by a thin, pinch-faced woman, dressed from top to bottom in a severe black dress. "Good day, Mrs. Hubbard," Peggy greeted the somber woman cheerfully, and, as it seemed with everyone Peggy spoke to, the mask fell way to a genuine smile.

"Mistress Peggy, come in! You just missed your father. He's off to the club."

Sarah's thoughts flashed back for a moment to Stewart's father, Travis Chamberlain. He'd been a guest for dinner at the

Slades' home several times, and Sarah recalled his dominating presence, despite his obvious age.

The family patriarch was clearly Stewart's father for both shared lean, hawkish good looks, although the senior Chamberlain's thick hair was silvery white.

It was apparent that Travis Chamberlain, a retired maritime attorney, was fond of the Englishwoman, often teasing her about his son's good taste. Knowing he had no idea of the hurt his ribbings could inflict, she took no offense, sweetly countering him with a nonchalance she did not feel.

Mrs. Hubbard's greeting did not extend to Sarah, however. The two had never met, but it was obvious that the housekeeper jealously guarded her charges. She eyed the unfamiliar woman suspiciously.

Seeing the piercing gaze, Peggy added quickly, "Mrs. Hubbard, this is Lady Sarah Tremont, our guest from England. She traveled over with Jeremiah and Stewart to Charleston, where Stewart remains, as you know."

"And how is the lad?" Mrs. Hubbard demanded suddenly. Sarah hid a smile, thinking how incongruous this woman's concern seemed coming out of the stony countenance. And considering him a "lad." Recalling his handsome, well-chiseled features, his thoroughly manly form, Sarah mused that Stewart was definitely a lad no longer.

"He's well, Mrs. Hubbard. Very well," she offered and Sarah's discomfort was there again for anyone to notice.

"'Tis good to know," Mrs. Hubbard sniffed. "He writes to his father of everything under the sun, except what his sire wants to know. The boy is much too independent. Nary a personal note as to whether he's eating well or taking care of the body God gave him."

Peggy clucked sympathetically, but Sarah only heard that he'd written. "You've heard from him, then?" she asked without thinking and instantly regretted her question, for both women looked at her curiously.

"Just this morning, it was," Mrs. Hubbard offered, but her expression stated that she would not abide any prying. Fortunately, Peggy intervened.

"So what did he say, Mrs. Hubbard? Will he be home for Christmas?"

Clearly disturbed by having to reveal privileged information to an outsider, Mrs. Hubbard ground out, "You should ask your father, Miss Peggy, but I don't believe Mr. Chamberlain was specific. He never is, the rascal. Said something about having to finish up some business and then expecting to travel by land this time. The letter was posted last month, the 27th, I believe."

Two weeks ago, Sarah calculated. So he might be home soon! But traveling by land in winter was a dicey proposition, so his arrival date could not be ascertained.

Oh God, why am I eager? Why do I care? She thought. *It's over.* But she knew it was a lie. It could not be over as long as she felt this way, as if she were incomplete without him.

As Mrs. Hubbard took their wraps, Sarah attempted to repress her unbidden thoughts once more. Peggy, thankfully, was chatting away, complimenting Mrs. Hubbard on all she did to keep the Chamberlain home in such fine shape.

And it was a beautiful home, Sarah agreed, walking with Peggy through the rooms filled with the smell of pine, as they took an informal tour. Richly appointed, the rooms had gleaming wood floors covered in thick, elaborately designed oriental rugs. The lines of the furnishings were unadorned, sparse even, from a woman's point of view. But then this was a man's house. Everything was sturdy, functional and meticulously cared for – a tribute to the severe and precise Mrs. Hubbard, no doubt. Expensive fabrics and sparse, Grecian lines provided a serene backdrop to the touches of Christmas greenery, dried berries and ribbons festooning the fireplaces and entryways. Being British, Sarah was happy to see some evidence of the special season in Stewart's home. Christmas had been a highly controversial holiday to the early Puritans, he had told her, and had, for nearly a quarter century, been banned in Boston. Fortunately that prohibition had been lifted years before and citizens were more openly celebrating again.

A portrait of Stewart's mother graced the formal parlor and Peggy smiled as Sarah studied the beautiful woman, regal and self-possessed, but with a faint twinkle in her dark eyes, as if she had found much joy and happiness in her life.

"Isn't she wonderful to look at?" Peggy remarked. "She was always so strong and capable."

"It seems to have been inherited," Sarah told her. "You and your brother both strike me that way."

Peggy eyed her, looking as if she badly wished to speak. "What is it, Peggy?" Sarah finally felt forced to ask, uncomfortable at being the target of her insinuating stare.

"You don't talk much about him. Stewart, I mean," and immediately Sarah stiffened. "I just wondered why. I mean, it's none of my business – well, it *is* in a way. He's my brother and I love to talk about him. And I've wanted to, but I can tell that you are not comfortable with the subject. And it's quite all right with me, but I just thought .... Well, Sarah, I just feel so close to you, and it's difficult for me to watch what I say around members of my family .... And ... Oh, my word. I'm so sorry. Sarah, you're crying!"

And she most certainly was. Crying as she had been unwilling to do since that last night she and Stewart had been together in Charleston. Crying for being such a fool, such a silly, lovesick fool, having burned all her chances for any happiness by reaching too far into the fires of her passion and his. Standing here in his home, being surrounded by his things, and all these wonderful people past and present who could never, ever be a part of her future .... It had become too much to bear in silence.

Sarah would have collapsed from her sobs had it not been for Peggy's supporting arms moving her to the settee beneath her mother's beautiful, satisfied face. Her grief was an ugly, jealous thing. For the Chamberlain women had it all. But Sarah could have none.

"I-I'm so ... sorry," Sarah finally managed to gasp, trying desperately to recapture her poise. "I-I don't know ...."

"Shh, it's all right," Peggy soothed, patting Sarah's quivering shoulder. "Don't talk until you're ready. Here, use my handkerchief. There, there. Go ahead. Blow your nose. Come now. Everything will be all right."

"I am being such a *child*," Sarah wailed. "And ... Oh my God. What if Mrs. Hubbard sees me?"

"Don't worry about her," Peggy insisted. "She's very discreet. She's closed the doors for us, see? We have absolute privacy so we can talk." Seeing Sarah's resistance, Peggy continued, "Sarah, you *must* talk to someone. I can help you, if you'll let me."

"No, you can't" Sarah moaned. "No you can't. Nobody can help me. I've made such a mull of everything."

But finally, with Peggy's gentle coaxing, Sarah told her. She began with the night she and Stewart met, at her sister's birthday ball, and how despite her denials, she had been attracted to him. And then when she assumed her feelings were under control, her father had named Stewart her sponsor on the trip to America. And then the pirate hijacking and the subsequent charade. Sarah told how their lives had depended on the well-played game...until it was no longer a game; she realized she'd fallen irreversibly in love with him. And how to avoid that truth, she'd insisted that they resume their former roles, only to see him rush into the arms of his beautiful lady-love.

Peggy listened attentively, but clearly she was puzzled by Sarah's conclusions. "Why are you so sure he doesn't care for you?" she probed. "It's not as if he expected or asked Felicia to come to America. She's his 'friend,' Sarah, not his love, if you know what I mean," she insisted but wasn't sure Sarah caught her meaning.

"Sarah, I don't wish to be indelicate, but it's not all that unusual – or meaningful – that an unmarried man like Stewart have 'friendships' with widows like Lady Felicia. Aside from the 'comforts' she might offer, she is a very powerful and connected woman of the ton. I am quite sure she has given him the introductions he's needed to be as successful as he is."

As Peggy did not know of the 'comforts' she herself had provided Stewart, her observations sent Sarah into another outburst of tears and weeping. "There, there, sweet," Peggy crooned, as the younger woman sobbed against her shoulder. "You are much too fine to let all of this overwhelm you. I wager that Stewart cares for you much more than you know."

"No," Sarah hiccupped, "you're wrong. You see things that aren't there because you're fond of me. But I tell you, I mean nothing to Stewart and I have got to stop dangling after him. It's making me sick," she choked.

Something was amiss, Peggy thought silently. Sarah's overwhelming reaction was violent to say the least. Why? And then it dawned. Her pretty face filled with concern, Peggy clutched Sarah's trembling hands and forced her to match her gaze. "Sarah," she whispered determinedly, "when you and Stewart were on the island, did he ... were you ... did you become ... lovers?"

For a brief second, Sarah thought she could dissemble. But Peggy wasn't looking into her eyes; she was peering into her heart, and there was no way the truth could hide there. New tears shored up in Sarah's crystal blue eyes as the two women stared solemnly at each other. Peggy had her answer. "Oh, my dear ...." she uttered as one who'd been forced to breathe.

Sarah jerked away, flinging herself to a standing position, her back to the woman. "I have been such a fool," she choked, clutching her arms about her thin shoulders ... "and I am so ashamed ...."

"Sarah," Peggy interjected sharply, coming to her side. "Do not do this to yourself. For God's sake, don't you think Stewart bears the responsibility?"

"No," she whirled around. "No! I behaved like a wanton. I let myself pretend our charade was true because that is what I *wanted* it to be. But he never forgot ... He never said ...." she gasped, the memories flooding her beleaguered brain. His fiery kisses, his all-consuming passion, his need of her that was clearly transitory. He had never made the mistake of calling it love. Why had she been so willing to pretend?

"Sarah, you're as pale as a ghost," Peggy announced. "Please sit down before you faint." As she led Sarah back to the settee, she murmured, "You haven't been well since we met, have you Sarah? Probably not since the ordeal."

"I've brought it all on myself," she croaked, closing her eyes in a desperate attempt to quell the queasiness in her stomach. "I have missed him so, and then I hate myself for even thinking of him. I have felt so guilty. Perhaps now that I have confided in you, I can begin to ... begin to ... oh, Peggy, I don't want to begin anything. I just want to end it all," she sobbed.

"No, please Sarah, don't talk that way," Peggy urged soothingly, though underneath she was boiling mad, angrier than she'd ever been at the brother who exuded charm as easily as others breathe. One look at this young girl and he should have realized she'd take nothing he offered lightly.

"I have to leave," Sarah was saying and Peggy snapped back to attention.

"Leave? What are you talking about?"

"N-now that you know, I couldn't possibly stay here. I-I'm not the sort of person who should ...."

"Balderdash!" Peggy cut her off, furious. "What in the world are you talking about? You think you're the first woman who's ever loved and been compromised?" Seeing so clearly the pain in Sarah's face, Peggy knew she believed it totally. "You are not! Darling, no one could ever judge you for what happened. You fell in love with him, and my God, you were forced to live as husband and wife!"

"'Tis no excuse," Sarah wailed, kneading her delicate hands in frustration. "I knew it was hopeless, that there was not a future for us. And I didn't care. I even thought I could deal with it, but being here, in his home, with his family ... and not *belonging* ... I just couldn't fight it anymore. But," she added hastily, seeing Peggy's pitying look, "I can and I will. But it is only possible if I leave soon – now, before I ever have to face him again."

"Sarah," Peggy spoke gently. "Did you ever think that perhaps a greater bond might have been forged between you two than you realize?" Seeing her puzzled look, Peggy drew a deep breath and plunged. "Sarah, might you be – with child?"

"No." It was a short, nearly silent rejoinder, filled with uncertainty. And then Sarah rose as if the settee had caught fire. "*No!*" She stared at the older woman for an eternity, as if her eyes alone could make the truth.

Quietly, Peggy persisted, seeking the evidence to support her surmise. "You've been ill, Sarah."

"Lovesick ... and guilty," Sarah snapped back.

"You seemed to have gained weight recently," Peggy quietly persisted.

"I have been a pampered guest – and only regained the weight I'd lost before."

"Your time, Sarah. The last ...?"

"Not since I left home. But," she hastened, on the verge of hysteria, "I was seasick, the ordeal, the traveling, so many reasons ...."

"Oh, Sarah," how can I tell you this?" Peggy moaned, rubbing her forehead. "The other day, Mrs. Leland helped you with your bath, remember? She asked me later if you were married. And when I said, 'Of course not,' she closed up and would not say why she'd asked the question. But now it makes sense, Sarah. She knows how a woman's body changes when she's in a family way."

"Oh ... oh God," Sarah whispered, frightened and humiliated. The effects of this revelation were too much to bear. They knew. They all knew what a fool she'd been and now every member of Stewart's family and household probably thought she was nothing but a bit of muslin, worthy of nothing more than their pity and disgust.

From far off, Sarah heard her name being called, but she could not seem to answer. All she wanted was to give way to the comforting darkness that was beginning to overtake her. The last thing she remembered was a distant scream as she limply slumped to the floor.

CHAPTER 35

The fresh air, though brisk, held unmistakably the promise of a lovely spring. The rolling hills surrounding the wide, low farmhouse and stables displayed observable hints of the green hue that would wash the meadow soon. Sarah walked contentedly along the rough fence boards encompassing the grazing lands of the country estate that Stewart had once confessed to her was his most prized possession.

Shading her luminous blue eyes, Sarah peered off to the west at the valley she had come to America to inspect for her father. There was no doubt the Tremont family would own the property. Much as she would have preferred not to do business with Stewart Chamberlain, the land was choice and with Stewart purchasing half the parcel to extend his farm, it would make a good investment for both families. Besides, it was a heady sensation to claim ownership to such fertile lands in the Colonies-turned-country. Sarah was eager to take title on behalf of her father, thinking of the pleasure she'd had describing in her last letter home the vastness and beauty of the 64,000-acre parcel that stretched 10 miles south and west.

With a bittersweet sigh, Sarah began her return to the farmhouse where a stout, light-haired woman was making preparations to hang wet laundry on a line that stretched from the long back porch to a post stuck in the middle of the side yard.

"Vell, you look pleased vis yourself today, *liebling*," the woman spoke as Sarah plodded up the plank steps in her borrowed boots that were sizes too big for her slender feet.

"You can just feel how lovely it's going to be soon, can't you, Elsa?"

"*Ja, ja.* Spring comes late to these meadows but ven it arrives, it iss so beautiful," the German woman smiled, her breath shortened by her labors to air the wash. Her crinkling pale blue eyes and rosy cheeks gave way to a full-mouthed grin as she glanced at the younger woman. "And how iss our *Kinderlein* today?"

Sarah smiled, stroking her rounded girth hidden beneath the somber woolen duster she used for chores. "Our baby is fine today, Elsa. Very active this morning."

"Dat's gut. You have a strong one in dere."

"That she is, Elsa," Sarah agreed, contemplating the trembling mound beneath her slender hand. Leaning against a corner post, she sighed contentedly.

Her pregnancy, now in its sixth month, was a good one after the initial weeks of queasiness and unhappiness. She had long since resigned herself to her fate, and now accepted it with a growing sense of anticipation. No longer did she worry about the future. Knowing she had survived so much gave her strength to look ahead with a calmness that sometimes surprised her.

This place had a lot to do with her feelings of well-being. And these people, she added, watching Elsa briskly go about her chores. Elsa and Johann Kemper were the caretakers of Stewart's farm. They had welcomed her as a daughter, showering her with love and affection, providing her with much more than a place to hide. Instead they had made for her a happy, simple home. For Sarah, who had lived in elegant luxury all her life, these plain, good, down-to-earth people had provided a foundation for her own feelings of confidence to be rekindled.

Sarah was very glad that Peggy and Jeremiah had convinced her to take up residence here to await the birth of the baby. After that horrid day when her pregnancy had been discovered, she had wanted only to flee to England as fast as possible. But the Slades had convinced her of the dangers of an arduous voyage in her condition and the futility of doing it merely to escape the baby's father. "Sarah," Peggy finally pleaded, "if we *promise* not to tell Stewart where you are, will you please reconsider living with the Kempers? Mind you, we still believe Stewart has an obligation and should be told, but we respect the fact that it is your decision."

Sarah had agreed to this at last, especially after Peggy and Jeremiah had promised not to aid Stewart in finding her. Hopefully she would have time to leave with the babe before his homecoming. She believed the Slades' complicity had a great deal to do with Stewart's complete lack of interest in her, which was obvious in his decision to stay away for over five months. Had he even considered the possible consequences of his actions on the island, he should have returned by now, if only to see what their tryst might have spawned. His avoidance of Sarah could only mean that he neither thought of her, nor cared.

Remembrances of Stewart were beginning to fade for Sarah. Her bitterness had been so strong for a while that it had started the process of forgetfulness – the only thing Sarah could count on to dull the pain of her unrequited love. And because of this abatement in her longing, she had recently made some important plans.

She had decided to lie about her pregnancy, rather than tell the truth to her parents. The truth would make her life miserable -- for her parents would not only demand a marriage, but would insist that she wed a man they no longer respected. Sarah and Stewart would be trapped in a loveless match, fraught with recriminations on all sides. She could not imagine a more difficult life.

To spare everyone, she had decided she would tell them that she had fallen in love with one of the officers on the voyage to America and that they had planned to marry but never had a chance because he had died in the pirate hijacking. She would console them with the fact that he had been from a good English-born family, and that for the sake of their friends, they could explain that their daughter was a widow. They would believe her, of course, for she had never been known to lie. It was the story she told to the Kempers and they were satisfied. Indeed, she had almost begun to believe the tale herself. If only her mind could separate her gallant sailor's appearance from that of Stewart's ....

"I think I will go and check on my bread, Elsa," Sarah stated, shuffling behind the woman as she made her way to the back door. "The dough should have risen by now." Not waiting for a response, Sarah entered the farmhouse kitchen, enjoying the enveloping warmth and sweet smells that surrounded her. She checked the bread, inordinately proud of the two pans filled with plump, smooth dough. After she split the tops and poured generous amounts of melted butter into the creases, she deftly swung open the iron door of the wood-fired hearth oven and slid the pans inside.

Thanks to Elsa, Sarah had become quite handy in the kitchen, learning to cook and bake several simple recipes, looking forward each day to improving her culinary skills. At times she thought this is what she would miss most upon her return to England – the simple and heretofore unknown pleasures of the kitchen.

Sarah left the generous kitchen, walking through the low-beamed parlor-dining room area for her comfortable bedroom on the far end of the farmhouse. The home was small by the standards of a successful landowner like Stewart, but it had been built with plans for expansion as years passed and circumstances changed. Right now it was basically one structure with three bedrooms: for the Kempers, Stewart and any visiting guests.

The Kempers had settled Sarah in the guest room. It contained a simple vanity, a wardrobe, a large featherbed and nightstand. Each piece was simply and beautifully made. Sarah was more pleased with the modest but comfortable quarters than even her own luxurious room in England, for she tended it herself.

In fact, she and Elsa shared nearly all the household chores. Sarah smiled, thinking how her mother would react to this, especially if she could see her daughter in her present condition. The English lady-of-the-manor supervised housekeeping but rarely participated in the more mundane chores of dusting, sweeping and washing. And certainly not when they were in a family way! But Sarah enjoyed her duties, and more than that, was pleased that Elsa did not consider her pregnancy a reason for confinement. Being cared about and kept busy was so much more rewarding than being coddled, Sarah decided as she removed Elsa's boots and hung the large man's overcoat on a peg.

Smoothing back her chestnut hair which was tied in a loose bow at the nape of her neck, Sarah fluffed her bangs as she reentered the parlor and began dusting the simple but handsome furniture. She was just finishing sweeping the colorful braided rugs that covered the wide-planked floors when Elsa returned, announcing that she was going to begin preparing the midday meal.

Some time later, as Sarah was slicing her prized bread into thick slabs, Johann Kemper returned from his morning's labors. A tall, large man with thinning brown hair, pointed nose and the same rosy cheeks as his wife, Johann Kemper was a somber fellow, but with gray eyes that spoke of a hidden humorous vein. Sarah had learned from him that he and Elsa had met Stewart in Amsterdam several years before when they were seeking passage to the New World. They and their young son were looking to carve out a better way of life than the one afforded them in their native Germany. Johann had served in the military but sought a less restricted life for his son who would have been forced to enter military training at the tender age of 12 had they decided to remain.

Stewart had offered Johann the job of helping him build the farmhouse and then, with his shipping interests taking up so much of his time, he asked the Kempers to stay on as caretakers. The situation was better than they had ever hoped for, and though Johann was not one to talk much, when he did speak of his employer, his voice was tinged with an emotion that one could almost call worship.

Elsa and Johann's son, Albin, was now married and living on a small farm several hours' ride from Stewart's farm. Albin and his wife, Lydia, were expecting their first child in April, and arrangements for this exciting event were the topic at their mid-day meal.

"I don't know why you are so concerned about me," Sarah teased them. "You have all the neighbors taking turns checking on me each day, you've arranged for Cecily and Tom Weeks to help me with the chores, and you've laid in enough provisions to see me through next winter! I will be fine. The baby is not due till summer. Remember, it is only April."

"*Ja*, I know, *liebling*, but iss not gut for you to be alone," Elsa cautioned as they ate a delicious venison stew.

"But I won't be alone that often," Sarah insisted, "and you've told me yourself nothing untoward ever happens. You've been here by yourself many times, Elsa."

"*Ja*, das true, but never with child," Elsa retorted, but smiled in spite of herself. "Johann and I would be happier if you vas to go vis us, to be vis Albin and his Mary."

"But you know I will be more comfortable here." Sarah responded for what seemed the hundredth time. "I feel fine, but not up to such a journey. We wouldn't want anything to happen to 'our *Kinderlein*' now, would we?"

Both Johann and Elsa chuckled at this, and the three silently reaffirmed the plans already made.

CHAPTER 36

April 6, 1810

The drops of rain, though light, were steady and cold. Sarah, bundled in her man's overcoat, her oversized boots, and a crumpled wide-brimmed hat belonging to Johann, was plodding through the barnyard mud, sifting grains through her hands to feed Elsa's hens. They, too, looked rather sorry, their brown feathers matted down by the rain. They clucked and fussed as Sarah walked through the flock, and fought among themselves for each grain.

The Kempers had been gone for three days. The Weeks children, Cecily and Tom, usually performed the barnyard chores, but today was Sunday and she knew they were not coming. And if the rain kept up, they would probably not be able to visit tomorrow.

Sarah didn't mind, however. She rather enjoyed the chores that had been left to do. Johann's small herd of cows was being tended by the Weeks' at their own homestead so she had little to worry about except feeding the chickens, the two goats, from which she got her milk, and collecting eggs.

Her wide, shallow basket nearly empty, Sarah shook out the last of the grain and was about to return to the house when she heard the slosh of a horse's hooves on the path between the farmhouse and the barnyard. Somewhat surprised to have a visitor, she whirled around, clutching the basket to her body ... and nearly choked on the gasp that escaped her as the vision of the rider rose up from the mist.

Stewart Chamberlain was obviously stunned by her presence but managed to recover enough to jest, "I hadn't realized the Kempers took on some help while I was away. How are you, Sarah?" he asked quietly, dismounting in a smooth, graceful motion.

"You ... you ... what are you doing here?" Sarah squeaked defensively, conscious of her gross appearance.

"This is my home, in case you've forgotten," he replied matter-of-factly, taking a kerchief from beneath his black cloak in order to wipe his face and neck. As he cocked his wide-brimmed black hat to the back of his head, Sarah was immediately aware of how much more handsome he looked than she had ever remembered. His strong, chiseled features, tanned by the Southern sun, the crop of springy dark hair, and those dashing brown eyes that missed nothing on her startled face – he was as striking as ever. It seemed, too, that he had gotten taller, but then she remembered the ugly, flat boots on her feet, and blushed.

Not knowing what else to do, she began walking toward the barn. Stewart joined her, leading his horse. "I thought you weren't returning to Massachusetts till the fall. That's what you said in your last letter," she forced out, clutching the round basket to her body.

"I felt I'd been away too long," he answered as they reached the dry dimness of the barn. "I have business to take care of here ... and I haven't been tending to it." He gave her a long, look. "I told your father I would see to your wellbeing, and from the looks of things, I've been neglecting my duties."

This remark infuriated Sarah and she lashed out, "I am absolutely fine, and have been well cared for by both your family and the Kempers. You needn't have returned for my sake."

His unexpected appearance shocked her to the core. All the longing that she thought had dried up was there again, as if it had never left. And to top it off, the baby was kicking up a storm, as if she, too, recognized her father's presence. Sarah desperately clutched the basket closer to her bosom.

As Stewart removed the horse's saddle, he echoed her sentiments. "Well, I must admit, despite your peculiar attire, I don't think I've ever seen you looking quite so beautiful. Perhaps you were always meant for a humble life. It does become you," he offered in that warm, sultry voice that always left her weak.

"I don't appreciate being mocked," she retorted, nervous as a cat. "Do you expect me to feed Elsa's chickens in a ball gown? In this weather?"

He ignored her ire, except for a slight twinkle in his brown eyes. "By the way, where is Elsa?"

"The Kempers have gone to be with Albin and Lydia, who's having a ... baby." She nearly stumbled on the last word, but covered her nervousness quickly. "The Weeks and other neighbors have been helping with the chores, until today that is."

"Why didn't you go with them?" he asked, rubbing down the horse with a dry blanket.

"I preferred staying here. The Kempers had enough to worry about without me tagging along. Besides, I can take care of myself."

"You mean you're here alone?" he inquired, his brow creasing in a frown.

"As I said," she retorted, as if talking to a slow wit, "the Weeks children are helping with the chores and other neighbors come by each day. I would not call myself 'alone.'"

"Well I would," he snorted angrily. "You are quite as stubborn as ever. I must speak to the Kempers about letting you have your way. You never did know what was best for you."

"I beg your pardon," she challenged sharply, "but you are in no position to determine my situation at this point! Why don't you just go back to Boston – or Charleston – and leave me alone!"

Stewart laughed at her outburst, further infuriating her. "Still jealous of Felicia, aren't you? But if you recall, it was your choice to end our relationship. Was I supposed to give up all feminine companionship as a result?"

"Knave!" she spat, wasting no time flouncing off in the direction of the stable door. But Stewart was finished with his horse and quickly caught up with her before she got outside.

"Sarah, wait!" he called but she ignored him. Like a shot, he grabbed her arm and in so doing, pulled her off balance, knocking the basket from her hand. Before she knew what happened, she was pulled up against his powerful length. "What in God's name..." he whispered hoarsely, as her hat tumbled to the dirt floor.

They stared at each other for an endless moment, and then, blue eyes snapping, she pushed against his chest with all her might. He released her but kept his hand on her arm to steady her as she stumbled backward, her lips pinched into a tight, defiant line. Immediately his eyes went to the mound covered by her coat. Their eyes met again, his wide with disbelief, hers challenging, hiding the dreaded apprehension that she felt.

"Sarah," he said, his voice rendered quiet. "You're going to have a baby?"

Sarah snatched her arm away from his grip, easy enough to accomplish in his present state of shock. But he managed to recover before she could escape him. With a sudden move, he blocked her path. "By God, Sarah, answer me!"

"Do I need to?" she taunted him. "I believe some things speak for themselves. And you were always quite astute. If you don't mind, I would like to return to the house."

This time, Stewart let her pass, and Sarah was filled with overwhelming pain. A warm tear mixed with the cold rain beating on her face as she returned to the farmhouse kitchen. She was furious with herself for fearing that he would saddle up his horse again and leave, riding out of her life again as quickly as he had entered it.

Well, it wouldn't be the first time a man flew the consequences of his appetites, and besides, her plans did not include the baby's father at all. It was just that seeing him reminded her of all the things she had worked so hard to forget – the most important of which was that she loved him, desperately.

CHAPTER 37

It was close to an hour before Stewart entered the farmhouse. But he hadn't left, and Sarah was secretly pleased that she'd taken pains to freshen up. She had fixed her hair in a feathery upsweep and had donned a fresh linen frock of dark green. It couldn't disguise the fact that she was pregnant, but at least if gave her a more elegant appearance than her raggedy work clothes. And she needed all the confidence she could muster.

It was hard to tell if Stewart was angry, miserable, or simply in a state of shock. His eyes rested for a moment on her as he removed his coat and all that she could discern was that the humor, the beguiling twinkle, was completely gone. He looked ready to attend a funeral.

"There's food ... if you're hungry," she offered as a way to break the uncomfortable silence. He nodded and Sarah left to dish up the vegetable soup she'd prepared earlier.

She laid a place for him at the head of the dining table, and one for herself at the foot, wishing she could eat in the kitchen, far away from his presence.

She'd taken only a mouthful when, his food untouched, he spoke in a tight, restrained voice. "Were you planning to let me know?"

The question surprised her, giving her no time for tact or evasion. "No," she whispered.

Stewart stared at her in silence. When she could stand his piercing gaze no longer, her eyes dropped again to her food. As she did so, his fist came down on the table with a ferocious bang. The pewter ware clattered and Sarah, strung taut as a bow, nearly jumped out of her skin.

"Hell's bells, Sarah. That is *my child!* You have no right to deny me the *courtesy* of at least letting me know of its existence. If you weren't pregnant, I'd wring your neck!"

Not nearly as frightened as she was infuriated by his outburst, Sarah shouted, "This is *my* baby, Stewart Chamberlain! There were no vows spoken between us. We are *not* married and you have no rights or responsibilities concerning this child. You can't even prove it is yours," she blurted, "but there is no doubt that it is *mine!*"

"I have no doubts about its parentage," Stewart rejoined angrily, daring her with his furious gaze, "and neither have you! I told you, madam," he added, his deep voice thundering, "that if a child should come from our relations, that I would take full responsibility. Surely you remember that!"

"Indeed I do!" Sarah retorted. "But I don't want your money. I don't want this child to have your name, and furthermore, I wish to God you had never shown your face here!" Immediately she burst into tears, totally relinquishing any advantage her words might have given her.

Sobbing into her dinner napkin, Sarah released all the emotions pent up within her since she had witnessed his totally unexpected arrival. The longing had not died; it had only lain dormant, and she was sick with the fresh pain, knowing that he would be forced now to deal with her honorably and that his actions would have nothing to do with his heart – only his conscience. And she was still so lovesick that a very large part of her was rejoicing that he was here and would have to stay because of what they had created in their breathless, heedless passion so many months ago.

But this child she was carrying had made her stronger than she ever believed she could be. Maybe, just maybe she could survive the onslaught of his overpowering presence – now that she wasn't alone to face it anymore.

Sniffling, she raised her head, wiping her red-rimmed indigo eyes in order to meet his gaze clearly. The look he returned was puzzling, a disturbing mixture of concern and bafflement – and something else that brought her quicksilver temper to the fore.

"Don't you dare, Stewart Chamberlain!" she choked. "Don't you *dare* pity me." Seeing his mouth drop open, she rushed on. "I have taken a lot from you since we had the misfortune of meeting, including your seed. And perhaps you haven't had time to notice, but I am a great deal stronger than that stupid young girl you once tried to seduce in my mother's gardens. No thanks to you, I have survived everything that has happened to me since we met, and until you galloped into my life two hours ago, I was handling my affairs very well, thank you. You can ride right out of here now and it wouldn't make one whit of difference to me," she lied. "Only a handful of people know whose baby this truly is, and I can live very comfortably and respectably without having her real father own up to his indiscretions.

"So," she finished, rising regally from the table, "don't you dare say or do anything because you feel sorry for me. You'd be better off to leave than to try."

Tossing her napkin on the table for emphasis, Sarah, her jaw set, turned abruptly to stomp toward the bedroom. Again, she was not followed, and this time she was relieved, for the effort to make her point had exhausted her. Closing the door firmly behind her, she sighed and practically fell onto the soft bed, shaking with emotional fatigue. As she drifted into a much-craved slumber, she thought again how every crisis in her life paled in comparison to the turmoil caused by the love she bore for the man in the next room.

The bedroom was dark, save for the dull glow of a solitary lantern on the bedside table. Sarah snuggled deeper into the fold of the heavy wool afghan that had been placed over her, as she woke to the persistent patter of rain on the window.

"I brought you some milk," a deep voice from the shadows spoke. "You did not touch your supper. I thought you needed something."

Sarah groggily pushed herself up from the downy soft bed, not ungrateful for the strong hands that quickly came to her aid. Moving in her present condition wasn't nearly as easy as it used to be. She avoided the dark gaze upon her as Stewart arranged the pillow more comfortably, then handed Sarah the tall mug of warm goat's milk. She drank without comment, waiting for him to speak.

When he did, it was with some relief that Sarah recognized a tenderness returning to his voice. "You are quite a woman, Lady Sarah Tremont," he intoned softly, watching her from the chair he'd placed close to the bed. "I admit I was more than a bit surprised to find you here today ...."

"Then no one told you?" Sarah asked, surprised. She'd assumed that Peggy had leapt at the opportunity Stewart's early return to Boston had provided to maneuver them into a confrontation, even though it was obvious that Sarah's condition had remained a secret, as she had demanded.

"Jeremiah told me you'd gone to visit relatives in Philadelphia. No doubt at your insistence," he added wryly, not expecting confirmation. "I was disappointed, a fact you may or may not wish to believe, and decided to come here for a while. To cool my heels, you might say."

Sarah's heart gave a lurch at the last remark.

"Damn it, Sarah," he sighed, moving forward to peer into her shadowed face. "God's truth is, I missed you. I remembered a lot more than I meant to about us, including what a self-righteous, arbitrary little spitfire you could be when you had your hackles raised. But that always seemed to pale when I remembered some of our better moments, like the night you begged me to ...."

"Stop it," Sarah cried out, covering her burning ears with shaking fingers.

"Why, Sarah? Why do you fight it so?" Stewart persisted, moving his large frame onto the bed beside her and laying a restraining hand on her shoulders as she tried to turn away. "Do you have some romantic notion that every man and woman find such rapture and fulfillment beneath a shared blanket? Do you think I am talking about something either one of us could find with anyone else?" He waited but she refused to take the bait. "Well, I'm not," he answered his own question. "And since I am the only one of us who could make a judgment, I am asking you to consider that it may be something worth marrying me for ... besides what I can offer you materially."

"You are loathsome," Sarah hissed, heartbroken at his crude offer of sex and money, when all she wanted, needed, was his love. "I do not need to marry for what you offer. I had one before we met and the other is the only reason you're asking at all. Tell me this: If I were not with child, would you have ever mentioned the word 'marry' today – or tomorrow – or ever?"

He didn't speak, so she continued, fueled by her disappointment. "You're such a blackguard. I am sure the thought of a bastard doesn't faze you. So what is it, Stewart? Are you feeling the need for an heir to leave your great fortune to?" she spat sarcastically. "Is that why you can offer marriage without gagging?" Furious, she tried to wrestle herself away from his suddenly painful grip.

But he wouldn't let go. "No you don't, you little hellcat," he ground out through clenched teeth. "Motherhood hasn't blunted your claws one bit, has it? You still believe I am a scoundrel and even an honest proposal won't make you believe otherwise. Well, since you think the worst of me anyway, I've nothing to lose by doing this."

And to her horror, he did what she most feared. His mouth came down on hers, hard and bruising, as he folded his arms around her in a captive embrace. He was ruthless, wasting no time in exploring the sweet depths of her mouth with his tongue. She struggled in vain to stave off his practiced assault, but in his anger he was devastating, using every sensuous onslaught he knew her to be vulnerable to. As she lay imprisoned, he managed to free one hand to stroke her cheek, her neck, and the sensitive places around her ear. And then, as she was swimming in the forbidden rapture of his kiss that had suddenly turned tender and teasing, she felt his fingers move down the buttons of her gown.

She sobbed, wrenching her swollen lips from his. "Stewart, you can't! Not now, not like this," she pleaded. "The baby!"

"That baby,' he whispered ruthlessly, 'is going to be a bastard unless I can convince you that marriage to me is not only something you can tolerate, but enjoy." His hand continued its relentless trail down over her breasts and protruding abdomen, exposing the chemise that remained between her and his exploring fingers. "Tell me you've forgotten," he taunted her, his full lips raining kisses on her face and neck, to the skin above her chemise. "Tell me you don't want me to make love to you ever again." For his answer, he took her lips in a soul-searching kiss as his gentle fingers explored the heaviness of her swollen breasts.

His ardor was too much to bear. He was bringing back all the feelings Sarah had willed herself to forget. "Please don't do this," she sobbed as his hand gently trailed along her full belly.

Stewart's dark eyes moved over her face that was illuminated by the candle's glow, but he wasn't seeing her. Sarah was strangely mesmerized by his far-off look that was fixed upon her – but not. And then he spoke softly, in an unusually muffled, emotion-filled voice.

"My son beckons for some consideration," he whispered almost reverently. And it was then that Sarah noticed that his large hand had stopped its sensuous movements and was spanning her belly, which was fluttering with the life it nurtured inside.

A slow, ridiculously proud smile overtook Stewart's face as he watched his fingers bounce and sway. "Look how strong he is," Stewart cried softly, completely overtaken by the miracle beneath his hand.

"She," Sarah replied gently, with a firmness that brooked no argument.

"What?" he replied distractedly, dragging his eyes back to her.

"She," Sarah repeated patiently. "It's a girl."

Stewart looked confused for a moment, and a grin creased his handsome features. "And how is it you know this for sure?"

"I am her mother and have borne her these past six months," Sarah rejoined smugly, but without rancor. "You may wish to call it sorcery, but I know it is a girl."

Stewart then chuckled indulgently. "I prefer to call it your contrariness. You think perhaps a daughter would disappoint me?" He paused, scanning her firm-set mouth for the truth that it indeed bore. "No, Sarah. 'Twill do you no good to lump me with those who consider females less desirable progeny. A daughter would please me well, even" he added intimately, "if she were only half as beautiful and intelligent as her mother."

He kissed her again, this time with a lovingness that stirred her immeasurably more than his passion had only moments ago. With a fateful sigh, her arms crept around his neck as he fitted himself more comfortably to her contours, letting his hands softly study her new shape. He had called her beautiful, and hadn't bolted upon seeing her with child. Indeed, he seemed most pleased about the entire situation. Sarah could not fight the feeling of delirious contentment.

No, he didn't love her, but his actions *were* loving, and Sarah admitted that they counted for a great deal.

"Sarah?" he called gently, bringing her out of her pleasant reverie.

"Mmm?" she answered drowsily, drugged by his tenderness.

"I'm going to get the preacher to marry us tomorrow."

"Mmm," she replied, feigning apathy, though her heart quickened with his words.

"For now," he continued in a husky, nerve-tingling voice, "I think I will spend the night convincing you not to change your mind ...."

CHAPTER 38

Sarah yawned sleepily, feeling smug and contented beneath the down comforter that fit like a cocoon about her bare flesh. Refusing to open her eyes to the pale light, she listened to the hypnotic rainfall outside.

Curling her limbs around her smooth, firm belly, Sarah hugged herself, quite convinced that nothing could ever equal the happiness she felt at this moment. Her soon-to-be husband had left earlier with orders to sleep as long as she wished, while he had gone to do the chores, which would be followed by a trip to the nearest village to invite the preacher to call in the afternoon.

Sarah smiled to herself, enjoying the delicious memories of the night before. Reluctant to make love because of the baby, nevertheless Stewart had persuaded her that there was much to do in the way of becoming reacquainted with each other's bodies. And they had, during what Sarah considered to be the most romantic night she had ever spent with her handsome, virile, considerate lover.

And today he was going to be her husband in a real marriage, not one that had been forged merely by two people signing a piece of paper.

It was going to be a wonderful marriage, Sarah mused, if last night were any indication. Stewart had been gentle, tender, patient, and when he wasn't concentrating on her, he had been most enthusiastic about the child they would soon have. No small wonder was this miracle to him, and he seemed genuinely eager to become a real father.

The sound of distant hoof beats suddenly broke Sarah's revelry, and with a gasp at her own laziness, she struggled out from under the covers. It must be quite late if Stewart were back already from the village! Pushing herself to the side of the bed, she scanned the room for a robe but could find none.

With a shudder born of the chill, she pulled herself out of bed and pattered to the wardrobe to find a wrapper. She was still shaking and searching when the door swung open and there was Stewart, looking damp and breathless but not much the worse for wear.

Surprised by his sudden appearance, Sarah blushed, pulling the skirt of one of her gowns out of the closet to cover herself.

With a hearty laugh, Stewart took a step toward her. "Do you have any idea how you look?" he grinned, enjoying the vision of her tousled hair falling past her shoulders, the long limbs peaking from beneath the fabric she held clutched in her hands, and the teasing glimpse of other places.

"Y-you startled me," Sarah gasped, overwhelmed by a sense of modesty. Last night was one thing, but here in broad daylight, and she being the only one disrobed, was quite another. "Let me dress. I will be but a minute."

Stewart advanced again. "A minute is too long, and perhaps I don't want you dressed," he said leeringly, amused by her shyness.

"Have a care, Stewart," Sarah cried, receding into the wardrobe as he moved closer. "I'm cold." In truth she was frightened that he would find her misshapen body distasteful in the light of day. And after last night, it was something she could not bear to suffer.

"What a fickle wench you are," he teased, lifting a lock of her chestnut hair and rubbing it against his jaw. "You allow me to worship your body all night, yet in the morn I find that the temple is closed? I think not ... " he murmured, skillfully snaking a hand around the materials she held against her, as his eyes locked hers in a heated gaze.

Timidly, she ducked her head, holding herself rigid beneath his gentle but purposeful touch. Pulling her away from the meager shelter of her hanging clothes, his soft mutterings brought a tingling to her earlobe. "Who's this stranger I hold in my arms? Where is the woman who tortured me to the brink of madness only hours ago?" His mouth found hers unwilling, but under his practiced movements, her lips became pliant and soon she was straining closer, wanting the intimacy his touch promised. He caressed her supple roundness with burning fingers as he trailed warm lips along the column of her throat. She sighed at the rough tingling sensuousness of his clothes against her nakedness, wanting again to drown herself in his pervasive virility.

"God," he whispered unevenly, "you are more a temptation than ever. It will be my undying pleasure to keep you with child, if only I can withstand this torture." To hear him speak of the future pleased her immensely, even as she reluctantly accepted his suddenly cooled ardor. With a sigh, he held her away from his body, noticing the attractive blush of her pale skin. "Get dressed, you wanton," he teased, "before we both forget the wisdom of our sacrifice." After one last abrupt, fiercely possessive kiss, Stewart released her suddenly and departed, almost as swiftly as he'd entered. Sarah was left staring at the door until a reactive trembling shook her body into action. But whether it was from the heat of his passion or the chill of the room, she did not pause to ponder.

"The road is a mess, and the bridge is awash," Stewart was saying between bites of the late morning repast Sarah had prepared for them. "I got only as far as the Weeks' farm before turning back. I'm afraid there's no point in summoning the parson today ... or even tomorrow perhaps. Until the river crests, traveling is out of the question."

Disappointment was written in Sarah's wide blue eyes, but she attempted to hide it by saying, "I expect the weather would have kept the Weeks away, too."

"Oh, they offered to make the journey, even in this deluge," Stewart replied, reaching for a slice of the fresh bread Sarah had warmed for them, adding, with a gleam in his eyes, "but I think we'll manage, don't you?"

Sarah blushed ridiculously, to Stewart's considerable amusement. He chuckled, "I have exhausted my imagination to make you a woman of experience, and yet you still color like a virgin. Look at you," he chortled, rising to place a kiss on her bowed head. Using a long finger to tilt her pointed chin upward, he spoke in gentler tones, "Come now, my sweet innocent. See me off. I'm going to bring in more firewood, and then we're going to barricade ourselves against this depressing storm."

As the day passed, Sarah experienced an increasing restlessness that had little to do with the steady rain outside. She knew its cause but was hard-pressed for a solution. Despite Stewart's seemingly complete commitment to marriage and family, there were still too many questions battering about in her mind.

Why had he remained in Charleston while she, accompanied only by her broken heart, had traveled to Boston? Why had he then stayed away so long? And despite the confession he had made about missing her, Sarah did not truly believe he'd come here to await her return from the fabricated trip to Philadelphia.

With each passing hour, she was more convinced that Stewart had found himself trapped into a situation with but one honorable solution – and she did not want marriage for that reason alone.

Oh, at first she had. Seeing him again after all those lonely months, feeling his intoxicating nearness, experiencing the joys that only his touch had ever provoked – those reawakened desires had proved powerful persuaders.

But where was the love? And how long could the marriage survive without it? Pretending to be his wife had been one thing, but the charade had been successful only because of the threat inherent in a poor performance. What were their chances under the present circumstances?

Could he be faithful to her? She doubted that very much. There was Felicia, of course, but what of the others she did not even know about? Stewart was a traveler, and there was no indication that the marriage would alter that fact. Could she stand the separations even if fidelity were not a concern? Their parting had nearly destroyed her once. It would be no less demolishing a second time.

As horribly difficult as it was going to be, knowing it would irrevocably splinter her heart, Sarah made a decision. The weather was cooperating, as if God himself was forcing her to make a choice. The parson could not come to sanctify the marriage, for there was no marriage to bless. And there wouldn't be.

Making the decision was one thing, Sarah knew. Carrying it out would be something much more challenging. But then something happened to change the course of events forever.

CHAPTER 39

It was nightfall when Sarah realized that the occasional contractions she'd been feeling during the course of the day were no longer sporadic or benign. Curiously fearful of alarming Stewart, she kept her condition to herself, as if sharing would make real what she did not want to be. It was too early, she chided herself; the pains would go away.

Finishing up a pure white muslin baby gown, she feigned absolute concentration over her work whenever her rounded belly tightened, praying that Stewart, who sat near her in the glow of the lantern, would not notice that she held her breath or creased her brow.

Fortunately, he seemed engrossed in reading Johann Kemper's journal which told of the success of the farm. It was hard to tell that there was so much unspoken between the two; they appeared perfectly, silently, in tune.

Immediately after the latest pain, Sarah decided that she must seek isolation for it was becoming nearly impossible to keep from gasping. "Stewart," she began nonchalantly, "I think I will retire now, if you don't mind."

"Is anything wrong," he responded, closing the ledger as he moved forward in his chair to look at her more closely.

"Of course not," she dismissed him lightly. "It's just that my eyes are tired from this stitchery, and I thought I'd go to bed, rather than take a rest. I can finish it tomorrow." Seeing that he was about to rise, she gestured hastily, "Oh please, don't trouble yourself. There's no reason you need to retire so early."

"Afraid that I may ravish you again?" he crooned teasingly, lifting himself effortlessly from the chair.

Ducking her head to hide her fear, she rejoined negligently, "Of course not! I'd given you credit for *some* sensitivity, if only because your efforts are ultimately fruitless. You know we can't ...."

He refused to be bated. "I was merely going to offer you a hand, my sweet, and tuck you in. You seem to have a bit of trouble moving around today." *Had he noticed after all*, she wondered.

"Please do not coddle me," Sarah retorted, even though she took his proffered hand. "Were I not perfectly capable of negotiating, I'd not have been left to fend for myself ... Oh my God!"

Sarah stood riveted to the floor as a gush of warm liquid trailed beneath her pantaloons. Clutching Stewart's fingers, she stared wide-eyed, her mouth shaped in an exaggerated *O*, her senses reeling.

"What is it, Sarah," he asked intently, his hands rising to her shoulders to steady her.

"I-I ... I don't ... I'm all ...." she struggled, and it was only because she cast her indigo eyes downward over her stomach that Stewart had any idea what she was referring to.

A faint suspicion developed as he lifted her skirts just enough to see her dampened pantaloons and drops of liquid on the braided rug beneath her. "The baby," he whispered, more to himself than to her. A flash of insight prompted his next words. "'Tis all right, Sarah. It's not unusual. It simply means that we're going to be parents a bit sooner than we'd expected."

"No!" she cried out, instinctively clutching the front of his shirt with both fists. "The baby's not due for three more months! Can't we stop it?"

Realizing Sarah was panic-stricken forced Stewart to maintain an aura of calm, despite his own unease. Rubbing her arms, he said quietly, "What we can do is get you into some dry clothes ... and then we're going to have our baby," he cajoled with soft, confident words. "Come on now. Put your arms around my neck."

Too stunned to do anything but follow his orders, Sarah let herself be carried into the master bedroom, down a small hallway between her own and the Kempers'. It featured a huge four-poster bed, and a stone fireplace that took up one entire wall. It was Stewart's room, of course, and had he not been carrying her, she still would have felt his presence here by the way the room was sparsely yet exquisitely furnished. Standing her on the plush Aubusson carpeting of browns and blues, he immediately pulled back the thick, downy comforter, ordering her to begin removing her clothes. "I'll get you a gown and some linens," he told her, and then proceeded to stir up a fire in the grate.

"Stewart," she whispered unsurely, as her fingers fumbled to open the row of tiny buttons on the bodice of her gown, "are you certain ... I mean, could it be a false alarm?" Suddenly she gasped for another pain had begun, and this time she had not the warning to disguise its effects.

He was at her side at once, supporting her as the contraction expanded and diminished, noting the beads of perspiration on her temple despite the room's chill. When it had passed, he took over the task of unbuttoning her. "That was not your first pain," he said, his eyes fixed sternly on her downcast lashes.

It was definitely not a question. He seemed to know much more about childbirth than she, and for once she found his greater knowledge quite comforting, though she was loathe to admit it to him. "How long have you been in labor?" he demanded as he helped her step out of her gown.

"This afternoon," she answered quietly, "but I didn't realize it until a short while ago."

"Then I think, madam, that you've answered your own question," Stewart replied as the folds of Sarah's undergarments loosed beneath his fingers. "This is no false alarm."

Shivering from his touch as much as the room's chill, Sarah was grateful for the quilt he threw round her shoulders before he turned to get her bedclothes. "You'll have to get Dr. Claremont then," she told him somberly. "He lives ...."

"I know where Dr. Claremont lives, Sarah. In the same town as Reverend Rushing who cannot possibly pay us a visit for at least a week. Get ready, dearest," he leveled at her from the doorway. "We're going to be on our own."

Stewart returned in moments to find tears coursing silently down Sarah's flushed cheeks. She was standing exactly where he had left her, huddled beneath the heavy quilt. "Another pain, Sarah?" he asked softly, throwing the linens on the bed beside her, before taking her arms.

"No," she choked, leaning heavily against him as if she had not the strength to stand alone.

"What is it, then?" he coaxed, brushing the tears aside as he cradled her head against his wide chest, his heart contracting painfully as he felt her distress.

"I-I am so frightened," she cried, her shaking voice muffled by his nearness. "I don't know anything about having a baby. Elsa was going to bring Lydia's scientific journal so I could read it when the Kempers returned. I thought I would have time. But now, and without a doctor ...." Her words broke off in an agonizing sob.

"Shhh," he whispered, as he curved her swollen body to his length, "you have nothing to fear. I told you a long time ago that I had developed some medical knowledge over the years. And it just so happens that birthing babies is one of my specialties."

"The truth?" she returned, her huge blue eyes fixing him with a gaze of undisguised hope.

"The truth," Stewart assured her, "including my own nephew, Ethan."

"You delivered Peggy's baby?" Her eyes filled with wonder at the thought.

"Her second son is named Stewart Ethan after me," Stewart smiled proudly. "Peggy was overwhelmed with gratitude," he added arrogantly, though his eyes expressed the teasing nature of his remark.

"However did ...?" she began, curious now.

"It's a very long and rather odd story – in hindsight, of course – and I promise to tell you all about it, but not right now. I think a matter of more pressing urgency is the need to get you into your bedclothes." Immediately Stewart pulled the quilt from her shoulders, reaching for the white brushed cotton gown he had tossed on the bed. Shyly she submitted to his ministrations, her heart nearly bursting with love for this man who was so gently and confidently taking over her life once again. As he tied the satin bows in the front, she was all too aware of his knuckles grazing her breasts, and she allowed herself a moment of pretending that he loved her and that they were married. It could be so good ....

Another contraction was forming and she winced in anticipation. Sensing her tension, Stewart took her hands, which she grasped tightly. "Relax now, Sarah. Loosen your grip and take deep breaths," he ordered. "Do you want to lie down?" She shook her head negatively, her eyes fastened shut, her lips a tight line. "Good girl," he said gently, "it's better if you don't, for now at least." His thumbs made soothing motions on the back of her hands for the duration of the pain, and when it was over, he placed warm lips on her fevered brow. "You're doing fine, just fine," he murmured, though it pained him to see her suffering. "Come over to the fireplace with me. And I'll try to warm up this place a bit."

Resting as comfortably as possible under the circumstances, Sarah sat in a winged chair next to the fireplace as Stewart added logs to the paltry blaze. Soon it was roaring and the heat felt good, especially on Sarah's bare feet. Stewart stayed with her while another pain wrought its torture, and then left to get water and instruments for the birth.

As the contractions increased in frequency and strength through the night, Stewart did his best to keep Sarah comfortable. At one point, he forced her to walk the length of the room for what seemed like hours, until she was crying with both pain and frustration over his cruelty. "Say what you will," he intoned, after she upbraided him for his cold-blooded tactics, "but you'll never see a healthy island woman taking such anguish lying down. They walk until the baby is ready to arrive."

In fact, however, Stewart's bravado was a two-edged blade, and both sides were cutting deeply. Sarah's suffering was his own doing. He had taken her again and again, only vaguely cognizant of the consequences, which paled in significance to the addictive joy her body promised and fulfilled. He kept telling himself that women had babies all the time, and though Stewart had managed to participate in more than a normal man's share of birthing experiences, he had always been completely detached.

Detachment in this case was a contrivance he could only hope for. Sarah's pain was his, and all the worse for he could not suffer it himself, but was forced to live it vicariously in the wounded indigo eyes that pleaded for relief ... relief that he could not provide.

And the other sharper cut was that what she was going through may all be in vain. He had wracked his brain recalculating the pregnancy, but the fact remained: the baby was grossly premature. If it should survive the birth, there was very little chance it would live.

As the night wore on and Stewart alternately attended, forced or cajoled the courageous woman whose life had been so affected by his, he pondered these grievous thoughts and prayed that his worst fears would not be realized.

Though it was morning, the only real light emanated from the fire that was blazing strong yet silently in the hearth. Attracted to the flames, Sarah's eyes moved slowly toward the light, coming to rest on a silhouette that would forever be emblazoned on her memory.

Two heads, one covered with unruly waves, the other tiny, round and smooth, were pressed together at the brows. The tiny form was serene and quiet. Peaceful. But the larger shape was shaking uncontrollably from the effect of deep, wretched sobs that were torn from lips glistening with spent tears.

Transfixed by the sight and the sharpness of the pain it wrought, Sarah closed her eyes again, hoping that the sinking blackness into which she was falling would culminate in a merciful death.

They buried her on the hill overlooking the low-slung farmhouse, in a beautifully wrought casket that Stewart had labored on for two days, stopping only to tend to Sarah's meager needs. She had no recollection that he'd eaten or slept.

With a calmness that belied nothing – for beneath the surface was a cool, hard stone where her heart had once been – Sarah finished the gown she'd once put aside and carefully dressed the miniature form for her eternal sleep.

With uncanny determination, she denied herself any sentimental indulgence. The baby was dead, and that fact would not change no matter how perfectly formed she was, nor how beautiful her pale skin appeared, nor how angelic her tiny face looked in repose. She would neither walk, nor talk, nor grow to become the apple of her father's eye.

She would be denied her mother's love beyond what they had shared these six months of her existence, and she would never know that she was responsible for the only time her father had ever cried.

They named her Mary, after Stewart's mother, and Catherine, after Sarah's, and she was laid to rest in the drizzling rain; the same rain that had started before she was born.

CHAPTER 40

"Sarah, please," the Duchess begged in an uncharacteristically harsh voice, her frustration at its peak, "you must eat something. You are starving yourself to death, don't you see?"

Hollow blue eyes trained themselves on the tearful green ones, and the Duchess recoiled in horror, seeing affirmation there. "Oh my darling," she finally cried out when she had regained her voice, "why are you doing this? Won't you tell me? Can't I help you? Sarah, I demand...."

"Mother, please," Sarah replied tiredly, directing her gaze to the garden below her bedroom window. *Where Stewart had first kissed her.* She winced and turned back to the distraught figure hovering nearby. "I am not starving myself, Mother. I assure you." *There are much slower ways to die.*

"You've told none of us anything that explains your behavior these past four months. I can only assume your captivity was radically more terrible than your account," the Duchess sobbed, wringing her slender hands.

"Believe me, Mother," Sarah answered through clenched teeth, absently rubbing her shadowed, sunken eyes, "I have told you everything there is to know about the hijacking, and you have the letter from Captain Slade to verify the events." By rote, she added, "I have lost Tegan and I suffered an illness on the boat. It simply takes time to regain one's strength...."

Sarah's mother interrupted. "That would explain your weight, perhaps, but not that look in your eyes. No, Sarah, you have changed; you are a stranger to all of us – and I will not rest until we learn its cause." Imperious though she sounded, she was not prepared for the effect of Sarah's icy hand grasping her forearm suddenly.

"Shall I assume this is some kind of threat?" Sarah asked coldly.

"You've left us no choice," her mother cried out, pulling her arm away shamefully.

"No choice but what?" Sarah bit back, suddenly unnerved.

"You were not supposed to know," the Duchess wept, "but we had to do something. Don't you see, Sarah? We want our daughter back."

Sarah ignored the heartfelt plea, but a creeping sense of dread forced her to pursue the other remark. "Tell me, Mother," she ground out, her hands shaking, "what have you done?"

"Y-your father has sent for ...."

"Who, Mother?" Sarah implored recklessly, frightened, angry, and filled with speechless dread. "Who?"

"M-Mr. Chamberlain," she sobbed, her beautiful eyes glistening with a tearful apology.

Though she was expecting it, the name hit Sarah like a blow to the stomach. Sheer survival instincts alone allowed her voice to maintain a semblance of calm. "You are wasting your time – and Mr. Chamberlain's – indeed if he does deign to come."

"He's coming, Sarah," the Duchess uttered as a parting comment, her words bolder in direct relation to her proximity to the bedroom door. "His business relationship with your father is at stake."

"Then you are being autocratic – and foolish," Sarah snapped back. "Stewart has nothing to do with me. If you'd but leave me alone, I would be fine!"

But there was no rejoinder as her mother solemnly quit the room. In frustration, Sarah tore at her dull, lifeless hair, a wave of nausea threatening to overcome her. *My God!* her brain screamed. *Haven't I suffered enough?*

"My God! Haven't I suffered enough?" She'd said those words once before in a fit of abject misery, and the utterance had closed, locked and barred the door against any future she might have had with Stewart Chamberlain.

Her body, a shadowy, fading appendage of an all but lifeless soul, was experiencing the tingling, painful rising of the deep hurt once again. Sarah dug her fingernails into her palms as she tried to stifle the awful thoughts, but this time, even the drawing of blood would not make her memory recede. "My God! Haven't I suffered enough?"

After Mary Catherine's simple burial, the farmhouse ceased its role as a haven for either of them. Sarah and Stewart became less than strangers; it was as though both had been struck deaf and mute. The pain was so sharp, it seemed neither could bear the risk of sharing it, and as the days wore on, Sarah felt in the deepest recesses of her heart that healing depended on her leaving ... leaving this house, this country. Leaving Stewart.

Her presence was his cross, and Sarah loved him too much to serve as a constant reminder of a dalliance gone awry. He had never misrepresented his feelings for her; yet he was willing to fulfill his obligations when they seemed inevitable. She loved him for that, and for his strength and comfort supplied so surely whenever she had needed it – until now.

The fact that he was now so distant proved his feelings of guilt, and Sarah could not bear to see him suffer so. She had to leave, so at least *he* could go on with his life, and she could ... exist.

So on a day that was incongruously bright and sunny, a day that marked two weeks since Mary Catherine's birth – and death – Sarah, with fear and trepidation, forced herself to confront Stewart with her logical, immutable plans.

She joined him for breakfast, an unusual occurrence in itself, and if he were surprised, he hid it well. Sarah, on the other hand, was visibly taken aback by his appearance. There were dark circles under his dull brown eyes; his face was gaunt. Though still handsomer than most, it was as if he'd aged before her eyes. For the first time, she noticed traces of gray in his dark, shaggy locks.

Unnerved by the sight of him she plunged into her speech before she completely lost her will. "The Kempers will be returning next week," she spoke quietly, somewhat hoarsely, watching the wake caused by her spoon stirring the cup of tea he had brought her. "I would like to be gone before they arrive."

He raised his eyes, unleashing a look of pure anguish before they glazed over with studied indifference. "Gone?"

Steeling herself, she continued, "Their daughter-in-law will have had her baby, and I think it will be difficult for them to restrain their joy in view of ...." her voice trailed off. "And I would not want them to. It would be better if I were gone."

"It's too soon for you to travel," he replied through gritted teeth, studying the plate in front of him.

"The bir ... the delivery was not traumatic," Sarah countered. "You told me yourself that very little harm was done. I feel capable of making the journey."

"It is very unwise. I cannot permit it," Stewart replied, his voice taking on a decidedly monotonous, stubborn tone.

"There is another reason," she persisted, detesting the need to resort to the second volley of her carefully planned argument. "The Kempers don't know ... about us. They think the father of the child is dead – a naval officer. I care too deeply for them to bear facing up to the truth. 'Twould be better if I were gone to avoid ...."

"Why did you lie?" Stewart asked suddenly, incredulously.

How could she explain that she'd made up the story for *his* sake as much as her own? The Kempers loved Stewart as if he were their own son. How much of their respect for him would have been lost had they known that the baby she was carrying was Stewart's illegitimate child? She could not have done that to him, or to them. With her gone, it would be *his* choice whether to reveal the truth.

"I thought it best not to complicate matters," she replied evenly. "Peggy and Jeremiah are the only ones who know, and I would prefer we leave it that way ... Not that it matters any longer ...."

"It matters to me!" Stewart choked angrily.

"Then tell them!" she gasped. "But I will not be here when you do!"

Stewart was livid, and Sarah trembled, fearing that she'd unleashed all the recriminations that seemed to haunt this house. "Where *will* you be?" he challenged.

"I want to go home."

"Your home is with me," he uttered raggedly. "We're to be married, or had you forgotten?"

Even though she had suspected that his guilt would force him to consider this option, she was shocked that he actually meant to go through with the marriage now that she'd supplied him with an exit. Her control snapped as she fought desperately against the irrational thing he was doing.

"I don't believe you!" she cried. "Your proposal – no, damn it – your *decision* that we marry was because I was carrying your child. That child is dead," she railed, tears suddenly streaming down her drawn cheeks. "And I will not be bound to you for the rest of my life as some warped form of penance you feel you owe to me – or to her – or to God himself! Let me out of your life!" she commanded in a sobbing decree. "My God, Stewart, haven't I suffered enough?"

As soon as the words tumbled out of her mouth, Sarah knew she had burned her bridges. It was true; she *had* suffered. But not because of anything he had done; rather what he had *not* done. He had not fallen in love with her. And for that he was not to blame.

But in her own pain, she had sought to hurt him, and saw with a deep sorrow that she had succeeded. She knew he had not been immune to her suffering but it was her only means of escape, and cowardly, hurtfully, she had taken it.

The muscles in Stewart's cheeks were vibrating with tension, and as he swallowed deeply, his eyes reddened. Then clawlike fingers raked through his thick, unkempt hair before they slid down his face as he emitted a totally defeated sigh. "We'll leave in the morning."

He had arranged passage for her to England immediately after their journey to Boston. She refused to stay the one night of waiting at either his home or Peggy and Jeremiah's, insisting that he not disclose her proximity. He honored her every request without discussion, even when she asked for a hired livery to take her to the ship. There were no words left to speak between them, and she did not want to make or hear an attempt when departure was imminent.

So, in the end there were no goodbyes. But when the ship set sail, she spied him standing off to the side of a crowd of well wishers, his wide-brimmed hat crushed tightly against his chest, his jaw set to the point of glacial hardness. Her heart leapt painfully at the sight of his ruffled hair and billowing coat, and she cried for nearly three days before it was possible to begin erecting the impenetrable shell that had so faithfully served her ... until today.

CHAPTER 41

"No, no *no*!" Sarah screamed, covering her eyes in defiance, squeezing her lids shut until droplets sprung from her sooty lashes. "I will *not* see him, even if King George himself commanded it!"

For once the calm, composed participant in an argument, Lady Juliana Tremont replied haughtily, "I believe Stewart would go far beyond such measures, Sarah, if you continue to refuse. He has already convinced Father of the importance of seeing you.

"I have not come to argue with you," she added coldly, "only to warn you that you'll accomplish nothing by barricading yourself in this damnable fortress you've insisted on creating." She gestured with a toss of her blond curls toward the center of Sarah's pink and blue bedroom.

With resigned disgust, Juliana continued, "I never would have thought you would be the one to put this family through such agony. Do you realize you have our own mother and father at war with each other?" Seeing the sudden uplift of Sarah's brow, she forged on. "Believe it, sister. Father thinks Stewart should be allowed to see you, and Mother is unrelenting in her efforts to protect you. From what, Sarah? Is *anything* worth what you've imposed on us?"

Sarah could not believe her ears. "You always were a selfish child," she scolded her sister. "You know nothing about anything. 'Throw Sarah to the wolves as long as I can have some peace and quiet and all the attention returned to me'," she mocked her. "That is the only reason you're here, isn't it?"

Juliana's beautifully shaped lips curled in a scathing sneer. "You are being loathsome. If you didn't already look done to a cow's thumb ...." she began, then abruptly switched her train of thought. "Downstairs," she muttered icily, "is the only man in this world who ever treated you like a woman. I don't know what has gone on between you two, but I'd wager the family jewels that you're running away from your one chance at any sort of happiness in this life. You think I don't know you love him?" Sarah winced visibly, folding trembling arms around her thin form as some cloak of protection from the truth Juliana was throwing at her. "There is only one person in this house who doesn't at least suspect you're shriveling from a broken heart – and that's Stewart Chamberlain. For God's sake, Sarah, tell him. What do you have to lose?"

"Stop it!" Sarah choked, "stop it. You do not know what you're saying."

"Don't I?" Juliana pursued relentlessly, moving closer to her weakening prey. "If he means nothing to you, then why won't you see him? Why won't you speak his name? Why are you literally wasting away? How could it be any worse to take the chance, to admit your feelings for him?"

"Because he doesn't love *me*," Sarah cried out miserably, "and I cannot bear to hear him say it. Knowing it is too much to suffer."

A satisfied smirk crossed Juliana's lovely features and she tapped her toe on the Aubusson carpet with glee, her fist balled on the rustling silk taffeta of her day dress. "It's true then, isn't it? Just as I suspected. Even the detached Lady Sarah could not remain aloof in the face of the Yankee's considerable charms."

"You-you tricked me!" Sarah gasped, a mixture of betrayal and sheer anger welling in her breast. "Juliana, you are horrid." Stumbling toward her younger sister, she moved to push her backward, but Juliana neatly sidestepped Sarah's clumsy tear-blinded approach. "Get out of my room," she sobbed, lunging onto her high, four-poster bed. "I hate you!"

Juliana, her green eyes immediately softening into a wide-eyed appeal, pleaded, "Sarah darling, I had to know, don't you see? Mother and Father are certain you were ravaged by some pirate, and I just knew in my very soul that it wasn't so. But you wouldn't confide in me." Raising her voice over Sarah's heaving sobs, she continued, "I meant what I said about telling Stewart. Do you think he'd set foot in our home if he didn't care? Even Father hasn't the means to threaten a man like him.

Sarah, listen to me!" she begged, reaching over the coverlet to shake Sarah's huddled form.

Catching the misery-filled blue-eyed gaze, she beckoned, "If you have an ounce of courage left in you, for God's sake talk to Stewart. I wasn't wrong about you, was I?" Without waiting for a reply, she said, "I am certain he loves you. I am absolutely certain."

"You are grasping at straws," Sarah choked back, wiping her wet cheeks on her sleeve as she sat up on the downy featherbed. "If I even suspected that he loved me, do you think I would be in such dire straits? You don't know anything, Juliana. You just don't know ...." Her thoughts threatened to dwell on things best forgotten until the sharp pain of longing forced her to stop.

"You're not going to do it, are you?" Juliana announced suddenly, her green eyes sparkling with characteristic impatience. "You're not going to take the one chance you have left in your life to be truly happy. Go ahead and rot in your misery then," she sniffed abruptly, turning on her heel toward the door, hesitating for a moment before turning the knob, she lashed out, "How I wish I could have made Stewart Chamberlain fall in love with me that night of my birthday party. He told me I was a coy little tease and he preferred women like you who wouldn't toy with a man's heart. But God help me, Sarah, I never would have treated him as callously as you!"

After the household had retired, Sarah crept down the hall to her parents' salon which her father used as an office when he could not sleep. She gazed upon his attractive, dignified features lovingly as he shuffled some papers out of his way. He was such a dear, wise man. She was ashamed of herself for the suffering she had caused him, for they had always been close ... until her return to England, after which she had become a stranger to all.

There was no need for preliminaries, and she gave none as she sat down in the comfortable chair beside his desk. "Did you truly ask him to come here, Father?"

His bushy brows quirked to attention, but he answered calmly, "Yes, but you must not misconstrue my involvement or my motives in this matter," he declared with an aura of both authority and benevolence. "Seeing Stewart Chamberlain or not is your own decision. My invitation was based strictly on business."

"But Mother said ...." and then she sighed wearily, her eyes closing in response to the aching struggle going on within her. "You know he has something to do with the way I have been acting, don't you?"

"'Tis a logical assumption. You've acted peculiarly since the day you met him," Tremont stated wryly. She could never accuse him of prying, she thought. If her father were to learn anything tonight, it would be because she had chosen to tell him.

But she was afraid, and ashamed. If he were to learn how completely she had made a shambles of her life, his disappointment would haunt her. He had not raised her to be a fool. "So how is it that Mr. Chamberlain is here? In England?"

"Not at my request, though I understand it is what you were led to believe," Weston intoned firmly. "I saw him in Town Tuesday last, and he asked to meet with me to discuss a business arrangement. We *are* partners, after all. I invited him here, for I've yet to learn why he should not be a guest in my house." His gray-blue eyes pierced hers deeply. "Have I a valid reason to rescind my invitation?"

She stared at him in wonder. "You would send him away if I declare? Without explanation?"

"I would," he replied pompously.

The offer was tempting, but to say yes would unfairly incriminate Stewart in her father's eyes. Her love would not permit that.

She changed the subject. "Has he said ... anything?"

"About you?" her father asked abruptly. The reluctant nod and accompanying spark in her eyes did not go unnoticed. "Not specifically. However ...." he began, hesitating for a moment before he added a completely subjective comment. "I have observed a change in the man that puzzles me. He seemed subdued, resigned perhaps. As though he had lost his confidence, his exuberance for life. 'Twere it the result of some disease," he leveled at her, "I would say that you, too, are its victim."

Ignoring her father's insinuation, her heart went out to Stewart at that moment; she realized her love was too great to allow his misguided guilt to continue. In that millisecond, she resolved to speak with him one more time; to let him know that she held him responsible for none of her pain; to conjure up a performance that would convince him that she had survived their shared past, and that with the record set to rights, he could survive as well.

Her decision made, she smiled fleetingly at her father as she rose from the chair. "I am glad that you've invited Mr. Chamberlain here, Father. We, too, have some unfinished business to discuss," she offered solemnly. "I believe I hold the antidote for this 'disease' you speak of.

"Mr. Chamberlain is a good and brave man," she added unexpectedly, "a man worthy of your trust and friendship. You needn't fear any longer that his presence would upset me. I will see him tomorrow."

CHAPTER 42

Words. So much more easily spoken than acted upon, Sarah mused groggily as dawn broke slowly outside her bedroom window. A niggling, awesome tremor began in the pit of her stomach as she realized that today was the day she would see Stewart again at last. Feeling terrified, but strangely, for the first time in months, whole, she stretched her long, slender body in a nervous, vigorous gesture. Eager, surprisingly so, to begin her toilette, Sarah threw back the downy warm covers and bounded to the softly-tufted carpet. *Today it will be over at last,* she told herself, trying to sort out these stirrings of life that had lain dormant, seemingly lost forever.

"Armor," she murmured aloud as she shook out her long, dark locks before her full-length mirror. "This scrawny body has but one more battle to fight, and then perhaps," she sighed, disturbed at the sight, "it can begin to regain some form."

Disgusted with her hollowed, wasted looks, her mind raced to thoughts of her wardrobe, trying to remember some gown that might aid her attempt to appear more voluptuous, and more healthy. As she mentally checked off day gowns, Sarah pulled the bell cord for the maid and within minutes, preparations had begun for a steaming bath. If anyone thought her interest in her toilette unusual, no one risked mentioning it, fearing perhaps that she would regress immediately to her former, apathetic self.

Scrubbing her limbs to a rosy hue, Sarah shook off dwelling on her bony appearance. There was nothing to be done about it now, and it would only interfere with the confidence she sorely needed this day. And despite her unusual slenderness, she felt alive, stronger, a growing excitement overtaking the months of lethargy. Raking her scalp, she washed her hair until the roots tingled, and when finally she emerged from the tub, dewy and deliciously sweet-smelling, she had decided on her attire.

Arrayed in fine white muslin undergarments and silk stockings, with the help of the maid Sarah donned a Turkey red printed day gown with cream lace around the low bodice and long-sleeved cuffs. The bodice was just narrow enough to hold her tightly, and she looked feminine and voluptuous. The small, well-spaced medallions of the print were a rich gold and blue, the latter matching her eyes almost perfectly. The maid who helped her brought wispy tendrils of shiny hair toward her face, and left the rest cascading in a loose knot from the crown of her head. Most unusually, Sarah's vanity forced her to touch up her dark circles with a light, tinted foundation and rice flour. She then softened her mouth with rose lip salve. After pinching her cheeks to force a bloom, she took one last look at her reflection and smiled. Her appearance would be no cause for distress today.

Feeling almost queenly in her fetching red dress, Sarah began the journey that would bring her to Stewart. Oh how benevolent she would be toward the man today. With kindness and calm dignity, she would let him know that she had survived well, the past was buried and that with her blessing he could freely take up his life again, guilt-free and confident. He would know that she, too, had survived their encounter – and the death of their child – without visible scars.

A smile threatened her full lips as she mused on the changes that would overcome this broken, hollow man as she absolved him of the pain he'd been burdened with since her departure. For the first and only time, she would have the upper hand with Stewart Chamberlain. She, the strong one, would aid and abet the recovery of the one who was suffering ... the man who had finally come upon a situation he could not alone transcend.

But that satisfied smile crumbled on her lips before it reached her eyes when, as she stepped down the main staircase, the entry door suddenly swung open and in tumbled a laughing, outrageously self-satisfied couple imbued with a vigor Sarah could only pretend to share.

"Cheat!" Stewart cried merrily as he tugged playfully at the back of Juliana's green riding jacket, causing her to fall backward laughingly into his chest, his arms closing around her waist in a much-too-familiar hug. As Sarah watched in shock, Juliana turned in his great arms and playfully pulled his thick, disheveled hair before resting her hands on his broad shoulders. "Did you think me so stupid as not to realize you could outrun me?" she giggled. "Tripping you was the only way I could win."

"What a sly feline you are," Stewart rejoined with an affectionate pat on Juliana's glowing cheek. Sarah's stomach lurched with a horrid jealousy at the familial scene. But by far the greatest shock was seeing the man only recently described to her as "subdued and resigned" brimming with vigor, his healthy, robust appearance causing Sarah's knees to turn to jelly as she involuntarily clutched the banister with quivering fingers.

Stewart Chamberlain had never looked more virile or more breathtakingly attractive. He was a dark, powerfully built Greek Adonis starkly contrasted by Juliana's pale loveliness. And in that second, she hated both of them with equal vehemence for setting her up to be the fool she'd almost made of herself.

Unable to escape, for she'd descended too far to retreat without notice, Sarah's thin shoulders stiffened in survivalist's resolve to take control of the insult thrust upon her. With her last ounce of courage, she swore neither would witness the mockery they'd made of her sacrificial act.

"Out riding so early, Juliana?" Sarah announced haughtily, beginning her march down the stairs. Smiling at the startled look in the two pairs of eyes suddenly locked on her descent, Sarah continued, "But of course, Mr. Chamberlain is here." Taunting her sister, she said sweetly, "What an unselfish hostess you are to depart from your normal habit of rising at noon." As she approached, the couple suddenly slid away from each other, Juliana looking chagrinned.

"Good day, Mr. Chamberlain. It was lovely of you to pay us a visit," she announced, proud of her ability to gracefully offer her hand in greeting.

But Sarah realized immediately that she should have known better. The look in those molten brown eyes told her that her leverage was fast approaching its end. "Sarah," he intoned intimately, ignoring her title. He took her thin fingers in his large hand, bending his head to place a searing kiss that caused a frisson of longing to nearly undo her. Nothing had changed, she realized, as his dark head rose to meet hers at eye level. *He affects me the same, and damn him, he's telling me he knows it,* she thought, her eyes widening frantically.

"Have you breakfasted yet?" she asked breathlessly, refusing to pull her fingers away from his, knowing what the withdrawal would tell him.

He did not let go. "No, will you join us?"

Though she had planned for a pleasant, dignified reunion over a leisurely repast with Stewart and her family, she had done so with the notion that she would have the upper hand. But the man before her was anything but desolate, broken. If anything, Stewart exuded more authority and self-confidence, not to mention an aura of heart-racing virility, than she had ever before remembered. Already her control of the situation was in jeopardy; another minute with the man would be her undoing.

"I had breakfast in my room" she lied, shifting her balance backward, "and was just on my way out."

"Out?" Juliana broke in skeptically, a hint of mischief in her cool voice. "Why, wherever are you going, Sarah? You haven't gone ...."

"Riding," Sarah retorted irritably, breaking the grasp Stewart maintained on her hand. "I am going riding," she announced without looking at either of the two people before her. "If you will excuse me?"

Juliana laughed merrily and Sarah clenched her teeth, a taste of pure venom welling up inside her. "In that costume? Don't be silly. Come join us, and do not be so rude to our guest."

Heedlessly risking additional embarrassment, Sarah leveled her sister with a scathing glare, ignoring Stewart's towering presence altogether. "Whose guest, Juliana? Surely not mine."

Moving quickly to the door, she jerked it open and flew down the front steps, practically colliding with Silas, as he was preparing to bring the horses Juliana and Stewart had ridden to the paddock.

"Come Silas," she ordered, ignoring his look of surprise, for he had not seen her in recent memory, "I want Serena saddled. I am going for a ride."

"Right away, Lady Sarah," the solemn little man answered, working quickly to match her pace with Fancy and Nubian in tow. The comical parade Sarah led advanced on the stable in record time, but it seemed ages before Silas had the mare saddled. Lacing up a pair of well-worn riding boots, her only concession to making her outfit more appropriate for a ride, Sarah grabbed Serena's reins as soon as they were offered. With Silas' assistance and a plea that she have a care for the animal and herself, Sarah took off through the training yard for a destination she herself did not even know. All she thought was that she had to get away from the couple who mocked her with their smugness.

"Blast," she hissed bitterly, leaning low over Serena's flanks as horse and rider hastened through the woods behind the Tremont estate. Angry tears blurred her vision as she sought to put miles between herself and the focus of her torture. Nothing had changed. She was again running from the pain and longing for a man who could promise her nothing but misery ... and the most brilliant glimpse of desire she had ever known.

As she raced across the sheltering terrain, her thoughts returned to the sight of Stewart and Juliana laughing and flirting, neither of them owning a care, while she was little more than a shadow bravely masking a savage ache. At that moment, Sarah's thoughts were so vengeful, she would have heartlessly mowed the couple down had they been in her path.

Sensing that her mistress had no specific destination in mind, Serena was, out of long habit, heading toward the Gables, the mysterious ruin where Sarah, Juliana and Jack often rode in brighter days. As the mare voluntarily slowed her pace upon sighting the retreat, Sarah raised herself up in the saddle, bent on restoring the composure she had lost. But her lungs were heavy with choking sobs, and when Serena stopped to taste the fragrant clover surrounding the Gables, Sarah dropped from the saddle and sank to the ground, too tired and miserable to fight for composure.

Hoarse sobs wracked her frail body as she sought to burrow herself in the cool turf, heedless of the havoc it was wreaking on her lovely dress. Her billowing dark hair was a protective canopy about her face and heaving shoulders, and like cat's paws, her thin fingers kneaded the sweet clover about her.

All attempt to exorcise the handsome demon who plagued her life had been fruitless, and seeing him again, so confident and sure, had completely undone whatever defense she had been able to muster in the months they had been apart. At this point, Sarah's will was so weak and vulnerable that she was certain she was losing her mind. And all because of one man ... one exciting, captivating, supremely attractive and intimately desirable man.

From his vantage point at the crest of the rise, Stewart, astride Nubian, sighted her, a pool of red fabric being gently nudged by her mount. His heart lurched in pain at the view of the crumpled, sobbing heap, and he quickly dismounted, bent on closing the short distance on foot so that Nubian would not startle Serena and cause her to harm her mistress.

Consequently Sarah did not know of his nearness until strong but infinitely gentle hands lifted her shoulders and turned her into his embrace. "No, no," she croaked, feebly resisting his comfort, her eyes squeezed shut as if to ignore the reality of his rescue.

"Are you hurt, love?" he demanded of her softly, as his practiced gaze noted her tear-streaked face and the hair plastered to her hollow cheeks. "Did Serena throw you?"

"No. Leave me," she sobbed, struggling as one coming out of a nightmare. "Please let me go."

But Stewart ignored her pleas. "No, Sarah," he pronounced, "not this time ... nor ever again." Tenderly, but with an urgency that could not be mistaken, he held her curving form against his broad chest, his cheek nuzzling her own as her face was pinned in the comforting hollow of his shoulder.

To struggle against his strength would be fruitless, and despite the foolhardiness of allowing herself the soul-searing pleasure of his dangerous embrace, Sarah could not deny that she was again where she belonged. As he quietly rocked her, satisfied that she was whole, her meager attempts to push away evolved into timid caresses of the sleek chest where his shirt gapped.

Sensing her acquiescence, Stewart's hands could not be denied the need to renew their acquaintance with Sarah's trembling body. As his fingers trailed along the soft gown from shoulder to knee, he whispered soothingly in the delicate ear beneath his warm lips. "You have run from me for the last time, my beauty. I cannot tolerate this emptiness you leave in your wake, and I will not attempt to try again ... even if I am forced to chain you to my side."

His voice, though soft, was sending shock waves through Sarah's body, and an undeniable flicker of hope was sputtering within, determined to seek fuel, even as she begged restraint. "What must this poor wretch do, Sarah, to convince you of his love? Tell me," he begged fiercely, "for it cannot be ignored, nor purged, nor left to die for want of a kindred emotion. I have tried all to no avail."

Hurt and sadness were too longstanding companions for Sarah to trust his words, though her emotions tore at her to cleave to them. "'Tis your pity that moves you," she choked. "And your guilt. From the beginning our roles were well-defined, and despite the complications, our motives stand as they are: different as night and day. I hold you responsible for nothing," she urged through gritted teeth, her face hidden in the warmth of his chest. "Why can you not leave me alone?"

"God help me, I've tried, Sarah," he said in a voice filled with desperation. Clutching her shoulder, he forced her gaze upon his own. "I know too well the sharp edge of that foolish matrimonial bargain, which I made purely out of a ridiculous notion that I could keep you in your place – a place I relegated all women – until I came to know you.

"Forgive me, Sarah, for my gluttony, but the charade we played out beneath d'Alava's nose was as much my means to an end as they were to protect you from that pirate bastard." The torment in his deep brown eyes was real. "I could not hope to surmount your stubbornness, but I knew you were vulnerable to me. I convinced Jeremiah that we needed to ratify the Special

License to keep you safe, but my intentions were selfish. I wanted you in my bed," he said, his voice harsh with remorse.

"But, my lady, you were not the only one to succumb. As surely as I stole your maidenhead, you captured my heart, and with foolish pride, I have been living a lie ever since, pretending that I did not love you with all my heart and soul."

Sarah stared at him, her blue eyes as round as full moons. "You love me?"

Stewart framed her face between trembling hands, tilting her chin closer to him. "Love you and beg you to accept my name as your own. I have known more happiness and fulfillment with you on that accursed island that I have ever felt as a man. Please let me return that joy. Let me give you a home, and nights as unforgettable as those we've already enjoyed. Please share my life with me, or know that I have no life."

Suspended in time, the two looked upon each other, each devouring the other's exposed yearning. Aching to bend her will with the touch of his lips on hers, Stewart forced himself to wait for a commitment that would be meaningless if not freely given.

Sarah, on the other hand, was awash with a torrent of emotions so sweet that she was paralyzed with bliss. But when her voice broke free, she gasped, "Oh my love!" before her arms flew around him and their lips met in a wild and joyful surrender that felled them to the sweet-smelling earth. Reveling in her abandon, Stewart opened his mouth to welcome her delicate, seeking tongue. She moaned in pleasure as firm hands pressed her body into the supple strength of his own, reacquainting himself with her slender waist and the softly-rounded hips that swayed across his loins in an urgent expression of desire.

Effortlessly Stewart rolled above her, his mouth sliding across her swollen lips to devour with fevered kisses the silky column of her throat. As his hand toured the length of her, his other cradling her in a fierce embrace, Sarah pressed her flushed face into the springy softness of his dark hair, whispering unintelligible endearments as he wove his passionate magic about her.

"You want me," he crooned, bedazzled by her fervor. "As much as I want you."

"Oh yes, darling," Sarah whispered, her body throbbing with the pleasure only he could give her. "I would have told you, shown you countless times, but I was hiding my love in fear that it would never be returned."

As his fingers moved against the buttons holding her gown together, his eyes seared her and he made his fierce confession. "Dearest Sarah, would that I could have spared you all the suffering my stubborn nature has caused. If you only knew how long I have been under your spell. I wrestled wildly with myself against sending you to Boston while I stayed in Charleston ...."

"Felicia," Sarah said, a flash of pain haunting her blue gaze.

"Felicia had nothing to do with it," he insisted, unconsciously squeezing the rounded breast beneath his exploring fingers. Her startled gasp made him aware of what he'd done, and apologetically he kissed the red fabric covering her breast, his warm breath scorching through to the aroused nipple longing for his naked touch. As he purposefully plucked away the offending layers of clothing, he continued, "I was plagued by the sight of you. Remembering how you had come to welcome me into our bed on the island, I was tormented by the time we arrived in Charleston. I admit I considered easing my lusts with Felicia, but God's truth, Sarah, I was incapable ...."

His pained admission caught Sarah completely by surprise. "You could not ...?"

"Aye, love," he muttered, recalling his discomfiture as well as Felicia's. "Men have been known to kill themselves over such a curse as befell me," he laughed without humor. "When I came to your room that night ...."

"And I sent you away ...." Sarah remembered, wincing.

"'Twas painful, but at least it proved the problem's cause. It was you I wanted, Sarah, only you. And that has been true since the day we sailed from London, I swear. But I refused to give my feelings their rightful name and sought to break the spell by sending you away from me." Her breath caught in her throat as she realized the depths of his own suffering, not so unlike her own. How foolish they had been!

Sarah realized that Stewart had become distracted by his success in parting her clothes. With flattering concentration, he was savoring the taste of the swollen bud revealed to him, causing Sarah to moan with desire.

"You are more beautiful than my tortured dreams reminded me," he purred, lovingly tracing the creamy contours of her ripe breasts. "I do not deserve this taste of heaven, but by God I would die were you to deny me now." As he caressed her, Sarah's trembling fingers found their way to the tactile delights of his chest, parting his shirt so that his warm skin could join her own.

Hugging him to her, she whispered, "I could no more deny you than I could deny the sun. I have loved you for a long time, Stewart, longer than I realized. Please let me show you how much."

Enflamed anew by her boldness, Stewart captured her mouth in a burning kiss as she slipped his shirt from his shoulders, then lighted a trail of fire as her fingers forayed beneath the flap of his close-fitting breeches.

With a groan, he lifted himself and pulled her up, bringing them both to their knees. Cupping her breasts, his thumbs wreaking havoc on her fevered nipples, Stewart rained torrid kisses on her jaw and the slender column of her throat, as she gently raked her fingertips across his lean torso. "You once cooled your desires because of an open meadow," she teased, her voice throbbing with anticipation. "Let me show you a place ...."

He was on his feet, pulling her up before she could finish, gracefully retrieving his discarded shirt in the process. "Hurry," he urged, pushing her toward the Gables. With a lilting laugh over her shoulder, she fairly flew across the grass, saucily hiking up her skirts to scale the litter of stones around the larger rock formation. Nimbly she plucked her way through the simple maze of hewn limestone chunks until they came upon a completely secluded patch of dried moss in the center.

Twirling about, her arms in their sleeves spread wide, her unlaced bodice sagging to reveal rosy breasts recently tasted,

Sarah offered, "Juliana, Jack and I used to play house here. Isn't it perfect?"

"Show me to the master's chambers, wench," he growled, his eyes sparkling with too-long abated needs, "and I shall pass judgment when I've sampled the hospitality." At once he sat and began removing his knee-length riding boots, his eyes following her every delightful movement.

"Sir, I beg your discretion," she giggled. "You are in the parlor."

"'Twere it the kitchen, I'd be about the same purpose," he declared, tossing the footgear aside and resting his elbows on raised knees, his fingers laced between them. His handsome face sobered into a smoldering stare. "Come here."

The quiet words beckoned her immediately and she knelt before him, resting her hands on his legs where they crept along the sinewy hardness of his thighs. With the wordless concentration afforded sacred rituals, Stewart slowly undressed her, finding the arousing revelation a bittersweet reunion.

Though more slender, her creamy, gazelle-like features were proportionately generous and his breath labored at the sight of firm breasts, small waist and gently curving hips. But he could not help but recall that the last time they had shared such bliss, Sarah was voluptuously rounded with his child. An unbidden flicker of remorse in his eyes did not escape her notice, and the reaction brought the back of her hand to her lips, her eyes blinking back the pressure of building tears. A single tanned finger reached out to trace one of the few, barely visible translucent lines that feathered along the side of her flat abdomen.

Sarah was frozen with uncertainty, mesmerized by the sight of him concentrating on the path of his hand. Finally he spoke, his voice low with self-recrimination. "The cruelest consequence of my selfishness. I never should have let this happen to you."

"Please, Stewart. Don't," she pleaded in a voice all but soundless. "I left Boston only because I could not bear your misplaced guilt. I loved you too much to serve as a reminder of some wrong you thought you'd done to me."

Urgently she pressed his hand against her smooth belly, beseeching him to return her gaze. At last he did, his eyes hooded with emotion. "I have never for a moment blamed you. When I think of Mary Catherine, I recall the beauty of her conception. Few women whose love was declared can share the rapture of *my* memories."

He was looking at her in stunned disbelief. Pressing on, she told him, "I recall that her father was there when I needed him most desperately. The help and strength you gave me that night – and many before we knew of her – are the reasons I am before you today. How many beloved wives can say as much?" He could not ignore that her moist eyes were glowing with a love that transcended any and all pain for which he felt responsible.

"I recall that you showed more joy and delight in the prospect of fatherhood than the most devoted of husbands. Had she lived, I would have required no other reason to stay with you. Oh my darling," she petitioned, moving into the circle of his body as his arms closed around her, "I had but few regrets ... and none now."

Her kiss promised all the relief of a cleansing balm, and Stewart eagerly partook. His mouth parted her lips to drink the fullness of the passion she offered, and with a shuddering moan, he welcomed the return of his fierce desire. With her help, the last of his clothes were removed and she gasped at the thrill of his nakedness in this ancient ruin. Cradling her beneath him, Stewart studied and teased her completely, with equal skill of both hands and lips. She gasped when he explored the wet heat of her womanhood, making whispered pleas for fulfillment until desire forced her to demand that which he held back.

Straining her body toward him, she pressed his lean hips with urgent fingers, groaning in frustration when he crooned teasingly in her ear. "Had I known what passion slumbered beneath me, I would have forced you to stay with me ...."

"'Tis your love that sets me free," she whimpered, the sweet ache of desire causing a beguiling throatiness to shade her voice. "My defenses are gone, and I beg you, my love, for relief. Please ...."

With the sound of a seductive, promising sigh vibrating in her ear, Stewart hesitated but for one breathless moment before joining them in the swirling, passion-filled ritual of love. Responding to his thrusts with mindless abandon, Sarah readily forsook control of her body, whose limbs wrapped around him in feverish desire.

Bringing her to the brink of madness with his knowing touch and practiced movements, Stewart wove her in a magic cocoon of love and longing, branding her irrevocably with his impassioned words of commitment, as binding as any marriage vows that would follow.

In response, Sarah cried out her surrender, vowing all the love and devotion her heart had borne silently these many months. And when fevered lips could no longer speak but sighs and fiery whispers, their bodies carried the message, a message shared only by those lovers truly one in mind, body and spirit. Lovers such as these.

CHAPTER 43

"I hope that your seed grows within me," Sarah told Stewart quietly, watching him lace up her worn riding boots while she relaxed, half-lying, half-sitting on the mossy ground. His eyes rose from his task with an obvious twinkle.

"I am quite sure I have given you all that I had – which was considerably greater than my own expectations," he chuckled, his hand moving up to caress for a moment one silk-covered thigh. "I knew you were a passionate woman, Sarah, but today you have proved nearly insatiable."

Despite her recent abandonment, Sarah blushed noticeably, dropping her chin to her chest to hide an embarrassed smile. "I've missed you so," her voice quivered.

"I know." The conviction of his response surprised her and immediately her eyes were upon him with the question. Moving his length to rest beside her on the ground, Stewart brought his arms around her in a tender embrace. "You may as well know that we have your sister to thank for bringing us together again."

"Juliana?" Sarah's voice rose indignantly, her feelings of jealousy and betrayal still raw. "She was all too eager to claim you for herself."

"You sorely underestimate her love for you," Stewart reprimanded gently, stroking her taut body into acquiescence. "Hear me out, all right?"

"Very well," she replied icily, recalling well the affection between the two and how it had hurt her so.

Settling himself more comfortably against the wall of their make-believe mansion, Stewart began his explanation. "While your parents were willing to believe your excuse of an illness and grief over Tegan during your return voyage, Juliana was too much of a romantic to be appeased. When she learned from her friends that they had seen me in London, she contacted me on my own."

"Why did you come here? To England?" Sarah interrupted, nuzzling her cheek against his strong chest, afraid to look in his eyes.

"I was so damned restless – and useless – after you left. I hated the farm for the memories it bore. And when I returned to my home in Boston, Peggy had set the whole family against me. She was furious that I had let you go. She told me that you were in love with me, but I truly believed any feelings you might have had died with Mary Catherine – or else you would have stayed.

"My life had become unbearable so I decided to take off. Actually I had planned to go to Paris, but when the ship docked in London, I felt compelled to be here. I took advantage of some opportunities to transact business ... and look up old friends."

"Felicia," Sarah spoke dully.

"I admit that I saw her, but believe me, Sarah, my relationship with Felicia has been platonic since the day you and I boarded for our journey to America."

"I believe you," Sarah sighed, letting go of the poisonous green monster once and for all. Stewart sealed her declaration with a generous kiss, filled with the promise of a lifetime of love and fidelity. When at last he lifted his lips from the heat of hers, she smiled into his glowing brown eyes. "Oh yes, I believe you."

"I shall enjoy proving my love for you," Stewart responded, lifting a glossy chestnut lock to his cheek and nuzzling it. "But let me finish."

Sarah settled herself back against his broad chest as he continued, lovingly stroking the strong arms that caught her beneath her breasts. "She came to London last week to see me, after we'd exchanged cards. I admit I was a tad skeptical – your sister carries more than her share of charm in her blood. I thought perhaps she was after what you appeared to be running from." Sarah giggled at the thought of Stewart nervous about being chased by a woman, stopping only when he playfully nipped at her ear.

"At any rate, I realized almost immediately that she actually knew nothing about us but suspected a great deal. When she revealed how frail and uncommunicative you'd become, I immediately contacted your father to gain an invitation to your home. I had finally admitted to myself why I was so miserable. I ached to be with you, to tell you that I loved you. I had to hope your troubles stemmed from the same malady. But I did not know for certain until this morning when Juliana and I went riding."

"So that explains why you were so jovial when I first saw you!" Sarah exclaimed, leaning back to look into his face. "My father told me you had changed, that you seemed to have lost your vitality. I was prepared to deal with a down-trodden man, but when I saw you laughing and fit, I thought I had been deceived ... and worse. I thought Juliana had finally caught your eye."

"You *were* in a pique," Stewart laughed. "Quite impolite, which only served to prove the truth of Juliana's words. She told me how she'd gotten you to admit your feelings for me. And needless to say, I felt like a new man."

"Oh Stewart," Sarah crooned, turning to wrap her arms around his shoulders, hugging him tightly as her lips brushed his neck. "When I heard how you had changed, I feared you were still laboring under a sense of guilt over Mary Catherine. I could not bear the thought that I had caused you such pain by the horrible things I said to you at the farm. I needed to make amends; to show you that I bore no contempt for you, and that you had nothing to feel responsible for."

"When I first saw you today," Stewart replied, "I thought I would burst. You were so beautiful standing there on the stairs, looking haughty and outraged. I fear I shall miss your indignation – it makes your eyes sparkle so. But then," he whispered seductively, bringing his hands up to frame her face, his thumbs gently stroking her high cheekbones, "it doesn't nearly match the fire that's kindled when I make love to you. All these lonely months, your eyes have haunted me. Sometimes I convinced myself that you must have cared a little – the way you could look at me when I held you in my arms."

"I have loved you for a long time, my darling." She turned her head to place a reverent kiss into his palm. "Only pride kept me from telling you – and then later, when I thought all you carried was guilt – I did not want to use it to force you into my life. I wanted your heart, not just your name. You told me once that men like you don't marry for the usual reasons. I knew we could never be happy unless you truly loved me."

"And I have been such an arrogant cad, expecting you to fall completely under my spell, without any commitment from me. It was a cruel game I played, and my only consolation is that I wounded myself more than you." Dragging his eyes from her face, his jaw tightened as he stared off into the distance. "When I saw you that day at the farm swollen with my child, I was actually relieved to have a reason to offer marriage. I refused to let you or myself believe my reasons were deeper than obligation – and lust. But after you left, and misery became my most constant companion, I realized my folly. And until this morning, I feared I'd lost any chance for real happiness.

"Forgive me, Sarah," he pleaded, turning his face back to hers, the urgency clearly reflected in his intense gaze. "I would do anything to take back the hurt I caused you."

"Stop." Her fingers pressed against his lips in a fervent command. "What's done is past, and we have so much to look forward to. Let's not cloud our future with regrets. Promise me."

For what seemed like hours, he stared at her with a passion that took her breath away. Then with his pledge given in a hoarse whisper, he took her lips in a savagely sweet caress that purged all the pain of their memories, leaving nothing but the exhilarating promise of a future filled with bliss.

CHAPTER 44

The afternoon sun streamed diffused light through the cloud cover as Stewart and Sarah ambled toward the stables, walking their mounts behind them. Even an inexperienced eye could determine how these lovers had spent their day. Conversation flowed easily in between warm embraces and teasing kisses. Despite their efforts to tidy themselves, Sarah's long, dark locks were decidedly tousled, with bits of moss clinging about, and their clothes were dotted with grass stains and creases.

But it wasn't until they neared the mansion, having left the horses with Silas, that Sarah voiced any trepidation over their dishabille. "Let's use the back stairs," she urged, as Stewart began leading her toward the cobblestone entrance in the front. "I would surely have much to explain if my parents saw us."

Stewart laughed at her sudden air of propriety. "If anyone were going to disapprove, Sarah, I'm sure a search party would have been sent out about five hours ago. Juliana knew exactly where I was going and I'm quite certain she informed your parents."

"Still ...." she bit her lip worriedly, "there is so much I want to explain to them before I make known the fact that we are lovers. And I would rather tell them after we are safely wed. You understand, don't you, love?" Her nervous blue gaze brought a kindly glow to his eyes as he squeezed her narrow waist.

"Of course I understand. And I respect and fear your parents enough to want to avoid flaunting our tryst. However," he concluded, cocking his head toward the pillared entrance to the estate, "I believe we've missed our chance for secrecy."

Sure enough, Sarah's head turned to see the Duke and Duchess coming down the steps, with Juliana smugly bringing up the rear. Sarah groaned in embarrassment, but Stewart pulled her along, a wide smile settling on his relaxed face. The much-prayed-for chasm in the earth did not open, and with a look of consternation, Sarah steeled herself to face their outrage. Thus she was quite taken aback by what followed.

"I have gone over the document and Jeremiah's letter, Stewart," The Duke announced as the two parties came within earshot of each other, "and I find everything quite in order." Sarah blinked curiously. Her whole family was looking quite pleased. No trace of disapproval clouded a person's eyes. Juliana was positively gloating. Sarah stared at all of them, speechless.

"Then you won't mind if I take Lady Sarah to our room," Stewart was saying. "We are both in need of tidying up." With a casual air, he pulled a piece of dry grass from Sarah's hair. Shocked by his audacity, she blushed bright red as she yanked her hair from his indolent touch.

"Not at all," Weston replied benignly. "I believe your things have been moved by now. I hope you and my daughter will be most comfortable," he winked.

"What?" Sarah suddenly found her voice, appalled by what she was hearing. "What is going on here? Will someone please tell me?" Glancing from one beaming expression to another, her eyes finally rested murderously on Stewart, who was smiling, too, obviously making light of her confusion. "Well?" she demanded, shooting warning sparks from icy blue eyes.

"A thousand pardons, madam," he smiled teasingly, ignoring her chagrin. "One would think I would have found a moment today to tell you what this is all about. But I admit I was much too preoccupied. I am sure you understand," he offered, turning his glittering smile on the Duchess of Weston, who actually giggled.

Her embarrassment turning to anger at their private joke, Sarah stamped her booted foot on the cobblestones. "Stewart Chamberlain, I promise certain harm if you do not tell me what this is all about!"

With an effort, Stewart sobered his features by a scant degree, unwilling to risk heightening Sarah's frustration. "My beloved Sarah," he told her, grasping her reluctant hands in his own. "I was about a very strange mission when I came to England this time. My first objective was to convince you of my love and my intention that we live as husband and wife for the rest of our lives. Fortunately I have a very persuasive nature – or it would have severely imperiled the outcome of my second objective."

"Which was ...?" Sarah asked archly.

"To tell your father I had drawn on the Special License he obtained from the Archbishop before we departed for America last year. And to request your parents' blessing for our marriage, which, coincidentally is one year long this month."

Sarah stood frozen, shocked by the dual revelations that pounded her like churning waves attacking a beach. "We are married?" she inquired of Stewart, and turning to her father added, "And you arranged it?"

The Duke spoke before Stewart could respond. "Sarah, I knew the situation between you and Stewart was liable to 'warm' if given the chance, and, as I was complicit in giving you two that opportunity, I ordered Mr. Chamberlain to carry the Special License in the event that it should be needed. You are my daughter and you were not to be trifled with. Stewart made a promise to treat you with care and respect – and he has kept it.

"But as I have learned, the license enabled Jeremiah and Stewart to save you from harm of the direst kind. Stewart could not have acted more rationally or bravely than to marry you over your own stubborn objections." The Duke glanced at Stewart, then returned his gaze to Sarah. "He saved your life, and your mother and I can think of no better way to show our love to you -- and our gratitude to him -- than to welcome him into our family as your husband and our son."

Sarah's mind was an absolute jumble. So many revelations. She clung to the only thing she remembered, addressing Stewart. "Jeremiah told me you had destroyed the license when our charade was over."

Stewart shook his head. "No, Sarah. He told you he had given it to me to take care of. I never destroyed it. On the contrary, I've kept it with me ever since it was placed in my care. And this morning, I presented it to your father, to ensure him that we had taken up the contract, and have since been true to it.

Though I did explain to him that you and I had some 'matters' to work out before we could begin celebrating our announcement."

Sarah's hands flew to her mouth. A torrent of thoughts whipped through her mind as she looked from one face to another. Finally her eyes came to rest on Stewart's countenance, and she could see that he was holding his breath. As confounding as it was to learn these secrets, she had indeed turned a corner today. No longer would she shrewishly doubt the intentions or the love of her family. And certainly no longer would she punish Stewart with her churlishness. By sometimes circuitous and arrogant means, he had always done what was right by her. He deserved her love and trust – right this moment, and forever.

With a sudden joyous shout, she was in his arms, showering his whisker-roughened face with exuberant kisses, exalting in the feel of his body shedding its tenseness as she demonstrated her happiness in a most convincing manner. Finally, after he had captured her fleeting lips in an enthusiastic kiss, holding her completely off the ground, he set her away to look deeply into her tear-filled eyes. Oblivious to their audience, Stewart spoke, his voice fraught with emotion. "Thank God you're not angry with me, though I would not blame you."

"Angry?" Sarah cried incredulously. "Stewart, I love you! I have dreamed of being your wife almost as long as we have been – married! Ever since ...." she stopped suddenly and Stewart smiled at their shared memories.

"Excuse me," the Duke's baritone interrupted and the couple turned abruptly, breaking their entrancing stare. "Son, do you mind if I kiss the bride ... or whatever word one would use to describe her," he chuckled, opening his arms.

"Happy," she rejoiced, rushing into her father's arms. "Deliriously happy." The Duchess and Lady Juliana joined in to echo the Duke's approval as they all hugged Sarah and Stewart, their good wishes mingling in a cheerful tumult of sound.

"Thank you, Julie," Sarah said with heartfelt gratitude as she embraced her sister for the second time. Walking a few steps ahead of the others on their way back inside, the two shared a private moment. "If it were not for you, I think I would have been the sorriest fool."

"You needn't thank me," Juliana insisted. "That man saved you from yourself. I only helped move matters along a bit faster."

"Just in time for our first anniversary!" Sarah chortled.

"Believe me, I had my own reasons for seeing this through. Now Jack and I can be married without worrying about how awkward it might have been for you."

Sarah stopped dead in her tracks. "You and Jack are betrothed?"

Juliana beamed smugly. "If you had taken a moment to join the living these past months, you would have known the prospects were imminent."

Sarah hugged her sister again. "Julie, I am so happy for you! Where's Jack? I am sure he must be beside himself. He has loved you forever."

"You may congratulate him tonight at the party."

"The party? What party?"

"Your anniversary celebration," Juliana grinned mischievously. "Thanks to your long absence today, Mother and I were able to organize a small gathering for this evening. If you and Stewart are not too exhausted," she teased, "you might want to attend."

Wrapped in a warm cocoon of limbs and soft covers, the lovers spoke in hushed tones as a fire flickered quietly in the hearth. "The evening was lovely," Sarah sighed, "but nothing can compare to this." Light, teasing fingertips played across the angular planes of the face above her as she reveled in the feel of their perfectly complementary forms. "'Tis a dream come true to have you here, in my bed."

"It pleasures me to know that I was in your thoughts," Stewart crooned, his warm lips sliding tender kisses along her cheekbone.

"From the very beginning. At first I would lie here wondering what it would be like to have your arms around me ...

and then, I was tortured by memories of just how wonderful it was ...." A cry of sheer pleasure escaped her swollen lips as he pressed his hips into the softness of her own. "Promise me, Stewart, that we shall never again be separated. I could not bear it, especially now, knowing that you love me too."

"'Tis done, my beauty," he whispered, nuzzling the pulsing cord of her neck. "We've been apart for longer than I could stand. If I must travel, I shall enjoy sharing my quarters with one who delights me so." To prove his words, his head lowered to capture a peaking nipple, his lips and tongue weaving a fiery magic within her creamy breast. "But it is my aim to confine ourselves to visits here and our homes in Massachusetts. I have circled the world in my restlessness for something to make my life worthwhile. And it was only in your arms that I ever found abiding contentment." Stewart raised his head, his eyes piercing her with the reflected glow of the fire. "I want to make a home for you. I want to give you more children; healthy, beautiful babies ...." His voice faded into a sigh.

"Yes," Sarah responded. "Yes, Stewart. We shall have children. Please don't let Mary Catherine's death discourage you. Though I do not know why, it was meant to be. But I know we will be blessed. And soon," she teased to lighten his mood, "if perseverance is any measure of success."

Fondly he gazed upon her delicate but remarkably strong beauty, his heart nearly bursting with admiration for the strength of her character. She was truly a diamond of the first water. "You have suffered so much and have borne it with a courage that would put men to shame. But still you are to me as fragile as a flower ... and as lovely. It is why I could never put you out of my thoughts. Forever you will intrigue me, I know."

His pliant fingers were beginning to explore the slenderness of her waist and the roundness of her hips. "I must have studied that Special License a hundred times, each time meaning to toss it into the nearest blaze. But I could not do it, anymore than I could imagine never seeing you again. I wanted to be bound to you for the rest of my life, even though I could not admit it aloud."

A questions suddenly entered Sarah's mind. "When we were at the farm .... Why did you go to the trouble of insisting that we get a preacher when you knew we were already legally married?"

Stewart grinned sheepishly, but the hesitancy was not matched by his touch upon her, which was sure and inviting. "I thought to ignore the license, seeing no point in using my claim and risking your indignation when marriage was to your advantage as well as my own. But then," he continued, his voice low with remembered pain, "I had no character to put an end to the foolishness and bare the truth when it would have served us both ...."

A soothing noise escaped Sarah's lips as she cupped his grim face with her hands. "You are yet too hard on yourself, my love. Had you told me of our marriage then, it would not have altered my course. I would not have consented without your heart's promise of love, and that was the very thing you were struggling against even then. We would have burned the contract together that day, I fear, and so would not be here like this tonight." Her last words were expressed with a purring seductiveness that was echoed by her body's questing movements against his own.

The blatancy of her desire pushed all dark thoughts from Stewart's mind as he raised himself to answer her siren call, his tongue making deep, symbolic forays into the welcoming moistness of her mouth.

Words lost their importance as Stewart and Sarah took each other to the stunning brink of fulfillment with their love play, their bodies undulating to the passionate waltz of desire. As one, they gave and received, their declarations of love and need spilling in rasping cries, until their bodies transcended conscious movements, drawing them unaided to the summit of rapture.

Stewart's triumphant gasp mingled with Sarah's joyous weeping as this most perfect moment suspended them in timeless wonder. And as they softly, sweetly tumbled into the starbright aftermath of their passion, the once-immured lovers shared the glory of captivity within each others' arms for now — and forever.